ONE TRUE PATRIOT

A NOVEL

SEAN PARNELL

wm
WILLIAM MORROW
An Imprint of HarperCollins*Publishers*

This is a work of fiction. Names, characters, places, and incidents are products of the author's imagination or are used fictitiously and are not to be construed as real. Any resemblance to actual events, locales, organizations, or persons, living or dead, is entirely coincidental.

First William Morrow premium printing: August 2021
First William Morrow hardcover printing: September 2020

Print Edition ISBN: 978-0-06-298658-0
Digital Edition ISBN: 978-0-06-298659-7

Cover art by Tony Mauro
Cover photograph © Surangaw/Dreamstime.com

21 22 23 24 25 BVGM 10 9 8 7 6 5 4 3 2 1

PRAISE FOR

ONE TRUE PATRIOT

"[A] high-octane thriller. . . . Relevant, relentless, and filled with the kind of authenticity you can only get from someone who's been there and done it, Sean Parnell's *One True Patriot* is a blistering, action-packed thriller that's perfect for fans of Mark Greaney and Jack Carr."

—The Real Book Spy

"In the climax, Steele and Kalidi square off in an exciting, bloody exchange around Washington's National Cathedral. . . . Parnell delivers loads of branded military hardware . . . and juggernaut plotting. The ending suggests big changes ahead for Steele and the Program. Military action fans will be well satisfied."

—*Publishers Weekly*

PRAISE FOR

ALL OUT WAR

"A fast-paced, all-out action-fest. . . . Steele is the kind of adventure hero whom everyone will want to see succeed, and here he's up against antagonists who define sheer villainy. . . . Parnell has jumped to the top of the military-thriller class, right up there with Brad Thor and Vince Flynn."

—*Booklist* (starred review)

"The mission becomes increasingly complex, dangerous, and engaging once Steele learns that the attack on his home is tied to assassination plans for some of the world's most prominent leaders. . . . A well-written and well-researched page-turner."

—*Kirkus Reviews*

"Sean Parnell continues to impress with his second novel, a timely action thriller that brings the pain in a big way. . . . Readers will enjoy following Eric Steele as he goes to work killing bad guys and trying to save the world."

—The Real Book Spy

"There is never any lack of action, and putting this thriller down is a tall order."

—Lima Charlie

"[A] rousing novel . . . [with] vivid, unrelenting action scenes. . . . A lingering mystery will leave readers eager for Steele's next adventure."

—*Publishers Weekly*

PRAISE FOR

MAN OF WAR

"An international thriller that delivers. Well-written, tightly plotted, fast-paced, and full of mind-twisting conspiracies and surprises."

—Nelson DeMille

"A completely gripping story."

—Clive Cussler

"A breakneck-speed thriller with enough action and combat to satisfy any reader. Eric Steele is a one-man army, and Sean Parnell uses his background in tactics and weapons to bust into the ranks of the best thriller writers out there."

—C.J. Box, #1 *New York Times* bestselling author

"A definite winner. . . . The main story line here, involving friends turned mortal enemies, is a grabber and will certainly please fans of Brad Thor, Brad Taylor, and Vince Flynn."

—*Booklist* (starred review)

"Falling somewhere between Brad Thor's Scot Harvath and Brad Taylor's Pike Logan, Eric Steele is a formidable new protagonist whom readers will love. . . . If you like conspiracies and bold, larger-than-life characters, *Man of War* hits fast, hard, and never lets up for a second."

—CrimeReads.com

"*Man of War* is a blockbuster that rages with high-speed thrills and suspense on every page. It has an authentic feel that can only come from someone who truly knows combat. And the intense action, the far-flung settings, and the well-drawn inside-dope on covert operations, all add to create a knock-out fiction debut by an author who has arrived on the thriller scene with a roar."

—Mark Greaney, #1 *New York Times* bestselling author

"Sure to be a long-running, exciting action series . . . Parnell's series can carry forward the torch of Mitch Rapp."

—*The Oklahoman*

"Nonstop action from the first page, a jolt of pure adrenaline. Parnell deploys the full arsenal in this high-stakes thriller."

—Joseph Finder, author of *Judgment*

"Setting, dialogue, and details create the ideal backdrop for the tension and intensity. . . . A marvelous debut from a talented writer to keep a watch on."

—Steve Berry, author of *The Warsaw Protocol*

PRAISE FOR

OUTLAW PLATOON

"A heartfelt story that shows how very different people can be thrown together in combat and find a way to make it work. Parnell and the soldiers who fought beside him are all courageous heroes—real bad asses. I really enjoyed the book."

—Chris Kyle, author of *American Sniper*

"An exceptional look into the mind of a platoon leader in Afghanistan; Captain Parnell shares his experiences of leadership, loss, and aggressive military tactics. You can really feel the bonds forged between these brothers in arms as the battle plays out."

—Marcus Luttrell, author of *Lone Survivor*

"An utterly gripping account of what our soldiers endure on the front lines—the frustrations, the fear, the loneliness."

—Tim O'Brien, author of *The Things They Carried*

"*Outlaw Platoon* is expertly told by a man who braved the heat of battle time and time again. An epic story as exacting as it is suspenseful, it reveals the bravery and dedication of our armed service men and women around the world."

—Clive Cussler

"Two of the most intense tales of courage under fire I own are *Black Hawk Down* and *Lone Survivor.* I now have a third, *Outlaw Platoon*. It's an absolutely gripping, edge-of-your-seat ride."

—Brad Thor, #1 *New York Times* bestselling author

"The range of emotions that Sean Parnell summons in *Outlaw Platoon* [is] stunning. A nuanced, compelling memoir. . . . Parnell shows he's a gifted, brave storyteller."

—*Pittsburgh Tribune*

"This is the story of a brotherhood of soldiers whose bond was forged in the fire of battle during an intense year of fighting. . . . [Parnell] relives specific battles, and his retelling of the stories reads at times like an adventure novel, full of adrenaline."

—*Library Journal*

"Parnell vividly captures the sounds, sights, and smells of combat, and proves most eloquent when describing the bond—'selflessness was our secret weapon'—that developed among his men. . . . [He] balances sentimentality with sincerity and crisp prose to produce one of the Afghan war's most moving combat narratives."

—*Publishers Weekly*

Also by Sean Parnell

Nonfiction

OUTLAW PLATOON

Fiction

MAN OF WAR
ALL OUT WAR

FOR MY CHILDREN

ONE TRUE PATRIOT

ACT I

CHAPTER 1

ALEPPO, SYRIA

At twenty-two thousand feet above sea level, Eric Steele was freezing his ass off. The night was black as a coal miner's handkerchief, the clouds were swollen with gumball hail, and despite two uniform layers and a low-porosity jumpsuit, a wicked headwind was driving his manhood back up into his pelvis.

Steele didn't mind jumping out of a perfectly good airplane. He'd done it a thousand times before. But this particular method sucked. High Altitude, High Opening. HAHO. Whoever had come up with that idea needed a lobotomy with a rusty blade, no anesthesia.

In theory, the tactic was sound. You'd exit the aircraft high up and miles away from the target, pop your chute, then fly the ram-air canopy in a long glide path and make a pinpoint landing on the objective—slick, silent, and deadly. But tonight, Steele had jumped from a special operations C-145A Skytruck in Turkish airspace, deployed his MC-4 parachute, and discovered to his warm-blooded horror that he'd be gliding through brutal arctic air for over half an hour and nineteen miles deep into hostile territory.

If he survived this, he was going to strangle the meteorologist.

He felt like a marionette in a meat locker. His arms and legs were already so numb that he wondered if he'd shatter like an ice sculpture when he landed. And right after that, he'd have to go into action. Solo. Against ridiculous odds. All the intel analyst geeks said the Syrian civil war was winding down, but all the spooks on the ground said Aleppo was still the most dangerous place on earth. Steele believed the spooks.

He wiped the fog from his helmet visor with a trembling glove, squinted down at the GPS screen mounted on his chest, reached up for the steering toggles, made an adjustment, and turned four degrees south. He glanced at his Russian Vostok watch and checked his altimeter. Eighteen thousand feet, and the damn needle was barely moving. The pull through his oxygen mask was still good, but it felt like sucking snow through a straw. And where the hell was that goddamn beacon? If it didn't show up on his GPS soon he could wind up landing in freaking Beirut.

Another ninety seconds crawled by, then it popped at the top of his screen—a tiny, amber, oscillating dot.

Thank you, Jesus.

Twenty minutes later, Steele rocketed into a tiny urban clearing in A'zaz on the northern outskirts of

Aleppo. It looked about the size of a CVS parking lot, bracketed by abandoned hooches. He hauled the toggles down to his hips, flared the parachute, barely missed a concrete retaining wall, thrust his boots straight out, and plowed up a furrow of scree. The fifty-pound ruck strapped to his thighs raked his spine across broken cinders, and his helmet bounced over stones. He reached up, yanked the Capewells, and the chute collapsed like a dying black jellyfish. His body hadn't shattered, but it ached like hell. He grunted, shook off the bruising, cranked himself to his feet, and checked his surroundings.

No one around but a wild dog. She stared at him, growled, and took off.

Time to go to work.

It took him five minutes to prep for action. He rolled up the chute and risers and doused the nylon clump with a bottle of liquid bromine, melting the MC-4 into a useless puddle. He doffed his helmet and parachute harness, set them aside, and stripped off his coverall, revealing a breakaway Russian Spetsnaz commando uniform.

He pulled a small, custom load-bearing rig from his ruck, left-thigh mount, with three magazines of 5.45 × 39.5 mm ammunition and two Russian F-1 grenades. Then came a Russian Krinkov submachine gun and an MP-443 Grach semiautomatic, both with Gemtech suppressors. The pistol went into his right-thigh holster, and he slung the subgun from his neck. Then he pulled on a maroon beret, stuffed the helmet and harness into the ruck, slung it over his back, and made off on foot.

Steele followed the GPS for two hundred meters,

turned a corner onto Khaled Ibn Alwaleed Street, stopped, and took a breath.

Aleppo had once been a jewel of the ancient Middle East. Now it looked like Dresden circa 1944. Assad's Alawite soldiers had battled with Free Syrian Army forces for years, with Al Nusra, Hezbollah, and ISIS all taking sides and lives. Barrel bombs had decimated civilian suburbs and poison gas had slaughtered innocents. Half the building facades had collapsed into piles of cinder blocks and shattered furniture, and with local power companies bombed to rubble, not a single lightbulb flickered. During the daytime civilians foraged for water and food. After dark, they were ghosts.

Steele moved carefully along the eastern side of the narrow street until the GPS signaled "on target." He looked up. A pair of two-story buildings, still relatively intact, faced each other across the road. He saw a slim, gleaming steel cable stretching from roof to roof, and checked to make sure each end drooped down to head height, and had a carbon steel carabiner attached.

That line better be stronger than mama's clothesline.

If it failed him on the extraction, he'd have no other way out.

Just below the left-hand snap link he found a dirt-slathered canvas tarp. He yanked it off, exposing an olive-drab, Russian Taurus fat-wheeled dirt bike, left there for him by a deep-cover Israeli intelligence agent. He pulled it upright and swung into the saddle, then spotted an envelope taped to the gas tank.

This better not be a goddamn stand-down order.

He opened it up, unfolded a note, and his green eyes squinted in the dark. It was a printed travel warning for tourists, from the U.S. State Department:

SYRIA–LEVEL 4: DO NOT TRAVEL

Do not travel to Syria due to terrorism, civil unrest, kidnapping, and armed conflict. No part of Syria is safe from violence. Kidnappings, the use of chemical warfare, shelling, and aerial bombardment pose significant risk of death or serious injury.

Just below the print was a hand-drawn cartoon smiley face. He smirked. Those guys in the Mossad were funny. But could he trust them?

There was only one way to find out. . . .

CHAPTER 2

Eric Steele was in Syria to kill some people. That was the job, and he had no reservations about doing it.

Steele was an Alpha, one of only nine special operators attached to the Program, a top-tier unit whose missions were outside the purview of CIA, NSA, the Pentagon, and all other "alphabet" agencies headquartered in and around Washington, D.C. The Program's heritage went back to the days following World War II, an interim solution for "dirty work" between the disbanding of the Office of Strategic Services and the standing up of the CIA. Composed of the operators and fewer than thirty support personnel, the Program was ensconced in the bowels of the White House, in a nuclear bomb–proof tactical operations center called Cutlass Main.

Missions could only be tasked directly by the president. The very few people in government who knew about the Program referred to it in whispers as TOA—"That Other Agency."

Almost all Alphas came from the ranks of the military. Steele had first served as a machine gunner with the 10th Mountain Division, then a demolitions sergeant with a Special Forces A-team. From there, he'd been planning on the assessment and selection process for Delta, but instead a mysterious civilian had tapped him for "something higher." You couldn't get much higher than Delta or the SEALs. The Program was above that; somewhere in the clouds.

In the course of seven years as an Alpha, he'd operated in scores of ugly hot spots all over the world. But this was his first time in Syria. He knew it might be his last.

He rode the chubby Russian motorcycle due south on Khaled Ibn Alwaleed, a long straight thoroughfare that passed the rail yards and went all the way down to the old industrial zone. He no longer needed the GPS or a digital map; he'd spent four days memorizing every infil and exfil route in Aleppo, using overheads supplied by the National Geospatial Agency to mentally mark off waypoints—much better than Google Maps.

His objective was a hotel called Boukra al-Quds, which translated ironically as "Jerusalem Morning." A five-story structure of steel and stone, the hotel had survived Aleppo's death throes, principally because it was used by the Russians as a command and control center. It was as if all the ordnance zipping around Aleppo never came close to the Boukra al-Quds. You just didn't screw with the Russians.

But Steele intended to screw with them tonight, big-time. A meeting was being held on the hotel's third floor. In attendance were nuclear warfare experts from Syria, Iran, North Korea, and Russia—

one each. Yet these three men and one woman (the Russian) were not theoretical physicists. They were all "missile mechanics," there to put the final touches on a cooperative venture.

This crew was building miniature nuke warheads to be mounted on an Iranian Qader anti-ship missile. Once they worked out the kinks, which would be very soon, the missiles would go into production and be distributed to Hezbollah terrorists in southern Lebanon. After that, no American or Israeli warship would be able to sail the Mediterranean without threat of annihilation by the mullahs in Tehran.

Steele's hide had been saved by the navy on more than one occasion. His niece was a midshipman serving with the Sixth Fleet. The idea of American sailors being immolated on an aircraft carrier was a horrific vision that churned his guts. Totally unacceptable.

Normally, the Israelis would have taken this crew down, just as they'd done with the Syrian nuclear reactor in 2007. But Israeli Prime Minister David Bitton and Russian strongman Vladimir Putin were just starting to get along—sort of—and using an Israel Defense Forces special missions unit to neutralize a top Moscow scientist could result in Russian paratroopers landing in Tel Aviv. So, the Israelis had appealed to U.S. President Rockford—promising to provide covert support—and Rockford had tasked the Program. In turn, the Program had tapped its best operator, Eric Steele.

But the mission had to be completely deniable.

No matter how it went down, no one would be taking the credit, the blame, or the shame.

Eric Steele was deniable, expendable, and ready.

He rode another half kilometer down Khaled Ibn Alwaleed, jinked left through an abandoned traffic circle, then zipped down Omar Abu Reesha, a median-divided two-lane road that continued south, with the railway lines glinting behind a row of trees on the right. A couple of cars cruised by, a battered Italian Fiat and an old Czech Škoda. Given the hour, he guessed they were occupied by patrolling "White Helmets," the crazy, intrepid rescue crews who braved artillery and gunfire.

He glanced at his watch and gunned the Russian bike, selected by the resident Mossad agent for its all-terrain balloon tires. That anonymous spy had also provided intimate details on the Boukra al-Quds hotel, including the precise positions of all rings of security personnel. He wondered if the guy had a trained cat with a minicam attached to its collar.

Then, precisely as stated in the mission brief, the Al Tawheed Mosque with its quartet of majestic minarets appeared on the left, and the Byblos Bank on the right. He slewed to the right onto Al Zohoor Street, and there it was—the Boukra al-Quds, three hundred meters straight ahead, a pristine structure hunkered in the midst of rubble. He wondered how many stars it was getting on Yelp.

The first line of security was an Entry Control Point set up in the middle of the road. Steele saw a pair of yellow construction sawhorses with a gap in the middle, and three Russian Spetsnaz operators wearing field camouflage, balaclavas, and airborne helmets. The two on the right gripped AK-74s, the one on the left had a shotgun. They were all smoking cigarettes, probably Balkan Sobranies. Off to their right, the hotel was dark, except for a glow from the lobby entrance and a spill of light from the third floor at the rear.

Steele set his posture to casual boredom and scrubbed all thoughts of anything but the mission from his mind. In another five seconds, it would be a matter of "speed, surprise, and violence of action." Emotions had no place in the Program.

He coasted up to the barrier, killed the engine, and swung off the bike. With the weight of ordnance gone from his ruck, it settled easily on his shoulders, and he stretched and smiled as the Russians turned toward him.

"*Dobryj vecher, tovarishch*," he said. Good evening, comrades.

"*Chertovski vecher*," one of them grunted. Shitty evening. Then added, "*Otlichnyj mototsikl.*" Nice bike.

"*Tebe nravitsja?*" Steele said. You like it?

Then his right hand blurred as he unholstered the silenced Grach and shot the two men on the right, one round each in the face. The Spetsnaz on the left jerked back, and Steele shot him in the groin so he'd drop the shotgun, which he did. Steele reached out and caught the weapon so it wouldn't clatter, then shot the man again in the throat so he couldn't cry out.

He stepped over the twitching corpses and trotted up the concrete stairs to the lobby. The glass front door was crisscrossed with orange shatterproof tape. He pulled it open and stepped inside.

To the left was the hotel desk, where no tourist had checked in for probably five years. A large mirror was mounted on the wall behind a Syrian officer who sat at the desk, grinning at something on his smartphone. Another uniformed Syrian was leaning over the top and laughing as he tried to see the object of his comrade's mirth.

Don't shatter the mirror, Steele thought as the two men turned to him and he switched the pistol to his left hand, leaned over the counter, and shot the officer in the side of his skull. Then, before the other man's shocked mouth could bellow, he shoved the silencer into his heart, fired one round, snatched the front of his tunic, and lowered his twitching form to the floor. Steele looked away from his dying eyes and just listened. The spinning shell casings had clinked, but not too loud.

He glanced up the flight of stairs directly at the back of the lobby. *Nothing yet.* The next ring of security was Hezbollah—not so easy. He tossed his beret behind the counter, gripped the front of his Spetsnaz tunic, and pulled. The Velcro seam at the back gave way and now he was wearing a Hezbollah camouflage smock. He yanked a *keffiyeh* headscarf from his side trouser pocket, wrapped it jihadi-style around his neck, holstered the pistol, gripped the Krinkov subgun, and headed for the stairs.

A Hezbollah militant appeared on the landing above. He was massive and bearded, wearing a *keffiyeh*, but his AK-47 was casually slung and he was carrying a rolled-up newspaper. Steele smiled up at him.

"*Masa al khyr, y'ach,*" Steele said in Arabic. Good evening, brother.

"*Al salam ul masayih,*" the terrorist replied. Evening peace.

Not tonight, Steele thought as he whipped the silenced weapon up and fired a short burst, center-mass. The man jerked upright and stiffened as his blood sprayed the walls and his mouth flung open in a silent scream. Then he started toppling forward. Steele rushed up the stairs and threw all his weight behind his left shoulder as the giant collapsed on him and moaned a final, gurgling curse in his ear—something Steele knew he'd be hearing for years.

He splayed the fresh corpse out on the steps. He was trying to be quiet, but things were getting bloody, noisy, and dicey. He had to *move*.

He jackknifed up to the second-floor landing, where the stairwell turned to the left. He hugged the wall and reached into his boot for a Fairbairn-Sykes, the classic SAS commando knife designed for mortal stabbing. Sure enough, he heard urgent footfalls as another Hezbollah came trotting down the stairs and took the corner.

Steele stepped out, grabbed him by the front of his magazine carrier, and with the overhand power of a railroad spike–driver, buried the Fairbairn hilt-deep in his throat. He held his gurgling victim upright until his arms stopped flopping and his eyes rolled back, but then he couldn't pull the Fairbairn out. The damn blade was stuck in a vertebra. He let it go, eased the corpse down, and took the stairs in pairs.

On the third-floor landing, two North Korean commandos were posted in front of a large wooden door. Dressed in black tactical gear from head to foot, they looked wiry and formidable, hefting sidearms and neck-slung Bizon submachine guns. Steele didn't try to chat them up—he didn't have Korean. Instead, he stopped at the landing, making frantic hand gestures and babbling Arabic in a panicky whisper. He motioned for them to follow him and rushed back down the stairs. The Koreans looked at each other, and took the bait.

Halfway down he spun around, just as they appeared at the top, then ripped into both faces with a silenced six-round burst and rushed back up to keep their weapons from somersaulting and making a racket. The Koreans tumbled onto their backs, their Bizons bounced on their chests, and Steele's shell casings pinged down the stairwell. He froze, but he could hear loud voices and laughter emanating from behind the wooden door—enough to cover the ruckus.

He sure wasn't cold anymore. He was pouring sweat and badly needed some water, but it wasn't exactly break time yet. He yanked off the breakaway Hezbollah smock, wiped it over his blood-spattered face, and tossed it over his shoulder. Then he reached back for a long *dishdasha* "man dress" from his ruck and pulled it over his head, covering the Krinkov. From a butt pouch under the ruck he pulled a brass *finjan*.

The small coffee urn was only a harmless prop, but it would buy him a few seconds inside. He couldn't just toss a grenade in the room. There might be some innocents in there, maybe a child. Kids were his red line.

He pulled out the pistol again, loaded a fresh magazine, press-checked the weapon, and tucked it under the robe. Then he gripped the *finjan* in his left, turned the doorknob, and hunched his posture like a submissive chai boy.

It was actually a pretty nice suite, with a glass-topped bar to the left and a flat-screen TV. In the middle of the room was a large low coffee table with a heavy Moroccan mosaic top, flanked by cushy green leather chairs left and right, and one at the far end, in front of a large picture window. It took all of three seconds for Steele to assess.

A Syrian general sat on the right, mustached with chest medals gleaming. To the left sat a Korean man wearing a black Nehru-type jacket, next to a fat Iranian in a charcoal business suit, no tie. The woman facing him across the table was a middle-aged blonde, wearing a Hillary-style mustard pants suit.

The table was strewn with blueprints and ceramic Turkish coffee cups on glass coasters. Right in the middle was a silver, foot-long replica of a Qader missile, mounted on a miniature launch vehicle. It looked like something from Toys "R" Us.

The quartet had been laughing about something. As Steele closed the door and shuffled over with his *finjan*, they stopped, glanced at him, then carried on with their conversation, all in Arabic.

He bowed twice in obsequious dips, muttered, "*Masa al khyr yasaditan*"—Good evening, masters—

and shuffled to the table. They ignored him. Except for the North Korean, who cocked his head to the side, looked down at Steele's boots, then back up to his face. Steele caught the flash of alarm in his eyes and knew the jig was up. He pointed at the missile model and said, in plain English, "That's gonna look great in my man cave."

He dropped the *finjan*, pulled out the pistol, and shot the Korean in the forehead. The woman screamed and the Iranian flipped himself out of his chair and ran for the bar. But he was too fat to hurdle the top and Steele shot him in the back of his skull. The Syrian on the right was already up and had decided to fight, but Steele backhanded him in the throat with the pistol butt and shot him twice in the chest.

The Russian woman was on her feet and still screaming. Steele didn't like killing women, and for a split second he thought he might just blow out her kneecaps and leave it at that. But then she came up with a Makarov pistol from her purse and fired a round point-blank at his chest. The .380 ACP bullet pierced his robe and clanged off his Krinkov, slamming the subgun into his ribs.

He shot her in the chest and then the bridge of her nose. She lurched backward over the chair, her black heels twitching in the air.

He heard shouts now from down in the lobby and the thunder of boots on the stairs. He pulled off the *dishdasha*, leaped for the doorway, armed a Russian F-1 grenade, tossed it down the stairwell, and slammed the door. The hollow bang shook dust from the ceiling as he yanked a thirty-foot length of nylon rope from his ruck and snapped the carabiner to one leg of the table.

Steele pulled his gloves on, stuffed the missile model and blueprints into his ruck, shattered the window with a burst from the Krinkov, tossed the rope outside, and was on the ground in another six seconds. But he didn't run from the back of the building to his bike. He walked, as he tried to calm his pulse and smeared streams of sweat from his neck.

Three Russian medics were squatting over the corpses in the street. They raised their heads as he walked right past them, mounted the bike, booted the starter, and took off.

The only comm device Steele had on his person was a Mini-LR-MIB—a Miniature Long-Range Midwave Infrared Beacon. He clicked the button hard with his thumb in his pocket and hoped to hell it was working.

He doubled back on his infil route but diverged when he got to the Byblos Bank and bounced from the road onto the railroad tracks. He thought he heard engines roaring up the parallel road behind him, but he didn't expect any sirens—just pissed-off Russians with guns. Sure enough, a flurry of wild shots zipped through the tree line, breaking off branches. He gunned the Taurus, the railroad ties making his teeth chatter.

He took the hard corner back onto Khaled Ibn Alwaleed and almost crashed the damn bike. A little kid in an oversize coat and sandals was standing in the middle of the road. *Christ!* Steele dumped the

Taurus, jumped off it, snatched up the bug-eyed boy by his waist, and sprinted to the maw of an alley. He sat the kid down, fumbled in his pocket for a Kind Bar, squeezed it into his little hand, tousled his dusty hair, and said in Arabic, Don't *move*. Then he ran back to the bike.

A minute later he was standing between the exfil buildings and struggling into his parachute harness. He ran to one side, snapped one cable carabiner into his right D ring, then did the same with the left as the steel line above went taut. He pulled on his helmet, kissed the Krinkov, and flung it behind a pile of rubble.

He looked up. Nothing yet.

At the far end of the road, a Russian ZiL troop carrier careened around a corner, roared like an enraged lion, and bore straight at him. AK-74 barrels appeared from both side windows of the cab and started spitting fire, lime-green tracers cracking through the air around him and biting off chunks of concrete.

Now would be a good time! he howled inside his head. And then he saw the twin spinning propellers.

The SpecOps C-145A was screaming above the road, just behind the truck and a hundred feet up, and he could see the jungle penetrator with its autolink whipping below the open cargo bay. A crew chief must have been lying prone in the bay with an M240-B, because as the aircraft passed the truck, it opened up on the cab with a wicked stream of lightning-white tracers.

He squeezed his eyes shut, folded his arms, and tucked his helmet into his chest. He heard the smack of steel snatching steel above, a short scream of whipping cables, and he was yanked like a meat puppet into the sky at 150 knots.

He opened his eyes at two hundred feet and looked down past his whipping boots. The truck had smashed into a concrete building and exploded in a yellow-orange ball of fire.

These foreign drivers never know when to yield, he thought.

And then he was up and away.

CHAPTER 3

NEVILLE ISLAND, PENNSYLVANIA

There were still some feathery wisps of smoke rising from the ruins of Eric Steele's house. He thought that was strange, given that two months had passed since the place had burned to the ground. But maybe that was how beloved homes gave up their last ghosts.

He stood in the gravel driveway, hands in the pockets of a navy peacoat, Steelers cap on his head. His green eyes were locked on the broken timbers and charred black walls, but they were seeing something else.

It was that day back then, when he'd finally gotten a short break after sweating through a battery of reassessment tests for the Program, and had come home to Neville Island for some R&R. He'd built that house with his own hands, renovating it from the old Dravo Corporation warehouse where they'd once manufactured landing craft for the Normandy invasion. It had taken him a whole year, and when he was done he thought he'd fashioned an island fortress on a par with Camelot.

The reinforced concrete walls had Krieger level-four blast doors, security cameras, motion sensors. He'd installed a state-of-the-art safe room with closed-circuit air supply, ballistic glass on all the windows, an armory that could rival Charlton Heston's private collection, and a kitchen to make Martha Stewart drool.

That day a couple months back was supposed to have been a nice quiet afternoon, hosting his mom with a couple of fat steaks in the broiler, a bottle of good wine, and some family nostalgia. But right after she'd shown up, so had Aleksandr Zakayev, along with two teams of Russian killers. He'd done his best to fight them off, killed a bunch of them, but his small armory was no match for RPGs and M249 Squad Automatic Weapons. He and his mom had finally had to book it in his 1967 GTO, which wound up peppered with bullet holes and upside down in a ditch. His adoring mother had gone into a deep coma, and he'd gone off for revenge.

The thing in Aleppo hadn't cured that rage, or quenched his disquiet about the recent past. Nor would any of it bring back the people he loved.

Bobby "Demo" Cortez.

Just saying the man's name in his head made him hurt from his guts to his furrowed dark eyebrows. Demo had been his "keeper," a term they used in the Program for what the intel spooks usually called a "handler." But to an Alpha operator, a keeper was much more than just a field manager. Demo had been his battle buddy for years, a mentor, a wise man much like a samurai's monkish guru. He'd also been Steele's best friend in the world, and he'd died in his arms in a bouncing, freezing Zodiac boat in the middle of the Arctic Sea, after a raid that had gone to shit.

Demo wasn't replaceable. And now that Steele had time to reflect on the loss, he wondered if he was just marking time continuing with the Program. He felt like a ronin—a samurai who'd lost his master, doomed to wander the world in search of a meaningful mission.

He blew out a long sigh and wished he had a cigarette, but he'd given up smoking way back in the 10th Mountain Division. Once in a while he still had a cigar, but you couldn't suck smoke and do the job. It required every healthy lung cell, and all of your heart.

Then he thought of Meg Harden. He suddenly saw her compact five-foot-five frame, her glossy black hair and turned-up nose, and those dimples and rare smile that could melt a man's shoes. He saw her in bed, flushed and purring and satisfied, at least for the moment, and he wondered if he loved her. He'd loved Demo, and he loved his mom. But he wasn't sure he had much left for anyone else.

He also wasn't sure that he'd loved his father, Hank Steele, because he'd never really known him. A Green Beret back in the day, Hank had hardly been in their lives. And then he'd disappeared, forever, filling Eric with an endless sense of longing and loss.

At the end of Steele's last mission, just prior to Aleppo, he'd finally caught up with Gabriel, the stone-cold killer responsible for Demo's death. And just before Steele put a bullet in his head, Gabriel had tried to barter for his life with some phony crap about knowing the secret of Hank Steele's fate.

If you kill me you will never find your father, he'd said.

It was a hard choice to make.

Truth, or dare? Redemption, or bluff?

He'd killed him anyway. And now, he couldn't help but regret it. Gabriel had possibly held the key to opening up Steele's Pandora's box of sorrows and heal his tormented soul. The idea of it made his eyes glisten as he stared at his decimated home and felt enraged by his burdens of loss and revenge.

That anger was something he'd have to learn to manage. But it was also the engine that made him the Alpha he was.

He started and snapped from his dark reverie when he felt a hand touching his elbow. His mom had been waiting for him in the brand-new 1967 GTO he'd bought and had apparently run out of patience. He turned and looked down at her. She was still such a lovely woman, and the long pink scar on her forehead was nearly invisible now, concealed by her brunette curls dangling over it. His chest swelled with gratitude that she was still alive.

His mom squeezed his arm and pulled him close, and she smiled that beatific smile and jutted her chin at the ruins of his house.

"I think those steaks are overdone," she said. "Come on. I'll buy you dinner."

CHAPTER 4

PARIS, FRANCE

The woman across the table from Jonathan Raines was absolutely stunning. Her name was Geneviève, the daughter of an Egyptian-born contemporary French artist named Emile Sadat, whose impressionist oil color works were the talk of the Parisian elite and featured in exhibitions at the Louvre. Geneviève worked as her father's curator and assistant, and turned more heads at the museum than the *Mona Lisa*.

Her long raven hair swooped across the back of her caramel neck and fell past her ample breasts to her waist. She had sleek dark eyebrows, large amber eyes, a small Roman nose, and lips so full that they seemed unreal. At five foot seven, her figure was that of gymnast who'd grown too tall for her sport, and the long, cobalt-blue slitted sheath dress she was wearing didn't have one wrinkle or bulge.

She was perfect. And for that reason alone, Jonathan Raines knew that he shouldn't have been there.

Raines was an Alpha with the Program—Stalker

Six to be precise—and he hadn't had a decent leave in the past two years, so Paris seemed like a prime selection. Fluent in Spanish, Portuguese, and French, Raines usually operated in Central or South America, and rarely had a chance to enjoy the luxuries of the Continent. Before being selected for the Program, he'd spent eight years as an air force PJ and combat controller, and before that he'd completed a master's degree in art history. So, Paris was the place to fill your eyes with breathtaking art, and apparently breathtaking women.

Professionally speaking, he was wary of Geneviève. He'd aced all the counterintelligence courses and briefings at Langley, the DIA, and in-house at the Program, where the cranky old instructor-spies warned you incessantly about "honey traps." Those were attractive women (or men, if you were gay) who'd strike up a casual conversation on a bus or park bench somewhere, get into your pants, and eventually lure you into an ambush. An Alpha learned never to trust a cold approach by anyone, not even a wrinkly old woman asking for help with finding her cat. Anyone could be working for the opposition, and the unbreakable rule about these ad hoc strangers was: If you don't absolutely know, don't go.

But it hadn't happened that way with this girl. Raines had taken a room at the Montmartre Bed & Breakfast on Rue Muller, a quirky little place where all the guests intermingled and any swarthy dangerous strangers would stick out like sausages in a punch bowl. He'd slept for two days straight, wandered the rain-washed streets of Paris, and had finally gotten over to the Louvre to take in a Monet exhibit. It just so happened that Emile Sadat was also displaying his works that day and giving a lecture to a hundred art tourists. Geneviève had been there by her father's side at the podium.

Raines had approached *her*—not the other way around. If that was a setup, it had to be the most miraculous honey trap in the history of espionage and special operations.

He invited her out for dinner. She demurred, brushed him off, then was suddenly standing there when he exited the Louvre. Then she offered a non-Parisian apology for being suspicious and rude. She'd agreed to a dinner date, but nothing more.

That was fine with Jonathan Raines. He didn't expect a one-night fling with a creature like Geneviève. Still, he thought it over one more time, almost changed his mind, then decided she was "clean."

He should have listened to his instincts. . . .

Her name was not really Geneviève Sadat. She was actually Lila Kalidi, an assassin and mercenary with Palestinian Islamic Jihad. And Emile Sadat was not her real father. He played that role well, but his artwork was cover for his true occupation as an explosives smuggler and gun runner for the Muslim Brotherhood in France. As a matter of fact, Emile couldn't even watercolor by number—his works were created by a trio of Algerian art students who were paid very well to paint and shut up.

Lila was, in fact, very knowledgeable about art. She had an advanced degree in the subject from the Sorbonne and spoke French fluently, along with English, Arabic, German, Spanish, and Russian.

However, her real father had been a founding member of Hamas, a bomb maker who'd murdered hundreds of Israelis and was called "the Plunger" for his affinity for TNT. His head had been removed from his body by the Israeli General Security Service, Shabak, when they'd planted plastique in his cell phone in Gaza, with technical and surveillance support from American intelligence assets.

That was enough to make Lila conclude that Hamas had grown much too soft for her tastes, which was why she'd attached herself to PIJ and a few other "subset" clients. She made them pay dearly for her wet work, though she thoroughly enjoyed killing American, Israeli, and British colonizer infidels. She had a second-degree black belt in Russian Systema and had aced the small arms and sniper school run by the IRGC outside Isfahan in Iran. In between jobs, she lived the high life, and made no apologies for it to anyone.

"You are very Parisian, Geneviève," Raines said.

They had taken a table in one of the grand inner rooms of Le Café Marly, on the ground floor of the Palais du Louvre itself. The walls were red and gold, the doors and wainscoting lacquer black, the plush chairs in royal blue brocade, and the dishes were all stamped with the café's moniker.

"How do you mean, Jonathan?" She sipped her champagne and regarded him with a twinkle over the rim of the glass.

He smiled. "You insist on speaking English, even though I'm fluent in French."

"I enjoy practicing my English." She shrugged

and tugged at a pearl choker. "And fluency is a relative term, *n'est-ce pas*?"

"*Comme vous le souhaitez*," he said. As you wish.

"So formal!" She laughed and chided him. "And I *wish* to have dessert."

She ordered a healthy fruit plate, and Raines a crème brûlée. He'd barely finished one glass of the Bruno Paillard, but she signaled the waiter and asked him to fill their glasses again. The young man couldn't help but glance down at her long legs, and as if she had a moment of self-consciousness, she turned to the side and crossed them. Raines couldn't help looking either. She reached out with her full glass and clinked it against his.

"You are not drinking, Jonathan," she said in her lovely French tones. "Are you afraid that I might take advantage?"

"I accept your challenge," he said. Against his better judgment, he downed half the glass as she grinned and did the same. She could have finished half the bottle and it wouldn't have had any effect. She'd popped a powerful amphetamine just before dinner precisely for that reason.

"So, where are you flying off to, after me?" she asked as she sat back and stretched her spine, and he was all but forced to scan her cleavage. "And when are you coming back?"

"I'm not sure yet, Geneviève." For this evening, he'd chosen his airline executive cover, because it would give him an excuse to return to Paris in the near future. Was he already falling for this woman? He'd barely spent two hours with her, yet she was totally magnetic, almost intoxicating. Her eyes burned into his and those lips looked like they could swallow him whole.

She pouted. "You are going to be one of those men who . . . How do you say? Loves them and leaves them, no?"

"No. And as I recall, you made it very clear that this would be dinner and nothing more."

She tilted her head and ran one glossy fingernail slowly down her dress, between her breasts.

"Well, since it appears to be late, and I must be at the museum in the morning . . . perhaps you should escort me home."

Raines called for the check.

She killed him in an alleyway just off the River Seine.

They had walked in the dark, from the café on Rue de Rivoli, past the Carousel Gardens down to the water, then northwest astride the glistening waves on Quai François Mitterrand.

They chatted quietly and didn't touch until they reached the Pont Royal bridge, and she took his hand and smiled at him, with her fingernails flirtatiously tickling his inner palm, as if already showing him how she wanted to be touched.

They crossed the bridge. It began to drizzle. She said she was cold. He took off his jacket, snuggled it over her bare shoulders, and pulled her close as they walked and her heels clicked on the pavement stones. On the other side of the river, they turned northwest again along Quai Anatole France, and the rain picked up and the few other people who were out and about quickly popped open umbrellas or chased after cabs.

Soon they were all alone, clipping along and laughing past the Caisse des Dépôts federal bank buildings, which were silent so late at night, and between that and the Musée d'Orsay, Lila Kalidi stopped him at the entrance to a slim alleyway and said, "I like being wet. Come kiss me."

She pulled him into the darkness. They both were soaked when she pushed him up against the heavy stone walls of the bank and kissed him deeply, with all of her tongue, and one stiletto heel cocked up behind her in the air.

He gripped her slim waist and swirled her tongue with his own, thinking how impossibly lucky he'd gotten.

She kneed him straight up into his groin.

Even with the shock of it thundering up to his head, Raines tried to fight. His arms came up and he slashed knife-hand strikes at her head, but she blocked both blows with her forearms and, driving her left hand up from below, palm-struck his jaw, smashing his skull against stone. Then her finger-nails dug into his eye sockets as she gripped him there, reached under her skirt for a dirk that was strapped hilt-down on her thigh, and drove it up under his chin and into his brain.

"*Merde*," she cursed as she yanked the blade out and a thin spray of blood spurted onto her dress. His body slid to the ground, and she kicked him once to make sure he was gone. She planted her heels on both sides of his head, bent over, sliced off his left ear with her knife, and let the rain wash it clean in her open palm before stuffing it into her purse. His jacket had fallen off her shoulders, and she picked it up, pulled out his cell phone, tossed the soaked blazer over his head, and walked off.

She was two blocks away when his cell phone rang. She answered it and a voice said, "Code in."

She smiled. "I don't know your code," she said. "And the man who knew it is dead."

"Who the hell is this?" said the frantic male voice on the other end.

She ignored the question.

"Your Program is just like a cat," she said. "But now you have only eight lives left."

CHAPTER 5

WASHINGTON, D.C.

By the time Eric Steele showed up at the White House, all the cherry blossoms were dead and clogging the Potomac River like the bloody scales of slaughtered fish. Steele wasn't much for signs or superstitions, but there was no way to avoid the visual metaphor of thousands of Japanese trees, their gnarled black limbs clawing at the sky, their lifeless flowers piled on the ground.

Spring was over, the summer was imminent, and Washington summers were always a bitch.

Standard Operating Procedure in the Program held that after any direct-action mission, Alphas were given ten days' leave. Steele had lasted three days, nursing a few of his Aleppo bruises, fending off fussiness from his mother, and consulting a contractor about resurrecting his burned-down house. He was supposed to recharge his mental batteries and get some decent sleep, but he kept waking up at dawn in his mother's spare bedroom and reaching for his 1911 under his pillow. That classic Colt

Government handgun was the only legacy he'd inherited from his father, and just touching the weathered frame triggered desperate thoughts about chucking it all and going off to find out what had happened to him. There was scant hope of going back to sleep after that.

On the third morning he heard in his head the voice of Demo, his departed keeper. *You can sleep when you're dead, mano.*

He'd packed it in and headed back to HQ.

His new 1967 GTO was a throaty beast, and already he'd felt better, cruising south on I-95 and cranking some old AC/DC tunes like "Hells Bells." His replacement ride was much like the one that had suffered a machine-gun fate, except he'd chosen an emerald-green skin so it wouldn't look too thuggy, and avoided the tinted windows because they often piqued the interest of state highway cops. His encrypted cell on the seat beside him was quiet. Cutlass Main had him slated as TDY and the thing wouldn't buzz unless the world was on fire. There were, after all, eight other Alphas on round-the-clock duty.

He parked in a municipal lot on K Street. No one in the Program used government lots, because the intelligence division of the Chinese People's Liberation Army had scores of spooks throughout the capital area whose only task was to slip into those lots, record license plate numbers, then hack into the Department of Motor Vehicles and find out which cars belonged to whom. The parking receipts made the Program comptroller nuts, which was probably why she looked like Dr. Ruth having a perpetual nervous breakdown. He made sure his pistol was secure in the steel box under his driver's seat, locked up the car, and walked.

Washington in May was already steamy and oppressive, much like the politicians who inhabited the place. Steele wore a pair of desert boots, Gustin jeans, an open-collar dress shirt, and a navy-blue blazer, with no lapel pins of any kind, not even an American flag. The double-thick jeans seemed a weird choice in the heat, but Alphas chose their wardrobes for tactical reasons—if one of your hands was mangled, you could still cock a pistol slide against the rough denim, one-handed. And his blazer had small lead weights sewn into the bottom hem. If you were using a waist holster, you could flick the jacket open and it would stay behind your hip while you drew your piece. Of course, he never went armed to the White House. It made him feel naked, but those were the regs.

He cut down Sixteenth Street NW through Lafayette Square, where the usual kooks were out banging drums and railing against "The Man." Black Lives Matter faced off against Blue Lives Matter, and a bunch of college kids in pink pussy hats pumped signs claiming that newly installed President Rockford was a Russian dupe. In truth, Steele harbored no animus toward any of these people. They were all Americans and could say whatever the hell they wanted, and that's why his country was great. But he did have the fleeting thought, *Try doing that in Tehran.*

At the northwest corner of the compound fence, he got on the line with all the other press people and tourists and approached the white shack and Entry

Control Point where uniformed Secret Service officers eyed everyone like Dobermans. A pretty coed in front of him turned around, looked him over, and smiled.

"Are you taking the tour too?"

"No." Steele smirked down at her. "I just want to see the bust of Winston Churchill."

"Who's that?" She stared at his dreamy green eyes.

"Never mind. You're too young."

He passed through the metal detector and showed his CAC card to an officer, who raised an eyebrow, then selected a press pass on a lanyard and gave it to Steele. He was grateful the guy didn't wink. The tourist group was summoned to the left. Steele turned to the right and headed down the gleaming floor of the West Colonnade toward Cutlass Main, an office that, technically, didn't exist.

The door was on the right at the end of the colonnade, just before the West Wing suites where the president and his advisors hustled around trying to run the country. It wasn't much of a door, but Steele knew that its gleaming silver veneer was made of battleship iron. A single close protection officer tasked over from DIA was posted there, but he looked just like the Secret Service guys in their dark suits, specially tailored so they wouldn't "print" their handguns. He nodded at Steele and stepped aside as Eric tapped his CAC card on the numerical reader, which glowed yellow at the top of its reactive bar, and then above that an orb that looked like a tenement peephole blinked, and Steele raised his left brow and matched it eye-for-eye. The door buzzed, the *pistolero* pushed it open, Steele went inside and closed it behind him.

Cutlass Main's Tactical Operations Center always struck Steele as weirdly magical. From the outside, the White House appeared to be large and spacious with endless great rooms and conference centers, but those who worked there knew that aside from the president's Oval and attached offices, most of the working areas were cramped, albeit impeccably designed. Yet somehow, Cutlass Main's TOC seemed to occupy a space that looked much larger than architecturally possible. It couldn't, of course, compare to the TOCs at CIA or Central Command, but it had a dozen workstations with superquick, multiterabyte computers, a huge flat screen that occupied the entire northern wall, and four additional workspaces called isolation cells, or "tanks," defended by further steel doors like the one he'd just walked through. He could never quite figure out how the whole thing was shoehorned inside the White House. He had a feeling that if the wrong person somehow opened the main door after midnight, he'd find nothing but a janitor's closet.

He stood just inside the main entrance and perused the place for a minute. The usual bustle of tracking worldwide bad actors was in play, but something else was going on as well. There were urgent whispers among analysts. Today's atmosphere reminded him of videos he'd seen of NASA mission control right after the space shuttle had burned up on reentry. He glanced at one of the side tanks that secured a secondary operation called Keyhole, where Meg worked these days on a DARPA project that involved virtual reality target analysis. He hadn't seen her yet since Aleppo, and his thighs tingled at the thought of her walking through that door, in which case they'd both have to be cool. PDAs, or Public Displays of Affection, were totally verboten at Cutlass Main.

"Stalker Seven, what the heck are you doing here?"

Steele looked down to see Ralph Persko, one of the Program's top geeks, staring up at him as if Steele were an atheist crashing a church. Persko was twenty-eight and chubby, with wild, curly brown hair, Elvis Costello glasses, and taco drips on his yellow golf shirt.

"First of all, Ralphy, I told you before. Don't use my handle unless it's on secure comms."

Persko slapped himself on the head. "Oh right, I forgot."

"You're going to slip one day when we're out at Starbucks, and every Russian spook in the joint's going to whip out a notepad."

"Sorry, Eric. But aren't you still on leave?"

"I got lonely. What's going on down here? Somebody lose a nuke?"

"Your keeper didn't tell you?"

Steele turned and glared down at Persko, who seemed to shrivel one full suit size.

"Oh God, I'm sorry." Persko groaned. "I forgot about Demo. It's just not real yet, ya know? To any of us. . . ."

"It's okay, Ralphy." Steele patted him on the shoulder. "But it's still too damn real for me."

Persko raised his palms apologetically. "I just can't brief you is all."

"I know. Go do some geek stuff and I'll catch you later."

Persko nodded and headed back to his workstation, just as the Keyhole door opened and Meg stepped out into the TOC. She was wearing a short black skirt, nylons, dark flats, and a prim, blue tucked-in blouse, but none of that could hide her athletic figure or the sheen of her tight black ponytail and stunning eyes. She stopped short when she saw Steele and he saw her. Their gazes locked across the large space, then she took a deep breath, looked at the ceiling, and silently thanked heaven. But that was all. She walked to a workstation and dropped a Special Access Program file on someone's desk, and when she turned to walk back to Keyhole she nearly tripped over a snaking cable on the floor. That's when Steele noticed there were three technicians in white Tyvek coveralls crawling around, unplugging computers and wrapping them up for a move. Then he spotted another one with a handcart piled with padlocked steel file boxes.

What the hell? Are we being evicted? Did somebody forget to pay the rent?

"Steele, you know you're not getting double overtime for showing up here when you're TDY, right?"

Steele turned and saw Mike Pitts, stalking his way toward him from his overwatch desk in the middle of the floor. Pitts was the Program's director of operations and had been so for more than a decade, starting a year after he'd lost a leg in Fallujah in 2006. A former infantry major, he wore his high-and-tight blond hair a little longer now for reasons of cover, but he couldn't hide the shrapnel scar that punctuated his grin, or the prosthetic left leg that ended in an incongruous brown loafer. Whenever he worked too much, which was often, he'd use a Fred Astaire cane. Steele liked Pitts a lot and he matched his smile.

"Morning, Mike. I realized after my post-Aleppo brief that I forgot to turn in some receipts."

"Really? Did you buy anything work related in Syria?"

"I had lunch on the objective," Steele quipped. "Nothing fancy, though. Hummus and a salad."

Pitts jerked a thumb toward one of the other four doors. "Well, you can go see Mrs. Darnstein, if you don't mind losing your head." He meant the harried Program comptroller. "She's got the sense of humor of a cadaver."

"I think I'll pass and just eat it. And what's going on here, sir? Are we expanding, contracting, or just getting our asses kicked out?"

"The latter, I'm afraid. Lansky's decided to move us."

Pitts meant the president's chief of staff, Ted Lansky, who'd worked for President Rockford when Rockford was still VP, and he had retained that title since President Cole had been forced to withdraw because of his terminal cancer and Rockford had assumed the office. Lansky was a former director of clandestine services at CIA, and while pleasant enough, he expected all of his directives to be obeyed without question.

"Did we screw something up?" Steele asked.

Pitts pulled a red felt-tip marker from his pocket, twirled it in his fingers, and jammed the end in his teeth like a cigar. He had a large whiteboard in his battle captain office on which he planned and tracked operations using multicolored markers, because unlike computers, whiteboards couldn't be hacked.

"Negative, at least as far as I'm concerned," Pitts said. "But Lansky feels that our profile's getting just a bit too large."

"Nobody ever complained before." Steele frowned. "And we've been here since the Nuremberg trials."

"Nineteen forty-six was a long, long time ago, Eric. The good news is, we're getting larger digs over on Q Street, not far from Dupont Circle."

"I hate moving," Steele said and felt his shoulders slump. But it was more than that. Being headquartered at the White House had always made him feel somewhat special, even though he spent most of his time in the field. And the Program's missions were always tasked directly by the president. Now there would be layers in between, which was never a good thing.

"I'm afraid there's another piece of bad news," Pitts said as he jabbed his marker at the head-down, whispering analysts. "We lost an Alpha yesterday."

Steele had been standing there with his hands in his jeans pockets, but now he slipped them out reflexively and his fingers curled into fists.

"Who was it?"

"Raines."

"Stalker Six?"

"Affirmative. In Paris."

Steele suddenly saw Raines laughing hysterically, when they'd both gotten lost together during assessment and selection at Fort Bragg while trying to sprint through a land nav course, at night, in the middle of a driving rainstorm. Jonathan Raines was the classiest of all the Alphas—highly educated, dressed like a *GQ* model, spoke multiple languages. But he was also a stone-cold hand-to-hand killer. He wouldn't have gone down easy.

"How many were there?" he asked as his jaw clenched. "Do we know how they got him?"

"Not 'they,' just one. And your new keeper will brief you."

That bit of news slapped Steele in the face even harder than Jonathan Raines's death. He pulled his head back and stared down at Pitts, who was regarding him with some sympathy, because he knew how Steele had felt about Demo. The relationship between keepers and Alphas was akin to police cruiser partners where the cops were working the most dangerous beats on earth. It was a balance thing, with both operators being carefully selected to match one another. It was a marriage where the spouses were both good guys and outlaws. Bonnie and Clyde, Butch Cassidy and the Sundance Kid. It was not an off-the-shelf kind of thing.

"It's too soon, Mike," Steele said.

"It's too late, Steele," said Pitts. His smile had faded and now he was issuing orders. "You haven't had a keeper for two months now, and you know we don't work that way. Play ball or retire. Clear?"

"Yes, sir."

Just then the main access door behind Steele's back opened, and a man walked through and slammed it shut again with his heel. He was shorter than Steele, cue-ball bald, fiftyish, and built like a fire hydrant. His eyes were polar ice blue above a boxer's bent nose and lips as tight as a chicken's. He looked like Ed Harris in *The Rock*, but not nearly as friendly.

"Excellent timing," said Pitts. "Eric Steele, I want you to meet your new keeper, Dalton Goodhill."

Steele just stared at Goodhill's eyes, which locked right back on his. Neither man extended a hand.

"And, Mr. Goodhill," said Pitts, "this is Eric Steele, also known as Stalker Seven."

Something like a sneer curled the corner of Goodhill's mouth.

"A fucking pleasure," he growled in a voice that sounded like marbles in motor oil. "Let's go for a ride."

CHAPTER 6

WASHINGTON, D.C.

The 1989 cream-white Ford Bronco bounced out of an underground parking garage on H Street, right next to the National Museum of Women in the Arts.

Dalton "Blade" Goodhill was behind the wheel and Eric Steele was waiting outside on the curb. Steele took a full step back as the small truck slewed hard to the right and slammed to a stop. He couldn't see Goodhill inside because the Bronco had gray-tinted windows, so for a moment he thought the Bronco's owner must be some twisted O.J. Simpson fan with a thing for serial killers. Then the passenger door swung open. Wrong.

Steele climbed inside, closed the door, and belted in. The upholstery was faded brown leather, the dashboard console featured coffee cup stains, and the interior smelled like stale cigars. Anyone who'd been alive in 1994 remembered how Simpson, the football legend, had murdered his wife and an innocent waiter in Los Angeles, then led the police on a wild chase in exactly that model truck. Now the sight of a white Bronco anywhere invoked images of fugitives and grisly mayhem.

Goodhill started driving.

"Interesting choice of a ride," said Steele.

"Nobody in our business would ever drive such an obvious POS, right?" Goodhill growled.

"Right."

"That's why I bought it."

Midday traffic in Washington was, as usual, brutal, but Goodhill just sat there relaxed in his seat and avoided using the horn. Steele glanced to the left and looked him over. His bald head was outdoor tan, as if he spent a lot of time on the water, but Steele had a feeling that Goodhill didn't sail like many of the Washington old-school elites. His skull had more than a few dings and dents, like a well-used soccer ball, and from behind his right ear a permanent red welt ranged four inches down across his bull neck, maybe a parachute riser scar. *Free fall junkie, probably Special Forces,* Steele decided. Goodhill's forehead sloped to a pair of thick blond eyebrows brushing his Ray-Bans and his pug nose had taken some hits. His anvil jaw stuck out over a button-down white shirt, no tie, and a blue blazer similar to Steele's. He was, however, wearing a lapel pin—Boy Scouts. *Wise guy,* Steele assessed. *But not a lot of laughs.*

"What's your handle?" he asked Goodhill.

"Blade."

"So you're good with a knife."

"No, they call me that 'cause I used to be a short-order cook."

Steele said nothing, but he'd already decided that this was going to suck.

"Look, kid," Goodhill said. "I'm not here to replace Demo."

"Good, because nobody can. Did you know him?"

"I knew *of* him, like everyone else in our world."

"Our world's pretty small," Steele said. "What's your glory story?"

"Seventy-fifth at Benning, Third Group at Bragg, then A-Squadron and Special Activities Division. Retired out of there and got sucked back in here."

Strong résumé, Steele thought, *though not unusual for upper-tier operators. Army Rangers, Special Forces, Delta, CIA.*

"But let's skip the first-date bullshit for now," Goodhill said. "We've got a man down and it's not like we're a full-strength platoon."

"Concur," Steele said. "What do we know?"

"Stalker Six, your buddy Jon Raines, was found in an alley on the Left Bank of the Seine. Paris Station recovered him from the Gendarmerie with the help of DGSE and called in a local medical examiner on the embassy payroll. He took a hard groin strike, a cranium fracture, eyeball trauma, both eyes, and then some sort of stiletto blade under his jaw and right up into his brain. That was it, lights out."

Steele sat there for a moment with those images uninterrupted by a throng of coed congressional interns crossing in front of them at a light.

"Raines was quick, and extremely capable," Steele

said. "No way he would have let some dude ambush him like that. Killer must've been one big bruiser."

"It was a woman."

Steele looked over at Goodhill's expressionless face.

"A woman. How'd they figure that out from the wounds?"

"They didn't. Cutlass Main was trying to make contact exactly at the time he went down. A woman answered his cell."

"So? That doesn't mean she was the one. Could have been a passerby."

"Right, except this chick mentioned the Program."

Steele felt the blood draining from his face, and suddenly the Bronco's air conditioner seemed not to be working.

"Say again?"

"You heard me right. Plus, the bitch gloated about killing Stalker Six, probably while his blood was still warm on her blade. Which reminds me, I forgot one detail—he was missing his left ear. And then she made a very clear reference to the Program, the number of Alphas we've got, and how now we'd only have eight operators left."

A tinge of nausea crawled up Steele's gullet. Someone, a woman, an expert female killer, had somehow honey-trapped one of the Program's most experienced Alphas, murdered him in cold blood, *cut off his ear*, then bragged about how she knew exactly who he was and where he came from, and hinted that more was to come.

"Did they get a voiceprint on her?" he asked with

a modicum of hope. Standard procedure was to record all secure comms and store them in an impenetrable "cloud," which was actually an armored server located three floors below Cutlass Main.

"Affirmative, but negative. They got it, but she doesn't match anything in anyone's database. Top nerd thinks she's using some sort of implanted voice chip."

By "top nerd" Goodhill probably meant Ralphy Persko. But an implanted device to disguise someone's voice wasn't something Steele had encountered before.

"You know what this means, right?" Goodhill asked.

"I know what it means," Steele grunted. "It means the Program is blown."

"Correct. Which is probably why you're getting kicked out of your digs."

"You mean *our* digs. Or are you just a tourist?"

"Okay, kid. *Our* digs. I'm new here, remember?"

Steele was in no mood to give a "Fuckin' New Guy" any slack. Goodhill turned right onto Rhode Island Avenue, instead of heading straight up Connecticut Avenue toward Dupont Circle. Steele jabbed a finger at the left-hand window.

"Dupont Circle's that way, up north."

"I know which way fuckin' north is, thank you. You *have* heard of countersurveillance driving, right, kid?"

Steele said nothing. He hadn't heard map references punctuated with profanity like that since his days in Special Forces, so at least that was somewhat comforting.

They drove another six blocks in silence, with neither man feeling the compulsion to break any more ice. Steele was thinking about the dire implications of an enemy agent knowing not only about the existence of the Program, but its manning strength as well, at least in terms of the spearhead operators. He had no idea what Goodhill was thinking, but the man seemed like one of those old-school, hard corps, Tier One operators who only thought about the next five minutes of his life. He remembered regarding Demo the very same way, before their working relationship turned from worthless lead into solid white gold, and eventually a deep, incomparable friendship. But that wasn't going to happen here.

Goodhill drove the Bronco around Dupont Circle, straight up Connecticut, and took a hard right onto Q Street NW. He cruised another three blocks, passing Hank's Oyster Bar on the right, which happened to be one of Meg Harden's favorites. In the middle of the block between Sixteenth and Seventeenth, he turned left into an underground parking garage and stopped at the drop pole. A sign on the slat said MONTHLY MEMBERS ONLY. Goodhill rolled down the window, carded the reader, and they descended into gloom.

A uniformed parking attendant was waiting at the bottom of the ramp. He looked much like such lot workers all over Washington, dark complexioned and presumably bored, except his feet were spread like a beat cop and he waved a glowing traffic baton. Goodhill stopped the Bronco, and both men got out.

"Morning, gents," the attendant said in an incongruous Bermuda British accent. "Show us the money, if you please."

Goodhill and Steele produced their Program ID cards, which the man examined carefully and returned.

"Very good," he said congenially. "Are we carrying today?"

"Nothing dangerous," Goodhill said as he opened his blazer and Steele saw an extremely short, cut-down Remington 870 shotgun, anodized in hard-coat black. A breakaway ring on the rear grip was clipped to a shoulder rig under his right armpit, and the shotgun's forward grip—nothing more than a three-inch steel rod—was secured by a Velcro belt loop. "It's only twenty-gauge. Just for those pain-in-ass geese on the Mall."

"I didn't figure you for a *Miami Vice* fan," Steele sneered.

"I didn't figure you for anything," Goodhill retorted.

"And you, sir?" the attendant said to Steele.

Steele opened his jacket.

"Just an empty holster. It's a metaphor for my effectiveness."

The "parking attendant" smiled and said, "Off with you, gents. And blazers buttoned, if you please."

They walked up the ramp, with Steele letting Goodhill take a slight lead. His new keeper turned left on the street and they were facing a pair of glass doors with a sign above that said GRACELAND IMPORT EXPORTS. Goodhill pulled the door open.

"Somebody's an Elvis fan," Steele muttered.

"Probably your ops guy, Pitts," Goodhill said.

"You mean *our* ops guy."

"You can stand down correcting me whenever you're ready."

"I'll take it under advisement."

There were a couple of white leather sofas in the lobby, unoccupied, and a hefty desk against the north wall under a large Robert Salmon painting of a merchant schooner braving rough seas. A pretty, twenty-something blonde in a business suit with her hair pulled back sat at the desk. Her name tag said MERRY.

"Good morning, gentlemen. May I help you?"

"We're here for the conference," said Goodhill, and both men showed her their IDs.

She pointed off right to a gleaming elevator. "Second floor, right above us."

"Nice," Steele said. "Low enough so we can jump if we have to."

The young woman cocked her head. "I don't know what you mean."

Steele smirked. "Of course you don't, Merry."

Up on the second floor, the elevator opened onto a submarine chamber, where Goodhill and Steele had to swipe their CAC cards, punch in their individual Program codes, and then have their eyeballs scanned. Another door slid open on bank vault rollers, and they were facing a large empty space that spanned the entire building floor.

The place was crawling with technicians and movers. They were all wearing white Tyvek coveralls stamped with the logos of a phony moving company. One group was hauling in Steelcase desks from a rear cargo elevator, while another group was down on hands and knees, routing electrical cables through narrow trenches in the slate stone flooring. Another crew was unfurling antistatic carpet squares upon which the workstations would perch, while another was assembling VariDesk units so the Program employees could stand whenever their glutei maximi ached. An enormous flat screen was being bolted in sections to the far north wall, while past that to the right, the thick transparent plexiglass slats of a Sensitive Compartmented Information Facility were being welded into place around a long, mahogany conference table. Electric drills whined, air compressors hissed, and the place smelled like a Formula One pit at Le Mans.

Steele noted that no one he knew from the Program was there. But that didn't surprise him. All of these young men and women were probably DoD support personnel seconded over from the Pentagon, or perhaps even JSOC at Fort Bragg. They all had TS clearances, yet that didn't mean they had any idea for whom they were building this TOC. The approximately forty Program officers, analysts, and security personnel wouldn't show up until all of the work had been completed and tested. After that, Ralphy Persko and his small crew of nerds would be the round-the-clock troubleshooters, for whenever someone's workstation belched. Steele jammed his hands in his jeans pockets and frowned.

"It looks cold."

"What do you mean, cold?" Goodhill said. "The AC's not in yet and it feels like ninety in here."

"I mean, industrial. Not like over at Cutlass Main."

"Get used to it. This is the new Cutlass Main. No Lincoln Bedroom, no commissary full of diplomats, and no nosy press flacks snooping around."

"I liked the old digs." Steele turned to Goodhill. "So what are we doing here? This place isn't going to function for a week."

Goodhill turned away from him and jutted his lantern jaw across the room. "She'll tell you."

Then Steele spotted Collins Austin, marching toward them from one of the multiple side offices he hadn't really noticed before. Austin was Stalker Eight, the only female Alpha on the team, and she had the perfect cover in that her looks instantly eradicated any suspicion that she might be anything other than a fashion model or Kennedy Center dancer. She was five foot seven, with flame-red hair, light blue eyes, and the figure of a Miss Universe contestant, and she could go from disarmingly charming to flat-out deadly faster than a methanol drag racer. But today she didn't look very pretty. Her face was drawn and pale, and her full lips were clamped into a tight scarlet scar. And Steele knew why. His stomach dropped as she approached.

"Hello, Maggie," he said. He wasn't going to use her real name within earshot of all these strangers.

"Hello, Max." She returned the cover courtesy in kind.

She was carrying a thick red file sealed with black security tape. For a moment Steele wanted to hug her but instantly thought better of it. Not with Goodhill standing there. He nodded at Goodhill.

"This is . . ."

"John Booth," Goodhill said as he extended a callused paw. But he didn't leer at Austin or look her over, as most men couldn't help but do. "The boss had me bring Max over here for the handoff."

Now Steele was beginning to understand. There was no reason for him to be getting a tour of the new digs, unless Mike Pitts had something special for him and wanted no other Program witnesses. With the killing of Stalker Six in Paris, apparently the ops director was taking extreme precautions. And there was something more. Collins Austin and Jonathan Raines had been very close friends, and then more than just that, only two years before. When Pitts had discovered their love affair, he'd nearly canned both of them, but Steele had intervened to save their careers. Sadly, none of that mattered now, except that Pitts clearly thought that if he could trust anyone with discretion on this particular matter, it would be Austin. There were tears in Austin's eyes. Steele had never seen that before, and it made him queasy.

"This is the file," Austin said as she handed it to Steele. "It's everything we have. Who Jon saw, where he was staying, all his movements as far as we know. There's some speculation about who that woman was, but nothing definitive at all. SOP on this, Max. Memorize it, but don't take it with you overseas."

Steele took the folder. "Where am I going?"

"Where do you think you're going?" Goodhill snarled at him. "Paris."

Steele swallowed the urge to smash Goodhill's Ray-Bans. Collins Austin reached out and gripped the lapel of Steele's blazer.

"Find her, Eric," she whispered as she pulled him close. A tear rolled down her cheek and she swatted it away like a plague-infested fly. "And when you find her, kill her."

CHAPTER 7

FALLS CHURCH, VIRGINIA

Meg Harden body-slammed Eric Steele less than five seconds after he walked through her door.

She had buzzed him into the condo and he'd taken the elevator to the eleventh floor, loosely gripping a bottle of 19 Crimes cabernet sauvignon because he knew she wasn't much for beer. He'd parked in her underground lot, recovered his 1911 from his car, and locked the red file in the gun box, and he was looking forward to a languid evening of maybe some good food, mild drinking, and mutually satisfying romance before boarding a plane for France. But this sort of welcome, he wasn't expecting.

Meg's front door was ajar, which made Steele's fingers switch the bottle from his right hand to his left and twitch toward his handgun. He toed the door open, saw nothing but hazy low-light gloom and a drawn shade over the far picture window, heeled the door closed, and advanced farther. Then the bedroom door on his left flung open and she came flying at him, with her black hair askew, her ice-blue eyes big and wild, and the only thing covering her athletic form a criminally short, silk black kimono splashed with combating dragons.

She hurled him backward onto her pin-striped sofa, grabbed the lapels of his blazer in both tight fists, and kissed him hard while she straddled his waist. The impact flung his arms to the sides and the wine bottle bounced on a cushion, but luckily stayed there intact. With her lips still locked onto Steele's, Meg tore off his jacket like a cop disabling a perp, pulled his 1911 from the holster, dumped the magazine, and racked the slide. A round went spinning off somewhere and she flung the gun and the mag in the couch corner—she hated Steele's "one-in-the-chamber" habit. Then she got down to business.

She released his tongue from her lips, slid back, yanked his belt buckle open, and snapped his jeans and briefs down to his ankles. Steele didn't need much more libidinous encouragement than that, but he was still somewhat shocked when Meg stared at him accusingly, as if he'd drugged her with Love Potion Number Nine, and then flicked her kimono sash open, whipped the whole thing off her gymnast's body, and mounted him with a weird small animal cry. He was still wearing his shirt and she clutched the white cotton over his chest muscles like a pair of reins and rode him so intensely he thought she might break something important, but he held back until she reared her head up and orgasmed, then he followed suit because he thought that was fair, and then she rode him even harder, like it was the last lap of the Kentucky Derby, until they were both hyperventilating and shiny with sweat.

She rolled off him, tucked her gleaming naked body close to his bare thigh, dropped her wild-haired head on his chest, and sighed. Steele looked down at her.

"I'm glad to see you too," he gasped.

"Just be quiet for a minute," Meg whispered.

That was fine with Steele. It was going to take at least that long for his heart to stop slamming his rib cage. Meg wasn't usually like this. She was controlled, reserved, and OCD neat. Their lovemaking usually occurred on a bed that looked like she'd measured the turned-down sheets with a slide rule.

But that didn't mean she was prissy.

She'd been a field operator for the Intelligence Support Activity, a branch of the Defense Intelligence Agency that tasked young men and women with laying the groundwork for Tier One special operations. ISA personnel had been on the ground in Islamabad prepping the hit on Osama bin Laden long before SEAL Team 6 showed up. Meg had multiple deployments in her army 201 file, including Ramadi and Mosul, and then she'd worked some very rough Middle East neighborhoods for the CIA, almost losing her life in Algiers. She regularly kicked men's asses in the hand-to-hand gym, but up until this evening, she'd been fairly bread-and-butter when it came to sex. Maybe this was the revelation of a wild side that she hadn't shown Steele before. He was looking forward to more.

"Are we cleared for conversation yet?" he asked at last.

"It's called afterglow," she said. "You need to read some girly books."

"I already am. I'm halfway through *Eat, Pray, Love.*"

"Ass."

She slapped his chest, got up, recovered her kimono, and quickly rewrapped herself. Steele felt a little silly with his jeans down around his ankles so he pulled them up, but he had to unbutton his dress shirt because his body was steaming. Meg picked up the wine bottle from the couch corner and inspected the label.

"Why's it called 19 Crimes?"

"It's an Australian vintage. Apparently, way back in Merry Olde England during the eighteenth century, being convicted of any one of nineteen crimes could get you a one-way ticket to Australia, which was nothing but a penal colony at the time."

"What were the crimes?" Meg walked into her spotless kitchen with the bottle and returned with two balloon glasses and a corkscrew.

"No idea. I'm an amateur drunk and only an occasional historian."

Meg handed Steele the glasses, sat down next to him, clamped the bottle between her naked thighs, and started driving the screw into the cork. His eyebrows went up.

"You're doing that on the couch?"

"I'm having it replaced tomorrow."

"Ahh, that explains why you didn't care about staining it."

"Don't be gross." She poured the glasses, set the bottle on the floor, and they both clinked and sipped.

"And I missed you too," she said. "And I'm pissed at you."

"Why?"

"I'm not exactly in the Program, Eric, but I knew where you were and have a good guess at what you were doing." The Keyhole project was not officially part of Cutlass Main, but Meg's shop supported Program activities with real-time intelligence. "I was worried, and I'm sure you knew that, and then you swing back in here, go TDY, and I don't even see you till you show up at the big house."

He reached out to stroke her raven hair, then leaned forward and kissed her forehead.

"I had to see my mother."

Meg laughed. "You're definitely the only Tier One shooter I know who's such a mama's boy."

"Well, she almost took one for the team. She deserves some attention."

"Fair enough."

They both sat back and sipped for a while. Then Steele broached the subject that was hanging right there in the air.

"I saw Collins Austin today."

"I'm glad I didn't," Meg said as she slowly shook her head. "I know she wasn't with Raines anymore, but she's still going through what I'm scared of every day."

Something about the way she said that set off an alarm in Steele's operator head. Meg wasn't his wife, and might never be, but he suddenly realized that having a ring and sworn vows didn't matter. They were not both Alphas—he was at the sharp end, while she was still part of the handle—but they were starting to cross that line where emotional attachments could cloud a man's brain. For him to keep on being a top operator with the Program, he could never find himself at the edge of some high-risk gambit somewhere and be thinking, *This could get me killed. And what about Meg?*

"That's exactly why Pitts is so adamant about interoffice relationships." Steele's voice was chilly.

"I'm technically not part of the Program."

"Doesn't matter."

She didn't say anything for a long moment. Then, "Well, do you think we should quit?"

"The Program?" Steele was certain that he loved her, but he was far from ready to surrender his career to love. He couldn't imagine going from what he did every day to having a Colonial house with a fireplace, a kindergarten minivan, and a brood of kids.

"No," she said. "Each other."

There was no way to answer that ambush question, so he deftly begged off.

"Let's just table that for now. I'm off to Paris in the morning."

She snuggled up closer to him. "Just watch your athletic ass. Whoever took out Raines had to be some big, bad, ugly dude. Maybe badder than you."

She's not read-on to the file, he thought. *Cutlass Main's strict compartmentalization policy's still airtight, just like it's supposed to be. She doesn't know the details of the kill. She doesn't know it was a woman, or how it was really done. Better that way.*

"What's for dinner?" he said.

"I was thinking Chinese."

"I passed Hank's Oyster Bar today."

She dragged her short fingernails through his chest curls and kissed him. "Believe me, Mr. Steele, you *don't* need oysters."

They ordered a pile of food up from Young Chow, watched one episode of *Stranger Things*, and went to bed. But they didn't make love again. They both knew they weren't going to top their reunion spectacular. Just before they fell asleep, Meg kissed him long and deeply, and whispered, "Just don't get stilettoed under your jaw."

"Not a chance," Steele murmured, and then he was off to dreamland.

Steele's internal cranial clock went off at exactly 4:00 A.M. It was one of his stranger talents, being able to wake himself up at any selected time, no matter his level of fatigue. All he had to do was envision a neon digital hour and minutes, with A.M. or P.M. glowing to the right, and that's when he'd sit straight up in bed. He'd been doing it since middle school, when he'd gotten his first underage job working a milk truck in rural Pittsburgh. Unfortunately, he hadn't taken advantage of the skill to get himself to school on time.

He slipped out from under Meg's sheets, pulled his 1911 from below the bed, tiptoed to the bathroom, brushed his teeth with a finger, stepped into the tub, and took a quick "whore's bath" with a washcloth—he thought the noise of a shower would wake her, and one long goodbye was enough. He dressed quietly in her salon, holstered the pistol, and checked his cell for secure messages; there were none. He locked himself out of her condo, took the elevator down to the indoor garage to recover his GTO, picked up a large burned coffee at an all-night McDonald's, and headed for Dulles Airport.

He parked the GTO in a short-term lot, outside. It would be harder for someone to screw with his car or try to jack it out in the open. Then he sat there for a full hour reading every page of the Stalker Six file, twice, though mostly he focused on Raines's last three days on earth, and he memorized place-names and Paris phone numbers. The autopsy report was in French, one of his best language skills, but still the words *énorme perte de sang*—massive blood loss—seemed worse in a romance language.

"You got sloppy, buddy," he whispered out loud as the bright orange ball of the sun rose above Dulles's massive runways and the early-morning jumbos careened up into the humid blue sky.

Then he felt bad about judging Raines, because he knew that any man who traveled like crazy, risked his life all the time, and was rarely home long enough to catch a baseball game could eventually develop a fissure that some wily adversary would penetrate.

"But she wasn't just some female assassin, right, Jon? She was beautiful, seductive, red-hot and ready, the type of woman any of us would go for."

He decided that he'd have to delve deeper into Raines's personal dating tastes—aside from Collins Austin—which might offer some clues. But there wasn't enough time for that now. He looked left and right out his car windows, making sure that no one was near. He reached back and pulled a black, nondescript REI backpack into the front seat, took off his holster and pistol, and zipped the 1911 and the red file into the ruck. Then he called Cutlass Main on his cell.

"Identify," said a sleepy female voice on the other end.

"Max Sands."

"Code in."

He recited an alphanumeric string, waited through some beeps and clicks, and the voice said, "What can I do for you, Mr. Sands?"

"I need a handoff, Dulles, Air France check-in. One hour, please. I'm tight to my flight."

"Absolutely. We'll find you." She clicked off.

He wasn't going to leave his handgun and the file in the car, not even in a lockbox that could only be opened with a thumbprint. If somebody really wanted his "jewels," they could tow his vehicle with a fake AAA tow truck and contract a safecracker to take his sweet time. He took his small rollaway from the trunk, locked up, and walked into the terminal clutching his bitter java and on the hunt for a cinnamon cruller.

Precisely one hour later, he was standing at one of those quick-ticket kiosks between Air France and KLM, inserting a Max Sands credit card from his wallet, when one of Cutlass Main's couriers cruised in beside him, also dragging a rollaway and carrying an identical backpack, which he dropped at his feet right next to Steele's. The handoff was easy. Steele's ticket popped out, he took the courier's backpack, which was packed with a laptop and plenty of Graceland Import Exports pocket litter, and headed for the security gates. The courier took Steele's backpack with his 1911 and the red file inside, and headed back to Cutlass Main.

One of Steele's well-kept secrets was that he loved to fly. All the other Alphas, keepers, armorers, analysts, and support staff bitched about it, claiming that they logged more miles than United Airlines flight attendants and federal sky marshals. Good soldier that he was, Steele crabbed right along with them, but the truth was that being on a long-range flight, even in economy class, was his favorite time. He could relax, watch a movie, read a book, and not have to answer some frantic call from HQ. To him it was like enjoying one of those sensory deprivation float chambers: no outside stimuli, other than whatever he chose.

But all of a sudden, he wasn't enjoying this flight at all. The 737 had taken off on time, and he was halfway down the cabin, sitting in an aisle seat, in a luxurious half-empty plane with plenty of leg room. He'd already ordered a Bloody Mary, yet his face was immobile as cold granite and he was staring at nothing.

And he was wondering how Meg Harden knew about the stiletto that had killed Stalker Six. . . .

CHAPTER 8

PARIS, FRANCE

Madame LeBarge, the night manager of the Montmartre Bed & Breakfast on 13 Rue Muller, wasn't a pretty woman. In fact she was fat, pushing eighty, and had worn the same muumuu printed with Normandy bovines for three days in a row. She had wispy white hair, wore pince-nez spectacles, and chaïn-smoked Gauloises. The minute Steele saw her, he felt like he was facing a gatekeeper from the last iteration of *The Matrix*.

As soon as he'd landed at Orly, just after midnight, he'd called over to the B&B where Stalker Six had been staying and asked for a room. She'd told him she had none. He'd asked to see one anyway.

"*À cette heure?*" she'd growled in a smoky Parisian patois. At this hour? "*Fou américain. Si vous insistez.*" Crazy American. If you insist.

Now he was sitting with her at a pink metal table in the courtyard of the Montmartre. The courtyard was large, festooned with fresh blooms, and Madame LeBarge's Jabba the Hutt figure was bathed in the yellow glow of overhead hanging lanterns. She was clearly displeased at having her reading disturbed. Steele noted her book was Albert Camus's *L'Étranger*, which happened to be about a murder.

"I assure you, Madame, I'm Mr. Raines's business colleague," Steele said in French fluent enough to keep her from responding in English, which Parisians often did out of spite.

"So you claim." She took a long drag off her filterless smoke, coughed, and folded her arms.

Steele then described Raines in detail. He knew Stalker Six had been traveling under his own name, which Alphas sometimes did when on leave. They were all "ghosted" and didn't exist on anyone's database, so occasionally it was safer that way.

"He has not returned to his room," the night manager huffed.

"Well, he's been having some family difficulties," Steele said.

"They are not *my* difficulties. There is a bill to pay."

"Do you still have his credit card information, Madame?"

"I do." Yet she shrugged, as if that was worthless.

"Feel free to charge it," Steele said. "And I'll cover any additional expenses. Have you rented his room?"

Madame LeBarge palmed her ample chest. "Do I look like a thief?"

"Of *course* not." Steele slipped a hand in his pocket and slid four fifty-euro bills onto the table. "I'd like to see his room. And then, perhaps I'll book it myself."

She looked at the cash over her pince-nez, then back at his jade-green eyes.

"You shall have to pay both his bill, *and* yours."

"*Avec plaisir*," he said. With pleasure.

She slipped the bills into her dress pocket, trundled into her small office, and returned with a brass key attached to a tag that said ROMANTIC ARTIST ROOM in English. She gave it to Steele, then pointed at a slim green door and said, "Third floor."

He slung his REI backpack, gripped his rollaway, and went up.

The room didn't match any of the nineteenth-century architecture he'd seen outside. It was minimalist, with cream-white walls, a black-and-white tiled floor, a Scandinavian king-size bed, and framed modern art all over the place. Left of the bed was a red plastic rocking chair, a minifridge, and an Art Deco electric fan atop an open wardrobe with a few wooden hangers. Right of the bed, a large modern bathroom was walled off from the rest of the space by plexiglass. Steele didn't much care for that kind of toilet exposure, but then he saw a brocaded purple curtain that could be pulled from both sides of the glass for privacy. Raines's toothbrush and shaving kit were still above the porcelain pedestal sink. Raines's rollaway was open on a wooden luggage mount at the far side of the bed.

Steele looked through the luggage but didn't expect to find anything revealing. The only unusual item was a music CD of Superchunk, lying atop Raines's neatly folded clothes. Alphas generally traveled "naked," meaning unarmed, and picked up whatever weapons or tools of the trade they might need from safehouses maintained by the Program in major capital cities. In the morning he'd head over to the safehouse in the 20th arrondissement and avail himself of an FN Five-seveN pistol in 5.7 x 28 mm, and a Smith & Wesson tanto folding knife. He figured he could get through the night without them.

Then he spotted one item that piqued his interest. Lying on the wooden night table was a four-color flyer, advertising the current Monet exhibit at the Louvre and a concurrent lecture by Egyptian-born French artist Emile Sadat. The date and time were circled in pen.

It was the same day on which Stalker Six had been murdered.

Steele tossed his rollaway on the bed, opened it, and changed from his blazer into a U.S. Navy G-1 leather flight jacket. Then he folded the art brochure, slipped it into the jacket, and made a local call on his cell. It took five European *brrrings* until a sleep-drenched voice answered.

"*Tu sais quelle heure il est?*"

"I know what fucking time it is, Claude," Steele snapped. "It's Max. Get up."

He heard rustling sheets and the voice became more compliant.

"I apologize. I didn't know it was you, Max."

"Meet me at Les Délices d'Istanbul café in twenty minutes. Know where that is?"

"Ah . . . Boulevard Barbès?"

"That's right."

"Are you staying near there?"

"*Pas de tes affaires*," Steele said. None of your business. Steele then clicked off.

He didn't much like Claude Fischer, a half-German, half-French informant who was on the Program's payroll and could be trusted with just about nothing. But the man knew everything and everyone in the underbelly of Paris, and might have heard some rumors about a recently murdered American and the woman who'd taken him down. The DGSE had kept everything about it out of the local news, but Fischer had shills everywhere, including the Gendarmerie. Fischer was a veteran of La Légion étrangère, the French Foreign Legion, and nothing scared him much. Except Max Sands.

Steele locked up, loped down the slim stairway, and found Madame LeBarge still reading Camus.

"The room's very nice, Madame." He smiled.

"I am so pleased you like it." She coughed and nearly rolled her eyes.

He showed her the Louvre brochure.

"Do you happen to know where this came from, Madame? Did your staff put these in the rooms?"

"My 'staff' is myself and the occasional Algerian whore." She flicked a finger at the brochure. "We don't advertise for anyone unless they pay. This one, I believe, was distributed by a woman some ten days ago."

Steele understood that whoever that woman was, she'd also bribed the madame.

"Do you happen to recall what she looked like?"

Madame LeBarge tapped her jowl and looked

up at the starry sky. "I might remember better at breakfast."

Steele nodded and put the brochure back in his pocket. He understood that her memory was only going to be spurred by more euros.

"In the morning, then," he said.

"Good night." She went back to reading her book.

Twelve minutes later, Steele was standing on the east side of Boulevard Barbès, across the way from the bright blue facade of Les Délices d'Istanbul, which curiously served Indian food. The waiters were outside, striking the white tablecloths from the chestnut café tables and folding up the chairs. The interior of the place was brightly lit, and Steele could see all the late-night patrons, but none were Claude Fischer. He looked at his Rolex Submariner and let another fifteen minutes tick by. Fischer never showed, and Steele knew if he called him he wouldn't answer this time.

Something had scared Fischer off. Something scarier to him than Steele.

It was starting to drizzle as he made his way back to the Montmartre B&B. A few street sweepers were out, and back on Rue Muller a tall blond hooker tried to make an approach. He had a twinge of empathy for her as he waved her off, said, "*Pas ce soir, mademoiselle*," and considered that their lives were similar—always on the move, hunting for action, encountering occasional pleasures and then sudden violence, all of which were part of the game. He was willing to bet that she'd also grown up without paternal guidance.

If you kill me you will never find your father.

He blew that tormenting phrase out of his mind and twisted his focus back to the mission at hand.

Something's rotten in Denmark, he thought, which was actually a reference to Shakespeare's *Hamlet* and had nothing to do with his current location. The whole point of the Program's effectiveness was that it had remained ultrasecret for decades. *Someone has figured us out. And once you've got a crack in that wall, the whole goddamn dam can collapse and we'll all go tumbling over the falls.* But he knew it was worse than just a simple breach of security, or a cyber hacker's intrusion, or, God forbid, a leak from a disgruntled member. For Raines's killer to have known about the Alpha headcount, she had to have someone on the inside, and he didn't even want to think about that.

He walked, and brooded, and suddenly decided that it was all probably something much simpler. Raines's killer hadn't been alone. Stalker Six had been ambushed in that alley by more assaulters than just that one girl, and they'd tortured him until he'd given up just enough for her to spew her poison into his cell phone.

I'm on a fool's errand. I'm swinging my pike at ghosts. It was just a one-off and they're having a ball making all of us crazy.

He felt better about all of it when he entered the courtyard of the B&B. Madame LeBarge wasn't there anymore, and he trotted back up the darkened stairway and turned the key in his lock. In the morning he'd start over again, go over to the Louvre, buddy up with some museum security guys, and see if they remembered anything.

He closed the door behind him, flicked on the light, shrugged off his leather jacket, and tossed it onto the bed. Then his brow furrowed when he realized that the purple brocade bathroom drapes were closed.

They flew open with the sound of a wind-ripped parachute and a man the size of a dump truck came flying at him from the bathroom.

CHAPTER 9

PARIS, FRANCE

It was like getting hit by a hundred-ton steam locomotive. Full speed, downhill, no brakes.

All Steele saw was this human bull encased in a giant purple corduroy jacket, with a massive head, arms like scuba tanks, and hands like bear traps, flying at him from the bathroom. Steele was at the left side of the bed, and only managed to snap a half turn and leap backward one stride. The flying monster was on the right side, and he stomped on the bed with one engineer boot the size of a gunboat, and launched his soccer ball–size left shoulder into Steele's chest.

Steele didn't fall. He sailed, backward, a full twelve feet, with the heels of his black Red Wing Oxfords leaving a double skid mark on the tile floor, and then his shoulder blades thundered dead center into a twenty-by-thirty-inch framed print of a Paul Klee painting, *Camel (in Rhythmic Landscape with Trees)*. Reflexively, Steele had tucked his head down and to the right, because that's all he could manage to do, and he knew what was coming. His assailant's head torpedoed over Steele's left shoulder and straight into the glass, which exploded, raining shards and splinters all over both of them. But the real damage was done to the man's crown, which gushed streams of blood, and as he stood up to his full height and shook it off, his face was like a mask from a horror movie.

He swiped the blood from his eyes with a sleeve, slapped Steele in the face with a sirloin-size palm, and roared "*Ubljudok!*" Motherfucker! That's when Steele knew he was a Russian, but for the moment, nationality didn't matter.

Steele kicked him straight up into his groin with the hardwood blade of his shinbone. It was a wicked strike that would have put any other man down, but it had no effect. *The guy's a friggin' sumo and can pull his balls back up into his pelvis* flashed through Steele's mind, and then his assailant obliged him by completing the Japanese metaphor.

He grabbed Steele's right arm with his left hand, underneath by the shirtsleeve, while he twisted inside to the left and jammed his huge right arm underneath Steele's right armpit. Then he spun around like a typhoon spout and executed a perfect judo *ippon seoi nage*—a one-arm shoulder throw—flipping Steele right over his head so his boots clanged off the ceiling. Steele's spine bounced off the bed like it was a trampoline and he was launched nose-first into the bathroom's plexiglass divider. He tasted blood as it gushed down over his upper lip, but there was no time for sensory observations, and he spun around just in time to duck away from the flying electric fan that missed his skull by an inch.

"This is for Kuznetsov!" the giant roared in Russian as he reached down for the footboard of the bed, lifted the whole thing up, and tossed it out of the way like a snack table.

Who the fuck is Kuznetsov? Steele wondered, but he wasn't going to ask; it just didn't seem like the time.

The beast hunched his bison-size shoulders and crouched into a Russian Systema stance, with his arms forming a triangle to his body and his bladed hands jutting forward. Steele responded with a Krav Maga stance, slightly pigeon-toed with his open palms hovering in defensive position beside his face. Even at six foot two and two hundred pounds, Steele could move like a bantam and strike like a jackhammer, but this guy had six inches' height on him and a hundred pounds. The only way to take him would be to feint for his head, burst his knees out with whipping side kicks, then blind him with both thumbs in his eyeballs.

Seemed like a good plan until the gorilla reached into his right boot and came up with a Kalashnikov bayonet. It looked like the standard-issue AK-47 knife with its honey-colored grip, blood groove, and wickedly curved blade tip, except that it also gleamed like it had just been honed on a diamond sharpener. The Russian spun the bayonet like a pencil, gripped it overhand, blade down, and grinned. He had teeth like dirty fingernails, the incisors tipped in gold.

Steele knew that once that blade started stabbing

down, it would never stop. He reminded himself to never, *ever* again, postpone swinging by a safehouse and getting himself armed up—not that he thought that anything short of a .50 caliber Desert Eagle could stop this guy. He jinked backward through the bathroom's plexiglass door. The man advanced on him, thinking he had him cornered. Steele spun and, in one swift motion like a whirling dervish, ripped the ceramic toilet seat off its mounts, kept on spinning, and hurled it like a discus at the giant's throat. From past experience with such things, Steele knew the monster would instinctively try to duck, which he did, and the toilet seat banged into the frontal lobe of his huge brow and shattered in half.

The giant roared, stiffened upright as if he'd just been shot through with high voltage, dropped the bayonet, and tumbled backward, crashing into the open wardrobe beside the smashed Paul Klee.

Then Steele was on him like a lightning bolt. He whipped a full-circle right foot roundhouse kick into the Russian's left knee, the sound of it like the whoosh of a baseball bat smacking a watermelon, and knew that he'd fractured the kneecap when the man threw his head back and roared like a gutshot lion. Then Steele stomped the floor with that same right foot and side kicked him in the solar plexus with the heel of his left Red Wing, bouncing him off the wall again, and the whole room trembled as if from a low-grade earthquake. Then he gave him two quick closed-fist strikes to the face, going for the temporomandibular joints, where that massive jaw was linked to the temporal skull bone, and hammering it left and right, which spiked a neural shock to his brain. And he was just going for the eyeballs with his thumbs when the Russian pushed off the wall and bear-hugged him.

It gushed the breath from his lungs like oversize pliers crushing a balloon. He palm-slapped the giant on both ears, but that had no effect. The Russian tossed him up into the air, spun him around like a ragdoll, and crush-hugged him from behind this time, and Steele felt his ribs bending like crossbows. He kicked a heel back as hard as he could up into the bastard's balls, and they both crashed forward onto the floor, but the grip didn't release one bit, and Steele felt his eyes starting to pop from his skull and he couldn't draw a breath. Another thirty seconds of this and it would all be over.

He saw Jonathan Raines's rollaway spilled all over the floor in front of him, next to the wooden night table. His fingers scrambled for the Superchunk CD as the giant hissed Russian death curses in his pulse-pounding ear, and he wrenched the plastic case open, somehow popped the CD out, gripped the gleaming disc with both hands, and cracked it in half on the corner of the night table, leaving two wicked half scythes of razor-sharp polycarbonate in his viselike-grip fists.

Steele flung his left hand back and sliced off half of the Russian's left ear. The giant screamed and turned his head to the left to ward off the blade, exposing his right carotid artery, and Steele whipped his right hand backward, stabbed the jagged disc two inches deep into flesh, and cleaved through the meat of that Brahman bull neck with everything he had.

The giant said nothing. He suddenly released Steele and staggered to his feet, trying to stanch the hose of blood from his neck. He gripped his own throat as if he were choking himself, but that didn't stop the gushing crimson, and he stumbled toward the bathroom, perhaps hoping that something in there might save him, and Steele lay there on his side and tried to regain his breath and just watched him careen. The Russian finally released his wound, reared his head back, gripped the purple brocade curtain, and tore the entire thing from its rings as he crashed face-first onto the bathroom floor.

Steele rolled up onto his rump and slid himself back against the wall. He dropped the bloody CD halves and looked at his shaking hands. Amazingly, he felt his cell phone still in his back pocket, and he pulled it out and tapped in for Cutlass Main. Out in the hallway, he could hear a female voice, Madame LeBarge, he was sure, yelling out in French and demanding to know just what the hell was going on in there.

"Code in," said the robotic tone from very far away.

Steele recited his alphanumeric code in a voice that didn't sound like his own. He was awfully thirsty.

"Yes, what can we do for you, Mr. Sands?"

"Know where I am?" He knew they'd have a GPS lock on him, but he wanted to make sure.

"Of course we do, yes."

"Good." Steele dropped his head back against the wall and closed his eyes. "I need a cleanup on aisle thirteen."

CHAPTER 10

PARIS, FRANCE

Eric Steele slapped Claude Fischer for the third time, and so hard that water flung from the Frenchman's eyes and made a spatter pattern on the filthy yellow stucco wall.

They were in the back hallway of a whorehouse inside the infamous Pigalle district, just two blocks from the Moulin Rouge. That's where Steele had been pretty sure he'd find Claude, and he was right, because the man had only two obsessions—drugs and sex—and it was too early in the morning for drugs.

"You fucking set me up, didn't you, Claude?" Steele's left hand was sunk like a crab claw in Fischer's throat and practically lifting him up off of his five-hundred-euro, Gianvito Rossi loafers. His right palm was cranked back and poised for another slap.

"I didn't, I swear," Claude gasped.

"*Menteur.*" Liar. Steele spat to one side onto the grimy runner carpet. "And who the hell was that Moscow monster?"

"I have no idea, Max, *really. Mon dieu*, I don't!"

A redheaded hooker in a terry cloth bathrobe and stiletto heels appeared, carrying a cup of espresso. She squeezed by them in the hallway as if such violence was par for the course.

"*Really?*" Steele snapped. "So who the fuck is Kuznetsov, Claude?" He jabbed a finger between Fischer's eyes as if it were a gun barrel. And it could have been, because by now he'd picked up the FN Five-seveN and the S&W knife from the safehouse, and he was sorely tempted to use them both.

"Kuznetsov? I . . . I don't know any Kuznetsov! The only one I've ever heard of is that Russian writer!"

Steele hauled off and slapped him again.

"Listen, you little shit." Steele jabbed the finger into Fischer's forehead, making his eyebrows scrunch and his eyes bug even wider. "I *know* you know the fat lady at the Montmartre. She pinged you on my arrival and you set me up for that goon, right? That's why you blew me off last night. You wanted me to hustle my ass back to my room so that fucker could play Ping-Pong with my head, *right?*"

"Max, I have no idea what you are talking about!" Claude began to keen from his throat as Steele squeezed harder. "I didn't mean to blow you off, I *swear.* Marianne and I were getting high when you rang, and after you hung up I simply forgot everything and fell back asleep. I'm sorry, I swear, I didn't mean anything by it and I know nothing about this Russian. And I do not know any fat lady at the Montmartre!"

Steele snarled, reached for his right-hand jeans

pocket, and came up with the black Smith & Wesson folder. He thumbed the grip and whipped it open, and then the terrifying tanto-style blade was a millimeter from Claude's left eyeball.

"Now tell me the *truth*, Claude, or I'm having this eyeball of yours in my afternoon martini."

"Max!" Fischer shrieked, and then his eyes rolled back and he went half limp, and Steele realized the former legionnaire was pissing himself. He looked down at the stain spreading through the crotch of his jeans, and he stepped back and released him. Fischer slid down the wall and slumped to the floor. Steele looked down at him.

"You know what, Claude?" he said. "I think I believe you."

He flicked the knife closed, clipped it back in his pocket, and stomped out the back door into the alley. Then he slapped some hanging laundry aside, popped out into the street, hailed a cab, and told the driver to take him over to the Louvre. The driver was going to make some small talk and angle for a nice early-morning tip, but then he saw the American's face in his rearview mirror and decided that silence might be the better part of valor.

Steele sat in the back of the Citroën and fumed. He wasn't going on much sleep, or any food for that matter, which left him with the surly disposition that Meg sometimes referred to as "hangry"—hunger-induced anger. But it wasn't just the lack of sucrose and caffeine. He felt like he was being wagged like a jingle bell on the end of a big dog's tail.

Thankfully, the "bleachers" had shown up at the Montmartre within twenty minutes after he'd made the call. There was such a cleanup team in every major capital where the Program worked, and if an Alpha was tasked to some out-of-the-way town in someplace like southern Africa, a bleacher team would be moved onto station there as well until the mission was wrapped and the Alpha exfilled.

The team was always composed of locally contracted emergency medical technicians—EMTs were used to blood and gore—and led by one American expat contractor who could be depended upon to keep his mouth shut no matter what he heard or saw. Bleach was one of the few substances that could effectively eradicate blood traces, thus the term for the teams, but the moniker also reflected the team leader's ability to erase the fact that an act of violence had occurred—which usually involved large sums of money.

A crew of four bleachers and a team leader had arrived at the Montmartre in a phony ambulance, dressed like Parisian EMTs, and had trotted up the stairs with two large black Pelican cases full of cleaning equipment and a rubber body bag, double-extra large. Steele left soon after they got there, having decided to sleep on the floor of the Program's Level One safehouse. An hour later, the bleachers exited, along with the corpse, leaving the Romantic Artist Room pristine and Madame LeBarge considerably richer.

There would be no police report, because the Gendarmerie had never been called. Steele sometimes wondered what the bleachers did with the corpses, but he never asked because it wasn't his need to know.

His mood was still on slow burn as the taxi wound through Paris traffic, but he told himself to cool off and analyze the situation. What was the train of recent events?

There was the job in Aleppo. Done, perfectly executed. Then, about a week later, and seemingly unrelated, Jonathan Raines had been murdered right here in Paris, ostensibly by a woman, who in turn knew forbidden details about the Program. This apparent leak had caused Cutlass Main to be moved from its historical location. Or, was that really the reason? Hard to know without hearing it directly from Ted Lansky, which he hoped to do as soon as possible.

So then, Steele had gotten himself a new keeper, that prick Goodhill, but that had no bearing on these events as far as he could tell. Then Pitts and Goodhill had sent him off to Paris to track down this alleged female assassin, and before he could say Joan of Arc, some Russian version of Odd Job nearly burst his heart right out of his chest in the same B&B where Stalker Six had spent his last night.

But were the events even related? Did this Russian have anything to do with Raines's death? And it was extremely rare that adversaries ever went directly after Alphas, because nobody knew who they were. Covers were airtight, trails were "dusted" electronically and digitally. For anyone to target Steele with this Russian, they'd have to know who he was, where he was going, and where he was likely to camp for the night. Who'd know that except for . . . ?

Someone in the Program.

We're not going there, Steele decided. *There's another explanation. We don't have a traitor or a mole inside. It's a disinformation operation, exactly what someone wants us to think. Somebody got me on facial recognition on some op somewhere, and that's how they're chasing me down. That's how they got Stalker Six as well. Yeah, that's it. . . .*

But he wasn't completely sure, and it was far from comforting.

He told the cabbie to first swing by the Paris Gare du Nord train station and wait for him outside. Steele trotted down the stairs to the gray metal lockers with their yellow numbered tags and stowed his REI backpack with his pistol and knife inside. He knew the Louvre had some serious security and metal detectors, so showing up with a piece and a blade wouldn't do. Plus, the Gare du Nord was a good location around which to center a backup exfil plan, so stowing his weapons down there seemed right.

Before making his way back up to the street, he tucked himself into a corner near the locker banks and made a call to the Montmartre B&B. He hadn't forgotten that Madame LeBarge owed him a description of the "brochure girl."

"*Comment puis-je ne pas vous aider?*" LeBarge answered in her gnarly tone. How can I *not* help you?

"It's your guest from last night," Steele said. "You promised me a description, Madame."

"I owe you nothing," she snorted. "And you made a terrible mess."

"And you were very well paid for the cleanup. But if you like, I can have the Gendarmes ask you the questions. I am already gone, but you are not. *N'est-ce pas?*"

The madame said nothing for a long moment while she considered the merits of courtesy versus the consequences of ill temper. Then she coughed and said, "*Casino Royale.*"

"*Excusez-moi?*"

"The girl from that movie. She looked like that actress, but meaner."

"But meaner," Steele said. "Good enough, Madame."

She hung up without a farewell, and right away his phone buzzed. It was Betsy Roth, Mike Pitts's adjutant, calling from D.C.

"Immediate recall order, Mr. Sands. You can head for the airport."

"I just got here. I've only just started my sales calls."

"You can argue about it with the boss. Would you like to?"

"Skip it," Steele said, and he clicked off and cursed under his breath. Pitts knew he'd almost been killed the night before, because he had to approve the bleacher tasking. Maybe Pitts was getting *really* nervous about losing another Alpha.

Well, he'd still go over to the Louvre, cold, without any sort of introduction. He had friends in Gendarmerie's tactical unit, GIGN, and could have them make a call to Louvre security, but he didn't want to alert anyone who might be on the wrong side. It was better to just pose as a guy lusting after a girl.

Twenty minutes later, the cab dropped him off in

the circular drive at the Louvre, where to the west the view of the Arc de Triomphe du Carrousel recalled the height of Napoleon's glories, but when he turned around the magnificent buildings of Phillip II's twelfth-century castle were now blasphemed by a glass pyramid plopped in the center of the museum's vast courtyard. Steele didn't care much for modernization of any sorts of classics, which was why he didn't like 1940s Chevrolets turned into hot rods, or, for that matter, Botox on aging movie stars. He thought the Louvre's pyramidal entrance was crass, but then again, he'd lost some of his enthusiasm for Paris ever since they'd let some nutjob torch the roof of Notre Dame.

He paid the cabbie and got out. Given the early hour, the usual endless ticket line that wound around the fountains was only fifty tourists long, so he waited his turn and paid his way instead of trying to muscle inside on some ruse. Fifteen minutes later, he was at the bottom of the escalator and hunting for the security office, which he located by following a guard who was munching on a chocolate croissant.

The office was tucked away beyond the magnetometers, where Steele found a chubby bald supervisor and two of his men, one of whom was the roll-muncher. The security personnel outside the museum all wore Kevlar and hefted G-36 subguns. These guys wore rumpled dark suits.

"Good morning, my friends," Steele said in French as he strode, uninvited, through the security station's door.

"And good morning to you, sir, as well," said the

supervisor. "How may we help? You're here at the entrance so you cannot possibly be lost yet."

The guard with the croissant smirked. The other one was more surly and sipped a *mélange*.

"Not lost, no," Steele said. "I'm actually looking for a girl."

"Aren't we all?" the supervisor said. "*Cherchez la femme!*"

Steele grinned. "This one was special." He pulled the art brochure from his jacket pocket and smoothed it out on the supervisor's desktop. "It was about ten days ago. I spotted her hanging around this exhibit and chatted her up, but then I lost her."

All three men peered at the brochure, and shrugged.

"Do you have any idea how many exhibits and lectures we have here, *mon ami*?" the supervisor asked. "Or how many beautiful women pass by?"

"Well, I thought maybe you'd still have security footage from that day," Steele said.

"If there are no significant incidents, we erase them after seventy-two hours," the supervisor said.

"And we certainly don't show them to tourists." The surly one sneered.

Steele ignored that and took out his smartphone. "Well, she looks exactly like this," he said as he googled for an image of the actress Eva Green. Her stunning visage and figure popped up and he showed the phone to the trio. "But perhaps a bit . . . crueler, if you know what I mean."

All three men peered closer.

"Yes, I remember a woman like this," the supervisor said.

"Who the hell could forget her?" the croissant man said.

"Even *I* would notice her," said the surly guard, "and I have no interest in women."

"I believe she was associated somehow with the artist Emile Sadat," said the supervisor. "Perhaps his daughter? Although with these kinds of men she could be a paramour. Did she hint at anything like that?"

"I'm afraid I didn't have a very long conversation with her," Steele said. "But I intend to, gentlemen. And thank you so much." He turned and made for the door.

"*Pas de problème*," the supervisor said. No problem. "And good luck."

Steele waved over his shoulder, took the escalator stairs in double leaps, and hailed a new cab. He told the driver to take him to the Gare du Nord. He'd have to return his weapons to the safehouse, book a flight, grab some food, and then head for the airport. He sat back in the seat and brooded some more.

Who the hell was she? A girl who looked like that should be easy as hell to track down, unless she was an expert in camouflage and disguise, or had a double. He'd have to have Ralphy Persko work his magic and run modified images of Eva Green through NSA-level facial recognition software, just to see if someone associated with Emile Sadat popped up.

That thought made him wonder what else Persko might be able to reveal. The *Taxi Parisien* Steele was riding in happened to be one of those old-style yellow Checkers that the French had purchased from New York. There was a plexiglass barrier between the driver and the rear passenger seat, and Steele leaned forward and slid it closed. He called Cutlass Main.

"Code in," said Ms. Artificial Intelligence.

"Texting," Steele said, and he tapped out the alphanumeric instead of saying it aloud.

A human came on the line. "What can we do for you today, Mr. Sands?"

"I've got a shipment needing urgent customs clearance. Can I talk to Mr. Wizard?"

"Just one moment, please."

Ralphy Persko picked up the transfer. "Morning, Max. How's it going over there?"

"Great, if you like mixed martial arts and you've got plenty of ibuprofen. Are you lonely today?"

"Do you want me to be?"

"Yes."

Steele heard a door closing and knew that Ralphy had gone into an empty tank with his phone.

"Okay, I'm lonely," he said.

"Tell me something. Who the hell is Kuznetsov?"

"You mean the Russian writer? Anatoly, as I recall from my lit classes. Wrote a famous novel about World War II called *Babi Yar*—"

Steele rolled his eyes. "Not *that* one. Another one somewhere, and recent."

"Wait one," Ralphy said, and Steele heard a laptop flipping open and Persko's chubby fingers flying across the keys. He was running a search through any raw intel that had flowed to the Program over the past sixty days, while simultaneously pinging for anything that might match Steele or his target packages. After about a minute he came back on the line. "Um, say, do you know any of the real names associated with your last sales trip to Damascus?" He meant the Aleppo job, and the four big players whom Steele had executed.

"No, none of us were introduced." Steele meant that he'd only been briefed on their IDs by descriptions and surveillance photos, but no names, in case he was captured. What he didn't know, he couldn't spill.

"Well, coincidentally," Ralphy said, "not long after your trip to Happy Land, a Colonel Valerie Kuznetsov was buried in Moscow. Quietly, but with full military honors. She was a Russian nuclear warhead expert. Ring a bell?"

Steele didn't say anything, but he slumped back in the taxi's rear seat, lowered the phone, and watched the Parisians strolling by outside his window.

Yeah, I rang her bell in Aleppo, he thought. *With a full metal jacket slug.*

CHAPTER 11

DRAMMEN, NORWAY

They called themselves Millennial Crude.

It wasn't a subtle moniker, but it encapsulated their youth, the raw value of their particular talents, and the fact that they had few morals and were always willing to go for the throat.

There were eleven of them to date, all hailing from countries that used to be part of the Eastern Bloc, or were allies thereof, but were certainly no friends to the West or any imperialist capitalist states. Each of them was not yet thirty years old, some barely of legal drinking age, and all had MENSA genius capacities and were ensconced in the security establishments of their respective nation states, for which they secretly had no respect, or a hint of fealty.

They could all program in C++, Malbolge, INTERCAL, Whitespace and Brainfuck. They could manipulate blockchains that were triple-encrypted and uncrackable, and they dealt only in cryptocurrencies such as Bitcoin and Ether. They played *Manhunt*, *Dead Space*, *Postal 2*, and *Helldivers*, often around the clock as they hunched in blacked-out rooms before multiple HD screens, wearing headsets and sucking Red Bull from CamelBaks. They listened to Mayhem and Gorgoroth, and sometimes Rammstein when they were feeling nostalgic. They scoffed at Facebook and Instagram, unless those platforms were necessary to entrap a particular target. They didn't do drugs, except for the occasional line of cocaine in mixed company, which meant only with one another. And they didn't make love. They only fucked.

They were killers with keyboards.

Dmitry Kreesak was the titular leader of MC. He was Russian, twenty-seven years old, the orphaned son of a Spetsnaz captain who'd been killed in Chechnya and a Moscow whore who'd died of an overdose when Dmitry was nine. He worked as the operational director of cyber security for a lieutenant colonel of the FSB, or Federal Security Service, currently headed by the notorious Alexander Bortnikov. Most of the mundane work of keeping the Service secure at its headquarters in Lubyanka bored him, but whenever the director tasked the lieutenant colonel, and in turn Dmitry, with something "outside the Service" and interesting, that's when he relished the game.

He'd come up with the concept for Millennial Crude while playing a seventy-two-hour video game marathon with a female counterpart in North Korea, and after that, he'd selected and assembled his crew carefully. They had to be brilliant, like him untethered to family, ambitious, and vicious.

Eventually he'd recruited government cyber security whiz kids from Iran, Syria, Bosnia, Pakistan, Nicaragua, the People's Republic of China, and more. None of them were any good with firearms, explosives, or WMDs, but they could rattle their keyboards, open the locks on a hydroelectric dam somewhere, and take out an entire town downstream.

They were hot. If you touched any of them, your fingers would burn.

Dmitry, whose MC comrades knew him only as "Snipe," was hunkered down at a desk in a suite at the waterfront Scandic Ambassadeur hotel, which was castle-ish and stuffy on the outside but appropriately minimalist on the inside. His lieutenant colonel boss, Ivan Kravchenko, had brought him to Norway for an economic conference, which the FSB was using as cover while they reconnoitered the beautiful blue-water fjord as a possible Russian submarine pen. Dmitry had taken one look at Drammen and suggested to his boss that in order for the access waterway to be properly utilized in the event of a global conflict, the bridges of Svelvik would have to be blown up and the water levels surreptitiously checked by Russian naval divers of the GRU.

"You're very clever, for a geek," his boss remarked.

"I believe they're synonymous, Colonel," Dmitry had replied with a grin.

But now Dmitry was buried head-down in his "real" work, which involved revenge for a terrible recent hit on a quartet of nuclear missile mechanics in Aleppo, one of whom had been Russian. Some time ago, Dmitry and his MC mates had unearthed a top secret American intelligence and special operations cell, apparently known as the "Program," and it was Dmitry's assessment that one of their operatives had pulled off the hit. In turn, FSB chief Bortnikov hadn't specifically ordered kinetic action, but he had emulated King Henry II and remarked, "Will no one rid me of this scourge?" Dmitry's boss had taken it to heart.

And Dmitry had an ace in the hole, something he hadn't revealed to his lieutenant colonel because it was just too delectable. A year prior, Millennial Crude, while trolling for U.S. government top secret–cleared employees, had uncovered a member of the "Program" and cleverly manipulated and turned that individual into an asset. They'd waited patiently, but now it was time to turn the screws.

"I like your skirt," Dmitry said to a young woman who was sitting on one of the suite's leather armchairs, long legs crossed and jabbing the air with a high heel. She was North Korean, a fan of leather, sleeve tattoos, and crimson lipstick. They spoke in English.

"You like what's *under* my skirt, Snipe," she said as she smoked a Virginia Slim.

"That too. But I've got to focus."

"Yes, make the call, boss."

Dmitry nodded and slipped something that looked like a Velcro collar with a microphone module from his black leather laptop satchel. He strapped it around his throat, donned wireless earbuds, and tapped on his iPhone. When he spoke again, his voice sounded two octaves lower and metallic. The North Korean girl, whose MC moniker was "Kendo," could hear only one side of the exchange.

"Good morning," said Snipe. Then his dark eyes became smoky and he ran his fingers through his gelled black hair. "Yes, I know exactly what time it is. So shut up and listen."

He sat back and smiled at his own brutality and allowed the other party to be obsequious for a moment. Then . . .

"We have had a modicum of success, but we're not terribly pleased with your level of information. There are still too many rough players on your board, which is decidedly unfair for the game. We've had one hit, and one dud, which are unacceptable odds."

The other party must have been protesting, because Dmitry rolled his eyes at Kendo, while she simply smiled, smoked, and nodded encouragements. Dmitry returned to the call, and even his harsh Russian accent came through the voice changer this time.

"You will do *exactly* as I say, no less, and no more. We want another piece. You can make it a rook, and then I'll let you know if I want a knight. Twenty-four hours is all you have. Are we clear?"

The other party must have acquiesced, because Dmitry popped a thumbs-up at his North Korean partner. She toyed with a silver teardrop pendant at her throat and seemed to shiver with pleasure.

"Good," Dmitry snapped at the iPhone. "Dead drop the particulars in the usual way, and then you can go back to sleep. But not for long."

With a flourish of fingers he tapped off the call, tore the voice-changing device from his throat, and twirled it up in the air. Then he reached for a bottle of Stoli on the desk and poured two tumblers, neat.

"I think it's time to call in the girl again," he said to Kendo.

"But isn't she very expensive?"

"Well, she was perfect the first time. Then we sent in the Bear, and he wound up in a box. She's worth the price. Just like you."

Kendo got up from her leather perch, gripped the back of Dmitry's caster chair, and rolled him back two feet from the desk. Then she slipped between him and the desk edge, sat on it, picked up her tumbler, and downed half the vodka. She squinted down at him and pulled up the front of her short black skirt with her long red fingernails. She wasn't wearing any underwear.

"That's why you're the boss," she said. "And I think you deserve dessert."

CHAPTER 12

WASHINGTON, D.C.

White House Chief of Staff Ted Lansky's pipe was empty. It had been that way for almost a decade, but he still had the thing jammed in his mouth most of the time, and there were days when he desperately missed the tobacco.

Lansky was "old school," a rumpled former intelligence officer who'd been raised on landline telephones, gas-guzzling Chevrolets, and peanut butter and jelly sandwiches before they were banned from kindergartens. He'd spent most of his life at the CIA, where he'd begun his career fresh out of Langley's basic clandestine officer training at Camp Peary, Virginia, aka the "Farm," and had risen to chief of the Directorate of Operations.

Lansky had started smoking that pipe during his first overseas undercover assignment to Algiers in the mid-1980s. It was, at the time, no more than an affectation chosen to enhance his nonofficial cover as an ESL (English as a Second Language) instructor, but he'd discovered that it somehow diffused the stress of the game. Plus, it was also a perfect prop to play with and delay a response, when you were trying to save your own ass by coming up with the correct answer.

After a decade in the field, and having become completely hooked on British pipes and the finest of Dutch tobaccos, Lansky had returned to CIA headquarters to discover that smokers were now the bastard children of the Agency. The intel analyst "caves" no longer swirled with that melodramatic blue-gray cigarette mist and now smelled like rest-room potpourri. God forbid you should try to light up even in one of the machine-tool-exhaust-filled R&D warehouses over at the Directorate of Science & Technology. If you wanted to smoke anything at all, from cigarettes to cigars or the occasional rare pipe, you were banned to a wooden bench outside in the Courtyard, where you could puff away while you stared at one of those weird octagonal fishponds bordered in cold concrete.

Lansky had endured it for another ten years, until he found himself one day trying to light his pipe while clutching an umbrella, in the midst of a wicked hailstorm, while his colleagues were inside at the commissary enjoying hot soup. So, he'd given it up. But he was still cranky about it.

And he was cranky today, as he sat at the head of a long polished mahogany conference table, inside the brand-new SCIF at the Program's brand-new headquarters over on Q Street. Sure, it had been his idea to move Cutlass Main from the White House to some nondescript office complex in the capital, but not for the reason that most of the Program's personnel assumed.

Yes, they'd lost an Alpha in Paris. The murder of Stalker Six was concerning, but you didn't turn an entire aircraft carrier around in the midst of combat because a single sailor had gone overboard. Lansky had simply decided that having a Special Access Program ensconced in the White House—literally a few doors down from the Oval—was just too risky for his boss, newly seated President John Rockford. Lansky had worked for Rockford when the president still served as director of the CIA over at Langley, and in all of his government service, he'd never admired or respected anyone with such a degree of conviction or loyalty. It was the same way that Rockford, as vice president, had felt about President Denton Cole, until a stroke had removed Cole from his desk.

In Lansky's mind, Rockford was still in a very tenuous position. Lansky didn't much care for many of the administration personnel his boss had inherited from Cole, and he suspected that if any of them finally discovered this supersecret kinetic special operations program hunkered down right under their noses, a leak could destroy Rockford's presidency and sully his entire storied career. It just wasn't worth the risk.

In truth, Lansky felt guilty about issuing the move order, but that wasn't something he would ever admit. He'd made a career of hard choices and had accrued a long roll call of enemies en route, but that was how things worked in Washington. He had big shoulders, both literally and figuratively, and he wasn't afraid to use them.

"Why the hell am I holding an Alpha Flash, Mike?" Lansky was gripping a slim file folder with a diagonal red tape strip across the upper left corner that looked like a Miss America sash. His dry pipe stem was clenched in his teeth, which always made him sound like Humphrey Bogart.

"Because this is the second such incident in fourteen days, sir." Mike Pitts was seated at Lansky's close right, with Dalton Goodhill across from him on the left. "We didn't issue one when we lost Stalker Six, but yesterday someone tried to take out Seven in the same location."

"So it's clearly a shitty neighborhood. Maybe you shouldn't be in there."

"It's *Paris*, sir," Pitts said. "And we're talking about high-end areas, not the no-go zones."

"Somebody's targeting our Alphas," Dalton Goodhill grumbled. Lansky looked at him sideways.

"Do I know you?"

"This is Dalton Goodhill, sir," Pitts said by way of introduction. "He's Stalker Seven's new keeper, took over for Demo Cortez."

"I assumed," Lansky said, but then he squinted at Goodhill. "But I meant, do I *know* you."

"You do, sir." Goodhill dipped his bullet head. "Special Activities, but we met first time in the Mog."

"Mogadishu . . ." Lansky rubbed his jaw, then grabbed his pipe bowl and jabbed the stem at Goodhill. "Hell yesss. I shoved a cash drop at you in a Blackhawk and you fast-roped out with it. Awful night, shitty weather, lots of ground fire."

"That was the night, sir." Goodhill didn't smile.

"I figured you for dead on that op, but you delivered."

"I figured me for that a couple of times too."

"Big stones," Lansky said by way of compliment, then he looked around the SCIF and frowned. Past the double-thick, lead-lined plexiglass walls he could see all the Program officers and support personnel scurrying around the main floor, still getting used to the new environment. "Mike, drop the friggin' shades, will you? I feel like a clown fish in an aquarium."

Pitts pressed a button on the conference table console and some very expensive miniblinds rolled down the transparent walls from the entire SCIF perimeter above. Lansky turned his attention back to the file.

"So, you had one hit on Six, which, from what I'm reading here, appears to have been a woman. Then, you send Seven over there to sniff the trail, and somebody goes after him as well. Do we have the details on that one yet?"

"Not yet, sir," Pitts said. "But we will in a minute."

"So, what am I doing here?" Lansky looked at his watch. It was a cheap quartz Timex. "Are you trying to tell me this all has something to do with the Italian Job?" Lansky was referring to the hit in Aleppo, which, like all Program missions, was titled so no one could possibly make a geographical connection.

"That's the only explanation we have at the moment," Pitts said.

"Oh, I get it now." Lansky slapped the file on the table and sat back, rocking intently on the heavy springs of the new leather "king" chair. "The president green-lit that mission, so *I've* got to be read-on to any blowback, and *he's* got to be back briefed. Is that right, Mike?"

"That's how I see it, sir."

"You friggin' spook types are slimy," Lansky sneered, knowing full well that he was one of those types, and always would be. It was in his bones.

The access door at the far end of the SCIF opened. The secure facility was slightly pressurized to enhance its cooling systems for the Seagate servers bolted beneath the carpeted concrete floor, and whenever the door opened, a white noise generator automatically kicked in to defeat any potential eavesdroppers outside the SCIF. Therefore, Eric Steele's entrance was accompanied by an ominous hiss and a sound like ghost whispers.

He'd come straight over from Dulles, after infuriating delays in Paris and finally a nonstop during which he'd failed to sleep even a warrior's wink, and instead had spent it thinking about his tours in Afghanistan and Iraq, his mother, Susan, who'd worked multiple jobs to support a fatherless family, the string of pet dogs he'd had who could never quite fill that void in his heart, his time and his missions with the Program, Meg Harden, then some more about Meg Harden, and finally whether or not Cutlass Main was getting to be like some Broadway show that had had a great run, but was in danger of losing its stars and about to go dark at last. Add to that the nagging suspicion that someone, or something, was worming its way into the Program like some Ebola virus, and he was in a foul frame of mind.

He was wearing his U.S. Navy G-1 jacket, which still had a few crusty bloodstains on the cuffs from the Russian monster's arterial spray, even though it had been lying on the bed during their battle, and the bridge of his nose had a scabby split where his face had impacted with the B&B's bathroom plexiglass. Steele quietly closed the door behind him, the hiss went away, and when he saw that the president's chief of staff was in the SCIF he remained at something like attention.

"Welcome back, Steele," Mike Pitts said.

"Gentlemen." Steele nodded at Pitts and Goodhill, then at Lansky, and said, "Sir."

"Have a seat, Stalker Seven," said Lansky. Steele took the closest chair at the table's end and Lansky waved the flash file. "Heard you had some trouble in Paris."

"SOP for the job, sir," Steele said.

"Give the man a quick and dirty AAR, Steele," Dalton Goodhill growled. "He's got more pressing stuff at 1600." Goodhill meant the White House address on Pennsylvania Avenue.

"Roger." Steele lasered Goodhill's bulldog mug with his eyes, then turned his focus on Ted Lansky. "I went over there to dig up some intel on Stalker Six's termination. Booked into his last known bunk location, got jumped by a Russian, size extra large, killed him, and called in a bleacher team."

"What's a bleacher team?" Lansky asked Pitts.

"Cleanup crew, sir," Pitts said.

"Right. Go on," Lansky said to Eric.

"After that I chatted with a local source."

"Chatted with?" Goodhill said.

"Queried aggressively," Steele said. "Got nothing. Then I hit the Louvre, talked to security and got a light lead on Six's alleged killer. Basic description only." He looked at Pitts. "Then you made me come back."

Pitts ignored the complaint. "Why do you say 'allegedly'?" he asked.

"Not convinced she acted alone, or was even the killer. Might have been nothing more than a lure."

"Honey trap?" Lansky posed.

"Yes, sir. There are some rough girls in our business, but I haven't met one yet who could take down Six."

"Anything deeper?" Pitts asked. Steele noticed that Pitts was taking notes in a leather-bound logbook. It was a curious habit, since everyone else seemed to use smart pads or laptops, but it matched his marker and whiteboard quirk.

"Negative," Steele lied. He wasn't about to reveal the Russian's blurt about Kuznetsov, not until Ralphy could tell him more, and certainly not in "mixed" company. He liked Lansky and had always had a good, albeit distant, working relationship with him, but Steele adhered religiously to compartmentalization.

"Is that all, Stalker Seven?" Lansky asked.

"Affirmative, sir," Steele said, but he felt Goodhill staring at him as if he were a lying thief. No surprise, since Goodhill had spent his life around tight-lipped special operators. Lansky dropped the flash file on the table and got up. Pitts, Goodhill, and Steele all rose in respect.

"Well, gentlemen," Lansky said. "I'm sure you'll run this down to everyone's satisfaction, and I'll brief the president *if* he asks. In the meantime, enjoy your new digs. We cut you all a nice slice of the black budget pie for this."

The three men murmured *yessirs* and *thankyous* as Lansky left. After the door closed, Pitts and Goodhill resumed their seats, but Steele remained standing. He was in no frame of mind for an interrogation, and they both sensed it.

"Get some rest, Eric," Pitts said. "Then come back in and give me a full After Action Review for the file."

"And don't fucking leave anything out," Goodhill snarled. "That was like a kid telling Daddy why he cracked up the family car."

"You said make it short, *Blade*," Steele fumed and they glared at each other.

"Boys, cut the mama drama," Pitts warned. "This isn't a team room at Bragg." He pressed a button, and the miniblinds rolled back up into the ceiling, revealing the Program officers and support staff flitting about and hammering keyboards like stockbrokers on Wall Street.

"You and me, Steele, 2300 tonight," Goodhill said, as if he were scheduling a back alley brawl.

"A pleasure," Steele said.

But he was thinking that, until he was able to dig down deeper into the implications of some Russian killer targeting him for a quadruple hit that no living soul should have known he'd committed, his AAR wasn't going to reveal much more than he'd already told Ted Lansky. He looked through the SCIF's thick transparent walls and saw Meg emerging from the Keyhole tank to the left of the TOC's huge flat screen, and realized that of all the officers, staff, and operators in the Program, there was only one person he still trusted.

And that person was dead.

CHAPTER 13

ARLINGTON NATIONAL CEMETERY, SECTION 60

It was a beautiful day for a graveyard stroll.

A morning rain had washed the rolling hills that had once constituted the magnificent estate of General Robert E. Lee's wife, Mary Custis, the great-granddaughter of Martha Washington, and the cemetery's tall trees and manicured lawn glistened like emerald jewelry. The temperature was mild before the onslaught of Washington's summer. A light breeze wafted off the Potomac, and across 624 acres of gardens of stone, tens of thousands of America's armed forces veterans, including the likes of John F. Kennedy, Audie Murphy, General Daniel "Chappie" James, and Lee Marvin, slept a hero's sleep.

One of those heroes was Eric Steele's former keeper, Bobby "Demo" Cortez, currently at rest in a southeast corner of Arlington reserved for those who'd fallen in the Global War on Terror, beginning in 2001. Section 60 was often called "the saddest acre in America" by much of the media, but

Steele didn't see it that way. Yes, the burials here were fresh, and many of the gravestones were decorated with cut flowers, children's toys, photos of young loving couples, and tearstained notes, but Steele knew that the same sort of mourners' icons and laments had taken place throughout Arlington during every period of warfare. Over the past century, the burial sections for World War II, Korea, and Vietnam had all been at one time the saddest acres. Section 60 was simply his generation's turn.

Steele walked out of the trees, hands tucked in the pockets of his jeans, and headed straight for Demo's marker. He had plenty of other fallen battle buddies in Section 60, but today he was here to see only Demo, and he knew they'd all understand. He wasn't carrying flowers, though he'd thought about bringing half a dozen roses just to piss Demo off, but he'd settled on a Casa Blanca cigar instead. As he walked he pulled the smoke from his jacket pocket, stripped the wrapper, bit the tip off, and stuck the end in his mouth. He wasn't going to smoke it, only soak it, because that's what Demo always did, a habit sort of halfway between using chew and actually lighting up. Pretty disgusting, actually. The memory of Demo doing it made him smile.

That faded when he saw a young blond woman, twenty meters off to the right, sitting cross-legged on a baby blanket in front of one of the graves, rocking slowly and listening to something on a pair of earbuds. Then off to the left, fifty meters or so, he saw an old man sunk into a folding camp chair in front of another grave. He was bent forward, fingers entwined on his lap and talking softly, maybe to someone he had lost. Steele sighed and carried onward. He loved them all at Arlington, on both sides of the graves, and thought they were probably the best people in the country.

Demo's gravestone was simple, like most of them here. The engraving said: ROBERT D. CORTEZ, SGM, US ARMY, 1960–2018, GWOT, SILVER STAR, PURPLE HEART, "SEND ME."

It might have seemed somewhat curt and cryptic, except to someone like Steele, who'd known Demo so well. His real middle name had been Emmanuel, which he hated, but he couldn't have his Program handle carved on a gravestone, so *D* was what he'd ordered in his Last Will and Testament. It was the same for his rank and branch of service—just a simple sergeant major in the army—and his dates of birth and death; the actual months and days would have given away too much to the foreign spooks who sometimes cruised Arlington looking to connect intelligence dots. Steele thought the mention of only the Global War on Terror was smirk-worthy, since Demo had fought in multiple theaters, from Panama to Syria, but there wasn't enough room for ten wars, both authorized and covert, so he'd chosen his last big game. He'd selected the two decorations that meant the most to him, and the quote from the Old Testament that was his essence.

"Then I heard the voice of the Lord saying, 'Whom shall I send? And who will go for us?' And I said, 'Here am I. Send me.'"

Steele stood there, looking down at the top of the gravestone, a smooth curving slab of granite. Visitors left all kinds of things on the stones at

Arlington and Demo's was no different. There was a can of Bandits chewing tobacco, probably from one of Demo's old Ranger buddies, one empty 5.56 mm brass shell casing, a sapphire stone, maybe from Demo's aging mom, a worn Special Forces tab, from another battle buddy, Steele guessed, and a challenge coin from someone in the 3rd Special Forces Group. He found a small spot between the Bandits and the bullet and laid the soggy Casa Blanca down. Then he stepped back, came to attention, and offered Demo a long slow salute. Right after that, in his head, he heard Demo's rasp saying, *Have a seat, mano,* so he did, right there in the wet grass facing the stone.

"I got lots of crap on my mind, brother," Steele whispered. He didn't bother to look around to make sure no one was watching and might think he was nuts. Everyone at Arlington talked to themselves, or to someone who wasn't there anymore.

Spill it, and don't leave anything out.

"Well, we lost Six, which you probably already know about. Then, they moved Main over to some prissy office complex up by Dupont. After that, I pulled off a job somewhere I can't say out loud, and the former Soviets sent some goon to remove my skull. And now, I've got more than a nagging suspicion that we've got at least a leaker, if not a full-blown traitor inside."

I knew the friggin' place would go to shit without me.

"And, you stuck me with this turd slice, Dalton Goodhill. I mean WTF? Really?"

Sorry about that. . . .

"But I've been thinking maybe it's just me. Maybe

I've been hitting it too hard for too long. Maybe I'm finally losing my mind."

Well, you didn't have much of a mind when we met. You were pretty much just cold steel, which is why I recruited you.

"Is that some sort of a pun?"

The dead don't pun, mano.

Steele thought that was funny, and could actually imagine Demo quipping something just like that. Or had Demo actually just said it? Somehow, from somewhere? He looked up at the heavens and the crystal-blue summer sky, and then he heard the all-too-familiar sound of helo rotors in the near distance, beating the humid air as they often did around Washington. And they took him back to that other time and place. . . .

Forward Operating Base "Turnbolt" was about to be overrun, and there wasn't a damn thing the men of Special Forces Operational Detachment Alpha 627 could do about it, except fight to the death. The alternative was to be captured, humiliated, tortured, and beheaded while some Haji asshole made a vid of it with his Samsung and posted it on the net for all their families back home to watch. Their A-team commander, Captain Brian Smith, had already made the decision to fight it out and had relayed that over comms, which was a good thing, because he couldn't talk anymore. He'd taken an AK-47 round through the right side of his plate carrier and had a sucking chest wound.

Some fucking moron, maybe in the Army Corps of Engineers back at Bagram, had decided that building an FOB in the ass crack of an Afghan valley only three klicks from the Durand Line and Pakistan's Taliban-infested Arandu was a good idea. It wasn't really a full-blown FOB with hardened structures, T-walls, guard towers, and a decent DFAC where you could at least enjoy a hearty last meal. It was pretty much a pissant Fire Base, with plywood hooches, a mortar pit, an ammo dump, and a perimeter of slit trenches surrounded by piles of sandbags and HESCOE barriers, which were nothing more than huge squares of heavy chicken wire filled to the brim with loose rocks and dirt. The heaviest armored protection was the team's own gun trucks, and their only secret weapon was a satcom so they could call in something with real firepower, like an AC-130 Spectre gunship or a pair of A-10 Warthogs.

It reminded Steele of Vietnam's Khe Sanh, and everyone knew how that one had turned out.

None of them had ever experienced this kind of incoming before. The Hajis were dropping 60 mm mortar rounds all over the place, which were inaccurate but scary as hell because you can't hear mortar rounds until they hit. RPGs were punching into the hooches from 360 degrees, and all the canvas sunshades were on fire. A Russian DShK "Dashka" 12.7 x 108 mm heavy machine gun was raking the FB and kicking up twisters of dust as the rounds pinged off rocks and the tracers went ricocheting around like burning pinballs, and the torrent of AK-47 fire from all the hills was like something from Al Pacino's last stand in *Scarface*. Everyone who wasn't dead already was deaf.

There were only twelve men on the team, plus the captain, his warrant officer shadow, some poor kid E-4 specialist from the veterinary clinic at Bragg who'd been dropped in to help treat goats and mules in the nearby villages, and one air force joint tactical air controller to call in air support. That man, Technical Sergeant Jason Flatley, had done everything he could before having his skull cracked open by a Haji sniper with a 7.62 mm Dragunov. But it didn't matter much now. A pair of valiant A-10 Warthog pilots had beaten back the Hajis with their 30 mm cannons until they were "winchestered" and had no choice but to fly back to Bagram for reloads. Flatley had then called in a 9-line for an AC-130, but the Spectre gunship had been called off because FOB Turnbolt was surrounded by Pashtun villages, and that's exactly where the Hajis had set themselves up.

The Taliban were nobody's fools; they knew the American Rules of Engagement by heart, and that lawyers were running this war from the Pentagon.

Master Sergeant Eric Steele was beginning to think he was the only one left on his feet. An AK round had bitten his right thigh pretty hard, but it hadn't cracked bone and he hadn't even bothered to bandage it. Another one had split his MICH helmet, but his MBITR radio still seemed to be working, except nobody was answering his calls. One of their SAW gunners, Tommy Spellman, was dead, so Steele had taken Tommy's M249 and all his drums and was hammering back at the Hajis over the sandbag walls as he sprinted from position to position, and the news just got worse and worse, corpse after corpse. His adrenaline level was red lining, but the good news was that he knew he was going to die, so at least he wouldn't have to console any of their families. Someone else was going to have to do that for his mom, but it wouldn't be anyone here.

Every time he found a frag on the ground, he pulled the pin and hurled it. Every time he found a LAW, he popped the tube open, squinted through his dripping sweat, and nailed some of the fuckers with a rocket. At one point a turbaned maniac popped up on top of a HESCOE, and Steele dropped the M249, reached up, gripped the bastard by his *salwar kameez*, yanked him to the ground while he whipped his Gerber StrongArm blade from his Load-Bearing Vest, and drove it so hard into the man's throat that he pinned him to the ground like a butterfly.

At that point he was covered with blood—his own, and theirs—and he passed into the realm of combat madness. The air stank of scorched cordite, dust, sweat, explosive smoke, fire, and piss from the corpses. Steele knew there were probably more than a hundred of them out there and no way to fight them all off, and nobody was coming, or if they were, they'd never get there fast enough.

He ran back to the mortar pit, where Captain Smith was lying on his back in the dust, and Sergeant Major Henry Hide was sitting next to him. Hide had pulled off Smith's plate carrier and was applying an Asherman dressing to his right lung lobe where he'd cut open his uniform top with a knife. Steele skidded to a stop and stared down at Hide, who he thought was doing an impressive job under the hail of gunfire, especially since Hide's right foot was completely gone. He'd applied his own tourniquet, and he was sucking on a fentanyl painkilling lollipop.

"So how's this Hearts and Minds thing going for ya, Eric?" Hide shouted up at Steele as he aligned the Asherman's "chimney" vent with Captain Smith's frothy pink chest wound. Smith was as pale as vanilla ice cream and his fists were clenched to bone white, but he was holding his own.

"This wasn't in the recruiting brochure," Steele yelled back. An RPG rocket whooshed over his head and struck a fir tree nearby, but he didn't even duck.

"Where's Tommy and BJ?" Hide asked.

"Gone."

"Like we're all gonna be in a few," Hide said, as if he were referring to a picnic where the hamburgers and hot dogs were running low.

"And I can't raise anybody else on comms," Steele said.

"I called Alamo back to Jalalabad," Hide said, meaning that their battalion now knew that they were being overrun.

"What'd they say?"

"Good luck and God bless." Hide grinned up at Steele and said, "All the gun trucks are fucked. Take Smith and go. Maybe you'll make it if you run south and don't stop."

Steele shook his head like a kid who'd just been told by his pop to go to bed early.

"Come here, son," Hide said as he crooked a finger at Steele. The sergeant major was the oldest man in the ODA. Steele took a few steps and bent closer, thinking that Hide might be losing so much blood his voice was failing. But instead, Hide grabbed him by the top of his chest plate and yanked him so close they were nose to nose. "Now you listen to me and you listen good. I'm bleedin' out, so I wouldn't even make it to a bird. You go *now*, and you take this fine young officer here with you, because otherwise every single one of us is going to die and our families will never know what happened to us. I am your enlisted superior and I am giving you a direct order. Are we fucking crystal *clear*?"

It was a moment before Steele nodded. Hide pushed him away, grinned, and pulled his M9 pistol from his thigh holster.

"Now haul his ass up and get moving, Eric," he said. "I'm gonna let these fuckers come in, send as many of them to their seventy-two virgins as I can, and save the last bullet for myself."

They shook hands. Steele could hear the victorious warbles and whoops of the Taliban as they started flooding the trenches at the northern side of the FOB. He dropped the M249, slung his M4 around to the front of his LBV with the strap around his neck so he could shoot one-handed, then bent and hauled Brian Smith up onto his shoulders like a firefighter. Hide tossed him a bottle of water from the ground and Steele jammed it into his side pocket. Smith groaned in his ear, "Put me the fuck down," but Steele ignored him. Hide gave him a snappy salute, and Steele turned and took off.

Steele never stopped. He killed five of the enemy with off-hand double-taps on his way out of the FOB, and another three in the woods of the southern downslope. A few more chased him for a while, but when he fragged their point man, they decided that the slaughter and ransacking back at the Americans' Fire Base was more than enough glory for one day.

On that day in Afghanistan, Eric Steele discovered that his body was a machine wholly governed by his mind. He erased the pain and walked, with the full deadweight of his unconscious captain bouncing on his shoulders and crushing his neck and spine, and refused to allow any construct of human biology to hinder his mission in any way. Hide's words were locked right there like the final credits of a film behind his eyes, and he was going to survive for all of them.

The kilometers clicked away, the water eventually ran dry, and he trudged through the parched wadis and rock-strewn valleys, always heading south, while the hawks and vultures circled in the purpling sky above and hoped for his final stumbles. But there were none of those; just one footfall after another. He never tried to call for help using his MBITR, because he knew the Hajis had interceptors and he wasn't sure how much fight he had left. He'd just kept on walking, always south, knowing that eventually he'd hit J-Bad.

He'd walked about sixty kilometers, or almost forty miles, and he was standing atop a small rise, getting his breath in the late-evening air, when he heard the helo. One thing he was sure about, the Hajis had no air assets, so the sound of those rotors was music to his gunfire-bruised eardrums. When the MH-60 Night Stalker Blackhawk set down in a roiling cloud of dust a hundred meters away, Steele finally fell to his knees. But he never dropped Brian Smith.

A warrior bristling with weapons jumped from the open cargo door and ran toward him, followed by a pair of medics hauling aid kits and a folding stretcher. They eased Captain Smith off Steele's shoulders, onto the canvas litter, and sprinted back to the bird. The man who'd led them to Steele knelt in front of Eric and grinned.

"You're Eric Steele, aren't ya?"

Steele cocked his half-delirious, weary head, wondering how anyone could possibly know that.

"Sorry about your team, Steele. Let's go home, such as home is." The man gripped Steele's arm, helped him to his feet, and guided him toward the rumbling Blackhawk.

"Who the hell are you?" Steele asked.

"Name's Bobby Cortez, but you can call me Demo. I'm gonna be your new best friend. . . ."

Steele knuckled a tear from the corner of his right eye and put his Oakley shades back on. He remembered his father's battle buddy, Bo Nolan, had once told him that "Special Forces soldiers don't cry," but he figured that one drop for Demo would be forgiven.

On that very last night in Afghanistan, after the docs at Craig Hospital at Bagram had patched him up, Demo had told him privately that a certain government covert organization had been tracking his army career for years. They'd been waiting to see if he'd accomplish something special while serving in SF, something that would show them he had the right stuff, and it looked like what he'd just done at Turnbolt was it. The last thing on Steele's mind that night was assessing for an outfit higher up the ladder than 3rd Group, especially with the gunfire still ringing in his ears and the stench of blood in his nostrils, but he'd had his fill of Afghanistan and figured he'd go for it.

It was his first inkling of something called the Program.

He stared at Demo's gravestone and the small row of memorial trinkets on top. For a moment he thought about taking the cigar away, because the first rain that came might make it stain the pristine granite with tobacco juice. Then he left it alone because he knew that Demo would like that.

"You were something else, brother," he whispered.

I was indeed, wasn't I?

Then Steele switched his gaze to the challenge coin. Lots of service members from all the branches carried them around, and the tradition was that if you pulled yours out and dropped it on a bar, and the guy next to you didn't have his on hand, he'd be the one buying everyone drinks. But a Special Forces coin meant much more than that. It was a touchstone, an amulet, the currency of courage.

He squinted at it and suddenly remembered something that Demo had once said to him while they were deep in the shit in a firefight in Africa and it wasn't looking good for posterity.

"If I don't make it out, and you do, mano, I'll coin you from somewhere."

At the time, Steele had thought it was nothing but a quip, cool bravado under fire. But now he got to his feet, picked up the coin, and stared at it. The front had the standard SF emblem of crossed arrows over a commando knife, with the surrounding banner that said DE OPPRESSO LIBER—To Liberate the Oppressed—and an emblazoned numeral 3. He turned it over, where the back had the Group motto, WE DO BAD THINGS TO BAD PEOPLE.

But Demo hadn't served in 3rd Group. He'd started out as a Ranger and had gone straight from there to Delta. So who'd left it there? Did it mean something? Steele examined the worn letters and symbols and numerals, but saw no "after market" message carved anywhere, and certainly no way to open the coin like a watch back. It was solid brass.

But now his heart rate picked up a pace, because he was wholly convinced that the coin was intended for *him*.

He slipped it into his pocket and headed back into the trees.

CHAPTER 14

NO ACKNOWLEDGED LOCATION

EYES ONLY

SAP (Alpha FLASH)

From: Alpha Ops Middle East

To: Cutlass Main

Subj: KRYTON NUCLEAR TRIGGERS
EN ROUTE CHABAHAR, IRAN

Source: IDF AMAN Mil Intel, Unit 8200

Confidence: High/Confirmed MI6, Venice Station

IMMINENT Iranian IRGC transport of 74 Kryton Nuclear Triggers, type Perkin-Elmer Components Corp., from Trieste, Italy, to Port of Chabahar, Iran, via Suez Canal. Vessel type, cargo; Vessel class, Delvar; Vessel#, 482;

Vessel name, *Chiroo;* displacement, 1,300 tons loaded; dimensions, 63.45 x 11 meters (208 x 36 ft); crew, 20; armament, 1 dual 23 mm AA (camouflaged); flag, Nigeria (false); color scheme, white over red.

Operational window, 13 hours. Alternative options, none, **kinetic only**.

Alpha response—URGENT.

CHAPTER 15

TRIESTE, ITALY

Collins Austin left the Greif Maria Theresia hotel precisely at midnight, because she knew the Iranian vessel *Chiroo* would be leaving the port precisely at two.

It was a struggle dragging herself from that five-star luxurious room, as it was rare that the Program would foot the bill for what their cranky old comptroller, Mrs. Darnstein, referred to as "excessive and unnecessary comforts." But in this particular case, Austin had had to move fast, and she needed an appropriate and "prepackaged" cover that would camouflage the mission tasks she was about to execute.

As Stalker Eight, she was going to blow up a ship. As Sabrina Quinley, she had to look like a woman who'd scoff at the idea of changing a flat tire for fear of breaking a nail.

Her keeper, Shane Wylie, had thrown this thing together at lightning speed, as soon as POTUS had signed off on the Alpha Flash. Austin had then grabbed a Program driver from the underground motor pool, had him break a couple of land-speed records en route to her condo in Bethesda, selected one of three "go bags" she always kept ready, and they'd hightailed it out to Langley Air Force Base, where Wylie had already commandeered one of the Program's Gulfstream G650 transcontinental business jets. Then they'd taken off for Trieste, which gave her and Wylie almost a full nine hours to chow down on fresh galley food prepared by a U.S. Navy cook and download encrypted mission intel flowing their way from Ralphy Persko's shop.

Among her other assets, such as a third-degree black belt in Okinawan Goju Ryu and a body that could make Bar Refaeli envious, Austin also had a photographic memory. By the time the Gulfstream landed in Trieste, she knew the precise locations of her accommodations, backup safehouses, emergency rendezvous points, and her infil and exfil routes and had memorized all of her dive tables. But she hadn't had time for a nap, which was why that enormous king-size bed was so damned tempting. *Ah well.*

This evening she was wearing a jade-green, sequined, sleeveless, misdemeanor-short dress, which, coupled with her flowing fire-red hair, ice-blue eyes, and a pair of matching Sergio Rossi heels, gave her the kind of aura that made the hotel staff (both men and women) swallow their gasps and blush when she appeared in the lobby. She was also carrying an Elizabetta clutch bag with a slim chain strap, into which she'd tucked her cell phone, lipstick, a modest four-inch switchblade, and an anodized black

Walther PPKS in 7.65 mm, with the smallest AWC Systems Technology suppressor she could rustle up from the Program's armory. Usually under such circumstances, she would have holstered the pistol to her inner thigh, but the dress was simply too skimpy. At any rate, the holster always itched her, and not in a good way.

She smiled at the hotel's valet as he helped her into a Fiat cab, and she said to the driver, "*Porto Franco Nuovo, per favore. Il ristorante Al Nuovo Antico Pavone.*"

"*Sì, mia cara,*" the driver said, and they were off along the Viale Miramare, the coastal road leading south to Trieste's upscale marina packed slip-to-slip with holiday motorboats, sailboats, and yachts.

Austin sat back in the cab and looked out at the lovely Gulf of Trieste, with its glistening inky waves, pinpoints of light twinkling from its coastlines, and the matching stars above. To anyone else, it would have been a romantic panorama, but she wasn't really seeing any of it. She was mission-focused, thinking about all of her waypoints and gear drops, mingled with a bit of pity for Shane Wylie. He was an older man, tall and slim and graying, and because of that he didn't remotely "match" her cover and was staying in a ratty B&B in the city center, over on the Slovenian side. But she also knew that he didn't care about luxuries and would be focused completely on ensuring her success and keeping her alive. Shane was widowed from the love of his life, Austin was openly bisexual, and their relationship was like that of a wise old gambler handling a crackerjack young pool hustler.

She got out at the Al Nuovo Antico Pavone restaurant, an upscale place just across from the marina, where the rows of fiberglass hulls were gently knocking together as they undulated in the midnight breeze. If Ralphy's operational intel was right—and it always was—the *Chiroo* would be anchored exactly 1.27 miles due west of the last marina slip at Porto Lido and the Corpo Piloti del Porto, the port's pilot station.

Per maritime practice, the Iranian vessel's captain had checked in with the pilot's office by radio the night before. The NSA had intercepted his transmission, passed the frequency to a contractor called HawkEye 360, which had then tasked its cluster of reconnaissance satellites with fixing the ship's position for "someone" over at the White House.

So, Austin's target was now a "floating duck," and she was inwardly crouched and ready to pounce, but she knew she couldn't rush it. First she had to run a tail check.

She strolled inside the restaurant, nodded at the stuffy maître d', and took a seat at the bar. She declined a menu offered by the admiring bartender, ordered a Campari and soda, nursed it through only three sips, and looked at her cell phone, until it flashed with a texted code word, THUNDERBALL. She almost laughed out loud at that, because Shane was so darned old school, but it meant "game on." She paid her bill in euros, went to the ladies', then walked right out the service door at the back. If she had a tail of any kind, she knew that move would panic her pursuers and she'd feel the upset in the atmosphere. But nothing happened. She was clean.

She walked back to the port, waited at the wide thoroughfare of Riva Grumula until the traffic cleared, and crossed the road. She could hear the dark waters lapping at the pier pylons as she took the slim stairway down to the marina. The air was a sweet mix of jasmine, sea salt, and marine oil, and she settled onto a bench facing the Pontile Istria slip, where there were so many vessels it looked like the boat expo in Vegas. She glanced at her TAG Heuer Women's Way dive watch, a timepiece elegant enough for her evening attire. Her time-on-target was getting close.

But it was holiday season in northern Italy, and despite the late hour there were still a few summer sailors fussing with their hobby vessels. She slipped off her heels, crossed her legs, and mimed searching in her purse for a cigarette, until one last trio of drunken college kids finally moored their skiff and left the pier empty. Then she strode barefoot over to the slip, skipped past the first seven boats, and spotted the sleek-hulled, six-meter Allegra 18 outboard. She knew it was the right one because Shane had tied a green neon ribbon to the steering wheel, just like a frequent flyer would do to his suitcase when too many of them looked exactly alike.

She untied the mooring, tiptoed over the prow and the boat's cargo cover, swung into the comfy leather pilot's perch, hit the starter on the Selva 40 hp whisper engine, backed out of the slip, and headed out to sea to kill the *Chiroo*.

Half an hour later, Austin's minidress was lying neatly folded on her pilot's chair, and she was a mile away from her anchored skiff and twelve meters below the waves, snug tight in a black Cressi Lido wet suit and zooming along on a TUSA Underwater Diver Propulsion Vehicle—basically an electric miniscooter that looked like a minitorpedo—with the caged propeller at the back between her diving fins and her muscled buttocks perched in its small seat. Lying horizontally, she only had to lean left or right to steer the DPV, which left her hands free out front to grip the 4.5 kilogram Limpet mine she was going to magnetically attach to the *Chiroo*'s hull, at the exact spot where she knew the vessel's fuel tanks were located.

On her chest she was wearing a Draeger LAR V closed-circuit 100 percent oxygen rebreather, which expelled no telltale bubbles. Strapped to her right calf was an Underwater Kinetics Blue Tang titanium diver's knife, and her Walther PPKS—silencer screwed on—was in a waterproof pouch buckled to her right thigh. A Scubapro heads-up display was attached to her mask and projecting her dive time, depth, air mix quality, and navigational waypoints into her right lens, so as long as she kept herself aligned with the digital moving spear, she'd find the *Chiroo* as easily as Waze would get her to the local Trader Joe's in Virginia.

The water was cold, but she wasn't. She was thinking about how awesome Shane Wylie was, and how he'd perfectly prepared everything for her, and it was all waiting right there in the cargo hold of the boat. If she'd had a father around as a child, Shane would have been her ideal model.

On the other hand, she thought as some sort of oblong sea creature blurred by her right flank, *if I'd had someone like Wylie as a dad, I probably wouldn't be in this game at all. I'd be a happy-go-lucky yoga instructor or something. Ah well.*

Then the hull of the Iranian cargo vessel appeared about a hundred meters directly in front of her, a long, black, bathtub-shaped silhouette, bumping up and down in the gentle waves above, which had the hue of ice-pop blue with a full moon glancing off the water. For a moment she was tempted to just attach the Limpet, set the fuse timer, and scoot, but she knew that wasn't proper procedure. What if she was way off course, and the boat was an innocent fishing vessel full of handsome Italian boys? That would suck. So she slowed the DPV's electric engine, arched her back, and it pushed her slowly to the surface. She killed the motor, gripped the handgrip hard so she wouldn't lose her ride, and popped her black-capped head above the waterline, just long enough to spot the ship's name glistening on its forward hull in the moonlight.

Fuck you, Chiroo, she thought as she slipped back under.

The Limpet mine made a little too much noise when its powerful magnet sucked it against the ship's hull on the port side of its shallow keel. Austin froze there in the shadows for a moment and just listened. The ship's engines weren't running yet, so she knew she'd hear stomping feet above her head if anyone aboard was alarmed by the hollow bang of metal against metal. But nothing happened. She reached up with her gloved left hand, switched on the OrcaTorch red lens minilight above her left ear, and set the Limpet's detonator for exactly 0200 hours. Then she doused the light and swam, very carefully, under the keel and toward the starboard side of the ship, with her sea sled shut off and hanging from a lanyard attached to her ankle. It had a small air bladder so it wouldn't drag her down.

There was another, much smaller hull bobbing five meters above her in the undulating waves, knocking rhythmically against the *Chiroo*. From Ralphy Persko's intel flow and Shane Wylie's careful briefing, Austin knew this was the "feeder boat" that had just delivered the nuclear triggers to the *Chiroo*. It was a 350 Outrage, a larger, European version of the Boston Whaler, and crewed by Corsican weapons smugglers who'd somehow gotten their hands on the triggers, perhaps by hijacking or bribery. But Austin hadn't been briefed on that and she didn't really care. The thing of it was, these slimy bastards couldn't be allowed to continue their nefarious activities at the expense of the entire Free World. In addition—Wylie had stated firmly—the Program couldn't take a chance that the deal for the trigger exchange might go sour at the last minute, and that the Corsicans might leave the area again with all, or part of, their lethal load.

"In other words," Austin had said to Wylie at his safehouse briefing that afternoon, "all these fuckers have to go down together."

"Indelicately put, but yes," he'd replied.

"If I were delicate, Shane, you'd have nothing to do with me." Austin had grinned.

"True."

Austin turned onto her back as she cruised beneath the Outrage hull, emerged on the far side, and scanned the surface above from a depth of three meters. In the silver moonlight she could see the cream-colored boat flank and a black gunwale above the shallow waves, and since no one was leaning over the rail, she kicked her fins, coasted up, breached the surface, dropped the regulator from her mouth so the Draeger wouldn't hiss, and detached the Crenova Dry Bag from her thigh. It was really no more than a fancy baggie, and she opened the seal, removed her PPKS, and gripped it at the ready. The safety was off and she already had one round in the chamber.

She cruised along the flank toward the bow, where she could hear two men chatting in Corsu, very much like Italian. They were talking about money, drugs, and sadistic sex, which made Austin's next moves even easier—not that she was having any pangs of conscience. She reached up with her left hand, gripped the rail, and pulled herself up. The two men, both with heads of black curls, wearing heavy fisherman sweaters and clutching Benelli shotguns, spun around to stare at her as if she were some kind of mermaid from hell, which she was.

She shot them both in the face, one after the other. When they collapsed to the Outrage's deck, their limbs twitching and boat boots kicking, she shot each one in the skull again. Her silencer made no more noise than a heavy-duty stapler.

She raked the PPKS's sight across the pilot house, but she didn't see anyone else aboard, so she slipped back into the water, swam to the stern, and checked that no one was looking down from the rusty flanks of the *Chiroo* above. She repouched her pistol, pulled her diving knife from its scabbard, and sliced through the fuel lines on all three Mercury outboard engines. Then she stuck her regulator back in her mouth, quickly submerged before the spilling gasoline could reach her lips, and headed back to her Allegra outboard.

She was back on board in ten minutes, and the return ride to the marina was glorious. She was naked, her long red mane whipping in the wind, her flawless skin being dimpled by the midnight air, with nothing left in the boat but her dress, heels, and purse. Shane had provided a large ripstop gear bag, along with a twenty-five-pound kettle bell, and she'd packed all of her diving equipment into the bag, including her pistol and knife, added the weight, clipped the bag to her DPV scooter, and dumped everything over the side. She was as clean as a newborn baby, though she looked like a Victoria's Secret model on a bender.

She reluctantly put the dress back on just before she docked at the slip. Then she removed Shane's ribbon from the wheel, tied the boat off, and tiptoed along the dock, carrying her heels, and she walked straight for the same bench she'd perched on an hour before and took a seat facing the water. She looked at her TAG Heuer, where the second hand was just ticking toward 2:00 A.M.

The sheet of light came first, as it twisted up into the sky like a rope of orange and yellow fire. Then came the boom, which doubled as it echoed off the shoreside buildings of Trieste and rattled all the nearby windows. And last came a stranger sound, like a giant gripping an enormous serpent and twisting it until a shriek emerged, and there in the distance, a pool of rapidly spreading fuel fire engulfed the *Chiroo*'s blackening hull, as its prow tipped up and it began to sink, along with its foul cargo.

A few late-shift restaurant kitchen people came rushing out onto the boulevard. For a moment, Austin considered trying to bum a cigarette, but then thought better of it. She stared at the raging inferno just a mile from the port.

"So *that's* what they mean by afterglow," she whispered to herself with a smile, and she stayed until the ship was gone.

CHAPTER 16

WASHINGTON, D.C.

Ralphy Persko had taken the day off. Eric Steele was about to ruin it.

"Ralphy, what are you doing?"

"Waiting for you to call me, of course."

"I tried reaching you at Main."

"They shouldn't call it that anymore. They should call it *Mini*-Main."

"Pitts said you had the day off."

"Yeah, my first one in two weeks."

"Where are you?"

"Buenos Aires. I had Scotty beam me down here for lunch."

"Where *are* you, wiseass?"

"Home."

"You got a microscope?"

"A what?"

"A microfuckingscope."

"I've never heard that particular scientific nomenclature before, but if you're asking for something to be enlarged and examined, I can probably accommodate."

"I'll be right over."

"Can't wait, Seven."

Ralphy lived on Sixteenth Street NW in Crestwood, halfway between Silver Spring and the National Mall, in one of those classic old brick brownstones where he rented a floor at the top. The neighborhood was diverse, like most of Washington outside the centers of government, and Ralphy was the only Caucasian living on a block of African Americans, Hispanics, and a sprinkling of Indians.

The brownstone was owned by the Jepsons, a black family who were kind to Ralphy, often invited him for Sunday dinners, and made no demands other than his timely rent checks. In turn he was a model tenant: no drugs, loud music, wild parties, or girls. The Jepsons thought he was a Smithsonian Institution computer geek from a wealthy Connecticut family, trying to make up for his privilege. He encouraged that belief, which worked well for cover, and certainly never told them that he'd been born into a poor Polish family from Fall River, Massachusetts.

Steele arrived at Ralphy's door after climbing three long flights, rang the bell, saw the peephole flash, and heard four different kinds of locks being turned as if the place were a flat in the South Bronx. The door opened and he slipped inside to find Ralphy wearing headphones and clutching a device in one hand that looked like an old-fashioned transistor radio, and something like a magic wand in the other. Persko locked the door behind Steele, held up a cautionary finger, and went back to what he'd been doing, which was a strange sort of dance along the apartment's perimeter.

Steele looked around. The place was unexpectedly neat, with an expansive wooden living room floor, IKEA pop art rugs, and lots of books on shelves, mostly nonfiction tomes about computers and coding, but also some Clancy, Ludlum, and Hiaasen. There were six large windows, all tilted inward due to the shape of the top of the building, and Ralphy's profession was revealed by one long table along the far wall, packed with laptops, monitors, motherboards, and soldering irons. In the middle of the living room a CD player was perched on a barstool, from which "Bamboléo" by Gipsy Kings was vibrating the window glass.

Steele waited while Ralphy finished dragging the tip of his magic wand along the walls, as if he were using a divining rod. Then he switched off the CD player and pulled the headphones down from his mess of sweaty curls. He was wearing a blousy Hawaiian shirt with leaping marlins all over it, cargo shorts, and no shoes.

"This thing works pretty well," Ralphy said.

"What the hell is it?"

"It's a multifrequency bug detector."

"You got roaches?"

"Funny, Steele. If somebody's planted an audio surveillance device while I'm out doing our dirty work, which is most of my healthy hours, this thing'll pick it up."

"How so?"

"Well, a device like that has to transmit my room

sound to somewhere else, right? This thing'll lock onto that signal and intercept the transmission, so when I'm running music from a contained device, like a CD player, if I'm being surveilled the tunes'll be picked up by the bug and I'll hear 'em in my cans." He pointed at the headset now sitting on his chubby neck. "Get it?"

"Yeah, right, got it," Steele said, though he wasn't quite sure that he did, and he also felt kind of bad that that's what Ralphy was doing on his rare day off. "But don't you have better things to do on your down day?"

"Like chat with you, you mean?"

"Point taken."

Ralphy put the interceptor and the wand down on a low glass coffee table in front of an IKEA couch, which faced a fifty-inch flat screen across the room. There was a high-tech joystick sitting on the table and, underneath it, a set of pedals that looked like the footrests from a rowing machine.

"You at the super pro level on *Call of Duty* yet?" Steele asked.

"I don't play video games. It's a flight simulator."

Steele was surprised. Every puter geek he knew was a game freak. "You don't say. How often do you crash?"

"Never. And I can land a Piper J-3 Cub on an aircraft carrier, not that anybody'd ever need that." Ralphy plopped down on the couch, picked up an open can of Izze soda, and sipped. "You want one?"

"Negative, thanks."

"So what brings you here, Seven?"

Steele noted that Ralphy's demeanor was a little different here than at Cutlass. This was his "cave," and his usual deferential manner was hued with impatience. Steele felt his respect for Ralphy tick up a notch. He took the challenge coin from his pocket and displayed it to Persko, palm up.

"I found this at Demo's grave today, over at Arlington."

Ralphy leaned forward and gingerly plucked the coin from Steele's hand, as if it were something hot. He didn't ask why Steele had been visiting his former keeper's grave.

"You mean, like, on the ground somewhere?"

"I mean on top of his headstone."

Ralphy pushed his big glasses up onto the bridge of his nose, turned the challenge coin over, and murmured the quote on the back. "'We do bad things to bad people.'" He looked up at Steele. "Hey, that could be the Program's motto."

"It's actually Third Group's. Ours would be 'People Need Killing.'"

Ralphy grinned. "That's a Vince Vaughn line from *Mr. and Mrs. Smith*."

"I know," Steele said. "Ralphy, somebody left that for me."

"How do you know?"

"I know."

The last thing Persko was going to challenge was Eric Steele's instincts. He got up, grabbed the can of Izze, walked the coin over to his worktable, set it down onto a square of green velvet cloth, and settled heavily into his office chair. Then he twisted a large magnifier on a corrugated metal neck into place, switched its light on, and hunched. After a moment, he emitted a low whistle.

"What?" Steele said as he moved closer.

"Now that's friggin' old school," Ralphy whispered.

"*What* is, Ralphy?"

"There's a period at the end of the quote."

"So?"

"It's not original to the coin. It looks like a microdot. Really ancient spy stuff, even from way before computers and shit."

Steele's mental cylinders were starting to fire more rapidly and his pulse rate rose.

"You mean like when they used to use film to reduce an encoded message down to nothing, and then glue it to a letter or something?"

"You were paying attention at Camp Peary," Ralphy said as he reached for a pair of needle-nose tweezers.

"I'm a history buff."

"Well step back, and don't breathe. These things were always stuck on upside down."

Steele stepped back as Ralphy gripped the tweezers and carefully peeled the dot from the coin, slid the coin off the velvet, and replaced it with a sheet of white paper. Then he held his own breath as he turned the dot over, laid it down on the paper, pushed the magnifier out of the way, and replaced it with a digital camera, which was also mounted to another corrugated neck. He clicked the shutter, sat back, cracked his knuckles, then rolled the chair down the table length to a computer with a large monitor. He pecked at the keyboard, maneuvered his mouse, clicked again, and the monitor glowed.

Now the dot appeared on-screen, but it was the size of a black dinner plate. It was covered with a full matrix of hundreds of white characters, all vertical lines and zeros.

"Well I'll be damned," Steele whispered.

"You were that when you volunteered for this gig," Ralphy murmured, but he was fully enthralled now by what he was seeing. "It's a binary code."

"Can you crack it, Ralphy?"

"Maybe. First I'll have to translate this into readable characters, which could turn out to form any language, maybe even some crazy dialect, or even Latin or something. Then I'll have to break *that* code, which'll be simple if it's a single primary, but if it needs a key I'll have to run a fuck ton of algorithms. . . ."

"How long, Ralphy?"

But Persko was already moving into a realm of obsessive curiosity and didn't answer. His day off had turned into something else. He now had three decrypt programs opening up on his system and was cutting and pasting sections of the microdot message.

"Okay, I'll stay out of your hair," Steele said. "Just give me a quick brief on that other subject."

"What subject's that?" Ralphy said without turning around as he slurped his Izze and hammered away at his keyboard.

"The intel on the girl."

"Oh, that ping you got from Paris?"

"Yeah, that one."

Ralphy waved a hand over his shoulder, as if the hunt for Stalker Six's killer wasn't really important right now.

"We've got that narrowed, but not enough to do anything with yet. Got thirty-two matches."

"You've got *thirty-two* matches on a girl who looks like a mean Eva Green?"

"You don't know how this facial recognition stuff works, Seven," Ralphy scoffed as he focused on the dot. "When a face is classically beautiful, you get lots of false positives, 'cause beauty's symmetrical. Most people don't realize they're subconsciously attracted to uniform features, which are common in, let's say, fashion models, which is also why those people often look so much alike. On the other hand, if a dude's ugly, the features are off-kilter, like a lazy eye or a busted nose. Much easier for FR to spot, right? But this chick ain't ugly. That's why so many hits. We've had thousands of feeds from Europol cameras, KBR and Honeywell units at airports and train stations, MI6 and Mossad street surveillance, even Jordanian intel. Gotta work it some more."

"Where are the hits, Ralphy?"

"Europe mostly."

"*Where* in Europe, Ralphy?"

"All over. Germany, France, Italy."

Suddenly Steele's skin was starting to crawl. He realized that when he'd shown up at the new HQ for his AAR, he hadn't seen Collins Austin, or, for that matter, Shane Wylie.

"Ralphy."

"What?"

"Where's Stalker Eight?"

"Austin? She's out of pocket. Just finished a flash in Trieste, while you were in Paris. . . ." Then he stopped working on the dot, pulled his chubby fingers from the keyboard, and sat back in his Naugahyde throne. "Come to think of it, we had one hit in Venice, but—"

"How fucking far is Venice from Trieste, Ralphy?"

"About two hours by car." Ralphy suddenly jerked upright. "*Jesus*, Seven."

He spun around in his chair, but Eric Steele was already gone.

CHAPTER 17

TRIESTE, ITALY

Collins Austin noticed the couple at the bar, because their eyes were burning her skin. It was that strange sensation she felt whenever anyone in close proximity was regarding her as a sexual object—which was often—sort of a seventh sense attuned to lustful transmissions. Yes, in between whispers, these two were definitely staring.

And why wouldn't they? She was sitting alone in one corner, on a plush red leather banquette with a small round table that couldn't conceal her long, tanned legs. Her red hair was twisted half up and pinned, with the curled ends teasing her bare shoulders. She was wearing a fringed, deep purple halter top revealing her cleavage and her muscled belly, above a short black leather skirt and high-heeled sandals that matched the top. She had dressed as a sensual lure this evening. But not for business; only for play. And the game was on.

The place was called Grotto, an upscale saloon and club where even the bouncers guarding the gilded glass doors looked like male Italian fashion models rather than thugs, and it was just half a block north of the Greif Maria Theresia hotel, where Austin was still staying. After vaporizing the Iranian vessel, she had run through her After Action Review with Shane Wylie, then taken the standard ten-day R&R that was granted after every kinetic Alpha mission. But she hadn't actually gone anywhere.

In almost all cases after a hit, an agent would exfil the Area of Operations as rapidly as possible. Yet Austin believed in the adage "hide in plain sight." If the authorities were searching for whoever had sunk the *Chiroo*, they'd be combing the airports, train stations, bus lines, and rental car agencies. Austin hadn't budged an inch. Her cover as Sabrina Quinley was solid, and there was nothing in her hotel suite or on her person to incriminate her, not even a weapon—except for her four-inch stiletto, which any wise, comely young lady traveling alone might carry.

Wylie didn't like it. He'd told Austin that sometimes she behaved like a goddamn rebellious teenager. She'd laughed, kissed him on his weathered old cheek, and told him she didn't much care. So he'd reluctantly headed off for Berlin to prep an upcoming mission while she'd shut down her Program cell phone and decided to party.

It was close to midnight, the music was pulsating early-1990s techno, and the Grotto was crowded with people of money undulating across a polished onyx dance floor through clouds of fruit-laced vape. The bar itself was a long glass affair, behind which rows of liquor bottles on frosted shelves were bathed in multicolored pin lights like dancers at Radio City. The couple was perched at the far-right corner, and they kept glancing her way and smiling; or at least the man did. Austin looked at them unabashedly as she sipped a pomegranate martini through a fancy glass straw, until they finally dismounted, politely shouldered through the bouncing crowd, and came her way.

Bingo.

The man was nothing special. Tall and slim, exceptionally thin wrists, frosted dark hair, a half-open black silk shirt, tight black trousers, and Gucci loafers—Eurotrash. The girl was more interesting. Short black bobbed hair with bangs, large-framed glasses, very full features. She was wearing a black cashmere roll-neck sweater, about a size too large, over a short, crimson velvet skirt and matching high heels. She was carrying a mismatched brown leather clutch, which told Austin she didn't get out much; maybe a librarian with a vivid fantasy life.

Austin was always cautious about blind approaches in the field, and "honey traps" were her own specialty, so she could spot one a mile away. But these two looked about as dangerous as Keurig salesmen.

They were carrying their drinks, and they pulled out the two chairs at Austin's small table and sat down. Introductions were made, followed by a few white lies and vapid small talk. The two were Slovaks and had good English. The girl kept looking down at her drink and glancing at Austin over the top of her glasses, then chewing her bottom lip and blushing. Austin noticed that her hands were trembling as she played with her highball glass.

"Leena is a bit shy," the man said as he stroked the woman's tense spine, then cupped her shoulder in what was supposed to be a comforting hug, and pecked her on her temple.

"I can see that." Austin smiled and cocked her head. "Are you shy too, George?"

"Not so much. But I am here mostly to please my wife."

"What a good husband. And how're you going to do that?"

"Well, she is . . . How do you say? *Curious.*"

Austin nodded, stretched out one leg, and let her high heel drag along Leena's bare ankle. The girl jolted a little and blushed again.

"Curious about what, Leena?" Austin said to the girl, who took a long sip of her drink and didn't answer.

"About you," George said with a grin.

"Ah," Austin said. "About the other side of the equation."

"Yes."

"Well, maybe I could cure her curiosity," Austin said as she reached out, took the girl's pale hand, and gently stroked her palm with one finger. Seducing her was going to be fun. If George was her only lover, she'd probably been faking orgasms for years. "Would you like that, Leena?"

The girl nodded, looked down, and whispered, "Yes."

Austin looked at the man.

"We'll come back later, George. It might be . . . *much* later."

"I shall be fine right here," he said, "just imagining."

"I'm sure you will," said Austin, and she slipped out of the banquette, took Leena's damp hand, and led her out of the Grotto. . . .

Austin's suite next door on the second floor of the Greif Maria Theresia was perfect for an explorative tryst. The decor was in deep crimsons, creams, and browns, with a huge, king-size four-poster in the bedroom and a well-stocked bar including always chilled prosecco. The bathroom was something that would have made Emperor Nero proud, and the large plush salon opened up onto a balcony through wide French doors hung with Egyptian silk curtains that billowed in the ocean breeze.

On the way over, Leena had shyly confessed her fantasy about luxuriating in steaming foam with a woman like "Sabrina," so Austin had started running a lavender bubble bath in the enormous tub. But then they'd moved to the wide white leather sofa in the salon and kissed, tentatively at first, and then with their tongues twining and their heart rates rising, until Austin slipped her fingers up inside Leena's velvet skirt and felt her wetness and the girl moaned and jerked her hips and thrust back against Austin's persistent strokes.

Then, panting and with her eyes gleaming, Leena pulled away and whispered hoarsely, "God, you are going to make me finish."

"Yes, I am." Austin grinned.

"First, I want to *see* you," Leena said as she staggered upright and sat down in a large leather armchair, facing Austin across from the sofa. "*Please*."

Austin smiled and slowly removed her halter. She wasn't wearing a bra. Leena gasped and stared at Austin's breasts, and then she quickly pulled off her sweater, and Austin almost gasped as well because the girl's body was stunning. She was wearing a black lace bra and her breasts heaved up from the cups.

"I want to show you something," Leena panted.

"*Show* me," Austin said as she started unzipping her miniskirt.

Then Leena, who was in fact Lila Kalidi, reached for her clutch purse, pulled out a small plastic pouch, and from that removed Jonathan Raines's severed ear and dangled it in the air like a greasy slice of salami.

"I believe this belonged to a friend of yours." She grinned like a panther.

It took only a millisecond for the horror to smash through Austin's brain. She growled, "Mother*fucker*," and sprang up from the couch. But Lila had already pulled a mini-Taser from her bag, and she shot Austin point-blank, full bore in the chest.

The shock sent Austin sprawling backward on the couch, her teeth grinding and her limbs flung wide and utterly paralyzed. Lila moved like a lightning bolt. She grabbed Austin's evening purse, leaped forward, whipped its chain around Austin's neck, twisted it twice, and hauled her half-naked, twitching body off the couch and dragged her across the salon's Persian carpet and into the bathroom.

Even with the Taser prongs still embedded in her flesh and the purse chain crushing her windpipe, Austin's survival reflex kicked into gear and her body tried to fight. With a gush of adrenaline and a banshee cry from her mouth she flung her arms up over her head and grabbed Lila's hair, but the bob haircut was nothing but a wig and it went flying across the marble tiles. Then Austin spun herself onto her stomach and almost got to her knees, but Lila snatched a large ceramic soap dish off of the sink counter and smashed it into Austin's skull—once, twice, three times. Then she hauled her over the edge of the nearly overflowing bathtub, kneed her in the spine with the force of a pile driver, gripped her red hair, and shoved her facedown under the roiling water, until at last Austin's fingers stopped clawing for air, her bare feet stopped kicking, and her beautiful body went limp.

Lila turned off the faucets, took a break for a moment, and waited to make sure Austin was dead. Then she dragged her corpse with her dangling bloody head from the tub and dropped her faceup on the puddled marble floor. She walked out to the salon, came back with her clutch purse, took out her favorite dirk, and sliced off Austin's right ear. She rinsed it thoroughly in the tub, dried it off with a hand towel, and added it to the bag with Stalker Six's. Then she collected her wig and spent some time in front of the bathroom mirror, fixing it back into place.

It took her a full five minutes to find Austin's cell phone. That Program bitch was clever; it was in a magnetic case stuck to the back of the minibar.

Lila walked the phone into the bathroom, pressed Austin's lifeless thumb onto the reader to open the phone, and changed the access code to "007," which amused her. Then she stuffed it into her purse as well, and got dressed.

She had a coiled length of 550 parachute cord in her purse, and a small steel descender—no worries, since her body weight was considerably less than 550 pounds. She checked once more that she had all her belongings, including her Taser, the wire leads, and the prongs. Then she walked out onto the balcony, gripped the purse in her teeth, clipped the cord to the wrought iron railing with a carabiner, locked the descender to the cord, and disappeared over the side.

CHAPTER 18

TRIESTE, ITALY

Shane Wylie was the first to make it back to Trieste.

Eric Steele's frantic message to Wylie, relayed in a flash comm through Cutlass Main II, turned him right around in Berlin before he ever left the airport. When his cell buzzed in his pocket and he saw the blinking black diamond icon, he quickly scanned the text, felt the heat flushing his face, and jumped off the people mover with his rollaway.

Wylie first coded in on a voice call to Mike Pitts, trying to get himself the fastest ride he could muster, but there were no Program air assets available in his immediate AO, so he clicked off without further formalities and went rushing headlong for the nearest Alitalia representative, who told him he'd have to go back out to the main terminals and buy a ticket at one of the check-in counters.

Wylie might have been old school, but he was also "quick school" and had decades of experience in the field. He took out his cell again, bought a ticket on the first nonstop to Trieste, downloaded the boarding pass, and went right to the gate. The gate agents, trained to be wary of such hastily purchased one-way tickets made by foreigners at the very last minute, called the airport's Flughafenpolizei. Wylie, anticipating just such a reaction, switched his standard U.S. blue passport for a diplomatic black passport, and haughtily informed the two young German airport policemen who arrived that he was about to call the U.S. ambassador to Berlin, who was infamous in Germany for his take-no-prisoners approach to bilateral relations.

"Would you like to meet him?" he asked the cops in fluent German. "After all, it's going to be your last day on the job."

They let him on the plane.

But that didn't quiet Wylie's desperate discomfort. He kept telling himself that this close-range facial recognition hit in Venice on Stalker Six's alleged killer was nothing but coincidence, and the fact that he couldn't raise Austin had been totally expected, because she was on R&R and therefore justifiably out of pocket. . . . Right? Still, he called her hotel in Trieste and asked the desk to ring her room, to which they protested because it was already the middle of the night, but he pleaded a family emergency and they rang him through. No answer, and now he knew that if he made a further fuss it would simply raise the ante, set off alarm bells, and risk getting the local cops involved, not to mention Austin's fury if it turned out she was perfectly hale and hearty and he was behaving like the doting old father she always accused him of being.

So, he rode it out, landed in Trieste, jumped in a

cab, and raced through the city to the Greif Maria Theresia hotel. He left his rollaway in the cab and told the driver to wait.

By then it was already morning, and as Wylie slipped past the front desk, trotted up the stairs to the second floor, and quick-marched down the hallway toward Austin's room, he could hear the *hee-haw* of approaching Italian police cars, and his stomach flipped over. The door to her suite was open and a maid in customary black-and-white service costume was bawling like a baby on the shoulder of a pale-faced security guard, and she was mumbling "*È morta*" over and over, but Wylie couldn't be sure until he saw for himself.

And then he caught a glimpse inside of the bathroom floor and Austin's red hair splayed over the bloody marble, and his knees turned to jelly and he knew there was nothing left for him there and he spun around, but the Carabinieri were already storming down the hallway, guns drawn, and they grabbed him and slammed him face-first into a wall.

Eric Steele was the next to arrive in Trieste, along with Dalton Goodhill, with whom he hadn't spoken a word all night. Steele had called into Cutlass while sprinting to his car from Ralphy Persko's place, had gotten Pitts on comms, and told him he needed to get to Stalker Eight asap because intel evidence was off the charts that she was "Primary One" on somebody's target package. Goodhill, who was with Pitts at that moment, had jumped on the call and told Steele to stand down and stop acting like some overprotective paranoid little brother, to which Steele had replied, "If you don't fucking clear this, *Blade*, I'll take out my credit card and get my own ass over there. And I fucking promise you this: if she's dead, and I could have gotten there sooner, whatever happened to her is going to happen to *you*."

Steele was steaming like a Spanish bull at that point, and he heard some harsh murmurs in the background, and then Pitts cleared the trip and the assets. Steele met Goodhill at Andrews Air Force Base at 1700 hours, where the same Program jet that had taken Austin and Wylie over to Europe was just landing to refuel and pick up some Program analysts for a training seminar sponsored by the CIA in Vegas. The kids were left cursing, albeit quietly, with their luggage, on the tarmac.

For Steele, the nonstop flight to Trieste was brutal. He couldn't sleep, had no appetite, and had to hold his alcohol content down, even though he felt like in this particular state of ratcheted-up tension, he could have downed a fifth of Red Label and not have felt a thing. He and Goodhill sat across from one another on opposite sides of the fuselage, while the female navy steward glanced at them occasionally like a kid whose parents were fighting. Steele looked over once and saw that Goodhill was reading a thick book by the historian Victor Davis Hanson, which surprised him, because he'd already decided the man's brain was the size of a walnut.

When they landed midmorning—a nine-hour flight plus six for the time change—Steele tried reaching Shane Wylie, who'd last made contact with Cutlass hours before. Nothing. And worse than nothing. All Alpha operators and their keepers had their phones linked by a TS DARPA app to their own biomorphic systems, meaning that the cells "identified with" their owners and "knew" if they were too far away from them. Wylie's cell was showing that it had been separated from him, which could not have been voluntary.

No one in the Program ever lost a phone. *No one.*

They jumped out of a cab in front of the Greif Maria Theresia, and Goodhill had to rush around the Fiat and slow Steele down. The place was crawling with police: at least six of the blue-and-white cars with their cobalt-blue lights flashing, an ambulance, and a SWAT truck. A semicircle of young female cops with white Sam Browne belts and white pistol holsters were keeping onlookers back from the scene, while chain-smoking detectives streamed in and out of the lobby, and they all stepped back and lowered their heads as the ambulance crew rolled a corpse in a green body bag on a gurney over the polished marble entranceway toward the open ambulance bay.

Steele knew it was Austin and he was trembling from head to foot, his breathing labored, his fists clenching. An Italian detective in a shiny pearl-gray suit watched the gurney pass by and side-remarked to one of the female cops, "Whoever the bastard was, he took her ear. *Maniaco.*"

Steele's Italian wasn't as good as his Russian or French, but he knew enough to understand that. And just as the poisonous bile surged up from his guts, he looked past the cops and saw the large glass doors of the hotel lobby, and through those he could see a long brown divan, and on that sat Shane

Wylie, bent over his knees, and handcuffed behind his back.

Steele grunted something and started to lunge forward. Goodhill grabbed him inside his left elbow and spun him around with remarkable power and slammed him up against the outside fuselage of the ambulance, where at least the cops were out of range and couldn't see them.

"Let go of me, Goodhill," Steele growled down at him.

"Get your head on straight, Steele," Goodhill hissed back up. "There's not a fucking thing you can do here."

Steele ripped his arm from Goodhill's grip.

"Maybe that's what they taught *you* wherever the hell you came from, but I don't leave men in the field."

Goodhill then took both hands and grabbed the front lapels of Steele's leather jacket, and bounced him off the ambulance again.

"She's *dead*, Steele. She's dead and she's not coming back. And Wylie's got diplo cover and he's somebody else's job now and he'll come out of it just fucking fine. That's how this thing works, and you know it."

"I said, *I* don't leave men in the field," Steele snarled, and he tried to pry Goodhill's fists from his jacket, but the man was all SpecOps muscle.

"Listen up, Steele, and listen real good," Goodhill said in a firm, but somehow much calmer tone, and he locked his ice-blue eyes to Eric's and wouldn't let go. "You, can't, save, everybody."

Eric Steele blinked. He suddenly felt weak, and

he dropped his arms by his sides and leaned back against the cold steel of the ambulance.

"That's what Demo always said," he whispered.

"I know." Goodhill nodded. "That's why I fucking said it."

Lila Kalidi was just waking up in her luxurious sleeping compartment to a first-class Continental breakfast.

The Nightjet's ten-hour high-speed train trip from Santa Lucia Station in Venice, Italy, to the Central Station in Vienna, Austria, was just what she'd needed to decompress after a stressful evening of killing. And with the sun breaking over the Austrian countryside, the rhythmic clicking of the big train's wheels, and the wonderful scents of apple strudel and *mélange* coffee, she felt justified in indulging herself with luxuries and was ready to collect her hard-earned pay.

She no longer looked anything like the "shy" girl Leena who'd been so keen to experience the pleasures of lesbian love. In fact, her latest disguise looked more like the pathetic American agent she'd just murdered. Her hair was now Irish farm girl red, and not a wig—she'd dyed it in the private compartment's bathroom. Her eyes were emerald green, owing to a pair of long-wear contact lenses. Her fingernails were now long and lacquered lime, since she'd had plenty of time to glue them on. And soon she'd be dressed in a tie-dyed blouse, hippy jeans, and Doc Martens, but at the moment she was naked under a thick, white terry cloth Nightjet robe.

She lay back on a puffy leather divan, watched

the scenery flashing by, sipped her *mélange*, and strapped on the voice-altering collar that looked like a velvet neck tattoo. Then she picked up the first of two cell phones lying on her bare thighs and made a call to Russia.

"Good morning, Mr. Snipe," Lila said in English. Russian was one of her languages, because her father had been educated long ago at the Patrice Lumumba Peoples' Friendship University in Moscow, but these self-impressed little idiots from Millennial Crude didn't need to know that. "The Italian property you inquired about has been purchased," she continued, "and now we kindly request the full amount. That's one million euros, just to confirm. And we'll expect it to appear in our Maltese account by close of business today."

Lila paused for a moment, sipped her coffee, and listened while Snipe said something. Then her arching eyebrows, which she'd also dyed red, knit slightly together.

"You're not really going to try to renegotiate our price, are you?" she said.

She listened again for a bit while Snipe stuttered and indeed tried to bargain, as urged to do by his lieutenant colonel boss. Then, she'd had enough.

"Snipe, let me ask you something," she said. "Do you ever suck on your toes?"

She smiled her panther's smile when he was clearly flustered by the question, and then she cut him off.

"I am simply wondering if you like the taste of your toes, Snipe. Because if that money is not in the designated account by the specified time today, all of your toes are soon going to be stuffed in your mouth, and they will no longer be attached to your feet. Are we clear?"

After giving Snipe enough time to comply while trying not to wet himself, Lila said, "Very good," and clicked off.

Then she picked up the second cell phone, the one she'd taken from Austin. She scrolled through the contact list, took a chance, and clicked on ICE, for "In Case of Emergency." She grinned when a tinny male human voice answered at Cutlass Main II and said, "Good morning. Code in."

"I'm afraid I don't know your code," Lila said, "and I just killed the bitch who did." She let that sink in for a moment, then dropped her voice to a vicious whisper. "But at any rate . . . now you are only seven."

She clicked off, reached over to the train compartment's window, slid it open, and hurled Austin's cell phone into oblivion.

ACT II

CHAPTER 19

WASHINGTON, D.C.

The funerals of all Program special operators were held at Washington's magnificent National Cathedral.

Yet unlike the final farewells for America's great statesmen and women, a fallen Alpha did not arrive in a motorcycle-led procession of armored limousines, escorted by honor guards on horseback. There were no crowds lining the great circular drive beneath the cathedral's spectacular twin Gothic towers, nor did pristine-uniformed military personnel carry the coffin through its Ulrich Henn bronze doors.

There would be no choir echoing Gregorian chants inside the grand nave, no one sitting in the pews to appreciate the spectral confetti of Rowan LeCompte's stained glass windows, and there wouldn't be a television camera or reporter in sight.

Alpha operators, whenever killed in action, were carried into the cathedral via a seldom-used side door, and had their last salutes raised to them not in the main worshipping space of the cathedral, but in a full-story underground in a chapel vault that most people had no idea was there.

Eric Steele had long ago learned to accept it, but it was still depressing as hell. And because this was going to be Collins Austin's funeral, he couldn't extinguish the fury in his heart. The rain didn't help dampen his ire, and it was coming down like a monsoon from clots of gray and purple clouds rolling above Washington, as if the capital's better angels, of which there were few, were weeping.

She wasn't supposed to go before me, he thought, feeling much like an older brother whose favorite sis had undertaken some risky profession that always made him nervous, which was basically true. *She wasn't supposed to go at all.*

Then he had a flash memory of an incident a couple of years back, when all the Alphas had been brought down to Fort Bragg and the Salt Pit for a physical fitness assessment. For the hand-to-hand module, USASOC had delivered a squad of paratroopers from the 82nd Airborne Division to "play" with this small group of strange "OGA" (Other Governmental Agency) civilians. Collins Austin had selected a twenty-year-old E-4 as her partner, a big kid and former cage fighter from Tennessee, and had thoroughly kicked his ass. Even worse for the battered soldier and his mates, she was wearing skintight black leggings and only a sports bra at the time, and she was barefoot.

"I think you just terminated all hard-ons in that platoon for the next thirty days," Steele had remarked with pride as Collins walked off the pitch.

"Naw." She'd grinned as she wiped some blood from her nose where the kid had landed one good one. "Those guys are all Airborne. They like pain. I think it actually turns them on."

"Good point," Steele had said with a smile.

And the thought of that now made him smile again, but only for a millisecond, until he returned to the present and the soul-crushing fact that Collins Austin was gone. He stood there beneath a gray marble portico on the northeastern end of the cathedral, just outside a pair of glass doors that looked more like an emergency room entrance than the respected portals to a final port of prayer. Hands in the pockets of his navy-blue funeral suit, he waited for Collins's hearse and looked up at the cathedral's spires, then down at its hidden rear doors.

Above are all the glories, below are all the stories, he brooded in a black poetic moment. Then his gaze drifted over to a circular mound of mowed grass about the size of half a football field, bracing the cathedral's north side off Woodley Road and Thirty-Sixth Street. And like all special operators everywhere, he reflexively assessed the space as a landing zone. A tall flagpole with the Stars and Stripes whipping in the wind jutted up from the mound's northern perimeter, but closer by and just off the south side, a black stanchion mounted with floodlights reached about thirty feet up to the sky.

A Little Bird could make it in here, he thought as he pictured the small MD-500 helicopter. *But a Blackhawk? Not so sure. Pretty dicey.* Then he chided himself, because he should have been thinking of nothing but Collins, yet the issue was solved as the hearse with her corpse arrived.

It was pearl gray, followed by a black limousine and two black bulky Suburbans, all of which barely fit into the tight little circular driveway. The doors of the last Suburban opened and a whole bunch of Program security personnel emerged like clowns from a circus Volkswagen and fanned out to make sure there were no nosy reporters or photographers around. Two of them headed across the grassy knoll and up the side drive toward the cathedral's visitors' entrance, where a pair of glass boxes that housed the elevators to the underground parking lot were spilling a few Asian tourists despite the downpour. The security men politely discouraged them from wandering down the hill, or using their cell phone cameras or Nikons until they were safely inside the church.

Steele took a deep breath, stepped into the rain, and joined the other five pallbearers to retrieve Collins's coffin. They were all wearing dark suits, sunglasses, and sundry hats, which reminded him of a macabre version of the Blues Brothers. Shane Wylie, who'd been sprung from a Carabinieri lineup by the U.S. ambassador to Rome, looked pale and sickly, and Dalton Goodhill's jaw was set even harder than usual. Stalker Two, an operator named Martin Farro, had been recalled from the field and, having gone through the Operator Training Course with Collins, had begged to be part of the funeral, even though Program protocol stated that no more than two Alphas and keepers were to attend such events at a time. Ralphy Persko and another analyst brought up the rear. Mike Pitts and Meg Harden got out of the black limousine, and Pitts, using his cane, stalked around to the other side and opened the door for a tiny, bent elderly woman.

She had curly red hair.

Just hold it together, Steele demanded of himself. *Special Forces soldiers don't cry.*

Most of the funeral itself was a blur for Steele. They carried Collins Austin through the glass doors, past the row of federal flags, and down the pale gray staircase into a gloomy corridor where signs pointed to the Bethlehem Chapel to the left, and to the Chapel of St. Joseph of Arimathea to the right. The Bethlehem Chapel was bright, airy, spacious, and even had its own pair of stained glass windows behind the podium, which was the lowest apex of the cathedral above, much like windows beneath a sailing ship's bowsprit. On the other hand, the St. Joseph chapel was set in the very middle of the limestone acreage, directly under the cathedral's intersecting "floor cross" above, but another whole story underground. It had no windows, scant light, one dreary mural behind the small podium, and a couple of dozen scratched old pew chairs. Wide slate staircases led down to its sunken floor from both side corridors, giving it all the architectural grace of a slop sink. It smelled of wet stone and felt like a tomb.

Only about twenty Program personnel were there. You couldn't clear out Cutlass II for a funeral, and besides, they were all back there going crazy and recalling everyone in from the field. Jonathan Raines's murder hadn't raised undue alarm bells, and even the attempt on Steele in Paris hadn't set anyone's hair on fire. But the killing of Austin, with a matching MO to Raines's death, had cinched it.

"Once is happenstance. Twice is coincidence. The third time is enemy action." It was an old Ian Fleming quote that Steele often remembered, but hell, he'd known it from the moment he'd heard about Raines. Not only was there some murdering banshee on the loose out there, but someone was also helping her from the inside, and she might even have support from one or more of the United States' arch enemies.

Steele hadn't taken a seat in a pew but was standing off to one side of the chapel on the third row of one set of wide-slab stairs. Half of him was listening to the meanderings of an Anglican priest who was standing behind Collins's coffin and talking about her as if they'd been buddies on the same high school swim team, while the other half of his brain was slinging out accusatory pinballs at every potential traitor in the room—and just as quickly decrying the suspicions.

Wylie?

Oh, for Christ's sake, it couldn't be Shane Wylie. The guy looks like he's about to collapse from grief. If he was responsible in any way for Collins's death he would have offed himself already.

Goodhill?

He's a hard-assed sonuvabitch, but he's been battling bad guys for this country since the freakin' Ice Age. He's new to the Program. Not likely that he came over to Cutlass to destroy it.

Pitts?

Oh, please. Mike Pitts has given his entire adult life to selfless service, not to mention half a leg. He's got two kids, Katherine's pregnant again, and he could easily go into private contracting instead of taking a lousy G-16 salary. Guy's a pure patriot.

Persko?

Yeah, right. If Ralphy was a traitor he'd be pissing down his pants leg every time he saw me, 'cause he knows what I'd do to him.

Meg?

Don't even go there. She probably knew about that stiletto that was used on Raines from some other rumor, or maybe from a flash file that came across her desk. She's the daughter of General "Black Jack" Harden and was raised on the Pledge of Allegiance and apple pie. She's clean . . . right?

Then he considered that it could easily be someone else, even higher up, like Lansky, or maybe some nameless baby analyst who'd just come over from NSA. On the other hand, his instincts were to protect his friends from the worst of all possible accusations, so maybe he just wasn't looking at them clearly enough. And instantly, he began suspecting each one of them again, including Meg.

Shit. That's why the counterintel guys are all paranoid and nuts.

He heard a soft sob and his stomach turned over, and he looked to the right at the first row of pews, where Mrs. Austin was holding a trembling handkerchief to her nose and Meg was holding her hand. That poor old woman from Iowa was probably totally confused, wondering why her gorgeous young daughter, who'd said she was super happy in

D.C. working as an import-export salesperson and keeping up with her dance lessons at night, was suddenly dead, and being buried by all these strangers who looked nothing like salesmen or dancers. Two months from now, she'd be getting a letter from the president. How the hell were they going to explain that?

Steele felt Stalker Two, Martin Farro, nudging up beside him. Farro was a big man, a former Ranger and SOCOM operator, with black curly hair, glasses, and shoulders like kettle bells. He was busting out of his suit, and not due to overeating.

"I hate this place," Farro whispered. "Feels like we were just here for Jonathan."

"We were, and so do I," Steele muttered back.

"Why the hell do we have to do these things here?"

"Security?" Steele shrugged. "Control issues?"

"It's bullshit," Farro hissed. "The place is depressing." He jutted his big chin across the chapel to a small bronze plaque mounted on the far wall. "Did you know that Helen Keller is buried here? Right under the floor."

"Well, she was blind," Steele said. "So she couldn't see how ugly it was."

Farro snickered softly and then dropped his voice even lower. "Sorry for you, bro. I know you and Col were close."

"We're all close," Steele said. "Hurts me no more than you."

"Right." Farro squeezed Steele's shoulder and walked away.

"Yea, though I walk through the valley of the shadow of death, I will fear no evil. . . ."

The priest was intoning the twenty-third psalm, which to Steele's relief meant that the thing was almost over. But then he felt a pang of guilt for wanting it to be so. He'd been to so many funerals, of so many people he cared for, had been responsible for, had led in battle or been led by in combat both official and covert. He should have been used to it by now, but he knew he'd never get used to it. Nothing ever actually healed, it all just added one more layer to the scar tissue squeezing his heart.

Collins Austin. A beautiful, talented, fiery, combative, hard-charging, and fearless woman. He'd seen her once on a playground with her college roommate's young daughters, laughing and playing as if she herself were once again seven years old, and he'd had a flash-forward moment, picturing Collins happily married, raising her own brood of tough, smart girls, a woman with a history she'd never be able to tell them, but somehow they'd know who their mother was.

Now that was gone, forever, and suddenly a line from an old Clint Eastwood movie, *Unforgiven*, sprang into Steele's head.

"It's a helluva thing, killing a man. You take away all he's got, and all he's ever gonna have."

Then he thought he was going to lose it, and quickly decided there was enough muscle down there to carry Collins out, and he turned and walked back out through the catacombs to the rain.

Twenty minutes later, they'd loaded Collins Austin's coffin into the hearse for her final trip to Arlington. She was one of the only Alphas who'd never served in the U.S. military, so she'd needed special dispensation to be buried at a United States military cemetery, which Mike Pitts was able to easily obtain from Ted Lansky. Once the secret procession crossed over into Virginia, there was going to be a full military honor guard, including a rifle salute and taps, and Pitts would present the folded flag to Mrs. Austin under a terrible brew of tears and rain. Steele desperately wanted to skip it. He couldn't, but he stalled for a minute with his car keys in his hand as the downpour soaked his hair.

Ralphy Persko waddled over to Steele from where his pallbearer duties were done at the hearse. He was carrying a tartan-patterned umbrella and his big glasses were totally fogged up. Steele looked down at him.

"I cracked it," Ralphy said.

"English, Ralphy," Steele said.

Persko looked around to make sure no one else was in earshot.

"The microdot. I cracked the encryption, decoded it."

Steele seemed to emerge from his gloomy stupor with that bit of news. He scanned Ralphy's rumpled, rain-stained suit. "You going to give me the readout?"

"It's short. You'll remember it." Then, like a sidewalk magician, Ralphy slipped Steele the challenge coin, which he didn't need anymore.

"Shoot," Steele said.

"It had only two items on it. The rest was chaff, just camouflage. It said 'Cole Knows,' and after that were two sets of numbers, 62, 46, 3.19 and 106, 14, 7.05."

Steele looked up at the purple spitting sky.

"Is that the Cole I think it is?" Ralphy asked.

"Yeah, I'm guessing our former president."

"And those numbers. Lats and longs, right?"

"Right," Steele said. "Map coordinates."

"So, what do you think Cole knows, Seven?" Ralphy asked.

"No idea, but I'm going to find out." Steele looked down again and put a hand on Ralphy's shoulder. "Thanks, Ralphy. You're an ace. But do me a favor and text me those coords. I'm foggy today."

"Yeah, you bet. Aren't we all."

Ralphy walked away to find his ride to the cemetery, and suddenly Meg was standing right there in his place. She had no hat or umbrella and her raven hair was soaking wet, but the rain seemed to only enhance the color of her pale blue eyes, and her full lips glistened with tiny droplets of water. She was wearing a dark blue trench coat, the belt tied at her slim waist. She looked up at Steele and their eyes locked, but even though both of them desperately needed to comfort each other in a crushing embrace, the Program frowned upon such PDAs.

Meg searched Steele's drawn and lined face, the pain behind his eyes, and she reached up and smoothed his suit lapel.

"Eric," she said, "I really think what you need is some serious downtime."

"I think what I really need, Meg," he said, "is some serious kill time."

CHAPTER 20

GREEN BANK MEDICAL FACILITY, WEST VIRGINIA

Former president Denton Cole was dying, and everyone around him knew it. But he'd be damned if he was going to admit it.

Nearly a year and a half prior, Cole had suffered a debilitating stroke while delivering his State of the Union address. Six months later, Vice President John Rockford had assumed the presidential mantle, yet for many months thereafter, Denton Cole's family, administration, staff, and fervent supporters all hoped and prayed he'd recover and be able to reoccupy the Oval Office.

In fact, Cole had recovered from the stroke, and with the best rehabilitation experts summoned over from both the Bethesda Naval Hospital and the National Institutes of Health, the symptoms of his neural debacle were barely noticeable. However, just as he was about to be discharged from the government's most highly secure medical facility in

West Virginia, a routine PET scan had revealed a suspicious shadow on his liver.

He'd never returned to Washington, and the only thing he occupied now was the presidential suite at Green Bank.

Eric Steele drove out there in his GTO on the same afternoon as Collins Austin's burial at Arlington. His heart was still gripped by that fist of sorrow and fury, but he went. It was a three-hour drive in the rain, during which he kept scanning for a radio station that might lift his mood, but when WJLS, "the Big Dawg" on 99.5, played Lee Ann Womack's "I Hope You Dance," he just gave up and let it ride. The long black ribbon of highway wound through rolling hills and valleys of lush emerald green, all misted in steam from the cool rain striking the warm macadam, and he knew that soon it would all be stunningly tainted by autumn, but his eyes weren't seeing much beauty.

The hospital didn't have a lot of patients. Green Bank was reserved for government officials with extremely high security clearances, and that didn't mean your average senator sitting on an Intelligence Oversight Committee. If a CIA deputy director got into a nasty car crash, that's where she went. If the chairman of the Joint Chiefs of Staff suffered a compound fracture while skiing, he wound up at Green Bank too. On occasion, the head of state of a foreign ally would be secretly whisked over to Green Bank after landing at Dover in the dead of night. Such patients could be released to other facilities, such as Bethesda, once they were in the latter stages of rehab, but not before.

People talk in their sleep, and they definitely chatter while anesthetized. All the medical staff had top secret clearances. Most of the doctors had served tours at Landstuhl in Germany or Craig in Afghanistan. They were all scalpel sharp, and tight-lipped.

It took Steele a little while to get through the hospital's Entry Control Point. The ECP was the standard, military base, hardened steel structure with bulletproof glass, but in order to approach it he had to first get through a rolling gate in a twenty-foot-high fence, then wind through a maze of orange water-filled barriers. The guards were uniformed federal agents carrying M4s, and they perused his ID carefully, but spent much more time admiring his car.

Then there was another rolling gate, and two Suburbans bracing the long driveway, from which a trio of subgun-hefting Secret Service agents spilled. He told them he was there to see President Cole. They raised their eyebrows, spoke into their cuff-link mics, and waved him through, after he assured them that he wasn't carrying, and they frisked him anyway and had a working dog sniff the GTO.

He parked, signed in at the front desk, left his cell phone in exchange for a numbered ticket, and took the elevator two stories underground.

The long gray hallway leading to Cole's suite was quiet and empty, except for one more Secret Service agent posted outside the door. Nancy Cole came out to meet Steele in the corridor. The former First

Lady was a tall, handsome woman with Texas grace, and she still had that schoolteacher smile that must have encouraged and comforted thousands of kids. But she'd obviously lost some weight, and her gray skirt and cream cable sweater seemed to hang on her frame, and her green eyes were dim and showed the strain. She was carrying a pencil and a book of crossword puzzles. She and Cole often passed the time that way, and they still laughed a lot over their silliest vocabulary guesses.

"How are you, Eric?" She hugged him briefly, then stood back and looked at him.

"Just fine, ma'am."

"And your mom?"

"She's fine too, thanks to you and the president getting her into this place after our . . . incident."

"That's a cute way to say it." Mrs. Cole cocked her head and smiled. She knew exactly what Steele did for a living, but the fact that his profession had nearly cost his mother her life didn't seem to faze the former First Lady. She was used to that sort of thing.

"And how are you doing, Mrs. Cole?"

She shrugged. "We're bearing up, Eric. I suppose everyone reaches this point in their lives, but I just can't picture it all without him, you know?"

"I know, ma'am," Steele said, though he really didn't, because he hadn't spent a whole lifetime with someone who he couldn't imagine living without.

"Would you like to see Denton alone?" she asked.

"If you don't mind, ma'am."

"Good." She grinned. "Gives me a chance to get out of here for a while." Then she reached up and patted his cheek. "And take all the time you want. He'll tell you when he's had enough."

"Thank you, ma'am," he said, and he watched her march off down the hallway. He knew there was a commissary up on the main floor, but he imagined it would be empty and he felt terribly sorry for her. It was that sort of day.

Steele pushed his way quietly into the room. It wasn't the usual hospital suite, not even of the kind you'd find on the very top floors of the most expensive facilities in Manhattan. This was expansive, with finely carpeted floors, heavy walnut dressers and French closets, an L-shaped mustard leather couch and recliner, brocade curtains hiding phony windows, and a hallway leading to a guest bedroom and a bathroom suite that could rival the Waldorf Astoria. The only thing that gave it away as a hospital room was the high-tech Stryker pneumatic bed on which Cole was lying and the headboard of muffled beeping monitors.

But the former president didn't stir when Steele entered the room. He was lying there wearing a pair of beige chinos, boat shoes, and a light yellow sweater, looking as though he was about to go out for a nice sail on the lake or some putting practice. Except his face was pale, his thick gray hair had grown wispy, and his eyes were completely closed. For a moment, Steele wondered if while he'd been chatting in the hallway with the former First Lady, the president had taken his last breath.

"You can stop standing there like some West Point plebe and have a seat, Eric," Cole suddenly said. "I'm no longer your commander in chief. I'm just some old fart in a hospital bed."

Steele smirked. "Roger that, sir," he said as he walked to the large leather couch and sat. "But you're still the C in C to me, and always will be."

"Sentimental softy," Cole said as he sat straight up like an electrocuted corpse and swung his legs over the side of the bed. His eyes were fully open now, and though ringed with the ravages of the cancer that was consuming his organs, they were still sharp and bright and deeply blue.

"I've been called lots of things, sir," Steele said. "That one's a first."

"Well, the walking dead have no filters." Cole grinned at him. "Don't tell anybody I said that." He pointed to a heavy wooden sideboard. "Black Label's in there. Pour us a couple."

"Yessir." Steele got up and executed his task, extracting the liquor and pouring two tumblers, neat. He handed one to President Cole, they clinked, and Steele resumed his seat as they both took long swigs.

"I see you're wearing a suit," Cole said.

"Yessir. Funeral."

"I know all about it. Condolences to all of us, for Austin, and for Raines before her. I told Rock I'd write that letter to Austin's mom. I knew her much better than he did. You Program Alphas are like my kids, you know."

"I know, sir." Steele nodded. "And thanks."

"Maybe *orphan*'s a better word," said Cole. Then he set his Scotch down on his rolling meal tray and coughed deeply and with a dark liquidity for a good twenty seconds until it subsided. He took a handkerchief from his pants pocket, wiped his lips, and picked up his drink again. "Sorry, it's in the lungs now."

"No need to apologize, sir."

Cole laughed. "I'm not apologizing. I'm just pissed it's in my lungs."

Steele laughed too, then they both got somber again.

"So," Cole said, "Ted Lansky's been briefing me, per instructions from the president. Guess they think my brain's not fried just yet and I might have a couple of insights left. My guess is you're here because the Program's under some kind of assault. Two assassinations on a couple of our best Alphas, another attempt on you . . ."

"It's not just that, sir. . . ."

"I know, I know." Cole slid himself off the bed, cranked himself upright, and straightened his spine. He was clearly in pain, but he wasn't going to verbalize it in any way, nor even let it show on his face. He walked with purpose toward the window blinds, and Steele was surprised to see him draw them open, revealing what certainly looked like a large picture window and the rolling West Virginia hills right outside, except that they were forty feet underground. "It's digital," Cole said as he looked out at a flock of black crows creasing the rainswept sky above the rows of green hills. "Works off a camera mounted up there on the roof. Pretty neat, huh?"

"Yes, sir."

"Anyway, you're thinking we've got a turncoat inside. That's the only way this killer, or killers, could know where our operators are working, how to get to them, their real-time vulnerabilities, correct?"

Steele was actually amazed at Cole's mental acuity, given his physical condition. Yet he still stood up from the couch and ambled toward the former president, just in case he lost his balance or suddenly had to sit down.

"That's how it looks," he said.

"Looks can be deceiving, you know that, Eric. What if that's just what the opposition wants us to think? What if all that's happened is that they've got some slick hackers who've cracked into our system and are gathering intelligence on us from our own communications? What if they simply want us to *think* we've got a bad apple? I'll bet you're tossing and turning at night, trying to figure out who in the family needs killing, while maybe nobody does at all. Am I right?"

It didn't escape Steele's notice that Cole kept using the term *we*, which told Steele that either he was trying to hang on to his former glories, or that he was much more endeared to the Program than he'd ever admitted before. But the thought that the former president might be right about this cat-and-mouse game both shocked him and pumped up some hope. Shock, because he knew that such unfair suspicions were how people got burned at the stake. And hope, because he wanted it to be just the way Cole was laying it out. He wanted to stop suspecting Meg, or anyone else back at Cutlass Main II.

"I sure hope you are, sir," Steele said.

Cole turned to him from the phony window, which actually wasn't phony at all. It was just a couple of floors lower down than it should have been.

"The other thing to consider," Cole said, "these killings are red herrings. They're feints designed to throw us all off from something else."

"Something else?"

"Something worse, Eric. But I haven't yet figured out what that is." The former president then had another long bout of coughing, and this time Steele took his elbow and helped him return to his bed. The skin under his sweater sleeve felt like it was hanging off his fragile bones. Cole recovered again, yet he wasn't about to surrender his bottle of Black Label, and poured himself another two fingers. Steele declined with a small wave, and figured he'd better move the conversation along before Cole no longer had the strength. He took out the challenge coin from his pocket and placed it on the food tray. Cole stared at it, then looked back up.

"I already gave you booze, son. You coining me for a beer?"

"I found it on Demo's gravestone, sir."

"I liked that young man. . . ."

"It had a microdot embedded in the back. I got one of our boys to decrypt it."

"A microdot. Now that's old school. I was never officially in the spy game, but I always liked the gadgetry and—"

"Sir, the message said 'Cole knows.'"

The former president sipped his Scotch, looked

up at Steele, and said nothing. Steele didn't mention the map coordinates, not yet.

"Someone left it for me, sir. I suspect that it was actually Demo, by way of someone else he tasked with instructions to execute if he died."

Cole still said nothing.

"What is it that you know, sir?" Steele asked, and now he'd put his drink on the table and was staring intently at his former commander in chief, for whom he'd soldiered on faithfully for years, without question, and to whom he'd become something of a surrogate son.

"Tell him, Denton." It was Mrs. Cole's voice, and it startled both of them, and Steele turned to see her standing in the door. "Tell him, hon. He deserves to know."

Steele turned back to President Cole.

"It's about your father, Eric," Cole said at last. "That's what I know."

CHAPTER 21

SIBERIA, RUSSIA, 1993

It was death in the tall grass.

Hank Steele knew it was going to be *his* death, if he didn't move fast. The guy facing him was six and a half feet tall, a master sergeant in the elite Border Guards division of Russian Military Intelligence, the GRU. He was wearing a camouflage tunic, brown woolen pantaloons, black combat boots, a bear fur hat, leather bandoliers crisscrossing his barrel chest, and, weirdly, a maroon tie. A jet-black walrus mustache drooped over his thick lips and his eyes were like charcoal briquettes under centipede eyebrows.

The uniform didn't intimidate Steele, nor did the AK-47 slung from the giant's left shoulder. It was the wickedly curved Gurkha fighting knife gripped in his bare right hand. It was about the size of a farmer's scythe, and Hank knew it wasn't there for harvesting wild roses. The guy was going to use it to flay open the man he was hunting, who happened to be Hank.

The only thing saving Hank Steele, at least for that moment, was the fact that he was wearing a similar uniform and spoke dead fluent Russian, thanks to the JFK Special Warfare Center and School at Fort Bragg and the Defense Language Institute in Monterey. Of course, his uniform was stolen and had been supplied by a Program contact in Vladivostok, but this oversize *Pogranichnya Ohrhana* couldn't know that. And there was one other environmental factor in Hank's favor: it was October in Siberia, and this open plain near the west bank of the Lena river, halfway between Yakutsk and Tiksi, would normally have been slathered in six feet of snow by this time in autumn. But Siberia was experiencing a rare warm spell, so the bullrushes and river grass were still about seven feet high.

He could hear the rest of this guy's search party running around out there on both flanks, along with their hunting dogs barking like banshees. But he couldn't see them, which meant they couldn't see him, or his soon-to-be mortal combat partner either.

The only weapon Hank had was a knife, a Choate Tool Corp. throwing knife with a weighted double-edge blade and a rubber-coated grip. He'd already used up all the ammo for his Makarov PB 9 x 18 mm pistol, so he'd tossed it away about half a klick back. It was a nice gun, but the built-in bulky silencer gave it away as an assassination weapon, and being caught with it would be like getting nabbed by a cop in a bank vault with a stethoscope and a safecracker's manual. He longed for his .45 caliber 1911, the one his father had used on Guadalcanal, but he'd left that at home for his nine-year-old son, Eric, just in case he never made it back. It wasn't much of a legacy, but Hank and his beloved wife, Susan, didn't own a mansion or a yacht. Government service was its own reward, right?

The big guy looked down at Hank and cocked his head like a Russian wolfhound, because Hank was breathing hard after his four-klick sprint from the perimeter fence of Russian Committee for State Security Technical Training Facility 722, which sounded somewhat academic, but housed a top secret camp for turning carefully selected orphaned youths, snatched up from all over the world, into robotic killers.

One of those youths had just been captured in Somalia by Delta, after leading the *shabab* in the murder and mutilation of a number of American troops in Mogadishu. Under interrogation he'd revealed the existence of Camp 722, and thereafter, President Clinton had ordered the Program to take care of the problem. Clinton never actually set foot in Cutlass Main and barely acknowledged its existence. He had Al Gore issue the order, which seemed etymologically appropriate to Hank.

What no one mentioned to Hank Steele—and what he only found out once inside 722—was that the "youths" in the camp weren't even teenagers yet. They were all children, some of them not yet nine years old, the age of his own son.

The Border Guard was asking Hank to see his identification card, since he obviously knew that this stranger wasn't part of his platoon. Hank smiled and said, "*Konyeshna, tovarich.*" Of course, comrade.

And while he reached inside his tunic with his left hand, he drew the Choate from his right-hand boot and in one fluid motion whipped it ten feet through the air and into the giant's throat.

The giant's eyes bugged out and he arched his back. A gush of blood frothed from his open mouth. Then he gripped the knife by its black handle, yanked it out of the torn flesh below his plum-size Adam's apple, tossed it into the grass, and charged at Hank.

Hank turned and took off, with the staggering giant's boots pounding the red earth behind him and the sound of the Gurkha blade whipping the air. Hank opened the distance until he sensed a gap between them of about twenty feet, slammed on the brakes, spun around, and charged right back at the gurgling Border Guard. It was like two locomotives bearing down on each other head-on, except that Hank then "slid into home," hard on his ass, with his right boot cranked to the left so he took out the giant's front ankle, and the big man crashed forward and down onto him like the steel drop-ramp of an Armored Personnel Carrier.

Hank snap rolled to the right and the giant slammed onto the ground face-first, and before he could shake it off and elbow himself up again, Hank had spun left and mounted his back. He jammed his right knee into the man's cervical C7, dove forward, looped his right forearm under his throat, gripped his own right wrist with his left hand on the other side, and hauled back as hard as he could, snapping the giant's neck.

The move might have won him a martial arts

tournament medallion somewhere, except that nobody saw it.

There were shouts now in the tall grass coming from maybe a hundred meters away, back in the direction of Camp 722, but they were moving Hank's way, and he heard a rank and a name and knew they were calling out to his "dance partner." His only chance now was to get to the river and if God and the luck that had always saved his ass before were on duty today, then Dmitry would be there with the boat and they might actually make it. But he had to move fast.

He rolled off the corpse and immediately thought to search in the grass for his throwing knife, then realized he couldn't fight off an entire platoon of GRU with a steel toothpick. So instead, he dragged the AK-47 out from under the dead guard by its strap. It only had one curved magazine in the well—thirty rounds of 7.62 x 39 mm, unless the Russians also didn't like overpressuring magazine springs, in which case, it would be only twenty-nine rounds.

You're actually doing ballistic analyses now, numb nuts? Hank chastised himself, then tried to turn the giant over to search him for more ammo, but the deadweight was like a damned Volkswagen. He knew he was out of time, leaped to his feet, and took off for the river.

He'd studied topical maps and stereoscopic U-2 surveillance photographs of the target area for a full month before being inserted into Vladivostok. He knew exactly where the river was.

It was too damned far.

Hank ran for his life, through the tall grass that

whipped at his face and sliced the skin of his hands and neck like the elephant grass that always cut you up on the drop zones in southern Taiwan and Thailand. He didn't have a compass, or enough time to use one anyway, but it was late in the day and he'd seen the ice ball sun sinking over the camp at his six o'clock behind him, so he kept on pounding east, always east, hoping he'd just run right off a cliff and wind up cannonballing into the Lena.

Didn't happen. They were gaining on him. He didn't know exactly how many, but they were directly behind and also on both rear flanks, and their dogs were straining and barking. He had no idea why the GRUs didn't just cut the beasts loose and let them rip him to shreds, but he figured that would come soon enough. His lungs were on fire, his heart slamming in his throat, and he tossed his fur hat away and breech-checked the AK as he ran.

You hesitated, Steele, and now you're screwed.

It was no time for some pitiable after-action analysis, but he'd always been a self-critical type, something he'd honed while in 5th Group, and then Delta.

You should've just executed the mission and taken out as many of those kids as possible, then exfilled nice and quiet, and this would've been a cakewalk instead of a friggin' fiasco. But you had to be Mr. Morality, didn't you? Did you actually think you could cut them loose and they'd follow you like some Pied Piper? Moron. Susan's gonna be pissed.

Then the gunfire started. He knew it was coming, but the bangs of multiple AK-47s firing at him on the run jolted his system. Kalashnikovs were always loud, but the hardpack landscape and thick clouds above were doubling their kettle drum echoes, and the heavy Russian rounds were cutting down shafts of grass on either side of his sprint. His spine hunched, nerves prepping for the inevitable punch, and another unwelcome sentimental thought flashed through his mind.

Is Eric ever going to know what happened to his dad? I love you, son.

He burst out of the grass into a wide clearing. It was the west bank of the Lena river, and it ran all the way north and south as far as the eye could see, a plain of much shorter grass and moss-covered boulders, and it was beautiful as hell. The rushing river slewed northward in a wide silver S, and the bank on the far side was steep and clear with nothing on top but more scattered rocks and scrub. A couple of AK rounds whacked into a boulder to his right and went careening up into the air, and he ran to the lip of the ten-foot-high bank.

There was Dmitry's boat, right below him, wallowing in the cold river water.

It was upside down.

It was on fire.

Jesus.

Hank spun around, threw himself down behind a boulder, flicked the AK's safety to full auto, and opened fire into the tall grass. He wasn't trying to spot proper targets and make every round count, he just needed to buy enough time to make it across the river, so he swept the barrel from left to right and let loose. At a rate of fire of six hundred rounds per minute, he emptied the entire magazine in three seconds, but he heard shouts and saw the tops of bullrushes whipping as his pursuers stopped firing and hurled themselves at the ground, and he left the AK where it was, pouring spent smoke like a steel cigar, and he got up, spun around again, tore off his tunic on the run, and launched himself off the edge of the cliff bank.

It was like jumping into an arctic bathtub. He came up sputtering and started clawing his way to the far bank, hand over hand like Mark Spitz on speed. He heard his GRU pursuers behind him reaching the bank from which he'd just jumped, but they were shouting epithets instead of firing, maybe even laughing, and he had no idea why but he wasn't going to look that gift horse in the mouth.

He reached the shallows on the far bank, burst out of the river, and started scrambling up through the sticky black mud of the low cliff above. Then he heard the rumbling engine and stopped.

A Russian six-wheeled BTR Armored Personnel Carrier was poking its snout down at him, with its Snoopy-helmeted commander grinning from the open hatch, behind a locked and cocked RPD light machine gun. And just arriving on either side of the frog-nosed APC was another platoon of GRU Border Guards, all aiming enough firepower down at him to leave nothing but his boots.

Hank Steele raised his hands in surrender.

He didn't know what was going to happen to him next, but one thing he was sure about.

He wasn't going home.

CHAPTER 22

GREEN BANK MEDICAL FACILITY,
WEST VIRGINIA

Eric Steele's breaths were rapid and shallow, but that wasn't because of any actual physical strain. They were in sympathy with what he imagined his father had gone through out there on the Siberian wastes. It was exactly the kind of thing he'd experienced himself on multiple occasions, except that he'd always made it, escaped by the skin of his teeth.

But Hank Steele hadn't made it. And this was the first time in his life that Eric had heard this tale of lionhearted courage, and he was filled with crossfiring emotions.

He sat there on the couch in the hospital's presidential suite, unable to move or speak. Mrs. Cole was next to him, her slim, pale hand resting on his forearm and squeezing it slightly, as if she were comforting a child after imparting sorrowful news. Former president Cole had somehow mustered his strength again, refilled his own tumbler, and climbed off the bed. He'd wandered back over to the faux window, where he was standing and gazing out at the rainstorm whipping the West Virginia mountains, two floors up and miles away.

At last, Eric managed to find his voice again, but it had the shellshocked tone of a soldier who'd just endured heavy combat.

"How long have you known all this, sir?"

Denton Cole considered that for a moment, then said to the window, "Since 1994," and took another sip of his Black Label.

Steele tried not to let the answer stoke his ire, but he was already starting to feel like a furious teenager whose parents had kept him in the dark about a family scandal for his entire life.

"And the details, sir," Steele said. "How did you know all those details?"

"NSA intercepts," Cole said, and then he turned back around from the window, almost as if he'd sunk deeply into some well of dark memories, and emerged again when he realized he had guests. "They picked up a full After Action Review of the incident from the Russian Committee for State Security, had it translated, then someone over there at Fort Meade remembered the White House was interested in anything popping up about a missing operator coded Stalker Twenty-Two. The NSA kids had no idea what that meant, nor anything about the Program, but they thought this capture might be relevant and sent it over to NSC, who relayed it to Cutlass Main."

"Stalker Twenty-Two," Steele almost whispered.

"That's right." Cole nodded, then his tone became weirdly wistful. "Did you know, Eric, that back in the day, when the Program was first stood up, instead of starting with the bottom of a numerical coding system, they called their first operator Stalker Fifty? That's why we're almost down to Stalker One. It'll all have to reset soon—"

"Darling," Mrs. Cole interrupted gently, "I don't think Eric cares very much about that right now. You've just told him that his father was an Alpha."

"Oh, yes. Of course, of course . . ." Cole trailed off, then looked down at his tumbler and swirled the amber liquid around the glass, as if he expected some answers or absolution to appear, like a Magic 8 Ball. "I'm sorry I could never tell you that before, Eric. But that file was slammed shut and everything in it was assigned to an ultra–top secret server. The presidents who followed Clinton, including myself, were all told 'hands-off.'"

"But, sir," Steele said, "as president, you had the ultimate classification or declassification authority." He was trying like hell to keep a respectful tone and not "shoot the messenger," but his teeth were grinding. Still, he chastised himself in his head.

Dad was an Alpha. Are you going to pretend you never suspected it? You just didn't want to believe you were working for the same organization he'd worked for, and that the Program might have failed him, or maybe even betrayed him. That's the goddamn hard-ass truth.

"That's true, Eric," Cole admitted. "I did have that authority. But just remember that the JFK assassination files were supposed to be declassified after fifty years as well, and it never happened. No president would touch it. . . ."

"Are you telling me my father's file was as sensitive as *that*?"

"No, no, but the motivation for keeping it all locked up superseded your father's professional reputation, or my sense of responsibility vis-à-vis your mother. . . ."

"Or me," Eric said, and he could no longer just sit there and listen to Cole bob and weave and try to diminish the impact of something that had driven him to overachieve in every endeavor he'd ever undertaken in his life, and to emulate someone who'd been gone from it forever, and had disappeared when he needed him the most. He slipped away from Mrs. Cole's grasp, got up, and started pacing like a leopard, back and forth behind the leather couch.

"What else was in that file, sir? If he was captured, what happened to him after that? And why the hell didn't the Program do everything they could to get him out?"

Steele didn't want to shout, but if he didn't get some answers soon he was going to lose it. He didn't even realize that he'd raised his voice at all until the Secret Service agent in the hallway stuck his head inside and Mrs. Cole waved at him and said, "It's all right, Peter," and the agent eyed Steele and ducked back out.

Then Mrs. Cole turned back to her husband and issued a spousal order. "Denton, tell him all of it. You're not going to live forever."

Cole nodded, polished off his Scotch, and set the tumbler down on the phony windowsill.

"Hank Steele disobeyed a direct order, Eric. And he was right to do so. It was an illegal order. His instructions were to eliminate as many as he could of the assassins-in-training inside Camp 722. But as I described before, once he entered the compound, he discovered that all of them were kids, some no older than nine or ten."

The former president then had a spate of coughing, while Steele stood there with his fists in his suit pockets and stared at him until he recovered and wiped his mouth again with his soggy handkerchief. Cole wheezed out a long breath and went on.

"After he was captured at the Lena river, he was imprisoned for a while in Lubyanka in Moscow. The KGB interrogated him for a full six months, but didn't get much out of him, certainly nothing about the Program. After that, he was sent to a maximum security prison in Siberia, some hellhole they called . . . What was it? Black Dolphin. We knew this because we had some intel on him through CIA, after a GRU officer defected in '98. We think he escaped after about five years."

"Five years." Eric was starting to hyperventilate again and his knuckles were clenching white inside his pockets. He didn't dare pull them out because he thought he might pound a fist on the furniture. "Sir, why the *hell* didn't the Program send in a team to get him out?"

Cole closed his eyes for a moment, drew in another raspy breath, and looked at the floor.

"Because the administration court-martialed him, Eric."

Steele was so utterly stunned that it took him a full fifteen seconds before he growled, "Excuse me?"

"I'm afraid you heard me right, son. They court-martialed him."

"For *what*?"

"For allegedly disobeying his orders."

"But the mission parameters changed on the objective," Eric protested, and he couldn't help himself now and his hands were out and slashing the air. "He found out the killers were still only kids and he *had* to refuse that order. It was his call to make."

"No, Eric. His fatal mistake was that he called it in. He had a satellite phone on him and contacted Cutlass. In turn they consulted with the national security advisor, and then they instructed him to carry on. He refused."

"As he damn well *should* have."

"I have to say I agree," Cole said.

"But, sir, why didn't he just come home after he escaped?" The pain of an abandoned lonely child was still in Steele's voice.

"Brace yourself for this one, Eric," Cole said. "He was tried in absentia, an in-camera hearing at Blair House, across the street from 1600, and convicted. But it was all an arrangement between the administration and Boris Yeltsin's government. Clinton and Yeltsin were engaged in détente negotiations, and the Russians had just captured an American assassin. They thought he was CIA, and they agreed to keep it all quiet, as long as Camp 722 was never mentioned, and your father was thoroughly punished, by *both* sides."

Steele felt dizzy. His head was swooning and he'd broken out in a sweat. He wanted to sit down again but his feet were telling him to get out of there as quickly as possible and find some fresh air.

"But my father *escaped*. It still doesn't answer why he didn't find his way home."

"Because he knew if he did, he'd wind up in Leavenworth for the rest of his life, and you and your mother would be disgraced and destroyed."

"But how could he possibly *know* that, in a prison cell in Siberia? How could he have known about his own court-martial and conviction?"

"He knew it, because his KGB interrogator told him. At the time, that man was a lieutenant colonel in Russian counterintelligence, and probably broke the news to your father with that same arrogant, wolfish expression you always see on his face on TV."

"Vladimir Putin," Steele whispered.

"The very same."

Steele was reeling, nauseated, but then he suddenly remembered the challenge coin. He stalked over to the former president's food cart and snatched it up again, and he recalled the number set that was the other part of the microdot message "Cole knows." He looked down at Cole, who'd once again managed to make it back to his bed and was sitting on the edge, slouched and rumpled and now fully wrung out by all the emotional effort of releasing so many demons that had haunted him for years.

"There was more to that microdot message, sir," Steele said hoarsely. "A number set. Coordinates . . ."

"I have no idea, Eric," Cole said. "Truly I don't. I have no more secrets to keep from you, son, nor any reason to do so." The former president reached across the tray and squeezed Steele's bicep with a surprisingly powerful grip. "If I had to guess, I'd say they point to a location in Siberia somewhere. But as a man who greatly admired your father . . . and I feel just the same about you . . . I need to caution you with a simple suggestion, since I can no longer issue you a directive. Don't go there."

But Steele had already pulled away, kissed Mrs. Cole on the cheek, and was heading back to the surface of the earth.

CHAPTER 23

NO ACKNOWLEDGED LOCATION

EYES ONLY

SAP (Alphas/Duty Stations/Support-FLASH)

From: Cutlass Main II

To: All OCONUS PAX

Subj: Ops Lockout

Source: Staff Ops/Duty Officer

Confidence: Level III

IMMEDIATE, all OCONUS Duty Stations, emphasis EUROPRO, AFRIPRO, SLAVPRO, SAPRO: Cease all activities ops PAX and support PAX; Recall all Alpha PAX Main II; Freeze and secure all SH locations; Blackout comms traffic. Emphasis, Do Not Relay to Bleacher PAX.

STATUS: No change pending Main II lowers DEFCON Status Red to Amber.

Operational window: Immediate Execute

Alpha response—URGENT/ACKNOWLEDGE

Additional WARNO, see Subnet incoming on [TRANSMISSION TERMINATED/TRANSMISSION TERMINATED/TRANSMISSION TERMINATED/TRANSMISSION TERMINATED/TRANSMISSION TERMINATED/TRANSMISSION TERMINATED/TRANSMISSION]

CHAPTER 24

CUTLASS MAIN II, WASHINGTON, D.C.

Mike Pitts's flash warning to all worldwide Program Alphas, duty stations, safehouses, and support personnel squeaked under the wire just before the lights went out.

Pitts had already recalled all the remaining Alphas and keepers from their various locations outside the continental United States, some of whom had attended Collins Austin's funeral. But one of those still at large, Stalker Five, was thirty fathoms below the surface of the North Sea in a U.S. Navy Virginia-class submarine and preparing to lock out, infil a small island, and kill an ISIS bomb maker. It would take a while to cancel Five's mission, and Pitts had to decide whether to just let him carry on. In the end, he'd decided against it, because this female assassin thing had him on edge, and he couldn't be sure that Five wasn't swimming into a trap.

The idea of losing another Alpha had cracked Pitts's usual cool, so he'd decided to freeze all OCONUS—Outside the Continental United States—activities everywhere, until they figured out what the hell was going on. It turned out his instincts were spot on.

The first thing that happened at the new location on Q Street was that the underground garage doors slammed shut. That was highly unusual, because they were NASA blast doors recessed into the concrete walls on either side of the vehicle entrance/exit, and were never used. The underground garage looked "normal," with the usual ticket dispenser and gate poles, and the Program's "parking attendant" kept a LOT FULL sign outside at all times, which the outfit's personnel ignored. The doors were for emergencies only, like an assault by Russian Spetsnaz commandos (highly unlikely) or Antifa protestors (slightly more likely).

When the doors suddenly whined and slammed closed—nearly decapitating a Program geek riding a Vespa—the friendly attendant with the Bermuda British accent was annoyed but not alarmed, and he called Merry at the desk of Graceland Import Exports. Merry, in turn, called upstairs to Ferris Copeland, a former navy nuclear aircraft carrier tech who ran maintenance for the Program. Copeland went down to the garage and tried to use his keys in the door overrides, without success, and then changed all the fuses in the circuit breakers. Nothing. He went back up to the second floor, scratching his head, and suggested to Pitts's adjutant, Betsy Roth, that she might want to warn the personnel that they'd all be taking Ubers home.

That was when the main flat screen in the TOC started to flicker.

By this time—a month since the Program had

relocated from the White House—everything was looking pretty slick at Cutlass Main II (or Mini-Main, as Ralphy Persko had been calling it in his impersonation of Dr. Evil). The indoor-outdoor carpets were down, the cables buried out of sight, and the dozen workstation VariDesks popping up and down like prairie dogs on the plain. The isolated tanks on either side of the TOC had also been furnitured up, and the electronic locks on their steel doors tested and linked to Internal Security's mainframe.

The vast, six-panel flat screen adorning the northern wall was functioning so well that sometimes when it broke into a hexagonal split-screen displaying multiple images, Pitts had to remind everyone to get back to work and stop watching the damn thing like a soap opera. The SCIF was complete, the HVAC systems were maintaining a computer-friendly environment, and all the appliances in the kitchen off to the right were working well enough to keep morale steady.

All in all, the roughly forty personnel ensconced at Cutlass Main II seemed settled in and adjusting to their new digs, despite having been banished from 1600 Pennsylvania. The only thing that still bothered Ralphy Persko about it—a lot—was that such a physical move meant that the firewalls he'd developed and implemented to protect the Program were compromised by switching over to new landlines, routers, and wireless networks. Ralphy knew from experience that you just couldn't tell how well things were going to work until you were actually attacked, which hadn't happened yet.

No one told Ralphy that the garage doors had just malfunctioned. But the weirdness on the main TOC display was obvious.

The six-panel, 124-inch display had been showing the internals from six different safehouses in Paris, Madrid, Rome, Cairo, Rabat, and Addis Ababa. There wasn't much to see, but Pitts wanted to make sure that his flash instructions were executed, which meant that sweepers would soon appear on those screens to secure any compromising materials and lock down the facilities.

At first, the panels started to flicker, as if from transmission interference. A minute later, all six panels turned a different, solid, primary color, which caused a number of personnel to raise their heads from their workstations, including Ralphy, who slowly rose from his chair, though he continued chewing his tuna hero. A minute after that, all six panels turned into digital three-dimensional boxes and started rotating, so the whole thing resembled a gigantic Rubik's Cube.

"What happened to my feed, Persko?" Pitts asked Ralphy through his headset, so he didn't have to shout.

"No idea, sir." Ralphy popped his VariDesk up, because he knew he wouldn't be able to sit still for this one, and started pecking away at his keyboard in an effort to troubleshoot the transmissions.

Betsy Roth walked out of the kitchen, over to Ralphy's desk, and stood there, staring at the weird cubic phenomenon. She was in her mid-thirties, had long, straight blond hair, chic Warby Parker glasses, and dressed like a prim State Department spokesperson. But she'd been an instructor at CIA's Camp Peary and had a mouth like a submariner.

"What the fuck, Ralphy?" she whispered. "Are we gonna get a freaking Halloween mask now and a message from Anonymous?"

"I don't *know*, Betsy," Ralphy sputtered. "I switched all the incoming satellite comms from the main wireless config to a backup, but that cube thing just followed me over, and now I'm trying to just shut down the display but it's not responding to remotes. . . ."

"Mr. Persko, I'm beginning to get a bit concerned over here." Mike Pitts was no longer using his headset, and he'd pushed the slim boom mic away from his lips and was calling out to Ralphy over his shoulder.

"I'm trying, sir," Ralphy called back across the room.

"Wow, never seen that before, except in the movies." Ferris Copeland had arrived at the other side of Ralphy's workstation, after returning from another failed attempt to fix the garage doors. He was tall with salt-and-pepper hair and looked every bit the ex-sailor. "Want me to go home and get the remote for my Sanyo?"

"Very funny, Ferris," Ralphy muttered. "Take the day off."

Suddenly the huge flat screen went blank. Ralphy's shoulders sagged with relief.

Then all the electronic door locks on the four flanking isolation tanks fired, at the same time, sounding like gunshots in a walk-in freezer. Those doors had no windows in them, and within seconds the occupants trapped within started shaking the doorknobs and pounding. Miles Turner, an ex–Special Forces ODA captain and chief of Program Internal Security, came flying out of the men's room, still hiking his pants up, which was made all the more awkward by the holstered Sig Sauer strapped to his belt.

"Mr. Turner," Mike Pitts called over to him. "I don't know what's going on here, but I strongly suggest you arm your personnel."

"Yes, sir." Turner spun back around and jogged the other way toward his corner security office, but his on-site two men and one woman were already bursting out onto the main floor and breech-checking their MP-5K submachine guns. Turner snapped out some orders and all four of them fanned out to secure the main elevator entrance and emergency exits. So far this appeared to be only cyber mischief, but it might be followed by something kinetic.

"We're fucking under attack," Betsy Roth spat.

Pitts heard that and said, "Ya think?"

Then the isolation tank locks slammed back open again, the doors swung open, and all the personnel came streaming out onto Main, including Meg Harden, who looked just as bewildered as the rest. One of those who'd been working on a surveillance package in the Keyhole project was Dalton Goodhill, who barreled his way toward Pitts and said, "Mike, this is all part of one big bag of shit."

"I concur," Pitts said.

"And where's Steele?" Goodhill demanded.

Mike Pitts looked at Goodhill as if he'd left his own toddler sitting in a locked car on the freeway.

"You're his keeper, Blade. Why the hell are you asking *me*?"

At that juncture, Ralphy had just finished downloading the last thirty minutes of activity history from the Program's main server and dropped it all onto his laptop, because his good sense told him that, in short order, he wasn't going to be able to do very much in this space anymore.

Then, all the screens on all the workstations went blank, the dishwasher in the kitchen turned on, the blinds on the SCIF windows dropped at full speed, the lights went out, and the overhead sprinklers fired, causing a spate of curses, tumbles, and stubbed knees in the dark.

The doors to the elevator wouldn't open, and neither would the emergency exit. Ferris Copeland switched on the light on his iPhone, gripped it in his teeth, fetched a sledgehammer from his office, and battered the door's push bar until the whole thing broke from its hinges.

But no one panicked, and no one left. They were all Program employees. Ferris just wanted to keep their options open.

"People, remain at your stations until we figure this out," Pitts called out to the TOC through the sprays of cold water from above. "And don't worry, you'll be getting a clothing allowance," he quipped.

"Over my dead body," Mrs. Darnstein, the comptroller, muttered from somewhere.

And because they were all in the dark and anonymous, someone commented, "That can be arranged," and the ensuing laughter was a brief relief.

But Ralphy Persko wasn't laughing, or staying.

He snatched his laptop, stuffed it into his messenger bag, and turned to his two best sub-geeks, a young man named Kilo and a girl named Frankie, who were both holding up cell phone flashlights and staring at him as if they were all lost at a rock concert.

"You two, follow me," Ralphy ordered, and he ran for the emergency door.

CHAPTER 25

CRESTWOOD, WASHINGTON, D.C.

Mrs. Jepson was sweeping the front porch of her family's brownstone on Sixteenth Street NW when her top-floor tenant, Ralphy Persko, showed up in a blue Hyundai with Uber and Lyft stickers in the windows. She stopped sweeping, arched her aching back, adjusted the green bandanna hugging her salt-and-pepper dreads, and watched Ralphy get out of the car with what appeared to be two young friends.

One was a tall skinny blond fellow with a long ponytail, the other a petite young Caucasian girl with a crown of tight black curls that Leah Berkowitz, one of Mrs. Jepson's best friends, would have called a "JewFro." It wasn't a term that Mrs. Jepson would dare use nowadays but had been perfectly all right back in the 1960s, when they'd all been free-thinking hippies.

All three of the young people were burdened with oversize laptop cases and grocery bags, from which Mrs. Jepson could see Red Bull six-packs and frozen taco meals bursting. The car pulled away and Ralphy and his crew headed for the wooden front stairs, which were badly in need of a paint job.

"Ralphy, please don't tell me you've been fired by the Smithsonian."

"Oh, no, not at all, Mrs. Jepson." Ralphy smiled as he hustled up the stairs. "Just got off early today."

"That's good news, then," Mrs. Jepson said. "Had a little worry there about rent on the first."

"Have I ever been late?" Ralphy said.

"Nope." She cocked her head to look past his shoulder. "And who might these fine young people be?"

Ralphy stopped and his Program compatriots nearly smashed into his back.

"Oh, this is Kilo, and Frankie, my friends."

"Frankie." Mrs. Jepson nodded at the ponytailed youth, then did the same at the girl and said, "Kilo, that's an unusual name for a young lady."

"It's the other way around, Mrs. Jepson. He's Kilo, she's Frankie."

"Ahhhh." Mrs. Jepson nodded up and down but was obviously confused. "Are you having a party this evening, Ralphy?"

"No, we're just working on an after-hours project, writing a video game together."

"I see." She was satisfied as long as Ralphy wasn't turning from a model tenant into a hellion. "Well, have fun."

"See ya later."

Mrs. Jepson went back to sweeping, and Ralphy led Kilo and Frankie through the stained glass front door, and they all headed up the long stairwell.

"The Smithsonian?" Kilo whispered.

"Whatever," Ralphy mumbled.

"What game are we writing?" Frankie scoffed. "*Cutlass Heart Attack II*?"

"Shhh!" Ralphy hissed.

He was already thumbing a fob on his key ring as the trio panted onto the third-floor landing, and then all four locks on his door fired and they were inside and dumping their gear. Frankie looked around at Ralphy's expansive apartment, six slanted windows, pop art throw rugs, and extremely nice furniture—for a generally slobby geek—and whistled.

"Wow, epic digs, boss." She was wearing a Nationals T-shirt, though she'd never been to a game in her life.

Ralphy ignored the compliment and pointed over to his long workbench along the apartment's far wall.

"All right, people, set us up over there, all three machines. Anything on that bench that looks like it's safely removable without doing me damage, move it over here." He pointed to the coffee table in front of the couch with his flight simulation setup. "Pull the plugs on all my desktop stuff, and I mean *everything:* my routers, PC, Mac, even those two wireless printers and the freakin' TV cable. I want us dead, connected to nothing, like we've been hit with an EMP. Got it?"

"But how we gonna uplink and work this problem," Kilo said, "if we got no water pipes?"

"Hot spots only, from our cells," Ralphy said. "I've got repeaters and boosters, but we're not going to use a single freaking thing that I've been using before. If Main II's been compromised, then we're going to assume that I've been too. Clear?"

Kilo and Frankie looked at each other with buggy eyes. They'd never seen their ketchup-stained team lead act like this at the office before, and certainly not at their regular Starbucks over a cream latte, so this was super weird.

Ralphy had taken the grocery bags into the kitchen and was sticking tacos in the freezer and Red Bull in the fridge. Then he ran the sink and filled up the glass tank on a Lebanese hookah he'd picked up the year before at a cyber security conference in Doha. When he emerged from the kitchen with the hookah and a box of French tobacco, Kilo and Frankie were still standing there, staring at him.

"What the hell, people? Get your asses in gear, we're under attack!"

They nearly leaped from their gym shoes, grabbed their Alienware laptops, and scrambled to the worktable. . . .

Two hours later, the apartment was completely dark, the only illumination coming from the oversize laptop monitors and the orange bleeds from their keyboards, through which swirls of smoke from Ralphy's hookah curled like giant spiderwebs. Ralphy had drawn all the window blinds, just in case some adversary was out there somewhere and using a laser window-glass vibration reader to eavesdrop on their conversations. The long workbench was strewn with taco wrappers, Red Bull cans, stained paper napkins, and bowls of sunflower seeds.

Ralphy had set himself up in the middle of the worktable in his office chair, with Kilo to his left and Frankie to his right, both perched on wooden barstools and hunched before their humming machines. Each was deep in the World Wide Web (via the latest version of Tor, The Onion Router, to mask their IP addresses) through a boosted hot spot on a burner smartphone, of which Ralphy always kept a handful over at Main II and had stuffed a bunch in his bag. In the background, Insane Clown Posse banged out "Hokus Pokus."

After two hours of brain-breaking work, they'd eliminated international "black hats" (computer hackers) of certain geographic origins, based upon historical talents and the unlikelihood that any of those not only would have discovered the Program, but also would be so bold as to launch an overt assault. So, on a large whiteboard mounted on the wall, Frankie had crossed off South and Central America, North and Central Africa, Southeast Asia, the Philippines, Japan, Israel, and all the "Stans." This didn't mean that the attackers couldn't be physically located in any of those places, but that they would not likely be of those origins, making it somewhat easier to uncover their footprints by using linguistic patterns and algorithms.

Ralphy was leading his team with queries, instructions, and self-checks, and they were all speaking in a vernacular that would have sounded like an alien language to anyone but a graduate of the NSA's cyber warfare school.

"Okay, recap this logic train," Ralphy said as he stared at his monitor. "Servos, pneumatic, first things to fire down in the garage, controlled by Pentaur Bravo, the second server in Copeland's realm."

"Affirm," said Kilo, "and that's the first of a series of waterfall triggers, which could have been inserted as a logic bomb, or might be a zombie drone, active, real time."

"Which means," said Frankie, "that because our physical systems and controllers came over from DoE, designed for nuke power plants like Calvert Cliffs, our cracker out there figured out how to bypass NEST protocols."

"Or he got in through a sloppy back door the DoE geeks forgot to shut down," Kilo said.

"Or, he Trojaned an ass crack and left a time bomb so it'd open up today."

"Why 'he'?" Frankie huffed. "Could be a she, ya know."

"Okay, *they*." Ralphy rolled his eyes, which were getting blurry and stung from all the squinting and smoke. His laptop was displaying all the Main II activity logs, from all the computers in the TOC and all four tanks, from five minutes prior to the garage doors slamming until the moment he'd unplugged and beat feet. "Can we move on, please?"

"Hey, is it possible it was just war driving?" Frankie posed, meaning that a group of malicious hackers, of which there were hundreds worldwide, had simply stumbled upon a faulty crack in the Program's computer defenses and decided to party. "I mean, that happened over at the DNC. . . ."

"No effin' way." Ralphy shook his head vigorously and took a long pull on his third round of Bull. "My cans are plugged into my malware scanners, and every time some a-hole pings us, even by accident, it goes off in my head like an ambulance siren."

"But who, boss? Why?" Kilo was twisting his long blond ponytail in front of his neck and had already chewed out an ounce of hair. "They manage to drop a payload on a supertight locked-down government bat cave, and all they do is slam some doors, kill the comps and lights, and get us all soaking wet?"

"For now, Kilo," Ralphy cautioned. "For now."

"We're never gonna backtrack this mother," Frankie brooded, but she continued to examine the same lines of code that were on Ralphy's screen, and she ran search matches for previously examined bona fide lines that might reveal a comparative anomaly. "Whoever got inside spoofed the hell out of their footprint, after first using ten iterations of Tor."

"Yeah," Kilo agreed, "and we're not talking here about some Iranian script kiddies."

"That . . . is . . . correct." Ralphy was suddenly speaking in a *Twilight Zone* tone, and he'd taken another long drag from his hookah, so a double stream of smoke was rising from his wide nostrils and spookily fogging his glasses. "We're looking at a rootkit. Maybe something even planted from inside. We're looking at a rootkit, and a polymorph, so that every time my bug bots looked for it, it changed its freaking spots."

"Holy shit," Kilo said, and at this juncture no one was moving, typing, or fingering a mouse anymore. "Are you serious, boss? Inside?"

"Don't quote me on that, or even think it out loud," Ralphy warned. "Not until we burn these a-holes and we've got no-bleed, no-smudge fingerprints. Got it?"

Kilo and Frankie both nodded and muttered "Uh-huh" at the same time.

"We're going to go back now, and look at every friggin' line of code in every friggin' comp, server, lap, main- and subframe, from five minutes prior to zero, till we walked out the door. And we're going to find that trigger. It could be something totally small, like half a line of binary, like three ones and a zero. But whatever the hell it is, it opened the door, and then the friggin' joker jumped in and shot up the nightclub. And once we find that trigger, I'm gonna hunt down this a-hole's botnet, and they're gonna tell me all about his master program, and *that's* gonna tell me who the hell he is." Ralphy turned to Frankie and added, "It's not a she, or a they. It's a he. Gut call."

"Okay, on it," Kilo said and turned back to his laptop.

But Frankie was looking at Ralphy in a different way than before. She'd never seen him quite so intense and always thought of him like some chubby, awkward, older sibling who'd still be living in their parents' basement long after she went off to conquer the world. Frankie had a pretty face, with very full lips, a small nose, and deep brown eyes, and those eyes were drinking in Ralphy's combat composure, and then she turned and went back to work.

Five minutes later, she jabbed a finger at her monitor and said, "There."

"What?" Ralphy said.

"Binary. Doesn't really belong in this stream. And it was in the freakin' HVAC system."

"Call it," Ralphy said as Kilo stopped pecking and mousing and looked over.

"One, zero, zero, zero, slash," Frankie said as Ralphy jotted the code down on a menu from Fridays. "Then, three ones, slash, three ones again, slash, and two ones."

Ralphy handed the menu to Kilo and said, "Change the ones to dashes and the zeros to dots, and tell me what it says in Morse code."

"Huh?" Kilo pulled harder on his ponytail.

"Morse code, genius. The stuff your granddaddy used in the navy during World War II."

"My grandfather was in the army. . . . But why?"

"A hunch," Ralphy said.

"I got this," Frankie said as she reached across Ralphy and snatched the menu. She'd already called up a sheet of Morse code from Wikipedia, and after a few seconds, she leaned back and whispered, "Holy shit."

"What's it say?" Ralphy asked.

"It says . . . 'Boom.'"

Ralphy nodded, cracked his knuckles, leaned into his Alienware again, and said, "Come to Papa, motherfucker."

CHAPTER 26

MOSCOW, RUSSIA

Millennial Crude did not operate out of FSB headquarters. In fact, Dmitry Kreesak's boss, Lieutenant Colonel Ivan Kravchenko, never discussed MC operations with him while they were within the walls of Lubyanka.

Whenever Kravchenko wanted to consult with Snipe on a matter of importance that required kinetic action of the cyber or "contractor" sort, he'd walk by his desk and casually drop a matchbook from one of the many small Moscow cafés that hunkered outside the Kremlin ring. An hour later, Snipe would find the lieutenant colonel sitting at said gloomy establishment at a corner table, reading a copy of *Izvestia*, and there he'd join him and receive his tasking.

Furthermore, Snipe couldn't run Millennial Crude operations during regular FSB business hours, because it would have been strange for a cyber security specialist to be away from home station for hours or days at a time. So, he did all of that at night—sometimes all night—far away from the Moscow center in a ghastly neighborhood called Kapotnya, which hosted twenty-seven thousand dirt-poor residents packed into low-rise brick apartments surrounding an enormous oil-processing plant. There was no metro station, the atmosphere was toxic, the teeming markets stank, and it was a pain in the ass to get to, all of which made it perfect.

So, Millennial Crude rented a large flat (subsidized by FSB—cash only) on the fourth floor of a dingy walk-up just off of Kapotninskiy Proezd, which made the trip down there bearable, because it was relatively close to the MKAD highway that ran back northward to civilization. The flat had one large central salon with curtained, oil-fume-stained windows, branching off into four small corner bedrooms and one Soviet-style 1950s "chic" kitchenette, with a tile slab floor and cinder block walls. The heating, which had not yet clicked on despite a late-summer cold snap, came from a local Kapotnya boiler station that pumped hot water up into the building's cast-iron radiators. But the outside temperature didn't really matter. Moscow's deputy mayor for Housing, Utilities, and Amenities decided whether or not you were cold or hot.

However, nothing else about the flat was typical of Kapotnya. The salon wasn't designed for living. Snipe believed that if you were sitting or taking a meal in a relaxed manner, you weren't thinking, and he wanted all of his brainiacs firing on all cylinders, always. It was bordered on all sides by long, Japanese onyx-topped worktables, which held massive LG monitors, all cabled to 8Pack OrionX PCs (their $30,000-per-system price tags were covered by FSB's black budget). The office chairs facing the workstations were self-adjusting Humanscale Freedoms, and every station had a pair of wireless Bose headsets. The overhead lighting was provided by recessed pinpoint spots, and the computers weren't connected to any commercial internet cables, but instead to an independent antenna array on the building's roof, which uplinked everything to a satellite bounce.

On this particular evening, there were four Millennial Crude operators sitting at the four workstations, all of whom had been flown in from various global corners for Snipe's latest project. They were Iranian, Syrian, and Bosnian—one of each gender—and Kendo, Snipe's North Korean cyber femme fatale and occasional pornographic paramour. At the moment, they were all having a wonderful time screwing with the mechanical servos and computer servers of a U.S. government black budget special operations and intelligence outfit in the middle of Washington, D.C., which was the ultimate sort of video game fracas for all of them, since in this case they were being very well paid to wreak havoc.

Snipe was not at any of those workstations but was ensconced in a Herman Miller mid-century modern hard-backed plywood chair, in the middle of the salon, facing Lieutenant Colonel Kravchenko in an identical chair. Kravchenko's thick gray hair and trim mustache gave him a distinguished air, while Snipe's messy black coif made him look like a nightclub DJ, but on first glance they could have been a Mafia don and his son. They were both wearing roll-neck sweaters, smoking Belomorkanal cigarettes, and sipping Ukrainian Nemiroff vodka.

Kravchenko wasn't concerned that Snipe's four cyber warriors might be able to identify him and tie him back to the FSB, because he'd informed them all upon first handshake that they should forget his face, or risk dying horrible deaths. They'd seemed amenable.

Given that the lieutenant colonel had tasked Snipe and Millennial Crude with this current assignment, he was pleased to see that it was going so well.

"I have no idea how you managed this, Dmitry," he said as he sipped his vodka, "but I am very impressed. Our sister comrades over at GRU seem to always be stymied by American countercyber defenses, and yet, here you are. . . ."

Snipe, feeling proud of himself, waved his cigarette in false self-deprecation and blew a stream of smoke at the pin spots above.

"We've had some luck, Colonel, but that was inevitable, given many, many hours of labor."

"Well, as they say, luck is simply when preparation meets opportunity."

"Yes, sir. Well put."

Snipe actually thought that Kravchenko was an apparatchik ass, but the lieutenant colonel was also Millennial Crude's walking wallet.

"And so," Kravchenko said, now that the niceties were over. "Tell me the nature of your 'luck.'" His smile had faded. He wasn't a man who tolerated being left in the dark.

"Um . . . would it suffice to tell you that the nature of it relates to blackmail?"

"Blackmail." The lieutenant colonel sat forward now and snuffed out his cigarette in a crystal ashtray sitting on the flat head of a two-foot marble gargoyle. "Are you telling me that you have someone on the inside of this organization?"

Snipe grinned and sipped his vodka, savoring the moment. "I am indeed."

"Stupefying," Kravchenko breathed and sat back again. "Absolutely stupefying. And is this how you cracked into their systems?"

"Well, it was much more than that, sir. . . ." Snipe didn't want his boss to think that his demonic whiz kids were only able to manage their coup because they had inside help. "Our mild extortion simply made the task easier. It required the planting of an invisible, undetectable, tiny line of pirate code. And then . . . voilà."

Snipe turned to Kendo, who was sitting nearby with her back to him, angled forward over her keyboard. She was wearing a long scarlet formfitting dress and large silver hoop earrings, with her sleek black hair piled up.

"Kendo, status please?" Snipe asked her in English.

"I think we've got them in the panic stage," she cooed. "They are actually, physically cutting cables with pinking shears and yanking electrics from the walls."

"*Hullyunghan*," Snipe said in Korean—wonderful—and then he added, in the same language, "I'm going to bang you like a waterfront whore later on."

She waved at him over her shoulder, and he returned to Russian.

"We have them on the run," he said to Kravchenko.

"Yes, I understood her English. I was posted to New York for three years, you know."

"Of course, sir."

"Now, Dmitry . . . tell me about our girl from Gaza."

Snipe was somewhat taken aback by the sudden shift away from his current triumph, but he answered frankly.

"Sir, I think she has outlived her usefulness."

"Really? How so?"

"Well, first of all, she is very expensive."

"This is true. But one million euros per target, when taken in perspective, is no more than the cost of a single Vympel air-to-ground missile. And with this crazy girl, we guarantee a kill every time."

"Yes, but she is also arrogant, sir. She makes demands. . . ."

Kravchenko lit up another cigarette, took a long drag, and waved Snipe off.

"Artists are often that way."

"We don't need her any longer, sir."

"*Do* tell, Dmitry." Kravchenko sneered. "Are you going to fly away from Moscow, track down these Program assassins, and kill them yourself? As a matter of fact, are any of you here, or any of your other computer idiot savants, capable of doing what that woman does? If anything, I would say that now, she doesn't need *you*. She's enriched herself so far to the tune of a sizable nut, and whether or not we continue to pay for her services, she might carry on with this for personal reasons and subsidize the project herself. She doesn't need our rubles anymore, but she might pin whatever she does going forward on us just the same. There are still a considerable number of operators left on that Program payroll, and I'd prefer to see that ledger balanced. Understood?"

Snipe shuddered internally. He remembered now how and why Kravchenko had risen to the top of his department.

"Yes, sir, but . . ."

"Continue to employ her, Dmitry, whatever it costs. Our leadership back at the office has, shall we say, made their desires plain enough. After all"—Kravchenko waved dismissively at all of Snipe's fancy workstations—"this is all very nice, and you are all delivering a fine display of mischief. However, there is quite a difference between kinetic, and cute."

That comment wounded Snipe's ego so badly that his face flushed and he forked his fingers through his thick black hair and almost stood up. He suddenly had a flash fantasy of telling Kravchenko to get the hell out, and that he'd submit his resignation letter in the morning, and that he'd forfeit his comfortable FSB salary and pension, and the lieutenant colonel could go straight to hell. But what came out of his mouth was a bit more muted.

"Sir . . . I . . . ," he stammered. "I object to that characterization of our operation and talents here. We are *far* more effective than you can imagine, and capable of *highly* destructive—"

And at that very moment, all the pinpoint spots

in the ceiling went dark, all the flat screens turned from complex, multiple, scrolling data streams to Disney cartoons, and all the hard drives on all the extremely expensive 8Pack OrionX computers spun into screaming overdrive, and burned out.

"*Bleht*," Snipe moaned. "Oh fuck . . ."

CHAPTER 27

VIENNA, AUSTRIA

As a child, Lila Kalidi had always loved the Austrian capital. It was a fairy-tale city of soaring architectures, classical music, and horse-drawn carriages, far from the fetid heat and violence of her home in the Middle East. Her father, Walid Abu-Marwan Kalidi, had often taken her to Vienna, where he'd meet with his beloved cousins, and afterward they'd all reminisce while laughing and enjoying fine Germanic dining.

"Baba" spoiled his beautiful little girl, cutting his meetings short to take her to the Prater amusement park, buy her funnel cakes, and ride with her on the largest Ferris wheel in the world, where each passenger bucket was a chamber the size of a small train car. He escorted her to the Vienna opera, and they stayed at the magnificent Hotel Sacher, devoured its famous chocolate cakes, and strolled through St. Stephen's Platz, where she came away with jewels and princess dresses.

Those times with her father had been ones of

beloved grace until the infidels had killed him. And Lila would only discover later that his "cousins" were actually high-ranking members of Hamas, like Walid himself.

Now she hated Vienna. The spoiled European lifestyle and snobbery reminded her of nothing but loss, and her visits only stoked her fires of vengeance. Nowadays she came to Vienna only to establish an alibi, or retrieve equipment from an Islamic Jihad dead drop, or, as was the case today, for psychotherapy.

Lila couldn't talk about her problems or stresses to anyone. She had no mate, no lover she trusted, no friends who couldn't be tortured or bought. Yet some years ago, she'd realized that part of keeping razor sharp meant also tuning her mind, which could be subject to clouds of self-doubt if one didn't clear the air once in a while. So, for the past three years, she'd randomly selected one psychotherapist in each of Paris, Rome, and Madrid, and paid for a single long session during which she unburdened herself.

The visits only occurred once. She never went back, for good reason.

This therapist's office was in his third-floor walkup on Schlachthausgasse (Slaughterhouse Street) in Vienna's dreary Tenth District. The salon was cozy, with overflowing bookshelves, a cream-colored patient's couch, and a low coffee table on which a small white porcelain rabbit struck a laughing pose next to a crystal ashtray. Across from that, the doctor faced his new client from a flowery antique armchair. His name was Heinrich Goldwasser, a kind older man and student, of course, of the school of the late Sigmund Freud.

Dr. Goldwasser was wearing linen trousers, a dress shirt, and a tie, and instead of the cliché pipe he was chewing a pencil, with which he occasionally took notes in a leather-bound notebook perched on his bony knees. He had a crown of wild white hair and wore gold-rimmed glasses.

Lila was dressed in snug jeans, running shoes, a baggy teal dress shirt, and had taken off her sunglasses and wide-brimmed hat, which she often wore to defeat Vienna's ubiquitous surveillance cameras. She had a large Coach handbag beside her on the couch.

Dr. Goldwasser had assured Lila that she could speak freely, though she wasn't actually worried about confidentiality. She had, however, asked him if he secretly recorded his sessions, to which he'd replied that such a practice was unethical without express permission. So she carried on, in German.

"*Mein Vater war ein liebevoller Mann*," Lila said. My father was a loving man. She'd been reliving her childhood for the doctor, which he understood had taken place primarily in the Gaza Strip, but also in various capitals of the world, to which she and her father had traveled via Cairo. "But, of course, he was also a terrorist." She smiled. "At least that is the term used by you and your kind, Doctor. We think of ourselves as freedom fighters, determined to liberate our homes from the Jews and their imperialist cohorts."

Goldwasser wasn't alarmed. He had patients who imagined all sorts of crazy things, and it was his task to sort it all out. This beautiful young woman's reference to "your kind" and "the Jews" did cause him to squirm a bit in his chair, yet he retained his kindly demeanor.

"Would you say, Ms. Kalidi," he asked, "that these painful aspects of your past have affected your personal relationships?"

"Please, call me Lila." She smiled.

"Yes, Lila." He nodded. Her response seemed a bit more friendly, though he found it curious that she was wearing fine leather gloves.

"I would say, Herr Doktor, that my past indeed has affected those relationships. I fuck all kinds of people, both men and women, but that's merely a physical need and is meaningless to me on a deeper scale."

"I see." The use of the term *fuck* didn't faze him. Patients often tested him that way.

"Do you still fuck once in a while?" Lila asked him. "I mean, given your age."

Goldwasser smiled. "This session isn't about my personal habits, Lila."

"Of course. I apologize. As I said, I lost my own father early on, which perhaps left some Freudian scars."

"Interesting. So, you've studied some psychology."

"Only as an amateur."

"Well then, let's pursue the heart of the matter." Goldwasser paused to sip from a rose garland cup. "Would you care for some tea?"

"No, thank you."

"All right. Then what, may I ask, has brought you here today?"

"Your reputation in the local journals," Lila said. "And I'm concerned that I might be a bit obsessive-compulsive."

"What brings you to that suspicion?"

"My vocation."

"Which is?" The doctor began taking notes. This was going to be fascinating.

"I am, in your vernacular, *eine Attentäterin*."

Goldwasser stopped writing and looked up.

"An . . . assassin."

"Yes. I currently work for an organization called Palestinian Islamic Jihad. You may have heard of it. But I'm also a freelancer and engaged at the moment by another small organization attached to the Russian FSB." Lila smirked. "That's basically the old KGB, with a new face."

Goldwasser offered a nod for her to continue, yet his pencil stayed poised above his pages and he wrote nothing further. He wasn't sure now if he was dealing with dementia, or something else.

"May I smoke?" Lila asked.

"Please."

He gestured at the ashtray. Lila reached into her handbag, came up with a silver cigarette box and electronic lighter, lit up, and went on.

"I am being paid very well, Herr Doktor. *Very* well. I could stop all of this right now and retire very comfortably, yet I feel compelled to continue."

"Compulsion, once recognized, is an affliction with which one can struggle successfully. If one has the desire . . ."

"Yes, well, I do, and I don't." Lila exhaled a plume of smoke at Goldwasser's ceiling. "You see, I discovered, only in the recent past, that it wasn't actually the Jews who blew my father's head off. It was an American assassin, with the aid of the Israelis, who committed the act. I've also discovered that he worked for a secret American intelligence organization called 'the Program.' That man, it appears, is no longer employed, or perhaps is dead. So, instead, I've been killing the other agents associated with that cavern of scoundrels."

"You . . . have?"

"Oh yes, and successfully. But you know, at times I wonder if there shouldn't be more to life than what feels like an utter compulsion to succeed. I mean, it's at the expense of true happiness, isn't it? Not that I really know what happiness looks like."

"Well, yes," Dr. Goldwasser agreed, though he recrossed his legs in the other direction, and despite the sweet tea his tongue felt thickened and dry. "And how do you envision . . . happiness, Lila?"

"Oh, who knows?" Lila laughed and waved her cigarette. "A partner of some sort, perhaps? Children? Though God only knows what I could possibly teach them, and you can imagine that I'm not much of a cuddler."

He tried to smile, though a shiver rose up through his spine. Lila cocked her head.

"Do you find me attractive, Herr Doktor?"

"In a physical sense?"

"Yes."

"I am sure you are aware of your physical attributes."

"Of course." Lila laughed. "Strangers sometimes tell me that I look like an actress."

"And . . . are you an actress?"

The question, and the thought, brought Goldwasser a brief sense of relief. He considered that this young woman might be nothing more than that: a girl with money and mental issues whose form of entertainment involved spinning tales to psychologists. And still, he decided that as soon as this session was over and she'd left, he was going to make a call to Cobra, the Austrian counterterror branch of the Federal Police, and to hell with the ethics.

"I suppose I am, in a way," she said, "but only insofar as those skills help with the kills. At any rate, I'm about to travel to America to complete my assignment, which, due to my recent discoveries, will be expanding to include some . . . shall we say . . . very important persons. But I'm wondering if I should just quit."

Goldwasser closed his notebook. "Well, my dear . . . my assessment would be that you should pause in your endeavors and take an extended vacation. Reassess, so to speak. You might consider Switzerland."

Lila's sleek eyebrows furrowed, and she dipped her face at him.

"You mean a sanatorium, don't you." It wasn't a question.

"No . . . I simply meant . . ." But he stammered because he'd been caught. "I think anywhere removed from your current environment, Lila. Someplace quiet . . ."

"Peaceful," she said. "And perhaps . . . restrictive?"

"No, no, not that at all." He was backtracking as quickly as possible, and his trembling fingers loosened his woolen tie. "As a matter of fact, it might be better if you complete whatever it is that you think you must do, first, and only then consider taking a long sabbatical."

Lila snuffed out her cigarette and lightly slapped both gloved hands on her knees.

"That's what I think I needed to hear, Herr Doktor. Thank you very much. I believe you've definitely helped me."

"Good," he said, and he set his notebook on the side table next to his teacup, uncrossed his legs, and also lightly tapped his knees. "Well, it appears our time is up."

"It is indeed," said Lila, and she pulled a silenced Walther PK380 pistol from her handbag, shot Dr. Goldwasser in the face, and took his notebook as well as the cigarette butt with her lipstick smear on it.

But she didn't cut off his ear.

He wasn't an Alpha.

CHAPTER 28

LANGLEY AIR FORCE BASE, VIRGINIA

Eric Steele hijacked the Program's Gulfstream G650 at four o'clock in the morning. The pilots, however, didn't realize they were being hijacked until they were four hundred nautical miles out over the Atlantic.

There were two full crews for the Program's transcontinental jet, including a pilot, copilot, and navy steward, plus maintenance teams, always on standby in twelve-hour shifts down at the last hangar of Air Combat Command's 1st Fighter Wing. Langley's wing commander believed that these tight-lipped personnel, who occupied the small BOQ on the second floor of the maintenance hangar, rear side, were part of an air force black budget program. They, in turn, wore air force flight suits and carried bona fide air force CAC cards, so as not to embarrass him. To access the Program's restricted area, you walked through the hangar, past the arrow-shaped F-15s and science-fiction F-22s, up a stairway on the other side, and then you palm-printed a reader on the steel access door and entered a long hallway.

If you turned right, you were part of the Gulfstream's crew. If you turned left, you were Team Alpha.

Steele had entered the Program's team room at 0300, after first sticking his thumb in a scanner. And he was shocked to find Meg Harden standing there, all alone, sipping coffee from a hot mug and looking amazing as ever in tight jeans and a white roll-neck sweater. His first thought was that it seemed like a year since their erotic tryst in her apartment. His second thought was that the Program definitely had a traitor inside, and she was still on the list.

Behind her was a row of Alpha gear lockers, each with a nameplate stamped STALKER and the corresponding number—Jonathan Raines's and Collins Austin's lockers were still there, untouched. To the left was a substantial armory, with long guns and specialized ordnance stowed in upright Steelwater safes and handguns in MultiVault biometrics. To the right was the "wardrobe," which afforded Alphas a myriad of tactical clothing and civilian outfits with foreign labels.

"How did you know?" Steele said as he dropped a hefty duffel on a changing bench. He was wearing his navy flight jacket, a black commando sweater, black jeans, and tactical boots.

"You were the only one who wasn't there when Main II went down," she said. "Did you know about that?"

"Yeah. I talked to Ralphy."

"So did I." Her ice-blue eyes were examining his worn features like a concerned pediatrician.

"So Ralphy rolled over on me," Steele said.

"No, he just guessed you might have gone to see President Cole. I called over there and got the former First Lady. She wouldn't say much, except that she thought you might be heading 'somewhere east,' as she put it." Meg scanned his attire. "You're a little overdressed for this weather."

Steele said nothing. He walked over to the armory, spun the combination on one of the safes, took out a large black tactical bag, and started selecting and loading equipment. Meg watched him.

"There's no flash in the works, Eric. You don't have a mission."

"There's a flash in my head," he said.

And then she was there, behind him, and she turned him around and reached up, both of her small hands grasping the back of his neck, and she pulled him down and kissed him long and slowly, as if it might be their very last time. She pulled away and looked up at him. Her eyes were gleaming.

"I don't know what this is between us, Eric, where we're going, what we're supposed to be. But you don't trust me. I can taste it."

"I trust you," he said, though he wasn't sure at all. "I guess I'll find out how much in a minute." He knew she could stop his plans with just a few taps on her phone, and he couldn't stop her except with violence.

"I'm not going to get in your way," she said, "but I think you're off the reservation . . . emotionally, and professionally."

"Thanks, Doc." His sarcasm iced the atmosphere, and Meg took a few steps back and sat down on the bench.

"Go do whatever you have to do, Eric. I'll just wait here and read till you're gone."

He picked up his duffel and slung the tac bag. They were both heavy.

"I don't see a book," he said.

She showed him her cell phone. "Kindle."

"What are you reading?"

"*Five Years to Freedom.*"

It was a famous book by Colonel Nick Rowe, about his capture and long imprisonment in the jungles of Vietnam, and his ultimate escape. And then Steele knew that she knew, and he was wondering if, when he got to the other side, he'd be walking into an ambush. But he didn't say anything more and just left. . . .

The Gulfstream crew was surprised when he rousted them out for a flight to the city of Split, Croatia, but they certainly didn't make a fuss. Normally they'd get a WARNO from Cutlass Main prior to any mission, but they also had standing orders to respond to the requests of any Alpha, especially in the flesh. Stalker Seven wasn't the type of guy you'd say no to, and he waited politely while they washed up quickly, grabbed some coffee and doughnuts, and all headed out to the jet.

It was an hour later, over blue water and on a longitudinal track with Nova Scotia, when the first message came in from Washington, a flash from a keeper named Blade. The navy steward walked back to Steele, where he was sitting in the passenger compartment among his gear bags, staring out the window. She told him he was wanted in the cockpit to take incoming comms. He declined and said he'd return the transmission in due course.

Two minutes later, she returned and said, "Sir, the captain would like to have a word with you up forward."

Steele nodded, got up, and made his way to the cockpit. The captain and first officer were both in their mid-thirties, wearing olive flight suits and commercial aviation headsets and mics. The captain, sensing Steele's arrival, said to his copilot, "You have the controls." The copilot responded with, "I have the controls," and the pilot turned to look up at Steele.

"Sir," he said, "I have orders to turn this aircraft around and head back to Langley."

"Interesting, Captain," Steele said. "On whose authority?"

"Mike Pitts, sir, apparently via the White House chief of staff, Mr. Lansky."

"Ignore that order," Steele said. "Just keep flying to Split."

"I can't do that, sir." The pilot kept his eyes on Steele but shook his head. "That authority supersedes yours."

Steele reached back into his waistband and pulled out his father's Colt 1911. He didn't point it at anyone, but just showed it to the pilot, as if he were making an offer at a gun show.

"Isn't this a classic?" he said. "Original frame, only blued once."

The pilot looked at the heavy pistol, and at that point the copilot had seen it peripherally, and the airmen glanced at one another. The pilot pursed his lips and looked back up at Steele. "Sir, you know you can't fire a forty-five in an airplane. We'll depressurize and come apart."

"Actually, I had it retooled for nine millimeter," Steele said. "But you're right, it's extremely dangerous. On the other hand, we're not far from Hamilton, and I've got a HALO rig in the back. Do you?"

Neither pilot said anything else, and they carried on.

It was early evening when they arrived in Croatia. Steele deplaned with a curt apology and promised the pilots and navy ensign that he'd make it up to them over a steak dinner at the Capital Grille, if he ever returned. Waiting for him on the tarmac was a gray Fiat Doblo Cargo with smoked windows, and he hauled his two large gear bags over, shoved them in the van's rear hatch, and got into the passenger seat. The driver was a tough-looking blond American woman, with deep dimples, green eyes, and a well-worn A-2 flight jacket.

"Nice to be able to skip passport control, isn't it?" she said as she started driving.

"Allie, you look as crazy and hot as ever."

"Thank you, Mr. Steele." She grinned.

They had met a decade before at Bagram Airfield in Afghanistan, when Allie was flying Lakota helicopters for the army and Steele was still in Special Forces. At one point, in absolute defiance of all army regs, they'd gotten drunk together on Jack

Daniel's that had been smuggled over in someone's mouthwash bottle, and had wound up over at the Public Affairs' celebrity-visitor VIP B-hut known as "the Hotel California," screwing like young warriors who hadn't been laid in a year—which was the case for both of them.

It hadn't gone anywhere, but they'd remained good friends, and Allie had gone on to commercial helicopter flying all over the world. It was said of her that she could fly a lawn mower if there was nothing better around.

"Sorry about the short notice," Steele said as they headed across the tarmac toward a Russian Mi-8 multirole cargo helicopter. It was silver and had a large Road Runner cartoon painted on the fuselage beside the cockpit, but this Looney Tunes version was cracking a whip. "Who you flying this beast for?"

"Romanian oil company. And I don't mind the short notice, hotshot, but it doesn't give us enough time for fun."

Steele didn't pursue that, because he knew it wouldn't take much to tip them both over again. Allie, whose nickname was "Whirly," parked the van ten feet behind the Mi-8's tail rotor and together they hauled Steele's gear, chucked the bags behind the cockpit seats, and got in.

"Where we goin'?" Allie said as she fired up the APU and the large main rotor began to slowly twirl.

"Siberia."

"Si-fucking-beria, huh?" She laughed and put on her headset. "Now I get it. You're just using me 'cause you know I've got a license for Russian airspace. But do you also know how friggin' far that is, sport?"

"I know you've got something like a Robinson fuel bladder in the back. I saw it."

Allie snorted, "You make a girl feel cheap."

The big helo rolled forward on its fat tricycle wheels, Allie spoke to the tower, and they took off and banked hard right, heading toward Sarajevo, and then Serbia, Bulgaria, and the Black Sea.

"I owe you for this, Allie," Steele said in all sincerity. There were many people in his life with exceptional skills and talents, but few that he knew he could count on once he'd gone rogue.

"Well," she said, and she looked at him and grinned and reached over and squeezed his thigh, "you can check in anytime you want, baby."

Steele said, "Yeah, but then I could never leave."

CHAPTER 29

SOL-ILETSK, RUSSIA

There was nothing in the world like Russia's Black Dolphin Prison.

While many other countries had maximum security incarceration facilities, some of which could only be imagined by authors of dystopian fiction, the Russian Federal Penitentiary Service had certainly broken the mold after this particular design.

Remote was not the proper descriptive word. It hulked on the vast open plain of the steppes in the middle of nothing, somewhere north of the Kazakhstani border, where the summers were as long as a sneezing fit and the endless winters were so cold that a prisoner's tears froze before striking his food bowl.

Austere would have also failed in terms of an apt architectural description. Black Dolphin was the shape and color of a Maltese cross, with each of its concrete and rebar branches fifty meters in length, extending from a central circular fortress capped with a squat black dome. The four branches held twelve prison cells each, with a corridor between them, and the central roundabout held the administrative offices. Above ground there was only one apparent story. Below ground was the interrogation facility, known as "*temnitsa*," the dungeon, as well as the prison's oil-fueled power plant.

There was no gymnasium, common dining area, recreation room, library, or single television. There was no outdoor exercise area. Prisoners never saw the light of day, or the glow of the moon.

Secure, however, was an appropriate adjective. A Voronezh-class, slotted waveguide radar antenna was constantly turning above the central dome and could detect any incoming aircraft at ten kilometers out, as well as ground vehicles at a similar range. All the iron prison cell doors used digital locks, so there could never be an issue of a stolen or duplicated key. Three rings of four-meter-high security fences, topped with razor concertina wire, surrounded the prison, with a "sweep strip" sewn with PMN-2 antipersonnel mines bracing the first ring from the outside.

Inside the prison, FPS guards patrolled the hallways, armed with Bizon submachine guns, SR-1 Vektor pistols, rubber truncheons, Sabre pepper spray, and nasty attitudes. Outside, the hardiest of this lot patrolled the grounds beyond the wire, wearing fur hats, boots, and long coats, armed with AK-74s and leashed to Caucasian *ovcharkas*, bearlike mountain dogs bred to fight off wolves.

There was only one entrance to Black Dolphin. It was on the southern end of the south-facing wing and consisted of a "submarine chamber" of one pair of steel exterior doors with pneumatic locks, then another pair of two-inch-thick plexiglass doors, also remote-controlled, and a bulletproof desk station manned 24/7 by two FPS officers, who eyeballed a bank of eight flat-screen monitors and kept their Vektor pistols always chambered.

There were no visitors. Ever.

You didn't escape from Black Dolphin.

You simply hoped to die young.

The prison's warden, Major Mikhail Petrov, had recently celebrated his fortieth birthday, which made him one of the youngest such executive bureaucrats in the entire FPS system. He had a confident gait, a bit of a paunch, a swept-back Stalinesque haircut with mustache to match, and wore a Jaeger-LeCoultre watch and a pair of Gucci Urban eyeglasses—unusual choices for a uniformed Russian apparatchik. Petrov was also one of the most corrupt wardens in the Service, which was why he'd volunteered to manage Black Dolphin, because his superiors from Moscow or even Chelyabinsk rarely came to check up on him. When they did, the Jaeger-LeCoultre was quickly switched for a Russian Raketa, and the glasses for a pair of FPS-issue steel rims.

His office, behind a locked steel door on the north side of the prison's central hub, was more than comfortable and sported an enormous oak desk, a long plush couch draped in dromedary camel fur, and a very fine bar. When seated in his black leather "captain's chair," Petrov could call up any of the prison's security cameras on his desktop computer—which he rarely did because he was usually watching Italian porn. When he wasn't working, he resided thirty-two kilometers north in a stylish dacha in Livanovka, on the banks of the Ural river, where he was currently hosting a pair of beautiful Mongolian whores. At the moment the dacha was bathed in waves of creamy white snow, like something out of *Doctor Zhivago*.

Per Petrov's instructions, his officers and guards rarely knocked on his door, unless it was for a matter of urgency, and with the amount of snow on the roof and grounds of the prison, all the sounds reaching him this evening were muted and soft. The only things he was hearing were the strains of Tchaikovsky wafting from his iPod speakers and the orgasmic moans from his computer—which was why he looked up and frowned when he thought he heard something outside of the norm.

The sound was Eric Steele, killing Petrov's guards.

Steele had just arrived in the prison's bread truck, which he'd hijacked after waving it down, kneecapping the driver with a 9 mm round, crushing the man's Nokia cell phone, and leaving him zip-tied in an abandoned roadside barn. The truck was a 1980s UAZ-450 van, which looked particularly harmless with its cartoonlike "face" of bug-eyed headlamps, and because the snow had started to assault Sol-Iletsk with something akin to a blizzard, the two patrolling guards at Black Dolphin's main gate were hunkered inside their greatcoats, and off their game.

The bread truck was on schedule. Who the hell

else would show up at this arctic hellhole in the middle of the night?

Steele parked the truck twenty meters back from the rolling gate in the perimeter fence, because he intended to use the vehicle again and didn't want it damaged by what was about to transpire. He got out, and the two FPS guards turned from a close conversation they'd been having about the quality of Ukrainian hookers, stared at him, and their jaws went slack.

The tall dark figure standing in the swirling snow looked like Arnold Schwarzenegger's nemesis in *Predator.* The guards saw a black ballistic helmet and the eerie green glow of a PVS-14 monocular night-vision device, a black balaclava revealing only dispassionate lips, and then full Ratnik body armor festooned with ammunition pouches and bristling with Dutch V40 mini–fragmentation grenades, a pair of legs encased in ribbed Kevlar and Arc'teryx LEAF knee protectors, and black Lowa Gore-Tex boots. The figure appeared to be gripping an HK416 A5 assault rifle in 5.56 x 45 mm NATO caliber—no suppressor.

Steele said, "*Dobryj vecher.*" Good evening. But he did not add the courteous *comrades.*

The Russians said nothing, but they fumbled for their AK-74s and their massive *ovcharka* guard dogs strained at their leashes and snarled like mountain lions. Too late. Steele opened fire, raking a burst across the openmouthed gapes of the two guards, whose skulls exploded in clouds of crimson beige as they slammed down on their backs in the snow.

The dogs, still leashed to their fallen masters, barked like banshees and tried to lunge at Steele to tear him apart. He didn't like killing innocent animals, so he walked forward and butt-stroked the left-hand beast in the head, knocking him clean out. The second animal lay down in the snow and whimpered.

The gate wasn't locked. Steele chopped the latch with a gloved hand, slid it open on its creaking wheels, and was facing a thirty-meter concrete walkway leading to the prison's main entrance. He slung the 416 and swung an RPG-7 rocket-propelled launcher around from his back, then reached over his right shoulder for one of three rockets settled there in a quiver. In some cases, Steele preferred the RPG over any of the U.S. inventory's light anti-tank tubes, because the Soviet weapon could be reloaded and was purely mechanical. He shoved the rocket into the tube, twisted the phallus until its collar nipple met the tube's notch, shouldered it, yanked the ring-pin safety off the rocket's nose, thumbed the pistol grip's hammer down, took aim at the prison's double steel entrance doors, and fired.

The thunderous double booms of the launch and impact were nearly simultaneous at that range. The doors blew open, clanging like church bells as they were ripped from their iron hinges, and as the smoke cleared Steele saw another set of plexiglass doors deeper inside. He reached back for his second rocket, loaded it, armed it, and fired again. The plexiglass exploded in spinning shards of shrapnel, ringing off the interior walls. A few seconds later, the two trembling FPS officers who'd taken cover behind their steel desk popped up and started firing wildly with their pistols.

Steele now stepped to the left and took a knee beside the walkway in the snow. From a canvas pouch latched to his left thigh, he drew two LX-700K Liberator drones—each the size of a fat hummingbird and with three-gram payloads of RDX high explosive—and whipped them into the air toward the shattered submarine chamber. The drones came to life and, buzzing like furious wasps, zipped away from their "master" and into the scorched hallway. They were already preprogrammed to target only enemy skulls, and they each found the sweet spot between the FPS officers' brows and detonated on impact, blowing ragged holes deep into their brains.

Steele got up and headed straight in. At this point the prison's alarm bells were banging like ship's klaxons and all the emergency lights were blazing. He flipped his night-vision monocular up over his helmet.

He wasn't going to need it anymore.

CHAPTER 30

BLACK DOLPHIN PRISON, RUSSIA

Steele knew it wasn't going to be a cakewalk, but he didn't care.

Outside the prison the temperature was a bone-cracking –9 degrees Celsius, and now inside the corridor it was like a high-altitude airplane fuselage that had suddenly blown a window and depressurized. The icy wind corkscrewed down the passageway, taking with it smoking shards of debris and logbook pages from the guards' reception desk. And still he was sweating like a pig underneath all his combat gear.

The RPG launcher was a heavy weapon of steel tubing encased in a wooden cocoon. He unslung it and dumped it, along with the quiver and his last rocket, and he slinked rapidly forward in a tactical half crouch with the 416 at his shoulder. The prisoners in their cells on both sides started screaming and pounding on their doors in six different languages, and the heavily armed FPS guards turned the corner at the far end of the corridor and came at him.

At a range of fifty meters, Steele killed the first one as he came around the right-hand corner, "slicing the pie." Only the barrel of the Russian's Bizon subgun and an inch of his head appeared, and Steele took him with a single shot through the eyeball. He knew the next guard would come from the left, so he smeared his right shoulder against the wall, kept moving forward, and locked the red dot of his EOTech XPS2–0 sight at a spot on that corner, mid-height. Just as the second Bizon barrel appeared, he slammed one into the subgun's receiver from halfway down the corridor. His bullet ricocheted straight up into the Russian's throat, he lurched forward onto his knees, and Steele double-tapped him in the head.

He knew they'd get cautious now, and having no idea how many of them might be gathering in stacks in that central circular roundabout up ahead, he decided on shrapnel. He pulled two of the golf ball–size V40 mini-grenades off his Load-Bearing Vest, gripped them both and their spoons in his left glove, twisted the pins out with his right-hand middle finger, and curve-balled them both down the corridor, skipping them off the linoleum floor.

There was a lime-green octagonal control station in the middle of the prison's hub—wisely unoccupied at the moment. The grenades rolled up against its plaster wall and stopped. Men started yelling, boots began pounding, Steele flattened himself to the floor, and the minis detonated at the exact same second, slinging wicked shrapnel in all directions, amputating a bank of lights from the ceiling, and finishing off their performance with a chorus of screams.

Good time to move.

Steele took off straight down the corridor now, his gunfire-muffled eardrums assaulted left and right by the prisoners' bellows. He pulled a CTS 7290 flashbang from his rig, yanked the pin, and hurled it as a follow-up to his shrapnel carnage, and he squinted hard as out ahead the tremendous explosion and yellow-white flash sent the already panicked Russians diving for any cover they could find.

He switched his 416 to only his right hand, yanked his father's 1911 from his left thigh holster with his left hand, broke past the corridor corners where the two fresh corpses were sprawled, and burst into the middle of the hub. He saw a writhing FPS guard moaning and crawling away to his right. Then, another suddenly popped from the entrance of the right-hand corridor, and Steele raked him with a short burst from the HK. He sensed, more than saw, another FPS guard charging at him from the left-hand wing, and he felt the punch of a round slam into the left side of his Ratnik armor, and he shot the man in the face, off-hand and twice, with the Colt pistol.

Then he waited, turning slowly in place with both weapons at the ready. No one else seemed to be showing up. He walked around the control octagon to the green metal door at the far wall, behind which he thought he'd find the warden—confirmed by the nameplate on the door. His ears were ringing from his own gunfire, and theirs, and the powerful bangs of the grenades, yet the loudest thing pinging around the inside of his brain was telling him to chill.

Don't kill him. Make him talk.

Steele rapped on the door with his knuckles. There was no response from inside.

"*Otkroye*," he said in Russian. Open it. "Or I'll have to blow it open, and that will make me angry."

After a moment, the lock buzzed and clicked, and Steele slapped the latch and went inside, both guns up and looking like a Robert Heinlein nightmare. Petrov was standing behind his desk, sweating and shaking like a rabbit in a wolf's cavern. He was clutching a Makarov pistol in his right hand, but it looked so tiny and felt that way to him, and he wasn't really pointing it at anyone.

Steele lifted one boot and mule-kicked the door closed behind him. It slammed and Petrov let out a small yelp and dropped the pistol on his desk.

"Sit," Steele barked.

Petrov collapsed into his black leather chair as if he'd been Tasered.

Steele walked forward to the front of the desk. He back slung the 416 and switched the Colt to his right hand. The balaclava was still covering his face and only his blazing green eyes and tight lips were showing.

"Major Petrov," he said, "I'm only here for one thing, and I'm not going to ask you twice."

"How . . . How do you know my name?" the warden stuttered.

"It's on your fucking nameplate."

"Ohh," Petrov squeaked.

"You had a prisoner here, an American prisoner. It was some years ago. His name was Hank Steele."

"I . . . I do not know this name."

Steele backhanded Petrov's computer monitor onto the floor, leaned over his desk, and jammed the 1911's barrel into his forehead. The major pissed himself in his chair.

"How long have you been here?" Steele asked.

"About . . . perhaps nine hours!" The major's voice was getting very reedy.

"Not today, idiot. How many years?"

"I, for most of my professional career, perhaps twenty years. I began as one of the guards. . . . But, we have had many prisoners from many countries. . . ."

"I'll bet you have, *yubtvoyumat*," Steele growled, a reference to fornicating with the major's mother. Then he reached down into the top of his body armor and pulled out a faded color photograph. It was a photo of Hank Steele, taken in Bolivia when he'd served there as an advisor with Special Forces. He was wearing no head gear in the photo and his facial features were crisp and clear. "This man."

Petrov didn't dare touch the picture. It seemed to him that it might mean something holy to this horrible creature standing before him and aiming an enormous pistol at his head. He only leaned forward a touch, stared at the image, and sat back again.

"*Da*," he whispered. "I remember this man."

A wave of nausea mingled with joy washed up through Steele's adrenaline-pumped body.

"Tell it," he said. "All of it."

"He . . . I think . . . It was perhaps fifteen years

ago, when I was a team lieutenant here. He was in one of the lower-level cells for . . . I think a long time. . . ."

"How long?"

"Four or five years."

Steele ground the Colt barrel into that fleshy spot between Petrov's eyebrows again.

"What else? Tell me everything. And don't leave anything out."

"I don't remember more!" Petrov was trying to disappear into his chair and Steele could now hear shouts outside in the corridors. They were mustering for an assault. He didn't have much time. Petrov kept on stammering. "They brought him down here from Lubyanka and the KGB and then the FSB were very interested in him and sometimes visited to . . . you know . . ."

"Interrogate him?"

"Well . . . to speak and . . ."

"*Torture* him?"

"I . . . I was only a guard!"

"What happened to him, Petrov? And if you fucking lie to me I'm going to blow your slimy, worthless, ass-kissing, cowardly brains all over your goddamn vodka trolley."

"He escaped! I am not lying to you!"

"He escaped."

"Yes!"

"From here."

"Yes!"

"How?"

"He dug a tunnel. He dug a tunnel from under

the shithole in his cell and into the sewer and out under the third wire. They said it took him a year, but no one knew how he did it."

"He dug a tunnel." Just the idea of his father somehow managing that made Steele's chest swell. "What happened to him after that? Did you catch him, Petrov?"

"No . . . we tried . . . they tried. But he was gone."

"Liar."

"No . . . it is true."

"Did you catch him and kill him, Petrov?"

"No! I swear!" At this point the major slumped and began to hyperventilate, and Steele thought he might have a massive heart attack right there on the spot. That wouldn't do. He still needed him for one more task. He pulled the pistol away from his forehead and lowered the barrel.

"All right, Major, I believe you," he said. "Get up."

Petrov gripped his chair arms. "But why? I've told you everything I know!"

"We're going for a walk."

Three minutes later, they emerged together from Petrov's office. The major, still wearing his piss-stained uniform, was hatless, pale, and could barely stay on his feet. But Steele was there behind him to help him and encourage his progress.

His right hand was resting on the major's shoulder, with the Colt 1911 pistol barrel denting his right temple. In the major's mouth was a V40 mini-grenade, its dark green ball jammed behind his teeth, with the spoon on the outside. Steele's left arm was thrust under the major's left armpit, with his index finger hooked in the ring pin. The major was keening and snorting through his nose, and snot was dripping over his mustache.

Six guards were waiting for them in a semicircular ring, Bizons up and pistol holsters open and ready for the draw.

"Drop the guns and leave them," Steele said in Russian. "Or you'll be eating the major's brains."

They lowered their weapons to the linoleum floor, and all of them took three steps back. He knew that any one of them still might decide to go for a medal of courage, yank a pistol, and shoot him, but everyone also knew if that happened, Steele's finger was going to pull that pin, and there'd be lots of explaining to do.

He marched Petrov down the south corridor, with the prisoners still yelling and banging their doors, and then they walked out into the horrid wind and snow and headed for the bread truck. Steele opened the driver's door with his gun hand, and with his left finger still in Petrov's grenade ring, he maneuvered his 416 around and into the compartment, then slipped into the seat. He turned the engine over and looked at his hostage.

"I'm not taking you with me, Major," he said. "You'd just be a pain in the ass." He slipped his finger from the ring. "But be careful. Don't swallow that thing."

The major's eyes rolled back in his head and he toppled straight back in the snow, out cold.

Steele gunned the engine and took off. He had gotten what he'd come for, the first piece of the puzzle, a confirmation that what President Cole had told him was true. And, for all of those suffering prisoners in Russia's ongoing gulag, he'd also taken a pound of flesh.

He felt pretty good about all of it.

But he'd forgotten one thing in all the excitement. The RPG and the single rocket he'd left in the prison's first corridor were gone. They'd been snatched up by one of the youngest guards while Steele was still in Petrov's office. That guard had been a Russian paratrooper, was an expert shot with a rocket-propelled grenade, and had slinked from the prison to ambush the bastard who'd killed his comrades in the corridor.

He was kneeling on a snowy knoll outside Black Dolphin's third wire, where the access road made its last turn before heading north toward the Ural river, when Steele roared by in the bread van.

He fired the rocket, it blew off the back of the van, and the vehicle flipped three times and rolled into a ravine.

CHAPTER 31

SOL-ILETSK, RUSSIA

Something was dripping onto Eric Steele's head. It felt like freezing droplets of water. They were soaking his scalp, running off his forehead, and coursing down the sides of his nose and over his lips. But they weren't enough for him to drink and quench his roaring thirst.

And something else was dripping onto his chest. He knew that was blood from his smashed nose and a wicked rifle butt slash in his left temple. Those were the blows that had knocked him out. The ice water had woken him up.

He raised his head and squinted into the painful glare of some sort of light, but everything beyond that was utter darkness. Above him he saw a black concrete ceiling with slim runnels of silver ice, from which the frozen droplets fell in a maddening rhythm and pinged off a slimy cement floor. Looking down he saw his own bare feet, his ankles bound to the legs of a steel chair with multiple turns of green duct tape. He was sitting in that chair, wearing nothing but his black long underwear. His body armor, load-bearing gear, balaclava, boots, and gloves were gone. His arms were cranked behind the back of the chair, his wrists bound so tightly with the same green tape that his hands were swollen and completely numb.

His bullet-bruised ribs trembled and ached with every ragged breath, and he knew he was slowly freezing to death.

Welcome to Russia.

He didn't know exactly where he was, but he knew it wasn't Black Dolphin. They had dragged him out of the burning bread van and tossed him in the back of a KamAZ light truck, with no less than four sets of knees grinding down on his spine. Then they'd driven about four kilometers—a guess in his soporific state—stopped, tossed him out into knee-high snow, and dragged him through the drifts to a horseshoe-shaped construct that looked like some sort of barracks, most likely where the prison guards resided. But they hadn't taken him inside and instead had hauled him through the swirling white coils of the midnight blizzard, past the barracks, to another squat building on a small hill in the back. It was empty, like some sort of hand-to-hand training area—maybe where they learned to crack skulls.

Then they'd gone to work on him. Buckets of freezing water. Cigarette lighters under his earlobes. Boot stomps on his toes. Bitch slaps, face punches, whipping side kicks to his thighs and knees. There were six of them, and they were justifiably pissed after what he'd just done to their comrades. Considering all that, he thought the treatment was relatively civilized. They didn't ask him a single question, just took turns. Then the rifle butt, which had sent him to dreamland.

"*Bolshoyespasibah*," he said. Thank you very much, he'd groaned and passed out.

Now he had no idea how much time had gone by. It could have been an hour, or six, but it felt like it was still nighttime.

He tried to see past what looked like a blazing Klieg light mounted on a tripod, but it was like staring into the sun. There were no other lights in the square space of cavernous blackness, but he could hear the soft thumping of a generator from somewhere outside and figured that's how the light was powered. He heard low mutters, boot scrapes, and thought he saw the orange arcs of lit cigarettes, like fireflies on a summer night. But whatever was coming next, the guards beyond the Klieg were taking no action yet. It was like they were waiting for something.

Count your blessings, Steele thought. *If you're lucky, your heart'll give out before they get to the serious stuff.*

Then the serious stuff appeared in the form of Major Petrov.

Steele couldn't see the iron entrance door there beyond the floodlight as it opened, but he heard its rusty iron hinges screeching, and a slice of icy wind slashed his shivering form. There were some murmurs in Russian, boot heels clicking, and something like caster wheels rolling across the concrete floor.

A figure appeared. It was hunched over and maneuvering something past the Klieg and into its half-circular glow of light on the floor beyond

Steele's feet, which were turning a shade of bruised purplish blue. The figure was uniformed and small, almost like a dwarf, and he was wearing a greatcoat and pushing a rusty slime-green hospital crash cart. But the top tray wasn't laid out with sophisticated, sterilized medical instruments. It was piled with tools, like from an auto mechanic's garage.

The figure left the cart and scuttled away, and then Major Petrov stepped into the light. He was wearing a greatcoat as well, the shoulders dusted with fat snowflakes, and it was open in front to reveal a fresh uniform. Steele's precious .45 was tucked in his belt. A fluffy fur hat, earflaps pinned up, was perched on his head, and his black gloves looked brand-new, as if he'd been saving them for a special occasion and had just clipped off the price tags. He looked nothing like the sniveling coward who, only hours before, Steele had dragged from Black Dolphin with a Dutch hand grenade in his mouth. He looked so fresh and clean that Steele's first thought was that either this guy was Petrov's twin, or the major had gone home for a hot bath and a sauna before showing up here.

Petrov looked down at Steele with the beady dark eyes of a rabid raccoon. He removed his gloves, one at a time, smoothed his thick mustache, and smiled. Five of his guards then appeared behind him, hanging back at the farthest edge of the semicircle of light, but they were brandishing their Bizons, and Steele thought for sure that he saw one of them licking his lips.

"You humiliated me in front of my men," Petrov said in near-perfect English.

"I'd apologize, Major," Steele answered in kind, "but it wouldn't be sincere. The only thing I'm sorry about is not pulling the pin on that grenade or shooting you in the balls."

Petrov backhanded Steele in the face, snapping his head to the left and slinging blood from his nose across the floor. The major looked at the back of his knuckles, took a handkerchief embroidered with roses from his greatcoat pocket, and wiped them clean. Steele shook off the blow and smiled up at the major.

"I'm not going to talk, you know," he said.

"I sent your photograph to FSB headquarters. I know who you are," Petrov said. "I don't want you to talk, Mr. Steele. I want you to suffer."

"Don't you want to know where I came from? How I knew to come here?"

Petrov shrugged, reached inside his coat, and came up with a slim silver box. He slipped a Kazbek cigarette from the box, tapped it on the metal, lipped it, and lit up with what looked like an old-fashioned trench lighter. He blew a stream of smoke at the dripping ceiling.

"All right," he said. "Where did you come from? And how did you know to come here?"

"I came from Nunya-FB," Steele said.

"Nunya-FB?" Petrov cocked his head. "What does this mean?"

"None a ya fucking business."

The second backhanded slap was harder than the first, but from the other side, and this time Petrov's knuckles impacted with the ugly open gash in Steele's temple, so it really rang his bell.

Don't give this bastard even a wince, he said to himself as he deliberately slowed his breathing and fought through the pain. *If you're gonna die here, die well.*

Steele switched back to Russian.

"Do your men here know how you pissed yourself back in your office, Major? How you whimpered and cried like a little girl?"

Petrov's face flushed and he grunted and turned to the crash cart. He inspected the tools, as if making sure that whatever he chose would be the right size for a specific repair, picked up a long red C-wrench, stepped forward toward Steele, and swung it in a blurring arc, smashing the haft into the side of Steele's left knee. Steele's head whipped back against his right shoulder as the pain thundered up through his leg, into his chest, and shot a burst of saliva from his bloodstained lips. But he didn't make a sound.

"Would you like to tell them?" Petrov asked.

Steele coughed and managed to speak again. "No, you do it. I'm busy composing a string quartet in my head."

Petrov grinned. "It's so fortunate that you came here, Mr. Steele. You've given us the opportunity that we never fulfilled with your father, that piece of shit. His escape destroyed the career of the warden back then, which is essentially how I arrived at my rank and position."

"Keep blabbering," Steele said. "I'm almost done with the score."

At that point, Steele thought he heard something familiar. It wasn't really a sound, just a mild pulse in the air. Petrov dropped the C-wrench back on the cart and came up with something larger. It was a ball-peen hammer, probably a three-pounder, with a heavy wooden shaft and a gleaming stainless steel head.

"Well," Petrov said as he put his gloves back on and started bouncing the haft of the hammer in his left-hand palm, "this is something akin to karma, is it not? Your father escapes and never returns to you, which is why I assume you are here. And then you appear, like some pathetic child on an idiot's tearful errand, so we can do to you what we never got to do to him. Irony, isn't it?"

"It's pure fucking Tolstoy," Steele said.

"I think it is more like Kafka, but whatever," Petrov said, and then he walked closer and looked down at Steele's left knee, the one that was still sending ripples of pain all the way into his head.

That pulse in Steele's ears was growing more distinct. It was a helicopter of some sort, which was weird as hell, considering the storm. But then again, Russian pilots were used to flying in that kind of nightmare.

"At any rate, you'll soon be on your way to Lubyanka. The FSB has extended you an invitation, which I, of course, accepted on your behalf. They are sending air transport tonight. I did, however, warn them that you were badly injured after the murders you committed at our facility."

Steele was now hearing something else. A couple of the *ovcharkas* were barking furiously, and then they were quiet, and he could hear a faint but distinct and rapid clicking, like the sound of weapons bolts ringing behind heavy-duty suppressors. No gunshots; just that.

"As a matter of fact, I told them that you were crippled." Petrov laughed as he raised the ball-peen hammer high above his head. Steele glanced right and left, and in the overspill of the Klieg light, he saw the teeth of the guards grinning. "That wasn't true when I spoke to Moscow. . . . But it will be, *now.*"

And he opened his mouth, stretched the hammer up one more inch, and started to bring it down.

Then the iron entrance door burst open, and his brains exploded from his teeth.

CHAPTER 32

SOL-ILETSK, RUSSIA

Steele knew not to move, not even a millimeter. He sat there in the chair, rock steady as an ice sculpture, and even though he was slathered with putrid brain matter and slick, hot blood, he didn't close his eyes. If these were going to be his last moments on earth, he was going to see them in Cinerama.

He could have flung himself to the left or right, or toppled his chair over backward, but anyone who'd ever been in a shoot house when top-tier operators were working Close-Quarters Battle knew better. Steele had been on both ends of that spectrum hundreds of times, in training and on real-world missions, with Navy SEALs, Germans from GSG9, British SAS, and Program Alphas. If you were "playing" hostage in a CQB live-fire environment, from Range 37 down at Fort Bragg to the Israeli kill houses at Lashabiyah, you sat in that chair and you didn't fucking move, and you just let it all flow around you. Otherwise you were bound to be dead.

It sure as hell separated the boys from the men, and the girls from the women.

And man, it happened fast.

Petrov's ball-peen hammer went flying and clanged off a wall, his corpse bounced with a sickening *thunk* on the floor, and the rest of the shitstorm started. The soles of tactical boots came pounding into the space, the mouths of suppressor barrels bloomed white flowers of flame, and the upper receivers of automatic weapons clacked like somebody hammering the keys of a dead piano. Steele saw the Russians trying to react as they spun toward the assault, and one of them actually got off a shot with his pistol, which flashed and banged in the enclosed space like a magnesium grenade with a shotgun kicker. But then his head whipped back with a bullet to the forehead, and his nose came off as another round burst through under his chin, and then the room went totally black as the operators took out the Klieg light.

The rest of it was suppressed gunfire that sounded like half a dozen German shepherds sneezing, empty shell casings bouncing off the ceiling, floor, and walls like jelly beans in a clothes dryer, and terrible screams and gurgling grunts. And then it was over. Dead silence.

Steele realized he was hyperventilating. No surprise, since about two hundred rounds had just been winging around his head and body like pissed-off wasps, and somehow, miraculously, even with the ricochet factor very high, he hadn't been hit. In fact, his adrenaline score was so off the charts that he didn't even feel his flaming left knee anymore, which he reasoned might be good or bad. Then, lights started to fill the space, chemlights, of the kind that he and most special operators kept by the handful in their LBVs. They were eerie and green, and they revealed the bodies all over.

He squinted into the darkness to identify his rescuers, and wondered for a moment if they were indeed that, or maybe the operators of some rival Russian power, perhaps a Putin oligarch who realized Steele would be worth a fortune as a prize. But none of that really made sense—the Kremlin could have whatever it wanted.

And these men were no band of Russian ruffians. They were kitted up even better than he'd been, just a few hours before. They were wearing MICH helmets, not with PVS-14 monocular NODs like his, but with four-tube Ground Panoramic Night Vision Goggles, and the rest of their kit was the latest DARPA prototype body armor in that weird snow cat camouflage. And they were all carrying Heckler & Koch MP5SD 9 mm integrally suppressed submachine guns, because they'd obviously anticipated doing close-in work. Lung steam flowed toward the frozen ceiling from the hoods of their balaclavas.

There were no patches or identifiers of any kind on their uniforms, but Steele heard one of them say to the other, in Texas-accented American English, "Five mikes and we're outbound. Start pulling the rest of the squadron in from security, copy?"

"Roger," the other one said, and that's when Steele knew who they were.

Delta Force.

The Program could call on the 1st Special Forces

Operational Detachment "D" for support, but only in cases of dire emergencies, and only for work OCONUS. But Delta could not respond affirmatively to such a request, except by direct order from President Rockford.

Well, Steele knew where his vote would be going next time around. But at the moment, if he didn't get some water and a couple of ibuprofens real soon, he was going to pass the hell out.

An operator who appeared to be the Delta team leader came forward out of the swirling gun smoke and semidarkness. He was bulky and short, arm muscles bulging through his winter camo gear, and he kicked aside the fallen shattered Klieg light, walked up to Steele, slung his MP5 behind his back, and knelt on one knee. He pulled off his MICH helmet, and then pulled down the front of his balaclava.

It was Dalton "Blade" Goodhill.

"You know something, Steele?" he growled. "You're a fucking pain in the ass."

Steele just blinked at him. He thought he might be delirious, or dreaming. Goodhill pulled a curved-blade Emerson Combat Karambit from his plate carrier and started slicing through the duct tape around Steele's ankles.

"Medic, up," Goodhill said, but he didn't really have to. A Delta corpsman was already moving in next to Steele's chair, pulling off a glove, and checking his neck pulse.

With the door open and that Russian winter wind ripping into the room now, Steele could plainly hear the sound of big rotors turning outside somewhere. Goodhill was now in back of him, freeing his hands.

"Can I get some water?" Steele said in a hoarse whisper.

The medic bent over and fed him the end of his water carrier tube. Steele took a long pull, spit the tube out, and nodded thanks. He heard another senior operator snapping at his men.

"We're not doing an SSE here, boys. Just a photo record and let's get the fuck out."

Steele thought, *A Sensitive Site Exploration . . . intelligence gathering . . . They don't care about that. They just came for me.*

A small camera flashed a few times in the room; the color was muted amber. The medic peeled one of Steele's eyelids back and checked his pupil with a penlight.

"How the hell did you find me?" Steele said to Goodhill, who came back around in front of him and stared down like a pissed-off middle school principal.

"You've got a chip in your ass."

"A what?"

"A while back, before I came aboard, you had some sort of nasty incident at your house. You and Momma wound up in the ICU at Green Bank, right?"

"Yeah." The medic was checking Steele's bruised ribs where his armor had taken a round. He bucked in the chair and said, "Jee-sus."

"You were out long enough for Pitts to issue an order to the docs. They put a tracking chip in you somewhere, probably hid it behind a piece of shrapnel."

"Oh," Steele said, and thought, *Gotta get rid of that thing.*

"Boss, you ready to move yet?" the Delta leader called out to Goodhill. "We gotta go. Pilot's picking up inbound on radar."

"Roger," Goodhill said. "Get him some boots off a corpse." He looked down at Steele's feet. "Size nine."

"Eleven," Steele corrected.

"I figured small brain, small feet," Goodhill sneered. "Probably a small dick too. Okay, let's get him up."

The medic and Goodhill helped Steele stand, while another slipped his swollen bare feet into a pair of Russian boots. They were blessedly still warm. The two men gripped him under his armpits and guided him past the Klieg debris, broken glass, spent shells, and bloody corpses. Outside the wind hit Steele like a hammer blow. He was still wearing only his long underwear and nothing else, and his face felt like the cold meat that his mother would soften with a mallet on Sundays before their big evening meal.

Goodhill and the other operator half dragged him, with Steele stumbling like a drunk in the snow, up and over another small hill, where there on its cap a large helicopter sat with its main rotor cranking up to a screaming whine as more operators folded back from their perimeter security positions and started climbing aboard. The snow was being whipped into corkscrews by the big rotors, but some starlight was peeking through splits in the thick clouds above, and Steele could now see the nose of the big fat helo . . . and its cartoon Road Runner cracking a whip.

He stopped stumbling, stood stock-still in the snow, and stared at it. "Allie?"

"Yeah, Allie," Goodhill shouted in the rotor storm. "She works for the Program, dumbass."

Steele was totally confused. His reasoning and memories and logical thinking were all mixing and fading like a watercolor painting on a hot sidewalk. A crew chief was leaning outside the helo's cargo door and madly twirling his finger in the air at Goodhill, but Steele wasn't moving. "Blade" pushed the medic away toward the helo. The man took off through the snow.

"I came here to find my father," Steele yelled above the thunder of the rotor blades. He was hanging back from the helicopter, as if his feet were frozen to Russia.

Goodhill turned to Steele, grabbed the front of his black thermal top in one gloved fist, and yanked him close.

"Stalker Seven," he growled, "your father's not here. And if we don't get your ass back to Washington, Lansky's gonna disband the Program."

Steele shook his head. "I don't care."

"Ya don't, huh? Is this what you want? A fate just like Hank Steele's? Branded a renegade, never seeing your mother again, breaking what's left of her heart? There's a killer out there, ripping the Program apart, and a traitor inside, tearing our guts out. You've got a mission, and this ain't it. . . ."

"I don't know who to trust anymore."

"I don't either," Goodhill said. "Except maybe for you, 'cause you're nuts."

"But you don't understand, about my father. . . . I have to finish this."

And with both gloved hands, Dalton Goodhill gripped the sides of Steele's bruised and bloodied face, hard so the pain would focus him, and pulled him down so they were nearly nose to nose.

"I knew your father, Eric," he said. "I knew him well. You're not half the man that he was, but none of us are. And he'd tell you exactly what I'm telling you."

Steele just stared at him, dumbfounded, and then Goodhill finished his thought.

"Now get on the fucking bird."

CHAPTER 33

NASHVILLE, TENNESSEE

Lila Kalidi crossed the Canadian border at midnight, halfway between the tiny American towns of Pembina, North Dakota, and Roseau, Minnesota, along a stretch of two-lane highway that was virtually unguarded.

Both of those small towns had bustling official border crossing stations, with U.S. Customs and Border Protection on one side, and the Canada Border Services Agency on the other. Yet between those stations and their endless lines of vehicles patiently waiting to cross in both directions, there were forty miles of unpatrolled open forests and grasslands, except for a few cameras and sensors. Lila could never understand the North American lapdog mentality that made people obey "territorial integrity" in such a ridiculous manner.

Well, all the better for her.

Entering Canada through Montreal had been easy. The daughter of Emile Sadat had a perfect French passport and had used that to apply online while in London for an electronic travel authorization (eTA) to visit Canada, which had cost her a whopping seven Canadian dollars. It was almost as easy as the absurdly porous border crossings of the European Union, which had made smuggling weapons, drugs, and terrorists so easy that it was hardly fun anymore, thank you very much.

From Montreal she'd flown into Winnipeg, waited until evening, rented a Ford Escape, and started driving south on 75 toward St. Jean Baptiste, which was only an hour, then eastward on the 201 toward Menisino and Piney, another hour. At around 10:30 P.M. she'd driven the car into the Lost River State Forest, off the slim road into a shallow ravine, and had covered it up with fir fronds.

Then she took her backpack and hiked due south for five miles. It was early autumn in America's north country and freezing cold, but she didn't mind and was dressed for "hunting," in tight flattering jeans, SOREL hiking boots, a fur-collared purple North Face jacket, and a matching embroidered woolen ski hat with fluffy pompoms. Still on the Canadian side of the border just west of Route 89, she lay down in the tall wet grass, pulled a pair of binoculars from her pack, and trained them north on the highway, until she spotted some truck traffic heading her way. Then she dashed across the border, which was nothing but a small silver obelisk with US and CA stamped on opposite sides, kept walking south for another mile until she estimated that the trucks had gone through the customs check, jogged to the highway's shoulder, and stuck out her thumb.

The first truck driver probably thought that

this beautiful redheaded woman in the middle of nowhere was an apparition brought on by his beer consumption at the previous truck stop. The second driver screeched to a stop. She spent four hours on the road with him, and left him alive. He had no idea how lucky he was.

Lila bought a fireplug-red 2008 Toyota Camry hybrid, for cash, from a private seller on Craigslist, in Thief River Falls. Then she drove to Nashville, stopping only in Minneapolis to meet a Somali American contact who fulfilled her prepaid order for weapons. She slept in no hotels en route, only in the car, and got excellent mileage.

She found Stalker Two, Martin Farro, after reconning Nashville's music strip on Broadway for three nights, while staying during daylight hours in a cash-friendly Motel 6 out on Route 24, and only leaving once to do some targeted clothes shopping. She had enough intel on Farro to know where he lived, but she wasn't going to stake out his condo. Just like herself, Alphas were never really "on leave," and Farro would sense a tail in an instant. It wasn't necessary. She'd studied his photographs and nocturnal habits. He was a big, handsome man with thick, dark hair, blue eyes, and horn-rimmed glasses who looked like a Latino film star and cruised the blues venues. Even among the throngs of good-looking cowboys in Nashville, he'd be hard to miss.

Lower Broadway was teeming with honky-tonks, bars, clubs, restaurants, and live music joints of all scales, the avenue's sidewalks stained with spilled beers and vibrating with the echoes of boot heels and battling bands. Tin Roof was one of the most popular, and largest, with two floors of performance stages, wood plank dance floors, long chestnut bars, twirling disco balls, swinging pin spotlights, and effervescent inebriated line dancers. The prettiest rockabilly aficionados of both sexes packed into Tin Roof every night, and rarely went home lonely.

On the third night, just after 1:00 A.M., Lila spotted Farro perched at the bar near the back of the main floor, on the left as you walked in from Broadway. She cruised by him once, then again to make sure, and slid up onto a stool around the bar's back bend to make sure he could see her.

He was dressed in a dark blue rough plaid shirt, black chest curls showing through the open collar, jeans, and Justin cowboy boots. The glasses gave him away. She was dressed in a black halter top, her long red tresses turned into waves by a curling iron, a very small green sequined skirt, and Tony Lama snakeskin boots. Her wrists jangled with Native American bracelets. Farro wasn't going to miss her either.

She ordered a Scotch on the rocks from an admiring bartender (Tin Roof had a reputation for the friendliest barkeeps in town), and she didn't look at Farro but only at the dance floor. It was packed with bodies twirling and swirling to the live band onstage, Danny Schimmel and the Wicked Greens. Schimmel had a full row of stacked, glistening, green electric guitars behind him, like rifles in an armory rack, and was shredding a Joe Bonamassa tune called "This Train."

There were two couples seated at the bar between Farro and Lila, but with the way Danny Schimmel was driving that tune to an ever-climbing wild crescendo, they weren't going to be there long.

"This train, don't stop for no one. . . . This train, got a mind of its own. . . ."

The couples got up and hit the dance floor, leaving nothing but empty space between Farro and Lila.

He'd already assessed her, from the moment she'd walked in the door. She looked like a classic honey trap, but he'd just gotten an encrypted flash text on his cell from Cutlass telling him that that murderous Alpha-hunting bitch was dead, which was why he'd finally left the house.

> Cutlass Main II to all Alphas: Be advised, current priority female hunt subject—terminated—Black Forest, German Bundeskriminalamt, positive ID—Confidence Level III. End.

The thought did flash through Martin Farro's mind, briefly, that this still might not be a good idea. Yet Main wouldn't have flashed him a message like that if the coast wasn't clear, plus the German BKA was brutally efficient, plus *he* was going to make the approach, not the other way around. Added to that logic were four beers and a high degree of lust.

He waved at her, smiled a Clark Gable smile when she looked his way, cocked his head at the floor, and crooked a thumb as invitation. She looked him over, slowly, as if she were sizing up a slab of ribs at a deli meat counter, and crooked a finger back at him, an invitation to slide over, which he did.

Lila leaned into Farro's ear and said—in a perfect

Texas accent she'd learned from studying hours of *Dallas* reruns—"You ain't my type, cowboy."

He pulled his head back, feigning hurt. "Not even for a dance?"

"Nope. Look at your hands." She almost had to shout above the music.

Farro lifted both large hands and looked at the backs of them.

"What's wrong with 'em?"

"No ring." Lila grinned. "I like it simple."

Farro laughed, nodded, and took a long swig of his Coors. "I can pretend I'm married for just one dance."

Lila pretended to think about that for a moment. She speared him with her cold green eyes and unabashedly looked down at his muscular thighs, then she downed half her Scotch, slipped her small black purse string over her neck, and climbed off her stool.

"One," she said as she took his elbow. "And it better be good."

"I'm Marty," he said.

"I'm Sheila," she said, "and I don't care."

They danced for ten minutes straight without stopping. Farro had never seen a gorgeous woman like her with such amazing moves. She twirled and spun and fell into his arms, then pulled away instantly and kicked a two-step as if he weren't there. Her body was like some kind of slithering electrified serpent, entwining him as she raked her breasts across his chest and was then dragging her fingernails down his back. She gripped his waist and seemed like she was leaning in for a kiss, but instead bucked back and ground her flat belly against his belt buckle, then laughed and spun away again.

With the crowd going crazy and not yet willing to retreat, as if it were the last dance at a wedding, Danny Schimmel circled back for an encore, and Lila wrapped her bare arms around Farro's muscled girth, arched on her boot tips, and practically slipped her tongue tip into his ear.

"I hear they got single bathrooms in this joint . . . and I ain't gotta pee."

He practically dragged her to the back of Tin Roof and down a slim stairway that led to a long hallway, painted in flat black and adorned with framed pictures of Dolly Parton, Willie Nelson, and the like, and with six separate non-gender-specific bathrooms.

Lila pulled him into the third bathroom, kicked the door closed, locked it, glanced at the window that led to the street and quickly assessed its size (workable), turned to Farro, and kissed him deeply and hard. She backed up against the porcelain sink counter, pulling him with her, her tongue deep in his mouth, and she slithered up onto the counter and opened her legs. Her short skirt rode up her thighs, and Farro, genuinely breathing hard, as opposed to her mock panting, saw a thong that was so tiny it looked like green dental floss.

As he backed up and started madly unbuckling his belt, Lila pulled her stiletto from her small purse, gripped the hilt with the razor-sharp point angled down, cranked her arm back, and, with the speed of a Nationals pitcher, stabbed him in the heart. The blade got partially jammed against a rib halfway through his chest wall, which wasn't unexpected, given his size, so she instantly made a fist with her left hand and hammered the pommel twice, and the point burst through his aorta.

The only sound Farro made was a hissing grunt, in time with his rolling-back eyeballs. He slumped straight down and toppled backward over his folded knees, as if he were doing the limbo, with a thin spray of blood pumping out from the blade wound in rhythmic bursts as Lila twisted it out.

She slid off the counter, straddled his face, flicked his glasses off with the bloody stiletto, gripped the top of his thick black hair, and sliced off his left ear. For a moment she thought about removing the right one as well, because something about the lack of symmetry bothered her, but she thought Dr. Goldwasser would have regarded that as "psychotic." Instead, she turned to the sink, rinsed off the ear, dried it with a paper towel, and added it to the collection in her purse.

She took Farro's cell phone, which she'd shortly be dumping in the Cumberland River, then she stepped over his corpse and unlocked the window, preparing her exit. But before she left, she took out the burner phone she'd purchased at Montreal's airport and called the night duty officer at 1600 Pennsylvania Avenue, Washington, D.C.

"White House. How may I help you?" said a sleepy female.

This time Lila didn't bother with a voice-altering device. She knew that in just a few days, everyone would know her name.

"You may help me by passing something to Mr. Theodore Lansky," she said.

"Um, the chief of staff isn't on the premises at this hour. May I ask who's calling, please?"

"You may not. Get yourself a pencil and tell me when you're ready."

She heard brief rustling, and then, "Go ahead, ma'am."

"Give Mr. Lansky this message," Lila said. "Your Program's stock value appears to be plummeting. Now you are only six."

ACT III

CHAPTER 34

THE WHITE HOUSE, WASHINGTON, D.C.

White House Chief of Staff Ted Lansky stormed into his West Wing office, picked up a two-pound crystal ashtray, slammed it onto his desk, and bellowed so loud that his windows rattled.

"Where in the *hell* is Eric Steele?"

It was actually a rhetorical question, because everyone there in the chief of staff's workspace knew that Steele had gone rogue on some private mission deep inside Russia and was still out of pocket. They also knew that Lansky's ashtray—which just like his pipe had been dead for years—was no more than a prop he used to scare the crap out of subordinates.

But that didn't mean he wasn't duly pissed. He pulled the old briar from his teeth, flipped it around, and jabbed it like a rapier across the room at Mike Pitts.

"Well, Pitts? It's one hell of a time for Batman to come late to the party, don't you think? You've got *another* Alpha down. That's the third one in ninety days, which is un-freaking-believable given the Defcon level on these operators, and your top dog's still out there on some goddamn personal quest?"

"He's had a few issues, sir," Pitts said. He was planted in the middle of Lansky's office, one hand gripping his camouflage-patterned cane and the other twirling one of his famous whiteboard markers. He was wearing chinos and a Notre Dame windbreaker.

"Issues?" Lansky bellowed, and he picked up the ashtray and slammed it again. "He hijacked a fucking Program airplane!"

Pitts didn't respond. It was Lansky who'd gone to the president and urged him to approve tasking Delta Force to Dalton Goodhill so they could go rescue Steele, an extremely dicey gambit that risked destroying thirty years of Cold War peace. In addition, that op came with a $2 million price tag right out of JSOC's black budget, and the president had probably told the chief of staff that until Steele was brought back safe and sound, it was Lansky's ass on the line.

Mike Pitts had a lot of respect for Ted Lansky, and watching the COS pace behind his desk and tear at his tie knot made him feel somewhat nauseated. But he'd learned from experience that the former CIA director of Clandestine Ops just needed to vent and would probably stomp around for a while before he cooled off. It was wiser to just stand still and shut up—Lansky had a reputation for making inanimate objects fly. Pitts had the fleeting thought that maybe a few broken artifacts might improve the decor.

The chief of staff's office was just plain ugly, and had probably been that way since Nixon and Haldeman. It was a large square space about twenty by twenty done up in muted hues of beige and brown, with sloppy brocade window curtains and a mishmash of furniture, including an elliptical mid-century coffee table, a long conference table right out of *Mad Men*, and fifteen 1960s-style dining room chairs. The couch and twin stuffed armchairs were a weird orange-and-cream chintz, the walls were adorned with crooked framed photos of heads-of-state handshakes, and the only impressive feature was Lansky's two-hundred-pound mahog any desk, which looked like a reject from Franklin Roosevelt.

And yet, this was the "war room," a hallowed spot where much of the real business of the executive branch of the United States was conducted. The president's Oval Office was plush, beautiful, decorative, and ceremonial. The chief of staff's office was where the sausages were made.

"And who's this motley crew?" Lansky demanded as he raked his chewed-up pipe stem across the room like a machine-gun barrel. Maybe he'd forgotten that he'd ordered the Program's staff and cell leaders over to his office for what he called a "slam conference," which meant there wouldn't be much conferring and they were all going to get slammed. There were five more people standing behind Pitts in a ragged semicircle, and each of them seemed to have selected a piece of furniture to place between themselves and Lansky, as if they might suddenly have to take cover.

"Betsy Roth, sir." The brave young blond woman spoke up first. It was drizzling outside and she was wearing a belted trench coat, and with her blue eyes blinking behind her chic round glasses she looked like a *Women's Wear Daily* spy. "I'm Mr. Pitts's adjutant."

"Ralph Persko, sir." Ralphy was tucked as far back in one corner as he could get. He was wearing a Nikola Tesla sweatshirt, one of his Alienware laptop cases was slung from his shoulder, and he was almost trembling. "Geek squad," he said, figuring that was the most accurate and succinct description for his team.

"Persko." Lansky dipped his bushy eyebrows and pointed at Ralphy. "You the one who shut down that Russian hacker cell? The bastards who burned out our systems over on Q Street?"

"Um, well, with some help, sir. . . . And I'm not sure they're out of—"

"How'd they do that, Persko?"

"I . . . We're not really sure yet, sir," Ralphy lied.

"Well, at least somebody's actually thinking around here. Happy Cold War two-point-oh, Persko." Lansky swiveled his head at Meg Harden. "And you, young lady. Harden, right?"

"Meg Harden, sir. Surveillance and collections." Meg, who'd come straight from a run when Pitts pinged her and was wearing black spandex leggings and a tae kwon do sweatshirt, was silently praying that Lansky had no idea about her personal relationship with Eric Steele, and that no one would bring it up in this forum. If it came out here, she was toast.

"You?" Lansky thrust his chin toward a rumpled slim man standing near the other far corner.

"Shane Wylie, sir."

"Wylie was Collins Austin's keeper," Pitts said to Lansky. "He's chief of that section."

"Oh." Lansky looked at Wylie and offered a small nod of condolence, then he resumed his gunfire and jabbed his pipe over at Miles Turner, the Program's chief of security. "You're Turner, aren't you? Security cell?"

"Yes, sir."

Miles Turner knew what was coming and hated his life at the moment. It didn't matter how often he briefed Alphas on risks or reminded them of security protocols. They were headstrong and wild, like surfers or skydivers, but for Marty Farro's death on American soil he knew he was going to take the hit. He was an African American the size of a linebacker and a former Special Forces officer with five tours downrange, yet at the moment he looked as sheepish as a kindergartener.

Lansky came out from behind his desk and advanced on Turner. His move made everyone flinch and take a step back, as if a rabid dog had just breached its own cage.

"What the *hell*, man? Don't you brief these Alphas when they're back at home? One minute they're overseas and got all their neck hairs and radars up, and then they come back here and start dancing around like they're at Chuck E. Cheese?"

Neither Lansky nor Turner knew about the flash message to Farro that had lured him from his condo, because it hadn't really come from Cutlass

Main. And his cell phone had been taken, along with his life.

"We've never had a hit, sir, or even an attempted one on U.S. soil." Turner had stiffened to his full height of six three and was standing at brace, as if getting his ass chewed by the commander of USASOC.

"You've had one *now*," Lansky boomed. "And maybe if you'd banged on these operators' thick skulls some more we wouldn't be putting them on ice every two fucking weeks." He turned back on Pitts. "And who've we got chasing down that crazy killer bitch?" Lansky glanced at Meg Harden and considered apologizing for his language, then skipped it.

Another man, who wasn't part of the Program's team, raised a hand from behind Lansky's ugly couch. He was tall and lanky, his red hair buzz-cut, and he was dressed in a dark suit, white shirt, and a club tie.

"FBI, sir," he said. "John Loughran, special agent in charge.

"Oh, freaking wonderful." Lansky's voice dripped disdain. "Farro's dead, the barn door's already closed, but the G-men are here. Hallelujah."

Agent Loughran's face flushed crimson.

"And where's Farro's keeper?"

"She's down in Nashville, sir," Pitts said, referring to Valerie Fontaine, the Program's only female handler.

"Good. Tell her to stay right there, and have his funeral service down there too. We're not doing the National Cathedral underground coven for this one. We'll bury him at Arlington afterward, but on the total QT, roger?"

There were nods and murmured *rogers* from around the room.

"All right, you people." Lansky walked back behind his desk, dropped his pipe in the ashtray, stuffed his hands in his suit trouser pockets, and looked down at his pile of paperwork. He seemed to sag for a moment, as if he was about to relay further bad news and was reluctant to do it. Then he looked up again. "This is where it's at. I want that Cutlass Main II disaster over at Q Street completely shut down. It's freaking useless now anyway, and until somebody can tell me, with a bona fide forensic report, the who, what, where, and why of what happened, it's to be treated like Ebola central. I'm sending over a security team from DIA and I want nothing and nobody over there. You're all on stand-down until we figure out what the hell's going on here. Are we clear?"

Lansky's "guests" nodded, and also sagged, mimicking his posture.

"And you, Loughran." He glared at the FBI SAC. "I want that goddamn stiletto woman. I want her caught, or killed, don't care which. And if you nab her alive, I want her at Guantanamo Bay, not some friggin' federal resort. You can shave her head like a French collaborator and build her a women's wing right next to all the crazy male jihadis down there if you have to, but I don't want some bleeding-heart limousine liberal Harvard lawyer getting her off. Understand me?"

The FBI agent said nothing. Lansky's order was supra-legal and everyone in the room knew it.

"And now, somebody tell me . . ." Lansky threw his hands up at the ceiling as if his last appeal was to God himself. "Where in the goddamn *hell* is Eric Steele?"

No one said anything for a moment. Then, with a nod from Pitts, Betsy Roth spoke up.

"He's en route from Helsinki, sir." She finger-curled a lock of her blond hair and blinked behind her glasses.

"*En route*," Lansky snorted. "And with Goodhill babysitting him, right?"

"Correct," Pitts said.

"Helsinki. Jesus. What'd they do, stop over for a sauna and some fresh herring? And I've seen that guy Goodhill in action, Pitts. He and Steele are two peas from the same damn pod. It's like sending a dirty cop to bust his own drug dealer kid. And where are those D-Boys now?"

"Back at Fort Bragg, sir," Turner said.

"Well thank Christ for that. I'm the one who talked the president into ordering them on that op, though I've got no idea why. Should have left Steele in freakin' Siberia."

"Goodhill will bring him back, sir," Shane Wylie said softly from his corner. He still looked sallow and broken from the death of Collins Austin, but he'd insisted on staying at work and felt the need to protect his professional brothers and sisters.

"If he doesn't, it's all of our asses. Now get the hell out of here."

They all nodded, shouldered their various laptops and satchels, and headed for the door as quickly and quietly as possible. Lansky started gathering his briefing files from his desk.

"You can all take some time off," he growled. "Might be for the rest of your lives. I'm gonna go see the boss."

And after they were gone and the door was closed, he mumbled to himself, "Maybe I can keep us all out of Leavenworth."

CHAPTER 35

THE OVAL OFFICE, WHITE HOUSE, WASHINGTON, D.C.

President of the United States John Rockford was an unkempt man. Nobody outside his family and closest circle of friends knew that, because his fashion model wife had been managing his public appearances for years. She selected his suits, shirt-and-tie combos, shoes, and golfwear, and had everything tailored to perfection. She watched his weight, kept him away from greasy fast foods, and got him some sunshine whenever possible. She checked his fingernails and gel-combed his wavy blond hair before every press gaggle.

But it wasn't neurotic or controlling behavior. Mrs. Rockford was stunning, charming, good-humored, and unflappable, and they laughed about her fussiness often and he never resisted. She simply didn't want her husband coming off like British Prime Minister Boris Johnson, who they both liked very much, but who always looked like he'd just stepped out of a NASA wind tunnel.

On this particular afternoon, Mrs. Rockford was away in Houston pursuing her efforts to raise child literacy and healthy interactive behavior—she despised smartphones and social media and thought they were the devil's playground. The president had managed to spruce himself up for an Oval Office meeting with the PM of Poland, but now that Morawiecki and his minions had left—along with the press throng that Rockford called the "leeches"—the commander in chief had shrugged off his suit jacket, yanked his tie open, and finger-mussed his hair like a little boy whose mommy wasn't there to scold him.

He was slouching back in the plush leather throne facing the Resolute desk once used by men so much greater than he was, men with revered names like Kennedy and Reagan, and while he tried to review a slew of proposed executive orders, once again he couldn't help but think of himself as an impostor. Truth be told—or so he believed—he was nothing more than an old armored infantry officer who, in accordance with the purest example of the Peter Principle, had risen to a position he sure as hell didn't deserve.

President Rockford's secretary, Fanny Maeford, poked her gray head in from her side office.

"Mr. President, the chief of staff would like to see you."

"Only if he brings us both coffee," Rockford said. "And he'd better know how I take it."

Fanny smiled and withdrew, and three minutes later, Ted Lansky walked in carrying two steaming mugs. One had the presidential seal embossed on it.

The other said OLD AGE AND CUNNING WILL ALWAYS DEFEAT YOUTH AND EXUBERANCE.

"Which one's for me, Ted?" The president stretched out a hand.

"The seal, sir. If I give you the other one, some press flack'll get a pic of you with it and claim you're a fascist dictator."

"They say that already. Have a seat."

Lansky dropped onto the president's couch, took a wincing sip of hot brew, then placed the cup on the coffee table and turned toward his boss. Rockford sipped some coffee but kept the steaming cup in his hands. It was always too cold for him in the White House. He still preferred the weather in Iraq, but unfortunately that part of his life was over. It felt strange missing the bombs and bullets, but it had been a much simpler existence.

"You're here about the Program, aren't you, Ted?" Rockford said. "I saw that close-hold flash from Nashville."

"Yes, sir."

"Okay. Give it to me straight, no chaser."

So, Lansky told him all of it, and it was hard for him. He'd never quite gotten over leaving CIA, and to him the Program was like a miniature version of Langley without all the bureaucratic and political bullshit.

"Well, sir, it seems like it all started when Stalker Seven took out that missile quartet in—"

Lansky stopped himself and looked around. Inside the Oval you never knew when the recorders were running, and he didn't want the president compromised later by anything they might say to-day. Rockford smiled like a Cheshire cat.

"Go ahead, Ted. On your recommendation, I had that old system ripped out last week 'cause there were too many fingers on the record button. Now it's on fail-safe. Only works with my thumbprint."

"Very good, sir. . . . So, that thing in Syria. Not long after that, we lost our first Alpha in Paris. Then there was another failed attempt in France on Stalker Seven, and then we lost another in Italy. Now we've had a third Alpha killed in Nashville. This is over the line now. The killer's penetrated our borders."

Rockford rubbed his jaw and thought about that.

"So, we've got a stalker who's stalking our stalk-ers," he said.

Lansky blinked. "Yes. You got it on the first haiku."

"Failed that in college English. Go on."

"Well, if you recall, you and I decided that having the Program here in the White House wasn't any longer a practical idea. It was fine before the digital age, when there'd be time to quash rumors, or get friends in the print media to pull back on leaks, but not anymore. We don't have a lot of friends in the media. So we moved Cutlass Main over to a location on Q Street, but I think we were breached during that move."

"How so?"

"It opened a vulnerability. There's a window during such moves when you're in technical tran-sit. Main II was hacked, and I don't mean Tweety

Bird popping up on computers. A Russian cyber cell literally burned us down. They fried all the wires, hard drives, mechanicals, even set off the sprinkler systems and trashed the location. From freaking *Moscow*, sir."

The president was in the middle of sipping his black brew, but he put the mug down and stared at Lansky.

"Holy shit, Ted."

"Unholy shit, Mr. President. Our geek boys and girls executed a counterstrike, but the damage was done. Morale's in the toilet, all assets recalled to CONUS."

"And you think it's all related to that quartet thing you mentioned before?"

"I don't know for sure, nor do I think it matters. What we've got now is a female assassin out there targeting our Alphas. Steele was working that angle in France, got a partial ID on her in Paris, we followed up with Europol, and in turn they linked her to an apparently unrelated murder in Austria." Lansky paused for the next bit so the boss wouldn't miss it. "Sir, we think the woman is Lila Kalidi."

Something went dark on Rockford's face.

"You mean . . . *that* Kalidi?"

"Yes. Walid Kalidi's daughter."

The president pushed himself away from his grand desk and muttered, "When sorrows come, they come not single spies, but in battalions."

"Sir?"

"Shakespeare, Ted. *Hamlet.*" Rockford got up, turned, thrust his meaty hands in his trouser pockets, and stared out his bulletproof picture window.

"Ted, we might have to make this shutdown permanent. The Program had a great run, decades in fact, but there are too many eyes on us now. Leaking's no longer an acceptable risk. It's a culture. And it's not about me personally. It's about protecting the office of the president."

"All right, sir. But what about the personnel? Will they be protected too?"

"I'll cover their butts for anything that comes up, don't worry. They're national heroes, every one of them." He turned back from the window. "Where's Eric Steele now?"

"He's on his way back from Helsinki, sir."

"Well, I'm glad. I green-lit Delta for that mission because I knew that's what Denton Cole would have done. But to be honest? Disobeying directives, strong-arming a flight crew, going off half-cocked like that for personal reasons? Steele's one true patriot, but I think that young man's burned out. Program or not, we might have to let him go. Can't have that sort of thing."

"Understood, sir." Lansky picked up his coffee mug and slunk back on the couch, as if his next comment was going to be offhanded. "But, if I may remind the president . . . I seem to recall that once, long ago in Iraq, might have been Desert Storm, a young armor commander disobeyed orders to save the life of a brother he loved, and wound up getting the Distinguished Service Cross. . . . Just sayin'."

Rockford actually flushed, but it was matched by his grin.

"Okay, Lansky, shut up."

Lansky shrugged and returned an innocent smile.

The president looked at his watch, a moderately priced Shinola.

"Speaker of the House is going to be here in fifteen minutes to flay off some more of my skin," the president said. "So, last piece of business, which I hate to bring up. Denton Cole's about to run out of road. Where are we on that, Ted?"

"You mean the state funeral, sir?"

"Ghoulish, but yes."

"I've pulled in Protocol and they're quietly working on it, though nothing about it's a secret. All the papers have been tweaking Cole's obit for a year. He'll lie in state in the Capitol for two days, then we'll have the National Cathedral service. State's already making preliminary arrangements for foreign heads of state. It's going to be huge, and a security nightmare, but it's nobody's first rodeo. We'll get it done right. The only thing we can't control is the timing."

"That's right, Ted." The president sighed. "Only God or the devil can do that."

CHAPTER 36

INTERSTATE 395, VIRGINIA

Mike Pitts drove south out of Washington, D.C., on 395, heading toward Springfield and pleased at least that he'd made his escape before rush hour. Over the past decade the capital's population had bloated out of control and the web of highways that ringed the city was now known as the "circle of hell." If you lived outside, as he did, in some decent place like Lincolnia, you had to get up at the ass crack of dawn to avoid a two-hour inbound crush. And leaving work, if you weren't hitting the gas pedal before three-thirty, the chances of making it home for dinner were only fifty-fifty.

Pitts had a restored classic Ford Woody station wagon, circa 1969. He liked driving it because it reminded him of the simpler days his dad had always told him about, when the country's worst internecine squabbles consisted of hippies protesting the Vietnam War and grizzly curmudgeons telling them all to get haircuts. He also liked the old brown beast because it was slow, and sometimes, like this afternoon, he didn't really want to get where he was going.

The only comforting thought was that it looked like the Program was fading away, which meant he would soon be unemployed, but he'd also be released from a nightmare.

The past year had been nothing short of that. Katherine was pregnant again, the twins had turned eight and were rebelling against Mommy, just like most little girls, except that their mischief was doubled. His working hours had increased, along with the mortgage, while the federal employee cost-of-living raises had stalled because both parties in Congress were focused only on hurling bombs across the aisle.

The Program had had some major successes, mostly due to Alphas like Eric Steele, but then there were the losses of operators like Jonathan Raines, Collins Austin, and now Martin Farro, God rest their souls. The body count was piling up, and Cutlass Main had been turned into a Dumpster fire, and he shouldered the responsibility for all of that. He was a man between a rock and many hard places, had a raging ulcer that no one knew about—including his wife—and frequently vomited in the bathroom before heading off to work.

Pitts had joined the army fresh out of community college, more than two decades prior. He'd served in the U.S. Army's 1st Infantry Division, the glorious "Big Red One," and had led young men and women in combat on multiple deployments to Iraq. He'd lost his leg to an Iranian manufactured

VBIED (Vehicle Borne Improvised Explosive Device) in the waning days of the Iraqi "strategic withdrawal," and had still risen to the rank of major after refusing a medical discharge and fighting like a pit bull for a waiver.

He'd only left the army because the guy in the bed next to his at the military hospital in Landstuhl, Germany, turned out to be some shot-up spook who later recommended him for a deep black project called "the Program." They were looking to fill a slot in ops leadership, but it had to be someone who wouldn't always be itching to get back into action. They thought it might even be wise to tag some hard-charging combat vet officer who had physical limitations.

That was Pitts. He was a natural leader, yet his action days were over. He was tough, but practical. He was disciplined, punctual, and precise. He was relentless when it came to accomplishing the mission. He was the perfect Program ops manager.

And now he was broken.

Traffic was flowing smoothly about twenty-five miles south of Washington as he passed the signs for Manassas, where the first major clash of the Civil War had been fought in July of 1861. At the Battle of Bull Run, more than thirty-five thousand blues and grays had soaked the rolling summer fields with their own blood, portending years of ugly things to come. Pitts was an avid student of that historical period, and fervently wished that every congressman and senator could be time-traveled back to that bloodfest whenever they called for each other's demise.

He got off the exit at Potomac Mills, swung around onto Opitz Boulevard, and crossed back under the highway, heading for the Potomac Community Library. He'd never been there before, but these dead drops were always similar and were standard tradecraft in the intelligence game. Someone wanted to meet with you on the down-low. Maybe they had treasure, or maybe just dust, but you could never just say no. In the course of a decade with the Program, he'd gone to such clandestine meetings about once a year. You loaded your handgun, got in your car, made sure your life insurance was paid up, and prayed that it wasn't a setup.

He'd gotten a cryptic text on his burner cell with a time, a place, one additional word, and nothing more. In the black ops business that wasn't unusual procedure, nor would the incoming text raise any red flags for the Program's monitors, who were always checking everyone's comms. For today's drop, the location was a library, and the additional word was the name of an author. It was someone the kids weren't reading these days, when they read at all, so the volumes probably wouldn't be checked out. Besides, Pitts guessed that the drop would be made less than ten minutes before he got there.

He parked the Woody, took his cane, made sure his Glock 42 was properly concealed under his windbreaker, and stalked into the library. He made straight for classical fiction, where under Alexandre Dumas there was only one hardcover book, *The Three Musketeers.* He opened the front flap and found a typewritten note inside.

Fridays. Fredericksburg. 1930 hours. Marwan.
Last booth by the kitchen.

He replaced the book on the shelf and stalked back out, chewing on the note like a wad of gum.

It was dark and chilly when he parked the Woody again down in Fredericksburg, after another long hour and a half in traffic on I-95. He pulled the Glock from his waist holster, press-checked it to make sure it was ready to rock, tucked it back in, and got out of the wagon. He sensed this would be the end of the line. It wasn't a treasure hunt with a secondary drop. He didn't know Marwan, but he expected to find him.

He walked in the glass front entrance, past the college-age hostess in her Fridays red-and-white tunic, and headed straight to the rear through the tunnel of dark wooden decor, because he could see the gleam of aluminum sinks and the steam from the kitchen back there. Up to the right on a raised platform was the bar, then below that and closer, a row of dark booths, and to the left were tables. It was dinnertime and noisy. He didn't much care for Fridays anymore. He thought they were using too many prepackaged frozen entrées.

In the last booth on the right, a dark, curly-headed young man was sitting there facing Pitts and the door. He looked like that terrorist kid, Dzhokhar Tsarnaev, who'd blown up so many innocent people at the Boston Marathon back in 2013. But, of course, it wasn't him, because that little shit was still on death row. Pitts stopped, looked down, and said, "Marwan."

The kid looked up and nodded. He was nursing a Stella, which told Pitts that he either wasn't a devout Muslim, or that he was, but operating on what the Program called "infidel license," which meant that you could drink alcohol and bang whores just like the infidels did as long as you were going to kill them. Pitts slipped into the booth. He didn't like having his back to the door, but there wasn't another option here.

"Can I see your ID, please, Mr. Pitts?" Marwan had an accent—Egyptian or Palestinian.

Pitts pulled out his wallet and showed Marwan his U.S. government ID. It didn't say "Program" on it, but it had his photo, full name, a meaningless Washington, D.C., address, and a bar code strip.

Marwan leaned forward and peered at the card. Then he slid out of the booth, turned, walked ten feet into the kitchen entrance, then right out the back through a cloud of steam. For a moment Pitts thought that something had spooked the kid and this whole thing was over. But then, someone came from behind his left shoulder and slid into the booth, taking Marwan's place.

It was a woman.

A very beautiful woman.

It was Lila Kalidi.

CHAPTER 37

FREDERICKSBURG, VIRGINIA

Pitts froze like a man who'd been dipped in liquid hydrogen. He stared at the young woman, his breathing labored and coming in shallow drafts, as if the ghost of one of his combat-fallen brothers had just joined him for dinner. He'd never met her before, nor had he expected to meet her here and now, or anywhere else in his life. Yet he was as sure about this as he was about his blown-off leg and the phantom pain below his left knee. She didn't need to introduce herself.

She had long blond hair and dark blue eyes, the first most likely from a bottle, the latter probably from contact lenses. She had very full lips, glossed in pale pink, and a Marilyn Monroe mole, probably phony, near the right corner of her closed smiling mouth. A pair of bespoke sunglasses were perched in her coif, and she was wearing a belted, black leather waist-length coat over a short black skirt. Her skin tones didn't quite match her blond hair or eyebrows, because she was olive-complexioned, but her features perfectly matched the images sent over from Vienna by Cobra.

She put her elbows on the table, steepled her long manicured fingers, and perched her chin on them like a severed head on a pike.

"I know what you're thinking, Mr. Pitts," she said in a near-perfect American accent. "I watched you come in, and that Glock of yours prints through your nylon jacket. You'd do better wearing leather, like mine. But, if you use your pistol, you know exactly what will happen next." She cocked her head slightly to the left. "Don't you?"

Oh, he knew all right. The voice of some Russian motherfucker had been reminding him about it for a year. He had no idea how they'd found him, nailed him, tracked him, discovered where he worked and for whom. But they knew all about his personal life, his family, and that his wife and his girls were his Achilles heel.

They'd played him, used him, churned his guts inside out. At one point he'd almost turned himself in, hoping the FBI would put him and the girls into some sort of program like witness protection, make them all disappear. Then he'd realized that no one could ever make him completely anonymous. He had only one leg. Sure, there were thousands of war amputees, but that was easy to narrow down. A guy his particular size, with a prosthesis, a wife and soon-to-be three daughters of certain ages, two of them twins?

Checkmate. Dead. All of them.

He cleared his throat and said, "Maybe I'll just take that chance," and his right hand slid from the table.

Lila nodded, leaned back, and slipped a cell phone from her jacket pocket. She turned it toward Pitts and propped it up on the table with her fingernails at the top.

On the screen was an image of Mike Pitts's kitchen, a live color video feed from his own household security camera.

Leaning on the kitchen's cooking island, in the foreground, was a dark-haired man wearing a Dominion Virginia Power overall, the uniform of Lincolnia's electricity supplier. His dark eyes were turned toward the camera and his fingers were tapping on a large handgun lying on its side on the island.

Beyond that, Pitts could see Katherine seated at the kitchen table, along with Bridget and Caroline, who seemed oblivious to any mortal danger and were spooning mac and cheese into their chattering mouths, while Katherine tried to keep them occupied. Beyond them was another overall-clad man leaning against the doorjamb that led to the living room. He had a large cardboard tube tucked under one arm with the butt of a sawed-off shotgun protruding from its open end. He smiled and waved at the camera.

"Go right ahead," Lila said to Pitts.

His trembling hand returned to the tabletop, and Lila pocketed the phone as a waitress appeared to drop off menus and take their drink order.

"I'll have a Spanish Negroni on the rocks," Lila said.

"Water," Pitts barely whispered.

"Okie," the waitress said and left.

Lila examined Pitts's ashen face with all the pity of an ISIS throat-cutter. She tapped her glossy pink fingernails on the table.

"I have some good news for you, Mr. Pitts," she said. "Your work is almost done."

"How the hell did you get into the States?" he said. He desperately wanted to kill her.

"That would be telling. And I might have to do it again," she said. "But I must say your country is as easy to penetrate as a Bangkok whore." She cocked her head to the right this time. "Have you ever had a Bangkok whore, Mr. Pitts? I have. They squeal, which seems to be common among Asian girls."

The waitress returned with their drink glasses. "You folks ready to order?"

"We haven't looked at our menus yet," Lila said, and the beatific smile she offered the waitress so utterly transformed her face that Pitts felt a grim reaper chill running up his one good leg and into his spine. "We're having a little spat." Lila shrugged.

The waitress examined both of them as if calculating why this gorgeous hot thing would be with this middle-aged buzz-cut type. "Okay, maybe later." She looked at Pitts. "Sure you don't want a drink, sir?"

"Mike's driving tonight," Lila said, and she reached across the table and dragged her fingernails across the back of his hand. "And he can't hold his liquor."

The waitress grinned, cracked her chewing gum, and walked away.

"What do you mean, done?" Pitts said as he downed half his water.

"I mean, almost finished, Mr. Pitts. Just one more task."

"Well what the fuck is it?" His face flushed an angry pink. He despised being used like this—helpless, impotent, enraged.

"It's a termination. But it's more of a timing issue than an actual kill."

"You're out of your fucking mind."

Lila sat back, sipped her Negroni, and smiled like a lizard. "My psychiatrist suggested the same thing. In the end, I think he regretted it."

"Well, he was right," Pitts snarled. "You're one crazy bitch, and so are your Russian boy toys."

Lila's eyes went blank. Even behind her blue contacts, they suddenly looked as dull as a shark's. She put her drink down on the table and opened her legs. She slipped her right hand between them, unsheathed her stiletto from her right-thigh scabbard, and boldly showed the gleaming black blade to Pitts.

Beads of sweat popped on his brow just below his hairline. Lila stabbed the fat green olive that was floating in her Negroni, popped it into her mouth, wiped the blade with her napkin, and returned the stiletto to its sheath.

"I'm sorry," she said as she chewed demurely. "My hearing is a little bit off these days, despite my collection of extra ears. What did you say?"

He leaned forward, desperate. "How did you find me?"

"Meaning?"

"Why me? Why was I chosen? How was I selected?"

"Oh, that." She flicked a hand in the air. "It was a fluke, actually."

"A fluke?"

"You are a Catholic, aren't you, Mr. Pitts?"

"What the hell does that have to do with anything?"

"Well, you are, aren't you?"

"Okay so I'm Catholic, so what?"

"And you go to confession. Saint Michael's in Annandale, I believe."

Pitts said nothing. His heart was palpitating and his pulse was pounding in his ears.

"The FSB has planted so many bugs in confessional booths around the capital area that they can't even keep track anymore of all the spilled secrets," Lila said. "Much of what's recorded is salacious garbage, of course. Wives fucking pool boys, husbands fucking their daughters' cheerleader friends. But there's a fair share of federal employees who still trust their priests with dark tales that they wouldn't dare share with anyone else. Drone strikes on innocent Afghani villages. Drug smuggling operations to fund black budgets . . . Assassinations, Mr. Pitts?"

He thought he was going to pass out.

"I don't think they bother with synagogues or mosques. The Jews confess only to their mistresses, and we Muslims answer only to Allah. At any rate, it was only a matter of tailing you after that, discovering your residence and your place of employment. And you know the rest, don't you? I believe they sent you a picture of your daughters on a playground swing set, yes?"

He nodded, remembering how the next message

had said: "Play ball, Major, or bury your precious dead."

"So, the Russians contacted me, as a contractor," Lila went on. "At first I declined, until I realized that your so-called Program was responsible for my father's death. Then it became a labor of love, with substantial financial benefits."

"Why the hell are you telling me this?"

"You *asked.*" She snorted as if he were a fool. "And it's not as if you're going to share it. The consequences are obvious. Plus, I've almost got what I want."

"Which is?"

"Revenge. Destroying the legacies of all those who destroyed mine, including your Mr. Steele." She looked at her watch. "But I digress, and I really should be going." She raised a manicured finger. "Oh, I almost forgot. . . . Your one more thing."

He waited, grinding his teeth while she leaned forward, pressing her breasts on the table and lowering her voice.

"Your former commander in chief, Denton Cole. He's on his last legs, isn't he?"

Pitts just stared at her. He could smell her breath—cigarettes, liquor, and mint.

"I believe he is over at Green Bank," she continued. "Just a comfortable drive from here. He has descended into a coma. Organ failure, so I hear, and we're all just waiting for his final breath. Take a drive over there, Mr. Pitts. I know you have full access with your exceptional level of clearance. Visit him, please. Flick the switch on his life support. You'll be doing all of us such a favor. Pull the plug."

A bead of sweat slithered down from his left temple and dripped off his jaw.

"And what if I don't?"

"Then we shall be pulling the plug on *you*. Or more specifically, Katherine, your unborn child, and the girls."

She pulled a ten-dollar bill from her purse, tucked it under her empty drink glass, slid out from the booth, and leaned over and kissed him fully on the mouth. Then she walked out.

Pitts stayed in his seat for a minute, then staggered with his cane to the men's room, locked himself in a stall, and threw up.

CHAPTER 38

GREEN BANK MEDICAL FACILITY, WEST VIRGINIA

He arrived at the hospital just before midnight. The night was clear and cool and there hadn't been a rainstorm, nor the tornado he'd prayed for to blow him off the road. It was all smooth sailing toward hell.

At the Entry Control Point, there were two federal security officers, one older, one younger. They were wearing body armor, black woolen caps, and black uniforms, with M4 rifles slung from their necks and M9 pistols in thigh holsters. The younger one stepped out of the bulletproof booth. Pitts rolled down his window.

"Evening, sir," the officer said. "We're way past visiting hours."

Pitts handed over his Program ID card. There were pale rivulet streaks on his face. He'd been weeping.

"I'm not visiting." His smile trembled at the corners. "I'm briefing."

The officer flipped his card over and scanned the bar code with an infrared reader. The acronym "SAP" popped up in his window. It meant Special Access Program, which indicated a clearance considerably higher than top secret. With such an ID you could walk into any secure federal facility in the country, except for the underground nuclear missile launchers scattered across the western plains.

The officer returned the card as his older partner stepped from the booth.

"Nice car," said the elder. "My dad had one."

"Thanks," Pitts said. He was in no mood for automotive chitchat.

"May I ask who you're briefing, Mr. Pitts?" the younger one asked.

"The former president."

The two officers glanced at each other and back at Pitts.

"You know he's on life support, right, sir?" the older one said.

"I'm just doing what I was told. White House chief of staff's orders. Maybe he thinks President Cole can still hear." Pitts smiled wanly. "Call Lansky if you like, but you're going to wake him up."

They looked at each other again, thinking that one over.

"You carrying, sir?" the young one said.

"It's locked in my glove box."

It was true. The Glock 42 was secured in Pitts's glove compartment, but it almost hadn't made it there. Halfway to Green Bank, he'd pulled off the highway into a grassy copse and had sat there for a long time, with the loaded pistol in his white-knuckled fist, thinking it over.

He'd endured nearly a year of torment. At first it had been basic intel about the Program's structure and personnel, handed over at anonymous dead drops where he'd never met the recipient. But after the "Italian Job" in Syria they'd cranked up the heat, demanding Alpha IDs and their missions. And then they'd put that woman in play. She was sucking his blood like a vampire. He was helping her kill his own people. And now, *this.* He desperately wanted it over.

The only thing that had kept him from blowing his brains out at the side of the road was the absolute conviction that Lila Kalidi would then slaughter his wife and daughters, even if it was the last thing she accomplished on earth. She was that kind of horror.

He knew it.

She knew that he knew it.

She had a collection of ears to prove it.

"Okay, sir. Secret Service over there might want to pat you down."

"Wouldn't be my first time," Pitts said.

"You can park over by their Suburban," the older one said.

"Thanks, gents."

He parked the Woody and an agent got out of the black armored vehicle. He didn't have the usual sharp look about him, probably because his detail was protecting a principal who was already on his deathbed. Pitts exited the wagon.

"Evening, sir. Are you armed?"

"Negative. My piece is locked in the car."

"Okay, they're gonna put you through the magnetometer over there." The agent pointed at the hospital entrance.

Pitts nodded and walked toward it, muttering, "Can it beam me to another fucking planet?"

"Excuse me, sir?" the agent called after him.

Pitts waved over his shoulder. There were another two officers monitoring the magnetometer. He dropped his car keys in a tray, handed his cane to one of them, and went through. His prosthetic leg rang all the bells and whistles, but the men had his cane, had looked it over, and were respectful of his loss and handed it back to him like a cherished sword.

He checked in at the desk, surrendered his two cell phones, took a ticket, asked the whereabouts of the presidential suite, and stalked toward the elevator.

His one shoe with the living foot inside it felt like a twenty-pound dumbbell.

His other shoe was a ghost.

Two stories down, at the end of a long silent hallway, he saw another Service agent sitting outside a pair of mahogany double doors in a chair with a desktop that looked like something from his elementary school days. The agent was primly suited and reading a book. Pitts stalked toward him, the agent stood up, and he handed him his Program ID card.

"Evening," Pitts said. "They ran it at the ECP, but feel free to call up there."

The tall agent examined the card, both sides, and frowned.

"Haven't seen one like this, sir. But you wouldn't be down here if they hadn't cleared you upstairs." He handed it back. "Not a lot of harm you can do here anyways."

"I know," Pitts said. "Sad way to end things."

"Sure is. I was on the president's detail when he was solid. Now he's on a ventilator. Can't even breathe on his own."

"Well," Pitts said, "I was supposed to relay a message."

"Doubt he'll even hear you, sir, but you can try."

"Where's the First Lady?"

"Sleeping in the bedroom suite. She's all tuckered out these days. Turns in early."

"Okay." Pitts patted the large man's arm. "I won't be long. It's sort of private."

"Take your time."

The young agent opened one of the tall wooden doors for Pitts, then closed it behind him after he limped inside. The main room was very large, with a sofa and comfortable chairs, and the president's Stryker hospital bed and life-support machines were tucked into one far corner. The space was illuminated only by one table lamp with a low-watt yellow bulb and the seepage of light from the headboard monitors. Pitts glanced up at the room corners, searching for surveillance cameras, but saw nothing.

It didn't matter anyway. None of this would take very long. Half of him wanted to be caught and stopped. The other half knew that even if sirens went off, he'd do what he had to do before they dragged him away. He felt nauseated and weak, but he took a long breath and closed in.

The president's face looked blue. His wrists were tied down to the bed so he wouldn't jerk any tubes out, and a light purple blanket was pulled up almost to his throat. A white flex intubation tube, about half an inch wide, ran from a mechanical ventilation machine into his slack lips, where its plastic collar was taped to the skin of his face. His eyes were closed. His once-full gray hair looked like the cobwebs you'd find in an old basement closet. The machine, which had three levels of pressure and gas graphs peaking and dropping on its monitor face, sounded like a very relaxed scuba diver.

In, and out . . . Long pause . . . In, and out . . .

Pitts looked at the door to the bedroom suite. He'd met Mrs. Cole a couple of times. He prayed she wouldn't wake up and come out, and then he prayed for himself and for President Cole, and for Katherine and the girls. He asked forgiveness from Christ. He begged the Lord to consider this as euthanasia, rather than murder.

He reached over and switched off the ventilator. The scuba sound stopped.

Then he held his breath, half expecting the sudden lack of rhythmic sound to alert the agent outside. But nothing happened. Maybe the kid was taking a walk, or he really couldn't hear much through the heavy wooden doors.

President Cole's cancer-wizened body twitched. His lungs, which were no longer functioning on their own, tried to expand but only stuttered like an old jalopy on a freezing January morning in Montana.

Pitts had been born in Montana. He wished he was there. He wished he was anywhere but in this room. He wished he was dying, instead of Cole.

The president's back arched up once, only half an inch, and then all of him slumped and he lay still. Pitts waited another full minute, counting the seconds in his head, and then one more just to be sure. He reached out and touched the president's wrist. Nothing. No pulse. He waited one more full minute, which made a total of three, the amount of time a man of a certain age would never recover from, after oxygen deprivation to his brain.

He stared at the president's chest. Not a twitch. He turned the ventilator back on. It had no effect and the monitor graphs were all flatlined. The machine emitted a single long tone like the old TVs used to do at the end of the broadcast day.

Pitts crossed himself, turned, and slowly stalked back to the suite's entrance door. He stepped out into the hall, where the Secret Service agent was just sliding back into his seat. He was eating a Twinkie from a vending machine. Pitts looked down at him and sighed.

"I think he's just taken his last breath," he said. "You might want to get someone down here."

CHAPTER 39

WASHINGTON REAGAN NATIONAL AIRPORT

Steele and Goodhill's Finnair flight from Helsinki landed later than expected. They'd had to fly commercial because the Program air crews refused to have Steele aboard again, at least until they were assured that his hijacking days were over.

After the op in Russia, Allie had flown them and the D-Boys back to Split, Croatia, where the Deltas had changed into matching hockey outfits, stowed their combat gear in sports duffels, walked across the tarmac to a waiting charter, and were gone within fifteen minutes. Goodhill had given his gear bag to the Delta first sergeant and asked him to deliver it to the Program team room at Langley AFB.

Also in that duffel was Hank Steele's .45, which Goodhill had recovered from Major Petrov's corpse. Steele was so grateful to Goodhill that he found himself unable to thank him. Blade never mentioned it again.

From Split, the duo had boarded an Austrian Airlines flight to Helsinki and had gone to a Program safehouse, where a contract physician looked Steele over. The doc stitched up his temple wound, iced his bruises, and fitted him for a temporary knee brace. Then, they'd actually done the very things that Ted Lansky had railed about in his office—gone to a spa and sauna to "cool off" and had some decent Finnish meals, including herring. They'd also talked about Eric's father.

When they came through the gate at Reagan, CNN was on the first TV monitor they saw. Passengers were standing around watching, and the mood at the gate was somber and quiet. Anderson Cooper was talking about the death of former president Denton Cole, his upcoming lying in state at the Capitol, and the follow-on funeral service to be held three days hence at the National Cathedral.

Steele just stood there with his hands in his jeans pockets and watched. Goodhill looked up at Cooper and muttered, "Dude looks like Max Headroom."

"Who's that?" Steele asked.

"Never mind," Goodhill said. "You're too young."

Ralphy Persko was waiting for them at the end of the terminal hallway. He fell into step beside Steele and Goodhill, said nothing about Steele's limp or stitched-up face, and they walked toward baggage claim and the exit. Goodhill was slinging only a backpack and Steele had nothing on him.

"The TSA let you come greet us?" Steele said.

"Yeah, but they saw my ID card and frisked my privates," Ralphy said. "I think I've still got a wedgie."

Steele had pinged Ralphy from the airplane while still over the Atlantic. He wanted to hear what he'd discovered about the cyberattack on Cutlass Main II, but Ralphy had to tell him instead about the killing of Martin Farro. Steele went cold silent and told him the rest could wait until he arrived.

"Okay, Ralphy, so whatcha got on that Cutlass event?"

"Moscow cell," Ralphy said. "We took care of those dudes, but I still think they had an insider."

"Tell me more."

"I think somebody used a dongle." Ralphy meant a small computer thumb drive that could be used to inject lines of malicious code, which was why USB drives were absolutely verboten around DoD computers of any sort. "Could have been something as small as the remote for a mouse, or maybe a network booster."

"Let me know when you guys decide to speak English again," Goodhill growled.

Steele and Persko ignored him.

"Any idea who?" Steele said.

"Not a freakin' clue. I backtracked the codes to the caviar dudes, which is how we counterpenetrated and fried 'em, but I got no fingerprint on who physically dropped it. It only takes a few seconds to do it. In and out, and it's back in your pocket."

"Or purse."

"Yeah." Ralphy looked at Steele and wondered who he was thinking about. "If you wanna be an equal-opportunity paranoid, like me."

"Any word on Marty's last date?" Steele's question came through clenched teeth.

"Well, trickle-down intel is Europol pegged her as a PIJ gun for hire, Lila Kalidi."

"Doesn't ring a bell," Steele said. "But I'd like to ring hers."

They reached the luggage carousels where groups of passengers were standing around waiting for their bags, and since they hadn't checked anything, they headed straight for the exit doors. Then Steele slowed, and stopped. There was a large young man in a suit, ex-Ranger type, standing there with an iPad like a limousine driver. The name in all caps on the iPad display was GRACELAND IMPORT EXPORTS.

Steele walked over to him, with Goodhill and Persko trailing close behind.

"Who you here for?" he asked the big buff kid.

"Max Sands, sir."

"That might be me. Show me something."

The ex-Ranger type slipped a badge carrier from his suit and showed Steele Secret Service credentials.

"Who's your boss?" Steele said.

"Director Murray."

"He's in my cell phone contacts. I can call him."

"Feel free, sir."

"Okay," Steele said. "Where we going?"

The agent looked at Goodhill and Persko, then back at Steele.

"Not them, sir. Just you."

Steele didn't say much as the agent took him on an evening ride in a black BMW X1 SAV. He was bone-tired and thinking mostly about Russia and Helsinki, the things Petrov had confessed, and what Goodhill had told him about working with his father long ago in Mogadishu. The unfinished puzzle that remained his past still had many pieces missing, but he'd never dreamed that this man called Blade, who'd just saved his life, would also be the one to supply a few more amoeba-like shapes. Going forward, no matter what happened between him and Goodhill, he owed him and knew that from now on he'd trust him.

The big guy, who barely fit in the driver's seat, drove the car through Crystal City, into the Hilton's underground parking garage, out the other side, and then wove through the small streets of Aurora Highlands, checking his rearview for tails as he conducted a countersurveillance routine. Then he headed due west through Arlington Ridge, cut south for a while, circled around heading back north, and Steele realized they were entering the grounds of the Army Navy Country Club. They skipped the main entrance and stayed on the long main drive that cut through the golf course.

"This is you, sir," the agent said as he pulled over in the dark under the trees.

Steele looked out his passenger window. There was a single park bench planted in the shadow of a large willow tree. Ted Lansky was sitting there in a trench coat, chewing on his dead pipe and reading the *Washington Post* by the light of an old-fashioned streetlamp.

Steele got out and the BMW coasted away. Lansky slid over on the bench and patted the slats next to him. Steele sat down.

"Evening, sir," he said.

"Evening, Steele." Lansky looked at his stitched-up face. "Have a nice vacation?"

"I'd apologize for it, sir, but it's not in me."

"You don't have to." Lansky folded the newspaper. Steele saw the headline: FINAL JOURNEY OF A PATRIOT. "President Cole kicked you off on that questionable quest, God rest his soul."

"How'd you know that, sir?"

"Mrs. Cole told me." Lansky pulled his pipe from his teeth and looked at the bowl as if wondering why there was no tobacco. "She also said her husband wanted you protected from any consequences."

"I guess I've got friends in low places."

"More than you know. President Rockford personally called JSOC to get you extracted, after Goodhill practically begged me. I would have let you burn."

Steele knew that was a lie. Rockford wouldn't have done it if Lansky hadn't lobbied hard.

"Well, thank you anyway."

"The funeral's being held at the National Cathedral, but you won't be able to attend. Nobody from the Program can. Too much media and too many spooks. Germans, Brits, French, Israelis, even the Russians. Heads of state. Everybody but the designated survivor."

"Who's that going to be, sir?"

"Speaker of the House, which seems fair, 'cause Cole didn't like her."

"Who does?"

"Her grandbabies, I guess."

"Well, sir, understood." Steele sighed. "Would you please thank President Rockford for me?"

Lansky tilted his head back and looked over Steele's shoulder.

"You can do that yourself."

Steele turned to see headlights approaching on the access road from the north. Then he heard the throaty rumble of motorcycles and heavy vehicles. Four leather-clad cops on Harleys cruised by, then two heavily armored black Suburbans. Then they slowed, and the president's twenty-thousand-pound Cadillac limousine, otherwise known as "the Beast," cruised to a stop right there in front of the bench.

Four Secret Service agents appeared from the Suburbans and one strode to the Beast's rear passenger door. He scanned his surroundings, opened the door, looked over at Steele, and cocked his head. Steele got up and walked to the limo.

"You carrying?" the agent asked him.

"No."

President Rockford leaned over from the far side of the rear seat. He was wearing a tuxedo, and his blond hair gleamed under a dome light.

"Join me for a short chat, Steele," he said.

Steele slid into the seat and the Secret Service agent closed the door, but not all the way, so he could keep an eye on things.

"Good evening, Mr. President," Steele said. The way he was dressed compared to the commander in chief made him feel like a pool boy at a royal wedding.

"Glad you made it, son," Rockford said.

"Thanks to you, sir."

Rockford waved his big hand. "It was Lansky. I would've let you burn."

Steele smiled.

"Listen, Eric. I know how Denton felt about you. I'm inclined the same way, but there isn't a lot I can do here. I'm putting the Program on ice, and since you're their top dog, I thought I should tell you myself."

Steele felt cold, like he'd swallowed a frozen baseball. He knew the Program was under assault, and that wasn't his fault, but he also thought that maybe this final decision was because of him and the things he'd done.

"And no," Rockford said, "this isn't because of you. You're part of an honorable heritage, a long line of patriots. This nation is grateful. Maybe we'll find you something else. But for now, take some time off."

"Yes, sir. I understand." Steele offered his hand, which the president took in his firm grasp. "Good luck and Godspeed, sir."

"And to you." The president smiled through his golf course tan. "Now get out of my car. I have to go pretend I care about a speech and a fund-raiser."

A minute later, Steele found himself standing there alone. Lansky was gone too, and the only sounds were the breeze in the trees and a gaggle of honking Canada geese, wandering around and leaving their crap on the greens.

He walked over to the country club's main building and caught an Uber home.

CHAPTER 40

NO ACKNOWLEDGED LOCATION

EYES ONLY

SAP (Alphas/Support-FLASH)

From: NOLO

To: All CONUS PAX

Subj: ICE

Source: Staff Ops/Duty Officer

Confidence: Level IV

IMMEDIATE, all CONUS PAX, emphasis those assigned Cutlass Main II, plus/or, mobile, home stations, air assets, ground assets: Program is on Immediate Cease Extremis (ICE). HQ will advise re: comms, developments, compensations, recalls to duty, reassigns. Nothing further.

STATUS: No change pending.

Operational window: Immediate Execute

Alpha response—None

CHAPTER 41

THE NATIONAL CATHEDRAL,
WASHINGTON, D.C.

There were fourteen tourists aboard the enormous steel elevator as it rose up from underground parking level two and hissed into the glass booth facing the National Cathedral.

Eight of them were an extended Chinese family, chattering and arming their digital Nikons and Canons. Three more were a pair of tall blond Swedes and their poster-child Aryan little girl. Two were an oversexed, giggling college couple hoping to find some hidden dark corner of a belfry in which to desecrate the convictions of their parents' faith. And the last was a nun dressed in full brown woolen vestments from head to foot, carrying a typewriter case.

The elevator doors slid open and they all spilled out into a beautiful, crisp, late-autumn day. The cathedral's spires were haloed in blinding spears of sunlight, and its gray stonework gleamed a near purple. The funeral of President Cole was still more than forty-eight hours away, but already the vast slate drive before the edifice was being cordoned off with wrought iron barriers by scores of National Park Service laborers, and District of Columbia cops were directing the placements of cable news vans and trying to keep producers and grips from irreparably trampling the manicured front lawns.

An advance detail of Secret Service agents—fit men and women in off-the-rack Macy's suits—was already scouring the grounds for points of egress and ingress for their American principals, and the agents of the Diplomatic Security Service were doing the same for their protectees, who would be all the attending foreign heads of state. Both sets of *pistoleros*—the first from the Treasury Department and the latter from the State Department—were deploying countersniper scouts with high-powered binoculars to scan the surrounding business buildings and apartments for potential assassins' perches.

Shortly, their team leaders would begin to argue over who had jurisdiction over what. All of these gunslingers underwent the exact same training at FLETC, the Federal Law Enforcement Training Center in Glynco, Georgia, yet the Secret Service pros regarded the DS agents as lesser mortals, and the DS agents thought the SS people were snobs.

The event of national mourning was drawing near, but the grounds, the magnificent apexes, belfries, and vaults, the overpriced café just outside on the south lawn, and the two well-stocked gift shops hadn't yet been closed down to tourists. That would only happen twenty-four hours later. So, in the meantime, the domestic and foreign visitors would enjoy their explorations of the lofty castle on a high knoll where kings prayed and presidents were eulogized, and they'd also get some great selfies with stone-faced bodyguards, grinning cops, and bomb-sniffing German shepherds.

The Chinese, the Swedes, and the hormonal college kids walked into the main visitors' entrance, followed by the nun. They all purchased their tickets from the two friendly young women at the semicircular kiosk, palmed their cathedral brochures, and got in line for a security check. Normally the cathedral had no such arrangement, but given the upcoming event, the D.C. police had set up a magnetometer.

When it was finally the nun's turn, she waddled toward the tall metal frame with her typewriter case. She was a tubby woman, perhaps in her thirties, though it was hard to tell. Her habit was a long, brown woolen tunic girded over her stomach rolls, then draped with a black scapular and an olive wood cross. Her cowl was a light gray collar and snug facial halo, topped by another black veil. Her face was pasty and pale, her full lips unglossed, and she wore a pair of large steel spectacles over her dull hazel eyes.

"Morning, Sister," said a stout female cop, one of three D.C. uniforms manning the checkpoint.

"Good morning, my dear." The nun smiled without showing her teeth.

"I'm sorry, but would you mind setting your case on the table?"

"I would not mind at all."

The cop opened the thick, rectangular, black

typewriter case. Its thin leather cover was peeling, and the machine inside was an ancient Olivetti.

"Well now, that's an old artifact, isn't it?" the cop commented.

"I am completing a thesis about Anglican architectural history," the nun said. She had a slight foreign accent, perhaps Italian.

"No computers for you, huh, Sister?" one of the male cops said and smiled.

"They are the devil's work." The corners of the nun's eyes crinkled, the cops grinned at her, and she lifted her vestments an inch off the floor and walked through the magnetometer without anything ringing. The cops closed her case and handed it back.

"There ya go, Sister," one of the male cops said. "Save a prayer for us."

"Oh, I shall," said the nun. "Have a blessed day."

She walked into the cathedral's main space, crossed herself, and proceeded with her case directly down the wide aisle between the long rows of fine, heavy wooden pews. As she approached the very last rows up front, which would be the first reserved for funeral dignitaries, cathedral workers were assembling a stage and a large podium, as well as seats for the choir and orchestra, under the guidance of a handsome young woman in a long black skirt and modest emerald blouse. The nun stopped and looked up at the woman.

"Good morning, my dear," she said. "Bless you and yours during this difficult time."

The woman turned and smiled down at her from the stage. "Thank you, Sister."

The nun turned slightly to the left and waved her

small hand toward the front rows of pews. Her fingernails were clipped to the skin and unmanicured.

"May I ask, is this where the president and his guests will be sitting?"

"Oh yes." The young woman gestured left and right at two towering marble columns the size of space rocket boosters. "They'll be right there in the first two rows, between those two columns."

"It is so terribly sad." The nun shook her cowled head and crossed herself again. "Bless them in their hour of need."

"We'll do our best to care for them," the woman said.

"God will care for them too." The nun smiled, but without her eyes.

She raised her face to the cathedral's high apse, then looked down past her scuffed wooden clogs at the floor, took her typewriter case, and headed for the far corner stairwell that led down to the underground chapels. Her heavy wooden clogs clicked on the marble staircase and echoed in the empty cavern, and at the bottom she encountered a uniformed Secret Service agent in a white shirt and leather jacket. She smiled and blessed him with an air-finger cross, and he touched the brim of his cap. She turned to the right and, silently counting her paces, walked along the corridor, turned left, and descended into the Chapel of St. Joseph of Arimathea. It was the same chapel from which Alpha operators were carried to their graves.

She spent fifteen minutes there, alone in the second row of old wooden chairs, hunching and praying before the chapel's dreary mural and a waist-high stone bier that served as a stand for coffins. Her fingers were intertwined on the chair back in front, and an observer might have thought that her hazel eyes were closed. But they were scanning the modest fixtures, the walls, and, most carefully, the ceiling, which formed the base plate of the main floor above.

At last she rose, took her case, waddled up the stairs and out the chapel's other side and into the cathedral's sumptuous underground gift shop, which was fifty feet long and filled with memorabilia, both touristic and pious. She paid cash for a large 3D puzzle of the National Cathedral, tucked the box under her arm, retraced her route through the dreary sunken Chapel of St. Joseph of Arimathea, headed back past the uniformed agent, all the way down the corridor, past the Bethlehem Chapel, and out the modest wooden exit door to the rear grounds of the holy site.

She found herself in an open courtyard of slate squares surrounded by further high stone buttresses, archways, and halls of stained glass. In the center was a fountain of rushing pure water spouting from what looked like a giant black metal rose and cascading down into an elliptical pool. Another pair of Secret Service agents were there, these in dark suits with obvious handgun bulges, alongside a uniformed K-9 D.C. cop with his bomb-sniffing beautiful beast, a black-and-caramel German shepherd on a tight leather leash.

The agents and the cop turned to watch the nun emerge from the cathedral, and she walked straight toward them, nodding her quiet benedictional greeting. She stopped very close to the dog, whose gleaming black snout was sniffing the air, and she knelt, placed the cathedral model box on the stones, and her typewriter too, and extended her hand, palm up.

"He is a beautiful creature," she said to the cop. "May I pet him?"

"He's friendly, Sister, but he'll probably want to sniff you. That's his job."

The nun smiled. "We all have our tasks and talents, given by God."

The dog trotted forward to the kneeling nun and began scanning her puzzle box and typewriter case with his twitching nose. . . .

Semtex is one of the world's most powerful plastic explosives. It is manufactured in the Czech Republic by a company called Explosia, and has often been called the favorite Play-Doh of international terror. It is odorless, usually red-brick orange in color, moldable and malleable, extremely stable, and its main components are RDX (cyclonite) and PETN (pentaerythritol tetranitrate). Twelve ounces of Semtex hidden in a Toshiba cassette recorder blew Pan Am 103 out of the skies over Scotland in 1988, killing 270 victims in the air and on the ground. Semtex was used to utterly destroy the American embassies in Nairobi, Kenya, and Dar es Salaam, Tanzania, in 1998, killing 224 people and wounding more than four thousand.

Somehow, nearly a thousand tons of Semtex went missing from the Czech Republic and wound up in the hands of the late Libyan dictator Muammar el-Qaddafi. Curiously, ten tons of Semtex fell into the stores of the Irish Republican Army and was used for three decades to kill scores of British soldiers, policemen, and innocent bystanders. The PLO used it, the Red Brigades loved it, and Hollywood had no idea what it was or could do, but it sure sounded cool and made a big bang.

In response to these multiple terrorist bombings, Explosia finally agreed to lace all Semtex products with trace elements that would make the product easily detectable, especially to trained sniffer dogs. However, the horse was already out of the barn. Semtex was invented in the late 1950s. No one seems to know exactly how many pounds of *nondetectable* Semtex are still out there on the black market.

There was a pinky finger–size molded tube of Semtex 1A, the type primarily used for blasting operations, hidden inside the nun's Olivetti typewriter carriage. This particular batch had been manufactured in 1999, without any tracing or tracking elements, but even so it was cocooned inside a double sleeve of Saran Wrap.

The nun gently curled her fingers through the shepherd's thick neck fur as he sniffed her cathedral model, and then the seams of her typewriter case. As trained to do by the trainers and handlers who'd raised him at Lackland Air Force Base, he remained standing and would sit only if his highly sensitive nose detected some sort of deadly explosive.

He did not sit.

He finished his sniffing, returned to his master, rubbed up against his thigh, and was rewarded with a loving head pat.

The nun rose to her feet and retrieved her puzzle and typewriter. Streams of sweat were dribbling down from her underarms and over the padding of pillow foam she'd used to make herself fat. Yet nothing showed on her beatific face but a sisterly smile, as she offered a nod of thanks to the kind policeman, walked directly north from the cathedral grounds, and exhaled a whisper of thanksgiving.

"It is indeed a blessed day."

CHAPTER 42

WINCHESTER, VIRGINIA

Steele almost shot Meg Harden when she came out of the woods. He was all alone, or so he'd thought, banging away at a row of five steel disk targets with his father's .45. He was wearing a pair of Peltor ear protectors on his head, gripping the pistol two-handed, and focusing out there at twenty-five yards as he dropped each plate with less than half a second between hits. Whenever he trained on the range, his mind was clear of everything, like a meditating monk, which was probably why he felt her presence behind him and nearly killed her.

He spun around and aimed the handgun at her face so fast it was like the blur of a samurai's sword. She froze in place, ten paces away, her eyes placid and hands by her sides, waiting for him to assess. He raised the barrel, made the pistol safe, slid it into his drop holster, and took off the Peltors.

"How'd you know I was here?" Steele said.

Meg sighed and looked at the sky. "I missed you too, Eric."

Steele didn't apologize. He took in her fit form, her raven-black hair and crystal-blue eyes. She was wearing a green corduroy jacket with bone buttons, jeans, and small hiking boots. She looked like an L.L. Bean catalog model. He walked to her and bent his head, but she didn't offer her lips so he kissed her cold cheek.

"I figured you wouldn't take real R and R or go very far," Meg said. "And whenever you're stressed, you shoot."

"I don't get stressed, Meg," Steele said, and he turned and walked back over to his shooting bench and started loading magazines for his Troy Industries 300 Blackout M4. He wasn't so sure yet about the new cartridge, which basically turned the standard 5.56 mm round into a 7.62 x 39 mm Russian-type bullet and fired it from a modified upper receiver, but he figured he'd give it a shot. In general he didn't like weird ammunition that you couldn't find easily on the modern battlefield.

"I know," Meg said, "you just get focused."

"That's right."

She followed him over to the bench, not too close, and stood there with her hands in her jacket pockets.

"How's the knee?" she asked.

"Coming along." The bullets clicked into the magazine as he fed them in with his tactical gloves. "Did half of Hawksbill this morning."

He'd gotten up at 5:00 A.M., driven out to Shenandoah National Park, and hiked halfway up the four-thousand-foot peak of the mountain. The knee resisted, because Petrov's wrench had cracked a hairline fracture in the upper tibia, but that wasn't something you could cast. The climb back down was painful, more so because he and Meg had once summited Hawksbill together.

From there he'd driven north to Happy Creek and finally out to Winchester, where the Program owned a thousand acres of do-whatever-you-want training area. It had been donated by Thorn McHugh, late of the CIA and allegedly a member of Cemetery Whisper, a secret club of disavowed intelligence agents. Apparently, McHugh, who came from a family of wealthy Yalies, knew more about the Program than he should have, and liked it.

"You're the only man I know," Meg said, "who tortures an injury into healing."

"Maybe that'll work with us," Steele said.

"I don't think so."

He looked at her, squeezed the Peltors back down over his ears, and picked up the rifle. He said, "Gunfire," and Meg stuck her fingers in her ears and turned to look downrange. Steele fired off ten rounds in rapid successions of five double-taps, but the second round of each pair didn't ring because the first round had already felled the plate.

"Kinda loud," Steele said as he lowered the barrel.

"What are you using?"

"Blackouts."

"It's a copy of a Russian round," Meg said. "Louder, heavier . . . might even be dipped in vodka."

Steele's smile was no more than a lip curl, so Meg gave up on breaking the ice.

"She's gone, by the way," she said.

"Who's gone?" He was loading a thirty-round

mag now. He wanted to see what would happen on full rock 'n' roll.

"Kalidi."

That halted his activity and his fingers stopped dipping into his ammo can. His dark eyebrows furrowed down at Meg, and now she clearly saw the stitches from his left temple wound.

"What do you mean, gone?" he said.

"Not dead," Meg said, "but she took off, fled the U.S."

"Yeah, right," Steele scoffed. "What do you know about that woman, Meg?"

"Everything. FBI confirmed it with Europol, MI5, and Israeli Shabak. Lila Kalidi, daughter of the late master blaster, Walid Kalidi. She was on a vengeance spree for her father's death and got help from a Russian cyber cell. She killed Jonathan, Collins, and now Marty. The only reason she didn't get you was because you never stand still for a minute." She smiled weakly. "Impulsive apparently has an upside."

"You keep using the past tense about her," Steele said.

"She's gone, Eric. Maybe something spooked her after Nashville."

"Nothing would spook that murderous bitch," he said, and his eyes slitted like a panther.

"Well, FBI says she made it to the Florida Keys, hopped a drug flight, and the pilot crossed international before the Coast Guard or DEA planes could catch up. Guesses are she made it to Havana."

"I'll believe it when I see a selfie of her with Raul Castro."

"I've got the FBI Red Notice request to INTERPOL right here." Meg patted her pocket where she had her cell phone. "Want to see it?"

"No." If he asked her for proof it would be like calling her a liar. Part of him wanted to believe it, but the larger part wanted to kill Lila Kalidi, and her fleeing like this would make that harder. Well, Program or not, he'd find her someday. He had a comforting thought of slicing her ear off and showing it to her before blowing her brains out. "I guess it's a good thing."

"I still love you, Eric," Meg said out of the blue, as if somehow the departure of Lila Kalidi, or the fact that she'd gotten away, was all Steele's fault, yet forgiven.

At that moment, something turned inside him. It was as if Kalidi's leaving the picture might clear the heavy cloud that had been hanging between him and Meg. He'd been awfully suspicious of her, and of everyone else except Dalton Goodhill, and maybe Ralphy, but now it didn't seem fair. The Program was dead, soon to be buried just like its greatest benefactor, Denton Cole. What was left were the good men and women who'd sacrificed so much for it, in silence, without glory. Meg was one of those patriots. He owed her, and yes, it was more than that.

"I know," he said. "And I want to make it right."

"I said I still love you, Eric," she said. "I didn't say that I want to be with you."

She reached inside her jacket. He tried not to watch her hand. She came up with a tissue. It was chilly in the forests of Winchester and her nose was running.

"We don't know what's going to happen after this," she said. "The Program's gone, maybe it'll be replaced with something else. Who knows? But it's obvious to me that two people in this kind of life can't make it together. I used to be so tough."

"You're still tough."

Meg laughed softly. "I can barely breathe when you're gone. And you're almost always gone. It makes me feel like a whiny woman. I think *I* need to be the alpha in a relationship. Maybe I'll marry a kindergarten teacher, boss him around, make him raise the kids. He won't be as hot as you, but he'll probably live to be forty."

"You don't think I'm going to live that long?" He was smiling slightly, but it was phony.

"No," she said, and she walked to him, reached up, caressed the back of his neck, and pulled him down. Her kiss was modest, yet it lingered for a moment, as if imprinting a memory. She backed away again.

"I guess we won't be seeing each other at President Cole's funeral," she said, "since none of us can go. But maybe, sometime, I'll see you at his grave."

She turned and walked away, and Steele saw that she'd parked her car beyond a copse of trees and that's why she'd seemingly emerged from nowhere. The engine kicked over and soon the sound was gone, and he turned back to his shooting bench. He hesitated for a moment, then drew his .45 again, instead of using the rifle, and started firing away at the targets.

His father's gun felt better for closure.

Two hundred meters away, atop a small embankment covered with tall wild grass, Dalton "Blade" Goodhill packed up his Remington 700 sniper rifle and Leupold VX-Freedom scope. He was wearing a camouflage Gore-Tex suit, but he'd been lying prone and immobile for over two hours, and his old bones were a little stiff.

He'd been covering Steele all morning. Steele didn't know he was there.

And for the entire time of Meg's visit, he'd had her face right there in his crosshairs. He was glad he didn't have to kill her.

CHAPTER 43

ALEXANDRIA, VIRGINIA

The large ugly warehouse on McConnell Avenue was the most run-down building in the neighborhood.

Just down the block from Zeke Hookah Lounge and the Kabul Kabob House, it was a soiled white structure 150 feet long, 100 feet wide, and two stories high, and had the minimum number of windows required by local fire codes, though they were all soiled and oily and boarded up from the inside. A commercial black-and-orange sign was hung on the street side above the double entrance doors, which were padlocked with a heavy chain. It said NOT FOR RENT OR SALE.

The sign didn't matter, however, because the warehouse was thoroughly uninviting to any passersby. But it was the perfect staging area for Lila Kalidi and the ten men who, in fewer than twenty-four hours, were going to kill everyone attending President Denton Cole's funeral at Washington's National Cathedral.

Inside the musty, damp, unheated workspace, all of the remaining detritus left by the previous tenant, a fly-by-night trucking company—fuel lines, spare carburetors, and tires—had been pushed to one far corner at the rear, and the floors swept clean. Now the place looked very well organized for the upcoming slaughter at hand.

At the front the assembled model of the National Cathedral sat on a sheet of white butcher paper atop an eight-foot-long folding table. On the paper, Lila had drawn a schematic of the surrounding avenues and neighborhoods, with street names and tactical points of interest marked. Notably, there were large red arrows pointing to avenues of attack, but no such arrows indicating avenues of withdrawal. No one was expected to get out alive.

Next came a row of ten metal folding chairs facing the model in a semicircle, so all of Lila's attendees could have unobstructed views. On the left and right flanks of those chairs were four more long tables, two on each side, upon which suicide vests were being carefully assembled. The tabletops were OCD neat, with tin shears, wire cutters, spools of white and red fourteen-gauge electrical wire, solid pack electric Dyno Nobel blasting caps, miniature twelve-volt batteries, All-Bond dental glue, and waterproof plunger switches with ring-pin safeties. It all looked like an assembly line for toys in Santa's workshop, except that Lila was Mrs. Claus and her elves were from hell.

The vests were standard black, police-type, armored plate carriers. Inside each wide pocket (one in front, one in back), the ceramic plates had been glued with sheets of molded C-4 plastic explosive, facing out and embedded with steel ball bearings and lug nuts. The plates would protect the wearer from incoming rounds, which wouldn't detonate the C-4, but when he pressed his plunger switch, anyone within a fifty-foot radius would be shredded to bone and blood, and the imploding plates would launch his severed head to heaven.

Beyond the chairs and assembly tables, on a wide patch of open floor space, were ten slim foam sleeping mattresses, ten neatly rolled sleeping bags, ten small embroidered prayer rugs, ten boxes of Halal-certified Meals Ready to Eat, and a battery-powered boom box sitting on a wooden stool. The box was playing Hawaiian big man Israel "IZ" Kamakawiwoʻole's ukulele version of "Over the Rainbow"—much more calming than a white noise machine, and equally as effective for defeating listening devices.

Finally, toward the back of the warehouse, a heavily armored Lenco BearCat SWAT truck sat hulking like a crouching tiger. It was shaped like a swollen alligator head, painted flat black, weighed nine tons, and had multiple gunports, a roof hatch like a tank, and an upthrust steel snorkel for air circulation and deep-water crossings. Its armor was half an inch thick, and in addition to the two driving crew up front, ten more SWAT operators could squat on the benches in the back.

The BearCat was ubiquitous with police departments all across the United States. This one had been purchased, for cash, by one of Lila's men—

posing as a buyer from a movie production company prop house in Atlanta—from a Georgia PD that had become the beneficiary of government surplus MRAPs used in Afghanistan (Mine-Resistant Armor-Protected vehicles; overkill for SWAT teams, but they looked cool to chiefs of police). Its fresh decals were still drying. The ones near the nose said METROPOLITAN POLICE, then the MPD silver shields graced the side armor, and E.R.T. (Emergency Response Team) was in bold white caps on the back.

It was a beast. You'd need an M1 Abrams tank round or a Javelin missile to stop it.

Lila's ten brothers-in-arms sat in their folding chairs, listening attentively to her briefing. They were dressed in black tactical SWAT uniforms, head to foot, and had Smith & Wesson AR-15s in their laps, modified to fire full auto, some with suppressors, and Sig Sauer P226 pistols in their thigh holsters. They all had black MICH helmets, headsets, and MBITR radios lying in front of their US Patriot SWAT boots.

They were all of the Muslim faith, but you couldn't have discerned that by looks alone. Three of them were Chechens who looked like Muscovite Russians. Three more were Palestinians from the West Bank, but of Jordanian Circassian descent, which gave them their reddish-blond curls and green eyes. The last four were Spaniards, the sons of light-skinned, freckle-faced Berber immigrants from Morocco. They were all members of Palestinian Islamic Jihad and had come to the United States on bona fide student visas—some of them "sleepers" who'd arrived more than two years prior—and every piece of equipment in the room, including the weapons, had been legally purchased.

Except for the C-4 and blasting caps. Those had been hijacked off a truck that was delivering the explosives from a demolition company based in Chicago to the Bingham Canyon Mine in Utah. The ATF was still looking for that lethal stolen stash, and they weren't going to find it.

"*Aichwaihti*," Lila said in Arabic. My brothers. Then she switched to English because the Chechens weren't fluent. "I trust you all had good evenings."

The men dipped their heads once but didn't say anything. Lila had released them for their final farewells, but it was none of that cliché nonsense about strip joints, beer, and hookers in which the 9/11 hijackers had allegedly indulged. These men were all married to pious young women who knew nothing of their extracurricular activities, and the men had spent the night with their wives in various hotels and Airbnbs in the Washington area. Lila almost smiled, because she imagined those wives had gotten quite a workout.

Half of the couples also had young children. After the men's deaths their families would be cared for via life insurance policies held in Gaza, which all had waivers for "martyrdom." The premiums were paid for with American tax dollars from a fund intended for Palestinian humanitarian aid. Lila loved irony.

Today she was wearing a full-length black woolen dress with long sleeves, and a gray hijab. She didn't want the men distracted by her figure, and the garb also gave her the aura of a stern schoolmarm. She clutched a long elementary school pointer and tapped it on the butcher paper as the men craned their necks.

"So, these are your two optional assault points," she said. "The first would be a frontal assault, directly from the west off of Wisconsin Avenue, across the park grounds and into the cathedral's main entrance right here." She flicked the rubber pointer tip against the model's ornate front doors, then back to the butcher paper. "The second option would be to continue north along here on Wisconsin, past the entire grounds, take a right on Woodley Road, then another hard right on North Road—which turns back into the church's flank—and cut west again right across this large oval of grass and into the tourists' side entrance. Now, why am I suggesting this second course of action?"

One of the young men raised a hand.

"Yes, Tarek?"

"Because the front lawn and the circular drive will be completely blocked off."

"Correct, most likely with mobile water-filled barriers, as well as the armored limousines of the current president, the Israeli and British prime ministers, the German chancellor, and so forth. There will also be media vans. Your vehicle might make it partway through, but not close enough."

"Excuse me, *ha'sheihkuhtee*," another man said, using the respectful term for *my mistress*. "But won't the side tourist entrance up there also be blockaded?"

"Yes," Lila said, "but not as thoroughly as the

front. These security protocols are practical, but also for the benefit of media." She cradled the pointer in the web of her left hand and jabbed it at the model's side entrance like a pool cue. "I am confident that even if you cannot smash through these double doors here, you will get very close. We are not trying to drive this beast right into the church, although that would be wonderful for your legacies." She smiled and received a few back in kind. "Our objective is to use it as an Armored Personnel Carrier, as with armored infantry." She lanced the pointer at one of the men. "Dasha, repeat that plan."

"I will be the first to exit the vehicle from the rear," the white-blond Chechen said. "I will detonate at the entrance doors, killing as many of their Secret Service as possible, and then the rest of the comrades will disembark and rush inside."

"Very good." Lila raised a warning finger. "But, comrades, make sure you do not exit the beast along *with* Dasha in your enthusiasm, because his blast will kill you as well. Wait for his results."

They all nodded and someone clapped Dasha on his shoulder. Lila pointed to one of the Spaniards.

"Ricardo, you will be operating the drone from the front passenger seat, correct?"

The curly-headed handsome young man nodded and gestured off toward one of the assembly tables, where a large black "air spider" hulked.

"The transmitter range is a mile," she continued, "so if you can get a good overhead picture of the target before you all arrive on scene, you'll be able to make a last-minute tactical decision about where to breach. But if for whatever reason that flying machine fails, ignore it and proceed with option two. Are we clear?"

Ricardo grinned and gave her a thumbs-up. Another of his comrades raised a hand.

"Yes, Yassir?"

"What if the access roads are blocked? They do that sometimes with their police cars for such an event."

"Drive around them if you can, but note that if you do so, they will immediately radio their command center at the cathedral. So, if you are not close enough yet, they will all be alerted to some sort of threat, despite the markings on the truck. I'd prefer that you kill them all with your suppressors, push their vehicles out of the way, and continue. That will buy you some time." She looked at her watch. Evening was falling outside past the oily warehouse windows. "My brothers, I am certain that you all will do well. Be brave, be determined, be swift and with violence of action." She touched the top of her chest and headbowed. "I wish that I were going with you, but someone must continue to lead this struggle, and engrave your names in glory." She raised a fist and said, "For Al-Quds." It was the jihadi war cry to never forget Jerusalem.

"For Al-Quds," the men intoned. They were too smart to shout it.

"Good. Continue with your vests. You still have much work to do."

The men rose from their seats and went back to the tables to work on their suicide vests. Lila walked over to her private table and began her own preparations for the evening. She was going to need at least two hours, much of it in front of a mirror, and for once she was grateful for America's politically correct culture, because even a truckers' warehouse had men's and women's bathrooms. She began sorting through boxes of hair color, then looked up from her worktable at the throng of young, virile, handsome men who would soon be blowing themselves into fogs of gore.

She felt a bit sorry for them. She didn't expect them to get anywhere close to the cathedral's entrance, and they would probably all die on the front lawn.

They were nothing but decoys.

CHAPTER 44

WASHINGTON, D.C.

Eric Steele rarely got drunk, and whenever he did, no one could tell but his mother. He had a rare ability to imbibe all sorts of alcoholic substances without them having any visible effect, which meant that he could outdrink a Ukrainian arms dealer in some backwater dive in Sevastopol without secretly tossing his vodka into a planter. It was like a chemical switch he could flip in his head. However, turning it off again wasn't so easy. It made it really hard to just let go and get wasted.

Tonight, he was going to do his best to defeat it.

Meg was done with him, and it looked like she meant it. The Program was shut down, probably for good. The quest for his father had dead-ended in a Russian blizzard and a pile of corpses. Lila Kalidi was gone, which for most other men would have been a good thing, but it sucked because he very badly needed to kill her.

He wanted to smoke two very fine Arturo Fuente

cigars, make quality time with a full bottle of Knob Creek 120 Proof Single Barrel Reserve bourbon, and pass out long enough to miss Denton Cole's televised funeral. Sounded like a plan, and he decided to start it all off with a decent steak.

Actually, the idea had been prompted by Mike Pitts, who'd texted Steele over his Program smartphone, which hadn't yet been recalled by the outfit's quartermaster (she was a meticulous young woman named Penny whom Steele called "S," from the military term for her role, "S-4"). It was Pitts who'd suggested that both of them needed a bitch session, and the Lost Society steakhouse in northern D.C. on Fourteenth Street and U might be a good spot. Steele had been there once or twice before. It had a rooftop bar, a red-brick interior facade, butcher block tables, brown leather chairs, and sort of a dark retro vibe, like some joint from a Mickey Spillane novel. He said okay, because what else did he have to do? Nothing but laundry.

Strange thing was, Pitts never showed up. Steele got there first, just before their reservation at 8:00 P.M., and was led to a corner table that looked out over the street, up on the second floor. He sat, as always, facing the door, or in this case the access stairway that rose up from below and emerged next to the bar. It was raining lightly outside, and in the high arched windows he could see the restaurant's electric sign flickering like some noir film from the 1940s. At 8:13, Pitts texted him with an apology: "Sorry, my man. Twins are sick. No go tonight. Rain check." Steele texted back an "okay" icon and ordered his first round of bourbon. The evening was panning out just like the rest of his current life: stood up by a one-legged spook.

The waitress was friendly, in a quiet way, but he only noticed how pretty she was when she came back with his first tumbler of golden gasoline. She had on clunky waitperson shoes, a mid-thigh black skirt, a baggy white button-down shirt, and her Lost Society apron. She had a short blond pixie haircut, big blue eyes behind librarian glasses, high cheekbones, full lips, and no makeup. She was in her mid-twenties and seemed to be one of those people who have no idea they're attractive.

"Here you go, sir. Knob Creek, two rocks." She put the tumbler down on a coaster and met Steele's eyes for only a moment, then took out her order pad. He noticed she had a short plaster cast on her right wrist, but her fingers were free.

"I'm not sure what I want yet," Steele said.

"You mean in general? Or in terms of food?" The waitress giggled at her own joke, blushed, waved her fingers in front of her face, and added, "Sorry. I'm new." She had a slight southern belle accent.

He smiled in spite of his foul mood. "Food, but maybe in general too. Looking for a new job."

"Oh?" She cocked her hip and put her left knuckles on it. "What'd you do before?"

"Demolitions."

"You mean you blow stuff up?"

"Or knock things down."

"That's so exciting. I'm just studying nursing."

"Well, that can be exciting too."

"Only if I marry a rich old senator, give him a heart attack, and take all his money."

Steele laughed and sipped his magic potion. "How'd you break that wrist?"

"Rollerblading." She rolled her eyes. "I know, dumb, but it's great for sympathy tips."

He was still smiling. "What's your name?"

"Maxine, but most folks call me Max. What's yours?"

"Eric." He almost gave her his cover name, but it was the same as hers so it would have been weird.

"A pleasure, suh," she said like Scarlett from *Gone with the Wind* and made a little faux curtsy. "I'll leave you the menu. Take your time."

Steele watched her walk back to the waitpersons' station at the far end of the bar, where she almost T-boned a waiter carrying a full tray of drinks. He always assessed any friendly conversation as a potential ambush, but in this case confidence was extremely low. He'd made a random reservation at one of the hundreds of D.C. restaurants, this girl was an employee, and besides, she was a klutz. He kept on drinking and tried very hard to do less thinking.

He ordered the twelve-ounce Sirloin Herb Butter, rare side of medium rare, and had finished his second bourbon by the time Max delivered it along with mashed potatoes and pan-fried mushrooms. She was waiting on three other tables nearby, so she couldn't linger long to chat, but she entertained him with surreptitious eye rolls about one older couple who kept changing their order, and an exasperated mime of cutting her own throat when another customer sent his chicken back to the chef.

When he ordered his third bourbon, Max

brought it and said, "You trying to forget something, Eric?"

"Washington," he said.

"I get it." Max nodded and sighed. "I'm trying to forget Charlotte."

"Ex-girlfriend?"

"Nope, the city." Max snorted like a small piglet, which Steele thought was cute. "I'm boringly straight."

"Same," he said. "Emphasis on boring."

She waved and went back to work again, without any overt flirtation, which relieved him. He wasn't remotely interested in bedding some willing young woman tonight, and Max wasn't giving off those signals anyway. Waiting on tables was tough on the body, and add to that her nursing studies, she was probably more exhausted than anything else. On any other night, in any other life, it might have been different, but he was content to chat with her during her "drive-bys," drink until he was numb, and maybe imagine her in bed, six months down the road.

Sometime later, he looked at his watch and realized he'd been sitting there for more than two hours. He'd been cutting his steak and chewing the chunks like a robot as his thousand-yard stare blurred the room. Hundreds of memories came rushing at him, and he swatted each one away as if looking to snatch the one that really mattered. But none of them hit home. He was working on his fifth bourbon, and all he felt was a mild throb in his temple, which was probably from having his stitches removed.

What was the meaning of "service" anyway? He'd served his country honorably, taken lots of bad guys off the field, and watched his friends die doing the same. For all that he was getting a pink slip. His waitress was "serving" in a totally different way, but in the best case she'd wind up working a hospital night shift and spending her life on her feet. Were either of their services more valuable than the other? Nope. Lost Society.

Okay, that's enough booze.

He caught Max's eye over at the bar and signaled for the check. After another five minutes she came over with the leather bill holder.

"They're letting me go," she said.

He raised an eyebrow. "Permanently?"

"Nah, just for the night. I've been on since three." Then she clutched the bill holder to her chest, as if it contained a secret message, and bit her lower lip. "Could you do me a favor, Eric?"

"What would that be?"

"Don't tip me. Walk me home instead. It's just a few blocks, but I like to cut through Meridian Hill Park, and after what happened to that girl up there in New York, you know, I'm a little skittish about it." They both knew she was talking about the recent gruesome murder of a college student in Manhattan. "I promise that's all it is. It's not some weird come-on, I'm *way* too tired, and I'm not gonna roll you. Looks like you can hold your liquor and probably take me." She cocked her head and her eyes pleaded, but there was no eyelash batting.

Something about her little monologue, and request, and the way she said it seemed sad. It was the last thing he felt like doing, but now he had no choice. If he begged off and God forbid anything happened to her, he'd be drinking a bottle of Knob Creek a day for the rest of his miserable life. He could call her an Uber, but that would be cold.

"Okay, but I'm tipping you anyway, Max. I made you work hard." He held out his hand for the check.

"Awesome." She grinned and took off her apron. "Thank you, kind suh."

"A pleasure, ma'am." He touched his imaginary cowboy hat.

They walked down the stairway together to the first floor, where Max retrieved a black umbrella from a brass holder by the front door, and they went out into the street.

Inside Lost Society, a pair of male waiters watched them leave from the bar, where they were picking up another round of drinks and appetizers for latecomers.

"Who's that new chick?" one asked the other.

"She's not new. She's Brenda's cousin, just a fill-in. Brenda called in sick today and said her cuz was a pro and could spot her."

"No shit? And Frank went for that?"

"Guess he liked her ass."

"Pig."

They both laughed. . . .

Brenda, of course, had not called in sick voluntarily, but at the point of a stiletto.

And now she was dead in her bathtub.

CHAPTER 45

WASHINGTON, D.C.

They walked north in the rain on Fourteenth Street, past Busboys and Poets, a funky old bookstore-slash-café, and took a left on V Street NW. Steele was taller, so he took Max's umbrella and sheltered them both. She'd taken her jacket from a cloakroom hook. It was an imitation Harley motorcycle jacket, which just made her look more cute than biker-dangerous.

Once they were out of the restaurant, Steele expected her to chatter, maybe about her southern upbringing, or the dreams that a young pretty woman—who didn't really know she was pretty—had for this old cruel world. She didn't touch him or take his hand for a couple of blocks, but when a cab zoomed by and nearly soaked them both from a deep street puddle, he jinked to the right and took her along with a quick hand around her waist, and she laughed, and after that slipped her wrist with the cast through his elbow.

They kept going west on V Street. The rain was

coming down a little harder and Max pulled Steele a little bit closer. His left knee was feeling pretty good and he figured maybe it was the liquor. It was already late on a weeknight and there were hardly any other people around, and he had the thought that maybe that was due to tomorrow's day of national mourning, and they were all home glued to their televisions. He let the girl guide him, because she knew where she needed to go, and they took a right on Fifteenth past the St. Augustine Catholic Church and School, and he tried to remember the last time he'd prayed, and had meant it. Maybe it was at Collins Austin's funeral. No, on that day he'd only flipped God the mental bird. A block up ahead, he could see the high, dense, dripping trees of Meridian Hill Park.

"Have you ever seen Joan of Arc?" Max said, which seemed to be a non sequitur out of nowhere.

"Nope. I think she was burned at the stake during the fifteenth century."

Max didn't laugh. Her demeanor seemed to have darkened somewhat, maybe from fatigue or the weather.

"I mean the statue up here in the park."

"Don't think I have," he said.

"I'll show you. It's on the way."

They cut into the south end of the park and she gently tugged him onto a long concrete walkway. It was dark and the walkway was silver with puddles, and the looming shadows of the high trees looked like giant, undulating black amoebas. In the distance he could make out the statue, an iron warhorse atop a square stone pedestal, with one front leg cocked up high as it charged. Sitting atop the horse was Joan, the nineteen-year-old French heroine in full body armor. Her outstretched right hand gripped the hilt of a sword, but the blade itself was missing. It had been stolen by vandals and the city had yet to replace it.

They stopped at the base of the statue and looked up. Max slipped her casted wrist from Steele's elbow and moved a step closer to the statue. Steele was still holding the umbrella in his right hand, and he stuck his left in his jeans pocket and just waited. Maybe Joan of Arc meant something special to her.

"She is missing her sword," she said. "But I still have mine."

And in that instant, she turned back into Lila Kalidi, like some demon witch from a fairy-tale nightmare. Her right hand crossed in front of her chest, her fingers touching her left shoulder, and then her entire body whipped to the right like an unwinding spring and she backhanded him with the cast in the bridge of his nose.

It happened so fast he had no time to duck or parry the blow. He saw a flash of white lightning and heard his own nose crunch and the shock went straight to his brain. Lila's cast was actually a heavy steel cuff, smeared with just enough plaster for camouflage, and it felt like he'd been slammed with a hammer. An instant later, she'd leaped up onto the pedestal, grabbed the iron front leg of the horse, and back kicked him so hard in the sternum that he dropped the umbrella and smashed down onto his back on the concrete walkway.

Blood was gushing over his mouth. The back of

his skull had bounced on the concrete. His vision was liquid and blurry, but he saw her above him, her hand reaching under her skirt like some pornographic gymnast, and then she was leaping up into the air and flying down at him with a gleaming black stiletto clutched in her right fist.

She yelled something like a banshee. It wasn't English. He snap rolled to the left and the blade point sparked off the stone where his head had just been. He hadn't packed his father's .45 that night, but he had his backup Sig Sauer P365 microcompact in a waistband holster. He was on his knees and he tried to go for it, but she kicked him hard in the left ribs—the ones still bruised from Russia—and the pistol went spinning off over the walkway onto a patch of soaked grass.

He was drunk.

She was fast.

And she was going to kill him.

"Not tonight, *Lila*," he snarled as he willed his adrenaline to surge past his alcohol level, jumped to his feet, and both of his hands came up in a bladed Krav Maga stance, defending both sides of his bloody head. "I like my ears."

Lila screamed, tore off her glasses with her left hand, and leaped at him like a fiend, plunging down with the stiletto in an overhand strike aimed at his neck. He blocked it with his left forearm and short-punched her straight in the gut, but it was like hitting a marble mannequin. She jumped back, stomped down on her left foot, and kicked him in the groin with her right shinbone. Inebriation had its benefits and he barely felt it.

He slapped her with his right palm and it whipped her head around. She grabbed the top of his hair with her left hand, straddled him in the air like a black widow spider, and sunk her teeth into his neck. He saw the stiletto coming down again and he jammed his thick left bicep under her armpit and the blade off-angled and plunged through the back of his leather jacket and into his left shoulder blade and jammed right there in the bone.

Steele grunted with the searing pain, but he got his right hand between her legs, grabbed a fistful of crotch, and hurled her off him and over his head. Her spinning body missed the edge of the concrete walkway by inches, and as she bounced on the grassy shoulder something flew out of her Harley jacket, but she ignored it and was instantly up on her feet again and facing him in a crouch like a feral cat.

A woman screamed, but it wasn't Lila. It came from somewhere behind Steele's back through the trees. He heard a wailing siren in the near distance. He reached over with his right hand and yanked her stiletto from his back.

"You want this?"

He started toward her, then stopped as she reached inside her jacket and came up with something that looked like a silver pen. She clicked the button and an eight-inch steel pike sprang from the pen tip and locked. It was a heart killer, and she grinned like the devil's butcher.

"I don't want my knife," she said. "I want your *life*."

"You two hold it right there!"

The voice came from behind Steele, and he heard car doors slamming and spinning police lights were flashing the trees. Shoes were pounding closer, nightsticks and handcuffs jangling.

Lila straightened up, hissed a curse in Arabic, spun, and took off through the park. She was so fast she was gone from sight in five seconds.

Steele didn't turn toward the cops. His whole body was coursing with adrenaline, but he knew that was going to wear off soon and he'd be in a world of hurt. He staggered forward toward the grass as he slipped Lila's bloody stiletto inside his jacket and reached down for the object she'd dropped.

It was her cell phone. He jammed that into his jacket too.

He headed a few more feet over to his fallen handgun. He knew if the cops found him with it, he'd spend the next eight hours in interrogation, so he turned, plunked his ass right down onto it in the grass, folded his legs, and put his face in his hands.

Two cops ran up to him and stopped. An ambulance was crawling through the park along the concrete walkway. Steele lifted his face and looked up at them.

"Holy shit, buddy," one cop said. "What the hell happened to you?"

An EMT ran up to them, dropped to his knees beside Steele, and started fumbling in his duty bag for an ice pack.

"Don't get up," he ordered.

"Don't intend to," Steele said.

The second cop, older, and with his dripping cap pushed back on his head, pointed past Steele at the trees.

"Who's that chick who just booked it?"

Steele smiled his best dumbass smile.

"Hooker, I think. I was just trying to get laid. She just wanted my wallet."

The younger cop put his knuckles on his duty belt and grinned.

"Looks like she also wanted to kick your ass."

Steele nodded.

"Yeah, that too."

CHAPTER 46

CRESTWOOD, WASHINGTON, D.C.

"Ralphy, open the goddamn door."

Steele was on the top floor of Mrs. Jepson's brownstone on Sixteenth Street, hammering his fist on the multilock door and rattling the hallway walls. He'd just arrived from Meridian Hill Park in an Uber and, getting no response from Ralphy's buzzer, had jacked the entrance doorway with Lila's stiletto and charged up the stairs.

His nose was crisscrossed with bright white surgical tape. He had teeth marks in his neck like a scarlet vampire hickey. The blood was running down his back from his shoulder wound.

"Hold on, hold on, hold on . . ."

Steele heard Ralphy's voice from the other side and his bare feet slapping the floor. Then his peephole popped open, closed again, and he heard all four locks clicking and pinging and the door swung open.

Ralphy stood there in a ridiculous Mickey Mouse bathrobe, his hair all crazy. He was clutching a

Glock 19 and his eyes were huge and bugged open behind his glasses.

"Holy *Die Hard*," he gasped. "What the heck happened to you?"

Steele pushed his way inside and slammed the door behind him.

"Lila Kalidi," Steele said. "And put that piece up before you shoot somebody."

"Kalidi?" Ralphy backed up. "But I thought you said she was—"

Something started pounding against Ralphy's floor from below. It sounded like the end of a broomstick.

"Ralphy Perrrrsssko!" It was Mrs. Jepson's voice. "What's all that racket up there?"

She had her head outside her street-front kitchen window below. Ralphy hissed "Shit," dropped the Glock on his coffee table, ran over to one of his windows, cranked it open, and stuck his head out.

"Sorry, Mrs. Jepson! I ordered late food."

"You're not having a party, are you? It's a school night."

"Nope, nope, nope. Sorry!"

He closed the window and turned back to Steele. Then his bedroom door on the right side of the flat cranked open. Steele spun, drew his Sig P365 in a blur, and almost pulled the trigger. Frankie was standing there in nothing but Ralphy's only dress shirt. She yelped, threw her small hands up, and covered her eyes. Steele put the pistol away.

"Any more surprises?" he said.

"Negative," Ralphy croaked.

"*Jesus*, Seven." Frankie stood there with her bare

legs quaking, but she was staring through her fingers at Steele's face. With the white X in the middle and his green eyes blazing, he looked like a Hells Angels gangbanger.

"Is Kalidi dead?" Ralphy asked.

"Not yet." Steele pulled Lila's cell phone from his jacket pocket and tossed it to Persko. "I got this off her, and I want whatever's on it. Pull everything from the last twenty-four hours."

Ralphy caught the cell and looked at it.

"I . . . I don't know if I can do that, Steele," he said.

"It's passcode locked, for sure," Frankie said.

"Crack it," Steele said. "She's planning something, I don't know what, but it's not about me."

"Okay, okay." Ralphy took the phone and waddled over to his long worktable.

"You got some ice?" Steele asked.

"Um, we used all the ice," Frankie said.

Steele looked down at the coffee table and saw two wineglasses and an empty bottle of cabernet.

"You kids put ice in red wine? Barbarians."

"I got a bag of frozen peas in the fridge," Ralphy said over his shoulder.

Frankie hurried into the kitchen while Steele took off his leather jacket and pulled his shirt over his head. She came back with the peas, blushed when she saw Steele's naked chest, then covered her eyes again as he reached up, tore the bandages off his face, took the peas from her hand, and mashed them to his nose.

He turned and showed her the two-inch-deep, bloody gash in his scapula. She nearly gagged.

"Oh, God," she whimpered.

"You gotta close this up for me," Steele said. "Got a sewing kit?"

"Do I look like I passed home ec in high school?" she squeaked.

"I . . . I got one big sewing needle I use for popping SIM cards," Ralphy said. He'd turned around from his computer and was gaping at Steele's wound. "No thread, but maybe some real thin copper wire."

"Get it, Frankie," Steele said. "And some alcohol, but if he doesn't have that, use vodka."

"Oh, God," Frankie said.

Steele pulled a stool away from Ralphy's table and sat down. Frankie staggered away and then came back with a roll of paper towels and a bottle of Smirnoff.

"Clean it first," Steele said.

"Oh, God," she said again, but she did it.

Steele didn't even flinch when she poured the vodka into his wound. Then, when her trembling fingers threaded the huge needle with a long strand of copper wire, and she pierced the first lip of his fish mouth–shaped wound, he didn't even gasp, while she nearly passed out. She wondered if he was high on something.

"Don't close it up all the way," he ordered. "Just enough so the flesh can't shrivel back."

"Okay, okay."

Steele took out his cell and tried calling Pitts, though he didn't really expect him to pick up, and he didn't. Then he called the White House switchboard.

"Get me the chief of staff," he said to the operator.

"Mr. Lansky's not here right now, sir. May I ask who wants him?"

"Patch me through, tell him it's Steele, and do it *now.*"

Lansky was at home, but he wasn't sleeping. He had a big day ahead of him.

"Speak," he said to Steele.

"Sir, I just had a close encounter with Lila Kalidi," Steele said. "Took me by surprise, since I thought she blew out of Key West."

"What? Who the fuck said that?"

"Never mind, sir. We've got her cell and we're trying to crack it. Gut tells me she's moving on something big."

"Okay, what's your call?"

"You'd better call HRT and put them on standby." Steele meant the FBI's Hostage Rescue Team. They were the best counterterror team in law enforcement, and unlike Delta, they could operate on domestic soil. "I'll advise as soon as we've got something."

"Okay, here's my cell." Lansky read off his number and Steele plugged it into his contacts. "Call me directly, and nobody else."

"Roger, sir," Steele said and hung up.

"I . . . I think I did it," Frankie whispered from behind him.

"Good. Get a couple of Band-Aids and slap 'em on."

"Oh, God," she mumbled again and went off to the bathroom.

Ralphy threw his hands up over at his worktable. He started pulling on his wild curly hair.

"I freaking can't do it," he moaned. "And I don't think we've got the time to petition Apple."

Then Frankie stormed back out of the bathroom with the Band-Aids.

"Ralphy!" she snapped. "Break the freaking phone case open, yank her motherboard, and use the Rainwear on my comp!"

"What's Rainwear?" he begged.

"It's an app I wrote, for God's sake. If nothing else it'll suck off her GPS coords for the last twenty-four. At least that, puleeez!"

"Okay, okay . . ."

Ralphy did as she instructed, dropped the tiny board in a "toaster" that he used to emulate hard drives, and plugged it into Frankie's Alienware. He opened her Rainwear app and it started scanning the board, and he crossed his fingers on both hands and started rocking, as if he were praying. Two columns of "balloons" started dripping down the monitor display. The ones on the left held military times and the corresponding ones on the right held latitude and longitude readouts.

Ralphy blew out a sigh of relief, but then he glanced down at Lila's pried-open cell and said, "What the freak is that?"

"What?" Steele said.

"There's something vibrating in her cell, Steele. And there's also a weird little piece of, like, red clay. . . ."

Steele stood up. "It's a self-destruct."

Ralphy jumped up, with Lila's cell clutched in his sweat-pooled palm. He started running around the living room.

"Bathtub!" Frankie yelled.

Ralphy sprinted for the bathroom, ran inside, came out again, slammed the bathroom door, gripped the knob, smeared his back against it, and squeezed his eyes shut. There was a sharp hollow bang from inside, a flash of light haloed the door-jamb, and then a slither of smoke spewed out the bottom between his bare feet.

He opened his eyes.

"Shit." He groaned. "There goes my security deposit."

CHAPTER 47

ALEXANDRIA, VIRGINIA

The first gunshot killed FBI undercover Special Agent Terry Palamino on McConnell Avenue at 6:43 A.M.

Palamino had a wife, a kid, and a dog at home, and he knew he was the canary in the coal mine. He was dressed as a homeless vagrant, looked old enough to be a Gulf War vet, had a brown woolen cap on his head, a bushy gray beard, an M65 field jacket with the 25th Infantry lightning shoulder patch, piss-stained jeans, and battered Timberland work boots.

He shuffled along McConnell from west to east, past the condo complex on the south side, crossed over Shillings Street, and headed for the ugly industrial area that bordered South Pickett. When he hit the soiled white warehouse, he slung his garbage bag over his left shoulder, dragged his filthy right fingers along the concrete front wall, and headed for the double glass doors, muttering to himself about "stinkin' rich folk and politicians."

The doors were padlocked and covered up from the inside with butcher paper. He peered through the half-inch crack where they met in the middle, and pounded his fist on the glass.

"Anybody in there?" he hollered, and then coughed up a smoker's hack. "Anybody got somethin' to eat for a veteran?"

Palamino had multiple medals for public service and was a very brave man. Dasha, the Chechen, shot him through the door crack from six inches away with his AR-15. Now he was sprawled on his back in the street with half his face gone.

An FBI sniper was lying prone on the rooftop of the building across the street that hosted "Metro by T-Mobile." He was covering Palamino with an Accuracy International AW Magnum firing .338 Lapua cartridges, and the range was easy—less than a hundred meters. He had no clear sight picture through his Schmidt & Bender scope, but the second he saw the back of Palamino's skull blow off and the agent collapse, he took the shot anyway.

His bullet pierced the glass front door, bounced off of something right behind it, ricocheted back in fragments, and shattered the glass, which cascaded down and covered Palamino's twitching boots in glimmering razor-sharp shards. "Shit," the sniper hissed through his headset.

It appeared that Lila Kalidi was a firm believer in worst-case scenarios. One of the first things she'd done after renting the warehouse was to have her men cover the front doors from the inside with the butcher paper, then weld quarter-inch-thick steel plates to the frames. She'd also ordered her men not to initiate action unless they had absolutely no choice, but Dasha, her Chechen team leader, had battled the Russian NKVD and Spetsnaz and knew a probe when he saw one.

Since dawn, Dasha had been watching the sprawling Van Dorn Station shopping center, which was directly to the left across the street and had more than twenty-five restaurants and stores. It was already almost 7:00 A.M. on a weekday, but there was barely any traffic, and no one was out in the parking lot or passing by on McConnell Avenue.

It was clear to Dasha that someone had secured the entire area.

This "homeless" guy was a cop.

Boom.

Game on.

Also, by this time, all of Lila's men were thoroughly high. Committing suicide, even for a mission of martyrdom, takes some liquid courage, and while alcohol is forbidden by Shariah law, other mind-altering substances are not. Somali gunmen are enamored of khat. PLO terrorists are often pumped up on Quaaludes and sometimes heroin. Lila's men had spent the night smoking hash in their hookahs, laced with fenclonine. They'd also used one of the trucking company's power drills to make three-inch gunports in the warehouse's cement walls, at the front and on both flanks. It was like a landlocked version of the Civil War's ironclad ship the *Monitor*.

Now, with Palamino's fresh corpse lying outside the front doors in a crawling pool of thick blood, they cranked up their boom box to full volume, and a weird, ethereal tenor saxophone started wailing, followed by a brass section, hammering drums, and a Hammond organ vibrating all of the walls. Then came the raw, gravelly voice of Meat Loaf, howling the intro to one of his 1990s hits.

It echoed all the way west down McConnell and around the corner to the First Cash Pawn Shop, where the FBI had just set up their command post. Their radios were going crazy with "officer down" calls and ambulances were already screaming down Van Dorn Street from up north. FBI Special Agent in Charge John Loughran, who knew he was about to have the worst day of his professional life, turned around to Eric Steele and said, "What the hell is that?"

"'Good Girls Go to Heaven,'" Steele said with a grim smirk. "'Bad Girls Go Everywhere.'"

"Holy fuck," said Loughran. "This is gonna be a shit show."

And indeed it was. The FBI had no idea who was in that warehouse, nor how many. All they knew—from this mysterious and "ghosted" federal agent named Eric Steele—was that the murderous female terrorist they were hunting had spent 50 percent of the past twenty-four hours at that very location on McConnell Avenue.

And that hadn't been easy to glean either. Back at Ralphy's apartment, Frankie's Rainwear had struggled to create a mirror image of Lila Kalidi's movements, by mining them, of all things, through a Washington, D.C., mobile parking app that was running in the background on Lila's cell (terrorists have to park somewhere too). However, the activities of all of Lila's smartphone apps were also double-encrypted by an umbrella program called Chameleon, implanted there by Millennial Crude. It was four o'clock in the morning before Frankie realized that all of Lila's time stamps and GPS coordinates were reversed and transposed—after all, it wasn't possible that only one hour before attempting to kill Steele, Kalidi had been in Guatemala.

When Frankie jumped up from Ralphy's worktable and yelled "Epic!" they knew she'd unscrambled the scrambler.

Steele called Ted Lansky. Lansky called Special Agent Loughran. Steele then called Dalton Goodhill, who, remarkably, was in the middle of an all-night game of Texas hold'em in Springfield, Virginia, with four other vets from Special Forces 5th Group. Goodhill then called Allie "Whirly," who by stroke of luck had fallen asleep in the Program team room over at Langley AFB, after cleaning out her locker and preparing to look for another flying gig.

"I was just packing up all my shit," she said in a sleep-drenched groan.

"Well, unpack your shit and get your ass in the air," Goodhill said.

He told her to roust a ground crew, crank up the Program's 1998 model Bell 212 helicopter (camouflaged with a white body and blue tail boom, colors of the DC Metropolitan Police's "Falcons"), fly over to Sixteenth Street NW in Crestwood, and hover three feet above Ralphy's building.

"Watch the wires over there and don't set it down," Goodhill said. "Those old roofs are tar paper and timber and you'll put a skid right through."

"Roger, Blade," she said as she zipped up her flight suit, grabbed her helmet, and sprinted for the bird.

Allie took off and called Steele when she was one minute out. Steele grabbed Ralphy and they charged up the brownstone's stairwell, burst through the fire escape doorway, ran bent-over through Allie's roaring downblast, climbed into the bird, and banked high and away for Alexandria.

Frankie stayed back at Ralphy's place, hoping to crack something else on Lila's motherboard and mine some more crucial intel. She also had to deal with Mrs. Jepson, who was very unhappy.

Dawn was already breaking bright, crisp, and clear when Allie set the helo down in the northern parking lot of Jiffy Lube Multicare, just off of South Van Dorn Street in Alexandria, a double-lane suburban highway that ran north and south, bordering the target area on its western flank. The landing was a tight squeeze, because the Bell 212 is essentially the civilian version of the military's UH-1 Huey, with a forty-eight-foot-long main rotor blade that barely cleared the telephone poles, the whipping sycamore trees, and a YIELD sign. The Bell also has that same pounding rotor *thwop* as the Huey, which turned everyone around from where they were ordering their Egg McMuffins at the Mickey D's just next door. Mouths agape, they watched as a tall, black-haired dude in a leather jacket jumped from the "police" helicopter, followed by a pudgy curly-headed kid with a laptop case, who both sprinted across Van Dorn through morning traffic, headed for who-knew-where.

Then the rest of the cops had shown up, but there were no sirens or fanfare. Arlington PD set up the first cordons well outside the active perimeter, staying out of the line of sight of something farther south, and using whispers and hand signals rather than bullhorns to keep civilians from wandering past their blockades. The FBI rolled in shortly thereafter, in their sleek black Suburbans and black vans with spinning radar dishes and satcom antennae. But they too stayed out of sight of whatever was going on farther south, and gathered in clumps of whispering men and women and hissing radios outside First Cash Pawn.

That's when they'd sent in their canary, Terry Palamino—a move objected to by Steele, who told SAC Loughran that Lila Kalidi had a penchant for killing anyone who interfered with her lifestyle. But Loughran hadn't listened to him, and now Palamino was dead and Meat Loaf was wailing.

Another burst of gunfire—this time long and nasty—suddenly banged and echoed off the walls along McConnell Avenue, as from inside the warehouse Yassir let loose with his AR-15 and took out all the windows, and the kitchen, at the back of Mumbai Darbar Indian Cuisine.

And that wasn't the end of it. Dasha didn't want the cops outside to get the idea that maybe there were only a couple of lightly armed gunmen inside the warehouse who could be easily taken, so he had Ricardo thrust his AR barrel through a gunport on the eastern side and sprayed a full mag of thirty rounds across a parking lot, shattering the entire glass front of the Evolution Volleyball Club.

There was no doubt about it anymore. If Lila Kalidi was in there, she wasn't alone. It was HRT's turn.

The FBI's Hostage Rescue Team is not a group to be messed with. Based out of Quantico, Virginia, it is one of the foremost counterterror units in the world. Composed of three separate assault elements, the size of which are classified, HRT's operators are considered on a par with the U.S. Army's Delta Force or the Navy's SEAL Team 6 and frequently train with both of those top-tier units, as well as with the United Kingdom's SAS, Germany's GSG9, and France's GIGN. HRT's helicopters, vehicles, breaching tools, diving and parachute gear, weapons, and "battle rattle" are so similar to those of any other elite military squadron that the only thing to distinguish them, on the street or in the field, is their round black shoulder patch worn below a subdued American flag on the left sleeve, which features a flying eagle gripping a length of steel chain and the motto SERVARE VITAS, To Save Lives.

They rolled up in a couple of monster-looking black armored vehicles stamped HRT. One assault element disembarked outside the pawn shop, while the second vehicle cut high above the Van Dorn Station mall to circle around to the far side of the warehouse. The first element's leader climbed down from his vehicle—a Lenco BearCat similar to the one owned by Lila's wild men, but with a long assault ladder mounted on its roof—looked at Steele from under his helmet, and said, "Whatcha doin' here, Hotshot?"

"Hi, Smokey," Steele said and shook the operator's tactical-gloved hand. They had served together in Special Forces, long ago. "The bad girl's mine."

"From what I heard on comms, you can have her. What happened to your face?"

"Are you gonna go in?" Steele said.

"Yeah, but first we'll do the negotiator dance," Smokey said.

"Okay. Got some gear for me?"

Special Agent Loughran had been listening to the exchange and stepped in.

"Steele, you can't just join this team on the fly. I can't allow it."

"Really?" Steele said.

"Loughran," Smokey, the HRT leader, said, "once we show up, you lose your jurisdiction."

"Absolutely *not*." Loughran shook his head. "It's a no-go."

"Will it help if I have the president's chief of staff call you?" Steele said.

Loughran looked at his watch. It was closing in on 9:00 A.M.

"My guess is, right about now," he sneered, "the chief of staff is rolling up on the National Cathedral for a funeral."

"Right." Steele smiled. "Which is why he'll be supremely pissed if I interrupt him for this. Your call."

"Fuck you, Steele," Loughran snapped and walked off.

"Likewise."

At that moment Dalton Goodhill roared up on a Harley-Davidson Street 750. He was wearing jeans, engineer boots, and a sleeveless gray sweatshirt with a desert camo field jacket and flying goggles, no helmet. His short-barreled shotgun was nestled in his shoulder rig under the jacket.

Smokey said to Steele, "Go in the beast and get a vest from the trunk behind the passenger seat. What're you carrying?"

"A Sig, nine mil."

"Okay then, you're Tail-End Charlie. You want us to take her alive?"

"Yeah, so I can kill her myself."

"This chick must've *really* pissed you off, Hot-shot."

"Got any frags?" Steele asked.

"Frags?" Smokey's eyes bugged. "We don't use grenades domestically, my man. Think you're back in Kabul?"

"Right." Steele grinned. He climbed into the truck, stripped off his jacket, put on a Level 3 Kevlar vest, put his jacket back on, and started rummaging around until he found a hidden can of M26 fragmentation grenades in their cardboard cocoons and stuffed one into his outside jacket pocket. When he came out of the truck, Goodhill was trying to convince Smokey to let him go in with the team as well.

"Who the hell are you?" Smokey was saying.

"I'm Steele's uncle."

"You spooks are all nuts," Smokey said. "One of you's enough."

Ralphy was standing well back, clutching his laptop case, and not volunteering for anything.

Agent Loughran sent an FBI negotiator down McConnell Avenue with a bullhorn, but at least he was protected by one trembling agent with a mobile assault shield. It was a heavy curved slab of steel with a grip handle on the inside and a small slit window of ballistic plexiglass. They got within fifty meters of the warehouse, the negotiator called out proposals for a peaceful resolution over the bullhorn, and he and his escort were met with a hail of gunfire, which they only escaped because an HRT heavy weapons man had climbed onto the roof of Kabul Kabob Express and opened up on Dasha's gunports with an M249 Squad Automatic Weapon.

The residents of Arlington had never heard a machine gun firing in their neighborhood before. It sounded like a nail gun on speed. Nor were they prepared for Dasha's response, which was to have his men stick the barrels of their AR-15s through the holes in the western wall of the warehouse and open up on the three-story condominium next door. Windows exploded, children were being smothered on the floors by their screaming parents, one man leaped from his second-story balcony into the condo's swimming pool.

"Go! Go! Go!" Smokey spun around and yelled to his team, and they sprinted across McConnell Avenue to the south side, stacked up in a crouching posture, and moved forward in a quick step like a long green-and-black centipede bristling with weapons.

With Steele bringing up the rear of the assault element—at which point he realized that he hadn't even donned a spare helmet—all of his thoughts were of Lila Kalidi, the wire stitches tearing at his shoulder, and his wounded pride that he'd let her escape and hadn't finished her off. A man was lying out there dead in the street, which wouldn't have happened had he killed her, or so he thought.

When they reached the corner of Shillings, the gunfire from inside the warehouse suddenly ceased, Meat Loaf stopped wailing, and an eerie silence swept over the streets glistening with glass and brass shell casings. The morning air smelled like coffee, blood, cordite, and sweat. The HRT operator just in front of Steele said, "Well, we've got 'em contained. They're not going anywhere."

And at that moment, there was a ripping vehicular motor scream, the front of the warehouse seemed to explode, and a giant black Lenco BearCat armored assault vehicle rammed down the double front doors like a landing ramp on an LST at the Normandy invasion. The welded steel slabs of the doors crushed Terry Palamino's corpse to bloody butter as all nine tons of BearCat bounced over him, made a screeching turn to the left, and zoomed down McConnell Avenue.

The HRT operators threw themselves to the sidewalk and rolled up tight to the condominium walls. There was no point in shooting at the racing monster, because they knew their rounds would just ricochet wild, and the only one who was back on his feet within half a second of the BearCat passing by was Eric Steele.

He chased it, though he didn't expect to catch it. He raced past First Cash Pawn and yelled to Goodhill and Ralphy, "On me!"

They followed him on foot as he pounded across South Van Dorn, heading for Allie's helo, whose blades were already starting to whip into a blur. Allie knew a shit show when she saw one.

"Where the hell are we going, Steele?" Ralphy called out in a wheezing screech.

"Home Depot," Steele yelled back, and kept running.

CHAPTER 48

ALEXANDRIA, VIRGINIA

Allie pulled pitch and yanked the helo off the ground while Ralphy's legs were still hanging out of the cargo compartment. Steele and Goodhill had beaten him to the bird, leaped inside, and spun around to haul him in. But Allie waited for no man, and Ralphy was still screaming while they got him onto a bench.

Steele grabbed a headset off a fuselage hook and jammed it onto his head while Goodhill slammed the cargo door and Ralphy hugged his laptop and tried to breathe again. Steele pushed the mic module to his lips, thumbed the transmit button, and spoke to Allie.

"Home *what*?" she said.

"Depot."

"We're going shopping now?" She was flying from the left seat and pulled her helmet off. Her blond hair went wild in the slipstream rushing through her window and she crowned it with a headset like Steele's. "How're we gonna find that?"

"There's one in every town," Steele said as he whipped out his cell and thumbed the search engine.

"They're heading north toward the city, Steele," Goodhill shouted. He had his face pressed to the cargo-door window and wasn't wearing a headset, but he could see the BearCat racing north on Van Dorn, with a line of police cars wailing behind it. "Know where they're going?"

"I got a good idea," Steele said, then he jumped off his bench, fell to his knees behind Allie's seat, and shot his right arm over her shoulder. "Right there! See it? Big orange sign, about one klick east."

Goodhill turned from the door window, found another headset nearby, and jammed it onto his bald head. He reached out for Steele's shoulder, pulled him around, and then they were both on their knees on the helo's floor, face-to-face.

"What's your plan, kid?" Goodhill said.

"That BearCat's got a snorkel."

"A what?"

"A breathing pipe, rigged for deep water or chem-bio. I saw it sticking up from the roof." Steele pulled the M26 grenade from his jacket pocket, showed it to Goodhill, and put it back again.

"You're outta your mind." Goodhill looked up at the ceiling, where a fast-rope pintle mount was rigged, but there was no rope attached to it, and no fat coil in the compartment either. "And we got no rope."

"We don't know what's in that truck, Blade," Steele said. "Could be half a ton of ammonium nitrate. They're headed for the cathedral. We both know *that*."

"My money's on you, kid," Goodhill said. "Let's do it."

"I think I'm going to throw up," Ralphy groaned from his bench, but no one heard him.

It was closing in on ten o'clock in the morning. In Washington, President Denton Cole's casket had already reached the National Cathedral, wheeled on a fine black horse-drawn caisson, and followed by a single, magnificent, black cavalry steed, riderless and with a pair of boots turned backward in his stirrups. From the steps of the Capitol and all the way up to the church, thousands of mourners had lined the chilly but sunny streets, as the fifes and drums bleated and rolled, and nearly all of the Free World's leaders, and many of the not-so-free, walked and now filed into the magnificent building in solemn, silent procession.

The parking lot of Home Depot, which the franchise shared with the Trade Center Shopping Village at 400 South Pickett in Alexandria, was already packed with cars. There was nowhere for Allie to set the helo down, so she hovered the skids one foot above the roof of a Ford F150 while Steele and Goodhill slid down the truck's windshield and over the hood onto the asphalt, and then helped Ralphy down. Shoppers stopped and gawked as if the helo were a pterodactyl and they were all tourists in Jurassic Park.

Steele grabbed Ralphy by his Disney jacket and pointed across the lot to a Shell station.

"Ralphy, get over there and bring us back a can of gas," Steele shouted under the spinning helo blades. "Show them the bird, tell them it's a national emergency, but *don't* come back without it."

"Okay, okay." Ralphy took off and Steele and Goodhill sprinted for the store's main entrance.

"Rope," Steele said on the run. "Seventy-five feet."

"Quarter inch or half?"

"Half, if you can, and work gloves."

"Roger."

They split up by the cash registers inside and Steele whipped his head around until he saw the sign for tool rentals. He ran into the small showroom, where an older man was manning the deposit desk.

"Got a gas-powered chainsaw?" Steele asked.

"Right over there on the wall."

Steele ran over and was just about to pull the chainsaw down when he realized it wouldn't cut steel, and instead grabbed a Hilti PRO gas concrete saw with a fourteen-inch circular blade. He yanked it off the hook, called "Thanks," and ran out the tool rental exit door.

"Hey! What the hell?" The counter man chased after him. "You gotta pay up front for that, buddy!"

But Steele was already climbing back up onto the F150, tossing the saw into the bird, and crawling inside. Goodhill showed up seconds after with a seventy-five-foot coil of half-inch Manila twist rope and a pair of work gloves, which he'd blatantly shoplifted. Then Ralphy arrived, panting and hauling a red plastic two-gallon gas can, but he couldn't climb up onto the hood of the truck, so Goodhill had to climb back down and shove Ralphy's butt up into the helo. They took off again while the pickup truck's wide-eyed owner stood there below, snapping pics with his cell phone.

Steele jammed the headset back on as he opened the concrete saw's gas cover and Goodhill filled it from the can, remarkably not spilling a drop.

"Haul ass, Allie," Steele said through his mic.

"I love it when you talk sweet to me," she said, but she dipped the nose and raced the bird north over Arlington at less than a hundred feet, spooling it up toward 120 knots, while Ralphy gripped his bench with both hands and babbled prayers.

Steele shed his jacket, got rid of the Kevlar vest, zipped the jacket back on, stood up in the middle of the cargo compartment, spread his feet, and gripped the pintle above with his hands. Goodhill unwound part of the rope, took out his folding knife, sliced off a fifteen-foot strand, and went to work.

"Swiss seat?" he yelled at Steele.

"Yeah, with a chest knot."

"I got a visual," Allie said in Steele's headset. "They're in Arlington on 395, two miles out with about nine cruisers behind 'em, but I don't think they're going for the Pentagon."

"Nope," Steele said. "Close the range, Allie."

"I'm already choking the throttle, baby."

Goodhill looped the fifteen-foot rope around the back of Steele's waist, braided the two ends in front, dropped them both inside his thighs, fed them up through the rear waistband again, and yanked hard until they sliced up into both sides of his crotch, making a primitive sling for his butt. Then he braided them again in front, tied them off with a square knot and two half-hitch "keepers" to lock the whole thing in place. He cut off the long ends, tossed one away, looped the other around Steele's chest under his armpits, and tied it so tightly Steele coughed.

"Can you breathe?" Goodhill shouted.

"No."

"Good."

Goodhill then slid the end of the remaining sixty feet of rope down through the front of Steele's chest loop and tied it off to the Swiss seat with four hitches. He fed the rest of it through the pintle above, pulled his gloves on, and shot Steele a thumbs-up.

Steele slid the cargo door open on the starboard side and the compartment roared like a hurricane. He sat down at the lip of the deck, dragged the saw over to his side, stuck his face and his legs out, and was instantly whipped by the roaring wind, his cheeks flapping like a dog's poking his head from the family sedan. They were thundering along at a hundred feet and the BearCat was racing up the highway toward Washington about two hundred feet in front of their nose.

"They're going for the Fourteenth Street Bridge," Allie said.

"I see that," Steele shouted in the corkscrewing wind.

"That's your only shot, Steele," she said. "After that I got structures up ahead, like maybe the Jefferson Memorial and the Washington Monument. Nothing major, but ya know . . ."

"Oh my *Jesus*." Ralphy had crawled to the opposite cargo door, which was still closed, and smeared himself against it like a cartoon cat. His hair was doing crazy things in the windstorm.

"Shove over," Goodhill shouted at Steele and squeezed himself down on the deck beside him.

"Put me on the left side of the truck roof," Steele said to Allie. "Snorkel's on the right front corner."

"I'll be happy if I don't smack you into a pylon," she said, but she dipped the Bell's nose and crawled it forward and down, its twin turbines screaming, and then the BearCat loomed so large below, to Steele it looked like they were going to smash into it like a wrecking ball. Just behind them the police cruiser sirens were warbling like banshees. Out in front, somehow the bridge had been cleared of all traffic, maybe by roadblocks, but Steele didn't know or care.

They were just above the roof, maybe at eight feet, when the BearCat's heavy round tank hatch swung open. It clanged back on its massive hinge in the wind, and one of Lila's killers popped up with his AR-15 and whipped it around at the helo. Steele threw himself backward while Goodhill blew the man's face off with his short-barreled twelve gauge, and when Steele sat back up again Goodhill growled, "*Miami Vice*, my ass."

Someone inside the BearCat yanked the hatch closed again. Then Goodhill jumped back up inside the helo, hauled on the rope through the pintle until only ten feet of it was left to Steele, whipped the slack around his waist, braced his feet on the floor, and yelled, "Now!"

Steele tore his headset off, gripped the saw, and

dropped to the helo's skid. Then he jumped from that, fell six feet, and bounced at the end like a puppet. Right away he started spinning, because he couldn't touch the BearCat's roof with his boots and the wind was whipping his flailing legs. He saw the black blur of the upthrust steel snorkel as it came around for the sixth time, and he jammed the circular blade of the saw against it to halt his spin. Then he yanked the starter cord with every muscle in his right arm and it roared to life, spewing blue smoke, and it ground through the pipe in a shower of sparks until the top six inches with its sealed vent cap went tumbling away in the wind.

Steele hurled the saw over the side of the bridge, where it flipped end over end and splashed in the river. He yanked the grenade from his jacket pocket, pulled the pin, let the spoon fly off, and dropped it down the snorkel like a mortar shell.

He looked up at Allie, thrust a thumb high in the sky, and his chest felt like it was going to burst as she pulled pitch hard, banked to the left, and within two seconds had him at four hundred feet.

The BearCat didn't just explode. It seemed more like it disappeared in an enormous cloud of black dust, as if it had been carved from charcoal. Steele didn't know there were nine men aboard wearing suicide vests, but the sound was unearthly, like someone ripping a gigantic sheet of Velcro, and the flash was like videos he'd seen of Hiroshima. The concussion smacked him like an iron skillet. It left one concrete buttress of the bridge flank completely blown away, a huge black smoking hole in the road, and nothing else but a few clumps of bloody flesh and one lazily rolling fat black tire.

Goodhill hauled Steele back up into the bird. He fell on his face and just lay there for a good fifteen seconds. Then Allie turned around and tapped her earcup. Goodhill handed Steele his headset and he sat up, smeared it on, and looked over at Ralphy, who was white as a sheet and shaking like he'd just been Tasered.

"Steele, you copy?" It was Smokey the HRT team leader.

"Yeah, good copy," Steele said.

"My SAW gunner hit one of your jihadis, and his asshole buddies left him behind."

"Yeah? So?"

"We just talked to him," Smokey said. "Hate to ruin your day, Hotshot, but your girlfriend wasn't in that truck."

CHAPTER 49

THE NATIONAL CATHEDRAL, WASHINGTON, D.C.

The tubby nun appeared at the rear fountain entrance of the cathedral once more, and standing there were the two Secret Service agents and the K-9 cop who'd been there two days before.

This time, however, Lila Kalidi had no intention of performing a smell-test run. Her typewriter case was packed with twenty pounds of cellophane-sealed Semtex, a detonator and digital timer, and her brown woolen cloak was lined with ten more cellophane-wrapped Semtex bricks, replacing the previous foam stuffing that had made her look porcine. The nontraceable vintage of the plastique had already proved that its vapors wouldn't trigger the German shepherd's olfactory nodes, so she was certain that once again, she'd pass right by.

There was a cordon of uniformed cops lining the south side of the circular drive at the cathedral's rear, and inside the fountain quadrant, the two Secret Service agents saw "their nun" smiling and blessing the policemen. A white-shirted lieutenant turned around and one of the agents signaled to wave her through. The services would soon be ending. The choir inside, 120 strong, was singing "The Navy Hymn," and already the scores of male and female law enforcement officers were stretching and yawning with relief that the whole thing was almost over.

Lila crossed from the drive, through the granite archway, and into the fountain enclave. The water was sailing up from the steel black rose, spraying a lovely rainbow in the late-morning air and cascading down into the elliptical pool, adding the sounds of a waterfall to the magnificent choral voices echoing from the church's cavern of stone.

The two agents and the cop had receded partway behind a buttress, so they could smoke without supervisory disapproval. But they were still guarding the plain wooden door that led to the underground chapels, and she couldn't just pass them without being sniffed. She smiled, and stopped, and with the typewriter case clutched in her left hand said, "Good morning, my valiant young countrymen."

"Morning, Sister," the senior agent said as he dragged on his Marlboro. "I'm afraid you're going to have to wait till this whole thing's over. Won't be long."

"Oh, that's no fuss at all," Lila said.

But then she realized something was wrong. The dog had risen from sitting next to his policeman handler and was straining at his leash, his black nose aimed at her case. A flood of heat rose through her neck and she realized she'd made a mistake. It wasn't the Semtex. It was the detonator, which had a minuscule amount of fulminate of mercury inside its cap, and no doubt the dog had been trained to hit on that.

Sure enough, he whined, and then sat. His handler looked down at the dog, his brow furrowed under his cap, and then he looked back up at Lila.

"Oh," she said with a beatific smile, "it must be my sandwich," and she reached inside her cowl, pulled out a Smith & Wesson M&P Shield 9 mm pistol with an Obsidian 9 silencer, and shot each man point-blank in the face and the dog in the top of his skull, before he could even whimper.

She'd fired all four shots in less than two seconds, with all the emotion of using a staple gun to tack a garage sale poster to a telephone pole. The men toppled back like bowling pins, the dog collapsed onto his paws. She leaned over the cop, because he appeared to still be gurgling, and she shot him once more, put the pistol away, clutched her typewriter case, and walked into the doorway that led to the Chapel of St. Joseph of Arimathea. . . .

"This is gonna be tight," said Allie as she worked the Bell 212's cyclic and collective like a teenage competition video-gamer and swung the big machine onto the grassy knoll at the rear flank of the cathedral. The distance between the flagpole and that bank of lights *looked* like more than fifty feet, but she wasn't sure, and she figured she'd either stick it or clang the pole, shatter her rotor blade, and dice everybody nearby into bloody meat slices. "Five seconds, boys, and we're either heroes or zeros."

Steele, Goodhill, and Ralphy braced themselves in the back. Steele had told Smokey not to call in anything to his counterparts there on the ground, because if his instincts were wrong and Lila wasn't there, it would be like shouting "Fire!" in a crowded theater, and everyone inside the funeral service would go screaming and sprinting for their armored cars.

"Let's play it out," he shouted to Goodhill as the helo yawed, pitched, and rolled.

"Roger, kid," Goodhill shouted back. "But if she's here, we better find her fast."

Ralphy just moaned.

The bird whipped the surrounding trees like a giant eggbeater and cops' caps flew off as they stared, but the helo was marked as Metro PD, so they figured it all was kosher. The cargo door opened and the trio spilled out and started running as they waved their federal IDs from their wallets. Goodhill would circle around to the far side of the cathedral and search the café and support buildings. Ralphy would go in through the tourists' entrance and hunt for a woman he'd never seen before—and he was unarmed and scared shitless because he'd left his Glock at home.

Steele would flank the building and come in through the back.

He ran across the circular drive, waved his ID, broke past the cops and into the fountain enclave. He heard the thundering chorus through the cathedral's vibrating stained glass windows. He saw the three dead men and the dog lying in pools of muddy blood behind the buttress. He pulled out his

Sig, press-checked the action, yanked the wooden door open, and went inside.

The long marble hallway was muted and dark. He moved along the left-hand wall, gripping the Sig two-handed, and some instinct told him she wasn't in the Bethlehem Chapel, but he swept the open doorway anyway and briefly scanned the pews, then kept on going. He checked the marble stairway on the right that led down to the crypts from the cathedral above—saw nothing, felt nothing—kept on going, and without his pulse rate rising more than a beat, stepped over the legs of another dead uniformed agent sprawled in the hallway. He was on cold, autopilot fury.

Then he arrived at the Chapel of St. Joseph of Arimathea. He took a breath, released it, and sliced the pie as he entered the wide-open arch and the slab stone stairs that led down to the chapel's floor. His gunsight swept the rows of wooden chairs, the identical staircase and arch on the opposite side, and settled on a concrete bier, shaped like a small child's coffin, which sat on the priest's pulpit just beneath the medieval wall mural.

A brown cloak of some sort was lying on the top of the bier, carefully folded, and inside out. Its lining was ordered with ten bricks of dull red clay, but he knew they weren't clay. On top of those bricks sat an old typewriter case with the lid closed. A crumpled nun's veil lay on the floor.

He took one step into the space. A gun barrel slammed against his left temple.

"You should know when you're beaten, Steele," Lila said.

He slowly lowered his pistol, with only his right hand. And at that moment, in one of those strange compressions of time—which lasted perhaps only half a second—he thought about all the times he'd seen those stupid cinematic confrontations between heroes and villains, those ridiculous climaxes of verbal jousting where opposing philosophies were shouted and challenges hurled before the final gunshots, which always ended the very same way.

And he knew he wasn't going to say one damn thing to Lila Kalidi.

He dropped the pistol, and before it hit the floor, he shot his left palm straight up, smacked the right side of her pistol as he gripped it and pushed, jerked his head back as she fired and the round missed his nose by a millimeter, flashed his right hand inside his jacket, yanked Lila's stiletto from his belt, spun to the left, and plunged it into her heart, hilt deep.

He was still gripping her smoking handgun. Her fingers released it, and she stared at him, and her full lips parted like a fish. She was wearing a black, full-body leotard, with her own knife hilt vibrating like a tuning fork in her chest. She slumped to her knees and her head dropped forward.

Steele reached down, grabbed a handful of her short blond hair, jerked her head back up, looked into her glazed-over eyes, and said, "You look much prettier dead," and dropped her onto her back.

He picked up his handgun, but he didn't touch hers. His nerve endings were vibrating like strings on a steel guitar. He walked down the stairs, heading for the bomb, because he knew that's what it was. Then something moved behind him on the right and he spun with his pistol and his finger curled in the trigger.

It was Meg Harden. She was dressed for a funeral, in a dark blue suit jacket with a matching skirt and white blouse. Her raven hair was piled up on her head, and when she saw him she kept her hands at her sides, just like she'd done at the range.

He almost shot her, for the second time that week. The chorus above them started singing "Amazing Grace."

"If you're looking for your bosom buddy," he said, "she's right over there on the floor."

"Eric . . . what are you talking about?" Meg said. "And your face . . . what happened?"

"You told me Kalidi was gone, Meg, but she just killed four men and a dog. Drop to your knees, hands on your head."

"Eric, wait," Meg started to plead.

"Do it fucking now!"

She dropped to her knees.

Then Ralphy stumbled into the right side of the opposite archway, from the direction of the gift shop, which was dark and closed. He was breathless and had to lean on the jamb.

"I couldn't find her, Steele," he gasped, then he realized he was looking at Stalker Seven, about to shoot Meg Harden, and there was a female corpse behind Steele's left shoulder with a black knife sticking out of her chest.

"That's okay, Ralphy," Steele said. "I found them both."

"Both?"

The chorus above them was growing louder. The audience of family mourners, friends, and statesmen and women had begun to join in.

"'Twas grace that taught my heart to fear . . . and grace my fear relieved . . ."

"Put the gun down, Eric."

Steele flicked his eyes to the left, past Ralphy, where Mike Pitts had just limped through the same arch on the other side. He had his cane in his left hand and a Glock 42 in his right, a sub-compact pistol in .380 Auto. But the weird thing—besides the fact that he was pointing the gun at Steele—was that he was dressed in his Army Service Uniform, dress blues, with all his service ribbons, his major's ranks, and his mess dress cap on his head.

"Mike," Steele said through clenched teeth, "you got some 'splainin' to do too. You stood me up for dinner, and this corpse over there almost ate my lunch."

"I thought she was *gone*, Eric," Meg bleated. She almost had to shout above the thundering voices above. "Ask Pitts! He's the one who told me that."

Steele heard a shotgun racking a shell. He flicked his head around for a second and saw Goodhill standing two stairs up to his left. He was aiming his sawed-off twelve gauge across the chapel at Pitts.

"A Mexican standoff," Goodhill growled. "I love those."

"Oh my freaking God," Ralphy moaned.

"Pitts, you're aiming a piece at my Alpha," Goodhill said. "I'll give you three seconds to put it up, and the first two don't count."

"I didn't know Kalidi was still here, *Eric*." Meg was starting to cry. "I swear!"

"She's right," Pitts said. "She didn't. I sent her a phony Red Notice."

Everyone turned and looked at him. His face had gone chalky, his cheeks were trembling, and he was no longer gripping the Glock like he meant it.

"It was me, all the time." Pitts's eyes clouded over and he wasn't looking at any one of them really, just off into some sort of horrific vision in his head. "I tried to get out of it, but they wouldn't let me. They had me, and once they did, they had Katherine and the girls and the baby too, and then I was done. It was me . . . all the Alpha setups, the backdoor into Q Street. It's all here in a letter." He patted his uniform pocket. "I'm sorry. I really am." He lifted the Glock barrel and twisted it under his chin. "The National Cathedral," he whispered. "No better place to die." And he pulled the trigger, the gunshot muffled by his throat and his brain, and he toppled backward onto the floor.

Meg slumped over her knees, weeping. Ralphy slid down the jamb of the archway, both hands covering his eyes. Steele tucked his Sig into his waistband holster and turned to Goodhill, who had lowered his pump gun.

"Take her and get out of here," Steele said.

"Okay, kid." Goodhill walked over to Meg and pulled her up. She slumped against him and sobbed, and he half dragged her up the stairs. He turned to Steele at the top. "Sure you don't wanna come?"

Steele pointed up at the ceiling. "Amazing Grace"

was roaring into a gorgeous crescendo. Goodhill nodded and left with Meg.

Steele walked over to the coffin bier and Lila's typewriter case. He took a breath and opened the top. There was an old Olivetti inside, but nestled between the two black ribbon spools was a digital timer. Below that, through the strikers that held the metal letters, Steele could see a large block of plastic explosive nestled around a battery pack. Three thick wires—blue, red, and green—led from the timer to the pack, and from there, he knew another pair led to an embedded detonator. He smiled, shook his head, walked over to Ralphy, hauled him up off the floor, and dragged him over to the bomb.

"Get to work on this, Ralphy," he said. "We sent you to that EOD course for a reason." And he left him there, shaking and staring at the device, and he walked over to Lila's corpse, yanked the stiletto from her chest, wiped it on his jeans, and came back.

"But, Steele." Ralphy groaned. "The timer. Did you see this?"

"Yeah."

"The numbers aren't ticking *down*, Steele. They're ticking up!"

"I know."

"That means, we don't know how long it's set for. . . ."

"That's right, so you better hurry up."

"But, Steele." Ralphy slumped to his knees in front of the bier. His hands were trembling and sweaty. "I . . . I don't know which, there's too many, it's not binary . . . I *can't*."

Steele put his right hand on Persko's shoulder and squeezed it with something like affection. Then he placed the stiletto in his sweat-soaked palm, squeezed his hand closed around it, and bent to his ear.

"Ralphy," he said. "The president of the United States, the First Lady, and the entire Free World are upstairs. Just cut a fucking wire."

EPILOGUE

NEVILLE ISLAND, PENNSYLVANIA

There were some feathery wisps of smoke rising from the foundation of Eric Steele's house, but this time they were from the hot dog grill of the construction guys working on the renovations. They'd soon be taking a break for supper.

Slab by slab, the reinforced concrete walls were going back up. He'd had them shipped in from the same company that made T-walls for Bagram Airfield in Afghanistan, because he figured if they were good enough for Taliban rockets, they'd do for a remote forest fortress out here. The roof wasn't on yet, but the doorways and windows were cut, and the new Krieger level-four blast doors were lying nearby on their pallets. Brand-new kitchen appliances, security cameras, and motion sensors had all been delivered. Ralphy was coming up soon to help install all that stuff. The steel slabs for his armory were on the way. He liked welding, so he'd do that himself.

There'd been a battle with his homeowner's insurance company over paying for the loss of the house—a destructive assault by Russian terrorists wasn't listed in the policy. Then someone from the IRS had made a discreet phone call to the insurance company, and lo and behold, a bank check arrived. It paid to have friends in low places.

Winter falls hard in Pittsburgh. There was snow on the ground, ice in the long gravel driveway, and Steele was wearing his navy peacoat again and a black watch cap, and wondering how his niece was doing out at sea. Dalton Goodhill's Harley was kick-standed over on a slab of wet plywood. They were standing elbow to elbow, watching another wall go up and smoking cheap Macanudos.

"Heard anything from Meg?" Blade asked. "It's been a month."

"Negative."

"Well, kid. Put a gun to my head, shove me down on my knees, and call me a traitor, might take me a while too."

"Yup." Steele wasn't sure how he felt about that, but guilt wasn't on his radar.

"I actually thought it was Lansky," Goodhill said.

Steele looked at him. "Really?"

"Yeah. Never trusted anybody above the rank of E-8." Goodhill grinned and blew out a cloud of cigar smoke mixed with lung steam.

"Mike Pitts was the last on my list," Steele said. "Until he wasn't."

"Poor bastard. Just goes to show you, never go to confession."

They'd both read Pitts's letter. It was sad, and

tragic for Katherine and the kids. But the White House had covered it up. Pitts had been buried with full honors at Arlington.

"Lansky called me yesterday," Goodhill said. "President Rockford wants to give you and me some sorta medals."

"Can we decline?"

"Snub the boss? Sure, if you never want the Program stood up again."

"Think there's a chance of that?" Steele asked, though he wasn't sure he wanted it. A job where your best friends didn't get killed all the time might be better.

"Maybe. But don't worry, our honors'll probably be pinned on us in the White House kitchen."

"Okay, but only if Ralphy gets one too. And Frankie."

"Agreed."

Goodhill dropped the last inch of his cigar in the snow, where it hissed under the crush of his motorcycle boot.

"I'm gonna go see the family," he said.

"Somebody loves you?" Steele smirked.

"I didn't say that. I just said I was gonna go see 'em." Goodhill shook Steele's hand, hard, then walked to his bike, kicked it over, and rumbled off down the driveway. He wasn't wearing a helmet.

Steele watched as his mother got out of his parked GTO, hugged herself in the cold, picked her way through the construction debris, and came over. She was wearing a paisley scarf on her head and a pair of stylish sunglasses. Steele thought she was the most beautiful woman of her age he'd ever seen—maybe of any age. She stopped and smiled up at him.

"Can we go now, Eric? I'm getting hungry."

"Sure, Mom," he said. "There's some stuff we need to discuss."

She cocked her head and wagged a finger.

"No family therapy today. If you promise to shut up, I'll buy you dinner."

He laughed, and she took his elbow, and they walked off back toward his car.

"By the way," she said, "something came for you in the mail today."

"Yeah? What was it?"

"A postcard." She smiled. "From your father."

ACKNOWLEDGMENTS

Stories are always collaborations. It takes a village. *One True Patriot* would not have been possible without the steadfast dedication and contribution of several people. David Highfill, my editor, is flat-out incredible. I've worked with him for eight years now, and every day I'm grateful. He's the best in the business. Dan Conaway is my agent. He took a chance on me and I'm thankful for it. He strikes the perfect balance between career mentor, story consultant, and editor. Dan, thank you for your time and attention.

Next up is my battle buddy Steve Hartov. Thanks for being in the trenches with me, brother. You've become a wonderful friend, and you made this book better through your association with it. John Rokosz, my old friend, thank you. You are a fantastic writer and a talented storyteller. Your involvement in this story helped to elevate this book.

Melanie. As you say in your Twitter bio, you're my number one supporter! Thank you for always being there for me. I'm so lucky and blessed to have you in my life.

Ethan, Emma, and Evan. My three children. Being your Dad and watching you grow has been the privilege of a lifetime. You are the reason for all of this!

If you enjoyed *One True Patriot*,
keep reading for a sneak peek at
the next thrilling installment in
the Eric Steele series,

LEFT FOR DEAD

Available in hardcover Fall 2021
from William Morrow

CHAPTER 1

ZHAGANTU, CHINA

The helicopters arrived at midnight, and the men they carried killed everyone they met.

There were three of the machines, black and hulking, sleek as sharks, all emblazoned with the red stars of the Chinese Communist Party's People's Liberation Army. They were Harbin Z-20s, heavily armed, capable of three hundred knots airspeed at treetop level and each hauling a dozen assaulters. They looked much like U.S. Army UH-60 Blackhawks, but they were not cheap knockoffs. Their rotor systems had been expertly cloned from a crashed American stealth helicopter, given to Beijing by the Pakistanis after U.S. Navy SEALs had terminated Osama bin Laden.

The Harbin Z-20s were very quiet. No one heard them coming at Toqui 13, the most secret biological warfare laboratory in all of China.

The lab was a Level V facility drilled into the summit of a wind scarred butte that resembled Devils Tower in Wyoming. It was located in the absolute nowhere of the north central Chinese badlands, ten kilometers from the Mongolian border. You couldn't just stumble upon it, and if you did you'd be shot on the spot and no one would find your corpse. Toqui 13, whose name meant Spearhead in Mandarin, had been built to harvest only one thing: a genetically enhanced coronavirus called Gantu-62 that could kill a Notre Dame linebacker in fifteen minutes.

Dr. Ai Liang, a full bird colonel in the People's Army, was the laboratory's director, and up until recently she'd been fervently dedicated to the Chinese Communist Party. The daughter of a distinguished couple who made their mark in the Cultural Revolution, she'd graduated with honors from Changchun University of Science and Technology while pursuing her military career. Mao Zedong was her god.

But three weeks ago, something had happened that had flipped a switch inside Dr. Liang. Her research assistant, 2nd Lieutenant Chang Wu—a handsome young man with a lovely wife and three precious girls in Shanghai—had slipped on a spill of lubricant from an air compressor and had smashed the glass of an incubator with his elbow. The shards had sliced open his Military Oriented Protective Posture suit, as well as his flesh.

Lieutenant Wu instantly knew what was going to happen, and so did his mentor. Together, they had tested Gantu-62 on laboratory animals—first mice, then rabbits, and finally rhesus macaque monkeys. The viral storm had swept through Wu's bloodstream in minutes and his immunological response was explosive. It was like an Ebola reaction in hyper speed. Helpless and horrified, Dr. Liang had watched the poor boy retch up his own intestines, drown in his own blood, and choke to death on the laboratory floor.

Two days prior to this evening, she had finally emerged from three weeks in quarantine isolation, where she'd examined her life and its purpose and had wept until she had no tears left. She had firmly concluded that there should be no Level V biowarfare laboratories, or anything like Gantu-62, *anywhere* in the world.

Tonight she was going to shut the whole damn thing down. . . .

The numerical designation of all such facilities is a reference to how many segregated floors there are. Level I, at the very bottom of Toqui 13, held the effluent decontamination systems. Above that on Level II was the research lab with inflatable seal doors, autoclaves, Petri dish germ farms, and breathing hoses into which lab workers plugged their MOPP helmets. Next came Level III—the serious business floor—with buffer corridors, steel double-entrance doors, incubators for "arms-only" handling of samples, electron microscopes, more breathing hoses, and reverse suction pumps to keep the air pressure at less than one atmosphere.

Level III was where they carefully deposited the already deadly, naturally occurring viruses being farmed on Level II and genetically enhanced them to be fifty times more lethal. If you ripped a hole in your PPE on Level III—as Chang Wu had done—they took your corpse right down to the giant incinerator below the blending tank under Level I and sent a very nice note and the Medal of Loyalty and Integrity to your mother.

Levels IV and V were all about reprocessing air, with HEPA filters, exhaust fans, and breathing air reservoirs—two whole floors just to keep everyone alive. And finally, at the top was the last level, which didn't count numerically, containing the lab's administrative offices, cafeteria, sleeping quarters, one small amphitheater, and, outside past the entrance, a helicopter landing pad.

It was a large facility shaped like a giant steel travel mug sunk into the excavated rock of the butte, with only the top floor and its camouflaged roof exposed. To get there, you had to fly west from Beijing to Hohhot on a PLA aircraft, ride a blacked-out government bus all the way to Baotou, and turn north for Bayan Obo for another sixty kilometers until you reached the alpine tram that took you up to one of the most dangerous buildings on earth. It was like working at an outpost on Mars.

Now Dr. Liang—outwardly composed though her stomach churned—took her place at the amphitheater's podium to start her emergency briefing. She was an attractive woman in her early forties, petite and toned from the lab's daily tai chi sessions. She had long dark hair swirled up into a bun, hazel eyes, a small nose, white teeth, and wore fashionable purple glasses. She was also very pale, but everyone who worked at Toqui 13 was pale.

"I must apologize to all of you for waking you up," she began as she clutched a set of phony PLA directives that she'd forged on her own computer. "However, we have received urgent orders with which we must all comply."

She looked at the twenty-three wide-eyed faces

staring back at her. Almost everyone was dressed in PLA track pants and T-shirts because she'd rousted them from their beds. Six of them were women and none was older than thirty-one. They were lab technicians, analysts, biomedical experts, and maintenance personnel, and all were patriots and dedicated party members. She had dressed in her brown camouflage Military Medical Team uniform to emphasize that her words were blessed by officialdom.

"You are all aware of the unfortunate fate of Lieutenant Wu," she continued, "which has been reviewed by the Committee for State Security. The Party has now deemed Toqui 13 as a domestic risk beyond acceptability." She was lying. She didn't dare tell them the truth because she knew that soon they'd all be interrogated, and if any of them were suspected of conspiring with her, they'd spend the rest of their days in a reeducation camp with the Uyghurs. "Therefore, I am very sorry to say . . . tonight we are closing down this laboratory."

Her minions gasped as if a surge of electricity had coursed through their amphitheater seats. They looked at each other, then back at Liang. One of them clutched an ornate chess set to her bosom and another clamped his mouth with both hands.

"Yes." Dr. Liang nodded with a mournful expression. "It is a terrible blow, yet it is true. I know this is difficult, and you've all done spectacular work here, but the needs of the Party . . ."

She glanced over their heads past the heavy tempered glass entrance doors. Outside on the landing pad four internal security guards were pacing back and forth. They were armed only with Type 77B pistols. No one ever threatened Toqui 13.

"You have one hour to pack your personal effects, and you will leave everything else behind. We will assemble outside at the tram and begin our journey back to Beijing." She smiled—a nurturing expression, especially for a colonel. Her plan was to be the last one to leave. Later, after she descended below Level I, she would pour thirty liters of the generator fuel she'd been secretly hoarding all over the floor, slice through the high-pressure oxygen hoses, fire up the incinerator, and open its doors. "Just five minutes for questions, please, and then we must hurry."

A young man raised a trembling hand. He'd been Lieutenant Chang Wu's best friend at Toqui 13, and his heart was still broken.

"Colonel Liang, with respect, why can we not first complete the application analysis for weaponization? After all, it is nearly . . ."

Dr. Liang raised a hand to shush him because she'd noticed something strange outside. A vibration was shivering the entrance glass and she saw a red-orange glow flooding the tarmac apron. The guards were looking up at the sky, and stepping back, and two of their fur hats fluttered off their heads.

A helicopter appeared. There was very little dust and debris at the top of Toqui 13's private mountain, so there wasn't the usual brownout caused by these big machines. Her heart sank like a stone through dark honey, as she realized headquarters had dispatched a military contingent without advising her, which was never a good sign. Moreover, her treachery would soon be exposed.

But the helicopter didn't actually land. Its big fat wheels hovered a meter off the deck. Liang's audience followed her gaze and turned to watch as the cargo door slid open and figures began jumping onto the tarmac in the glow of the aircraft's tactical lights. Strangely, they were not regular troops. They were wearing sophisticated black MOPP suits and helmets, with oxygen hoses and their own compact air supplies on their backs. Their faceplates were tinted and above each was a pinpoint spotlight. They looked like spacemen, except they were all carrying QBZ-95 bullpup assault rifles in 5.8 x 42 mm, and the barrels were fixed with large thick tubes that resembled . . . suppressors.

"*Tien Tahng*. God in heaven," Ai Liang whispered as they shot the first guard in the chest. Then they spun on the other three, who were trying to draw their pistols, but the assaulters' muzzles flashed and the guards screamed and collapsed.

"Run!" Liang yelled as she saw the spacemen stomping toward the entrance doors. There were six of them, no, eight or nine, and there seemed to be more helicopters now and her young laboratory comrades leapt up and started howling and scrambling in every direction. The front doors flew open and the killers walked into Toqui 13 with the cold temerity of bored executioners and started mowing everyone down.

Submachine guns spat silenced fire, and bullets ricocheted off the metal seat backs, but there weren't many of those misplaced shots. As she turned to run, Dr. Liang had the fleeting thought that these bastards were expert killers.

A thundering sound came from above her as she

sprinted across the theater, thinking she might be able to make it out the rear doors, though she had no idea where she'd go after that. Then the landing gear of another helo crunched down on the roof and a second later the ceiling burst open with a flash and a *whump* that slammed her backwards onto the floor. She saw the girl with the chess set, Mingyu, a sweet young thing from Nanjing, go sprinting by her on the right just as one of the spacemen zipped to the linoleum on an assault rope, grabbed Mingyu by her ponytail, spun her around, and shot her point-blank in the forehead with a pistol.

Liang had nowhere else to go. She jumped to her feet and rushed Mingyu's killer, and as she hit top speed, she left the floor and slammed him in the spine with her boot. He crashed to his face and his helmet bounced but she didn't see or hear any of that because she rolled and kept on running for the glass exit doors at the far side, and as they got closer and closer, amid a torrent of screams and choked gunfire that sounded like a dozen madmen hammering a dead piano, the doors burst open and another five spacemen came stomping inside. Two of them were carrying satchel charges that looked like the thermite bombs she'd once seen at the EOD school at Kaohsiung, and one of them was hauling a gleaming metallic box the size of a large picnic cooler.

She knew immediately what it was: a lead-lined, temperature-controlled, vacuum-sealed system for transporting biowarfare weapons . . . like Gantu-62.

They gunned down Ju-Long, the young master sergeant in charge of the lab's pneumatics, then turned their weapons on her. She jinked hard to the right as bullets whip-cracked past her ears, and she charged through the door to her office, slammed the deadbolt on the other side, and flew across the room without stopping to catch her ragged breath. The previous director of Toqui 13 had devised an escape hatch for his office that Liang had always thought was paranoid and had never bothered to inspect. But now she found it there at the back of her closet, a small door with a twist handle, and as the killers pounded outside on her door and opened fire on the lock, she ripped the escape door open, grabbed the top of the frame, launched her feet through the hole, and crashed to the floor of the buffer corridor on Level V.

She expected a hand grenade to follow her, then realized these men were there to steal something volatile and deadly and wouldn't risk using explosives, but they would surely kill her as soon as they could. She felt blood running down the inside of her trousers from some sort of wound, the adrenaline flooded her veins like *baijiu* hard liquor, and she swooned and felt like she was going to vomit, but she raced for the corridor stairs.

Thank God there were no elevators at Toqui 13—no one could head her off. Access to all levels was via steel stairwells that could never fail, and that was also why all the workers had such strong legs.

Dr. Liang charged down the stairs.

The lights went out. She fumbled for her cell phone to use its flashlight and found it had bounced out of her fatigues pocket, but that barely slowed her pace because she'd loped those stairs a thousand times. She heard clanging in the darkness above her, sledgehammers smashing the door locks on Level III. She passed every level and kept on going until she reached the very bottom and the final door to the effluent systems, and below that, the giant incinerator.

It was pitch black. She fell down that last short set of steel stairs. She crawled on her torn hands and bruised knees along one cold stone wall. There was still the smell of incinerated flesh in the subterranean cave, but she managed to hold her bile down and felt her way to the expulsion hatch that was only opened for rare occurrences, such as extracting virus culture remnants after a three-hundred-degree-Celsius burn, or the charred remains of a comrade like Lieutenant Wu.

She had the only key to that hatch. Her hands were shaking as her slick fingers flipped through the key ring that was still on her garrison belt and she found the right one out of twenty. The lock opened after eighteen seconds of coaxing, twisting, and praying, and she hauled on the hatch. A blast of icy air smacked her face, and she saw a long black tube, and at the very end in the distance, starlight.

A minute later, she was lying on her back outside on a forty-five-degree cliff face of slippery rock, a third of the way down the butte with nothing but blackness below. It was freezing cold and the wind was threatening to whip her right off the mountain.

She looked up, where the fat wasp shapes of three murderous helicopters were winging away into the midnight sky. Suddenly the crown of her once-precious Toqui 13 exploded in a thundering fireball, and the top of the mountain was engulfed in raging flames.

CHAPTER 2

TRANSYLVANIAN ALPS, ROMANIA

Eric Steele fell ninety-seven feet and slammed into the side of a mountain. It was a vertical rock wall of black cosmic granite, and the only reason it didn't kill him was that he'd belayed himself with a two-hundred-foot length of Petzl Vector climbing rope. Still, he bounced off the wall like a whiplashed marionette, shattered his MBITR radio, lost his hip pouch of Dutch V40 mini-grenades, and it was only by pure miracle that his pelvis didn't crack in half.

Holy mother of God . . .

It was nearly impossible to quietly hammer a rock-climbing piton into a cliff face, so he'd jammed a hex nut anchor into a crevice, linked a titanium carabiner to its steel cable, clipped the rope into the carabiner, and had kept on climbing upwards. He'd been at it for more than two hours, repeating that process over and over, and had made it past the thousand-foot mark with less than five hundred to go, when he'd put pressure on what looked like—at least on this freezing moonless midnight—a nice strong toehold.

Negative.

Now he was swinging in the wind with fifty-four pounds of gear on his back, including an FN P90 submachine gun, two extra fifty-round magazines of 5.7 x 28 mm ammunition, a Sig Sauer P226 MK25 suppressed pistol, two combat knives, a tourniquet, a mini water bladder, a rear plate carrier, black mountain boots, tac gloves, MICH helmet, night vision goggles, and a hip harness of carabiners, ropes, pitons, hex nuts, rappel guides, and now . . . *no* freaking radio, or frags.

He was praying that the hex nut holding the rope would last just a bit longer, while the stretched nylon cable *thwanged* in the wind and yanked his climbing harness so far up into his crotch that he felt like a candidate for the Vienna Boys' Choir.

He hung there for a moment, arms drooping, while he mentally diffused the pain that came with smacking yourself into a concrete wall at the speed of a motocross bike. He looked down at the Argeș river where it wound through a forested valley far below, then up the other side to, of all things, Dracula's Castle.

That's right. This was the spot in Romania that the Millennial Crude jokers had chosen for their new hacker hideout, a nice little bombproof structure above Steele's head, with a spectacular view of the former citadel of Vlad the Impaler. Made sense to Steele, and gave him all the more reason to kill every last one of them.

He had many other reasons, of course, beginning with the deaths of three of his Program comrades at the hands of Lila Kalidi, a vicious female assassin. Kalidi had been contracted by Dmitry "Snipe" Kreesak, the leader of Millennial Crude, who in turn worked for Russia's Federal Security Service. However, both sides had suffered casualties. Steele's friends were dead, but so was Lila Kalidi, who he himself had killed at close range. So he'd figured "all's fair in love and war" and was prepared to let it go.

That is, until Crude really lived up to its name.

A month ago, the Russian FSB had decided to take out a Russian defector to the United States, Naftali Ostrovsky, who was making too much noise about Vladimir Putin's sexual peccadilloes to American media outlets in Boston. An FSB agent had slipped into the U.S. and poisoned Ostrovsky's tea with polonium, which had put him on a ventilator at Massachusetts General Hospital. But Ostrovsky wasn't dying fast enough for the Kremlin.

Millennial Crude was called in, and from their remote headquarters in the Moscow suburb of Kapotnya, they'd shut down all the electrical power to Mass General for two full hours, including the backup generators. Aside from Ostrovsky, who'd expired in ten minutes, four other innocent patients on ventilators had died, plus three newborn infants in incubators.

Steele might not even have known about all this if not for the Program's cyber guru, Ralphy Persko. The Program had been disbanded by order of President Rockford, but Ralphy had an obsession with Millennial Crude and had kept on tracking their activities. When he told Steele about the attack on Mass General, the news about the helpless babies boiled Steele's blood.

Steele knew there'd be no Program support for a hit on Millennial Crude, so he and his currently unemployed keeper, Dalton "Blade" Goodhill, had turned to an old CIA special tactics hand, Thorn McHugh, who happened to be as wealthy as Marc Cuban. The three men had met one night in East Potomac Park in Washington, D.C., and after hearing Steele and Goodhill's pitch, McHugh had simply walked away. The next day a FedEx letter had arrived on Steele's doorstep at Neville Island, Pennsylvania. It contained a black American Express card in Steele's name—no limit.

After the Boston slaughter, the Russians had decided that Millennial Crude should relocate for a while till the whole thing blew over. Romania seemed the perfect spot. The country had been a Soviet satellite for decades, but even after Gorbachev nothing much had changed. You could buy just about anything with oligarch money in Bucharest, including a modular ceramic tactical operations center shaped like a giant igloo, with double-thick tempered glass doors, sidebar living quarters, a Jamie Oliver kitchen, mini-gymnasium, banks of 8Pack OrionX personal computers and satellite uplinks, and all of it delivered by contracted heavy lift helos and assembled by FSB engineers. The nine bodyguards were Russian private military contractors from *Grupa Vagnera*, who slept outside in a trailer and never entered the dome.

Ralphy Persko knew all this because ever since

the Program had stood down, he was incredibly bored and had lots of time on his hands. He hadn't asked Steele for one penny for the intel. Nevertheless, Steele intended to add a fat tip for Ralphy to the Thorn McHugh budget.

Steele finally stopped swinging at the end of his rope, reached over and grabbed the main line, and pulled himself back to the vertical wall. The granite was slimy and slippery as hell and he didn't have crampons on his boots, but he'd file that memo for later—if there was ever going to be a "later." He spread his black-clad legs wide, found what seemed like two firm toeholds, reached for a couple of fingertip ledges, and started inching his way back up the cliff face like Spiderman—just much slower, and more cautious, and extremely bruised.

It took another hour setting belay hexes, paying out rope, inching upwards, and sweating in the icy night, and then he was peering over an onyx shelf at that salmon-colored dome, straight ahead on a summit clearing among a copse of Romanian pines. The moon had just popped up from behind a charcoal fur ball of clouds and it was so high and bright in the indigo sky that he wasn't even going to need the NVGs mounted on his helmet. He slithered on his stomach over to the left behind a long coffin-like slab of granite, took one long pull from his hydration bladder, and started quietly shedding gear—the rock-climbing hardware, ropes, harness, and carabiners. He came to his knees, slung the P90 subgun over his back, pulled the P226 from his thigh holster, screwed on the Knights Armament silencer, and press-checked the handgun. He wished he still had his radio so he could tell Goodhill he'd made it to the top. And oh yes, the grenades; he wished he still had those too.

Oh, well, FIDO . . . fuck it, drive on. . . .

He rose and moved forward at a hunched, graceful glide, especially for a large muscular man wearing mountain boots. The slab of granite on his left had a twin on the right, forming a roofless corridor, and suddenly at the end of it a figure stepped into view. It was one of the Russian sentries, a tall man wearing a Spetsnaz camouflage smock, black tactical pants, a fur hat, and slinging a Romanian AK-47 with its peculiar folding stock. He was lighting up a smoke and his back was turned to Steele.

For a moment, as he floated closer, Steele felt a twinge of remorse.

Dude's just a gun for hire, probably doesn't even know what he's doing here, or who these people are he's protecting. . . . Maybe he's got a wife, little kids, a faithful dog. . . . Maybe even a little old mamushka back in Moscow or Saint Petersburg. . . .

Steele shot him in the back of the skull.